DEVIL

or

ANGEL

& OTHER STORIES

OLD-STYLE SCIENCE FICTION AND FANTASY TALES

by

MATTHEW HUGHES

Devil or Angel & other stories
Copyright Matthew Hughes, 2015

Published by Matthew Hughes
ISBN: 978-1-927880-06-7

Cover illustration and book design by Bradley W. Schenck

CONTENTS

ACKNOWLEDGEMENTS

I want to thank the editors who originally bought these stories and put them out into the world: John Joseph Adams, Andy Cox, Pete Crowther, Gardner Dozois, George R.R. Martin, and Gordon Van Gelder.

And I especially was to thank fellow author of old-style science fiction, Bradley W. Schenck, who designs and formats all of my self-published books and who provided the cover for this one.

INTRODUCTION

Over the past twenty-or-so years–yes, it's been that long–I've made a modest reputation as a writer of Jack Vance-inspired science-fantasy novels, novellas, and short stories. *Booklist* went so far as to call me Vance's "heir apparent," which pleased me no end. My Vancean Archonate tales, which have gradually become separate elements of one grand narrative concerning the twilight of a far-future interstellar civilization as the universe arbitrarily switches from an operating principle based on rational cause and effect to one based on magic, have been a pleasure to write. I intend to do more of them.

But in between outings of Henghis Hapthorn, Guth Bandar, Luff Imbry and–lately–Erm Kaslo, I've written a slew of science-fiction and fantasy stories that have nothing to do with Old Earth and the Ten Thousand Worlds. Some of them are light and funny pieces, some are good-old-stuff space opera, and a few even trespass upon the borders of that dark land called horror. Some I wrote because I had a cool idea I wanted to explore, some because an editor invited me to contribute to an anthology, others because I could sell them to a magazine and thereby keep my name in front of readers until the next book came out and, maybe, attract some new eyeballs to my work.

If there is a common theme running through these sixteen stories, it will take a more perceptive mind than mine to work out. One quality they do share, I think, is that they draw their inspiration from the science fiction and fantasy I used to read as a teenager back in the 1960s–works that were mostly written in the 1950s and which could be found in paperback in second-hand bookstores.

In other words, this is old-fashioned sf. I hope you enjoy them.

DEVIL OR ANGEL

Back in the 1980s, I had some hopes of a career in screenwriting. I wrote some scripts, even got two of them optioned and made some money, though nothing much ever came of it. But there was this one afterlife-fantasy romantic comedy I'd written up as a treatment, and one day I noticed it resting in the back corner of my hard drive, and thought, "That would make a decent little novelette." So I wrote it up and sold it to Gordon Van Gelder at The Magazine of Fantasy & Science Fiction.

If you happen to be a film producer, the rights are still available.

LET'S START by making one thing clear: Michael and Jessica were among the top ten of the great love matches of the twenty-first century. About that, there can be no argument.

But when their friends say that it all began the night of Mike's twenty-first birthday party, when he was waiting for the restaurant staff to bring him his blazing cake and instead saw them take one to a far table, where they laid it down before a girl he subsequently couldn't take his eyes off–that was Jess, of course–that's where their friends get it wrong.

Great love match? No question. Begun over cakes and candles? Not even close.

———————⟡———————

For the real beginning, we've got to go back to the early nineteen-nineties—not quite stone age, but certainly before internet-savvy smart-phones and MP3 players. More to the point, we're going back to the days when if you wanted the latest and greatest hit single, you didn't download it from the web into your MP3 player. You went to an actual record store and bought one of those new-fangled CDs for your home stereo system. If you wanted to hear the music on the move, you bought a cassette tape you could pop into your Walkman or your car's dashboard.

And chances were, if you were buying the latest and greatest, the CD or tape would have had a label on it that said it was made by Fate Records, one of the top independents out of Seattle. And that meant you'd have been putting a few more dollars into the already overflowing bank account of Fate's founder and owner, Jason Flanders.

Jason is the centerpiece character of this story, but we'll get to him in a moment. Right now, let's zero in on Wally Kaminski. Age: twenty-two. Occupation: no need to disguise it, the guy's a gofer at Fate's headquarters. He fetches, he carries, he gets things out and puts things away. Interests: fantasy novels and role-playing games, in which he temporarily becomes Vlar of the Ax, a beefy barbarian mercenary. Personal status: virgin.

He has one real friend: Ted, Fate's sound engineer, who has been trying to help Wally fulfill a romantic ambition—to go on a date with Amy Beamer, the receptionist. But since Wally has never been on a date, has never even asked a girl out, Ted has been trying to roll a serious-sized rock up a very steep slope.

We come upon Wally as he is carrying Jason's bags from the boss's third-floor office down to the waiting limo. As he transits the reception area, he passes Amy's desk. Amy is the female equivalent of Wally, even to the fondness for fantasy novels, although she does her role-playing through the Society for Creative Anachronism, at whose fairs and jousts she assumes the identity of Eliadora, a Knight of Faery, masquerading as a serving maid in the kitchens of Arthur, king of the Britons—though not the lusty-wench kind of serving maid; like Wally, Amy is also an unplucked flower.

Amy's only friend in the world, if we don't count her cat, Snuggles, is Tina, who handles the label's advertising and public relations. Tina has lately got a serious thing going with Ted, and has come up with the idea of them double-dating with Wally and Amy. But Wally is still going to have to make the first move.

As he nears Amy's station, Wally cuts a quick glance her way. She, coincidentally, raises her eyes and their gazes meet. Now, if they could but hold that connection, who knows what magic the next few moments might weave? But they don't. They can't. He immediately drops his gaze, and actually raises a blush that she doesn't see, because she has instantly changed her own field of vision to encompass only the pink message pads, pens, and paper clips on her desk blotter. Plus the phone rings and it's her job to answer it.

"Fate Records, how may I direct your call?" She listens then says, "Mr. Flanders? One moment, I'll see if he's available."

She's about to buzz the boss's assistant's line when she sees Jason Flanders himself crossing the reception area, in a hurry. He's on his way to SeaTac to catch a flight north to Vancouver where Fate's newest discovery, a band called E*ville, will be launching its first tour. She raises a hand, catches Jason's attention, then points to the phone.

He shakes his head, smiles, keeps on moving. After him comes Krissa Bolide, as always in tight-fitting skirt and blouse that emphasize her considerable anatomical advantages. The undulant woman is assistant head of A&R for the Fate label, and way too ambitious, in Amy's opinion–which is a fair assessment; Amy may be mousy, but she's not dumb. She understands that Krissa's real ambition is not to replace Hank Billings as head of artists and repertoire, but to hear Jason Flanders say, in front of a churchful of witnesses, "I take thee, Krissa Bolide . . ."

The would-be bride shoots Amy an unpleasant glance. If asked, Krissa would say her opprobrium is for Amy's daring to delay the boss when he's in such a hurry. But the unspoken reality is that Krissa wants to kill any woman, even the little shnook of a receptionist, who attracts the attention of the catch she intends to land. It's a matter of instinct, mostly. That's because Krissa is mostly instinct.

Amy gets back on the line and tells the caller that Mr. Flanders has left for the airport, and takes a message. Wally comes back upstairs, having stowed the bags in the limo's trunk. Here's another chance for his and Amy's eyes to meet and their hearts to melt as one; but like the other hundred opportunities before it, this, too, is wasted.

Down in the limo, Jason and Krissa are settled into the back seat. But, to her chagrin, they are not alone. Waiting for them is a young man named Nick Caspian, a teenager from suburban Renton who has won a radio contest entitling him to an all-expenses-paid trip to the tour's opening night. He'll also get to spend some face-time with Wilson Proteus, E*ville's lead singer and creative force.

In the past week, since learning that he has won, Nick has described the anticipated events as "radical" eighty-seven times. He now makes it eighty-eight as he tells Jason Flanders how totally stoked he is.

"I'm glad you're happy," Jason tells him, and means it. "They're a powerhouse band. It should be a great concert."

"Dude, totally," says Nick, and begins to explain in detail why Wilson Proteus totally rocks. He's interrupted, though, by Krissa, who has been waiting for an opportunity to get Jason on his own. She asks the teenager if he'd like to be the first person in Seattle to hear the band's new single, a sinister remix of the old sixties pop hit, *Devil or Angel*, as reimagined by E*ville's dark genius.

"Dude!" says Nick, leaning forward so she can slip the big earphones over his ears. The woman slides a CD into the limo's sound system. A moment later, as Proteus's throaty rasp grates against Nick's eardrums, he breathes, "Whoa," and sinks back into the soft leather.

Krissa reaches into her slimline briefcase and brings out a couple of pages closely packed with columns of numbers. The movement brings her thigh into contact with Jason's. She does nothing to break the connection.

She says, "I've been going over the contracts of some of our acts. There's a provision for hold-backs on royalties that Fate is not taking full advantage of."

"I know," Jason says. "I wrote the contracts."

"But we're paying on a quarterly basis, when we could be paying semi-annually," she says. "And if we went to semi-annually, we could put the funds into short-term certificates of deposit and bank the interest. Over five years, that adds up to serious revenue enhancements."

Jason glances at the papers, then pushes them aside. "Nuh uh," he says. "I'm good with what we're getting. The acts are happy. Why screw up a lot of good relationships?"

She looks at him as if he'd just grown a new nose. She's a smart young woman, but not always smart enough to recognize a question that doesn't need an answer. "For the money," she says.

"Krissa, you're A&R," he tells her. "Leave the money to the accountants." He sees the way she's staring at him, and says, "Listen, I've been in the business long enough to see that what goes around comes around. When I started out, I ran some hustles, cut some corners. Now I'm thinking that, back then, I was not the person I should have been."

"You do what you gotta do," she said.

He holds up his hands in a way that says he isn't going to argue. "Whatever. Thing is, now I don't need to do that kind of shit. In fact, I'm thinking I should be doing something to put a little back."

"I don't understand," she says. Of course, she doesn't. If Krissa Bolide was a car, she'd come with only forward gears and no rear-view mirror.

He looks at her. "I know you don't," he says. "Don't worry about it."

Nick has made it through to the end of the single. He hits the replay button and continues to rock—in both senses of the verb—all the way to the airport. Jason and Krissa ride in a silence that couldn't be called companionable. She even shifts position so that her thigh is no longer warming his.

They're flying Air Canada to Vancouver, and they head for the airline's Maple Leaf Lounge, reserved for first-class passengers. E*ville is already there, the bass player and drummer making full use of the open bar, while the rail-thin lead guitarist is sleeping in one of the overstuffed armchairs. Wilson Proteus is at the floor-to-ceiling window-wall that looks out on the airfield, a glass of liquor in his hand. He does not turn as Jason, Krissa and Nick come in.

The reason he does not turn is that the man could give lessons on self-involvement to an oyster. A komodo dragon would have a better grasp of right and wrong. An interviewer once asked him if he had named his band after his home town of Everett, just up the I-5 from Seattle. "Yeah," said Proteus, "sure."

Nick manages to cross half the distance between him and his idol before he freezes. Jason comes up behind the kid, puts an arm around his shoulders and shepherds him the rest of the way. "Wilson," he says, "time to meet your number-one fan."

Proteus does not turn, takes a leisurely sip of scotch that's two years older than his number-one fan. Finally, he turns only his head and gives Nick the side-eye. He's a tall man and broad-shouldered, so he's also looking down.

"Nick Caspian," says Jason. "He won the contest. He's going with us."

The singer says nothing, just continues to look down at the teenager. Jason, his arm still around Nick's shoulders, gives him an encouraging squeeze that somehow forces words up the kid's throat and through his mouth, which has been hanging open for a while.

"It's . . . it's an honor . . ." He pauses to swallow dryly, then takes another run up the hill. "An honor to meet you, dude, sir."

Obsequiousness is seldom wasted on Wilson Proteus. The man turns and gives Nick the benefit of both eyes. If the kid wasn't so awestruck, he might notice that it was like being looked over by a bored basilisk.

"I'll tolerate your respect," Proteus says, "though I'd prefer fear and loathing." It's a line he's worked up for dealing with interviews on the tour, and this is its first try-out. He follows it up with another. "I don't give a pinch of buzzard crap if you like me, and if you cross me, I'll kill you."

Nick Caspian's mouth reverts to hanging open. "Uh," he says.

Jason's arm now becomes protective. He draws the kid away, saying, "Let's go meet the rest of the band."

They wake up the lead guitarist, although it takes him a while to get both his eyes pointed in the same direction. But the bass player is as laid-back as bassmen usually are, and the drummer's not as insane as most of his peers, so a conversation ensues and continues without too many lapses.

Krissa has been standing by the door. She looks at the group chatting amiably in the seating area, which includes the boss she is considering scratching off her list of possibles. Then she looks at the solitary figure by the windows. It doesn't take her long to make her choice. She adjusts her blouse in a way that removes any doubt that she is a mammal, and glides over to stand beside Wilson Proteus. Another conversation ensues, this one in subdued tones and punctuated by low chuckles. After thirty seconds, Krissa leans in so that the side of her breast nudges Wilson's elbow.

"And we're off," says E*ville's manager, an over-caffeinated twenty-something man who used to run a cabaret in Everett and who is now clinging by his fingernails to the tiger he thought would offer him a comfortable ride to riches. He has just come in, his hands full of passports and boarding passes. "We're all cleared for boarding."

He directs them toward a door on the airfield side of the room that has just opened to admit two uniformed young women with maple leaf insignia on their caps.

Jason and the others rise and head toward the boarding ramp. The singer remains where he is. Krissa, therefore, does not move either. The manager turns toward him with the worried look of a nervous dog that never knows whether it's going to get a kick or a cookie. "Wilson?" he says.

"Surprise," Proteus says, deadpan. He waits for everyone to give him their full attention, then a little longer to make them sweat. "I leased a Gulfstream."

Several eyes blink and the manager lets out a pent-up breath. Jason is the one who answers. "You've got a pilot's license?"

"Yep. Been taking lessons. Passed my solo on Wednesday."

The manager brings Proteus his passport. "Vancouver's got complicated airspace," he says, in the tone of someone who foresees the possibility of having his head chewed from his neck.

"I can handle it. I flew there and back Thursday."

Jason says, "Well, that's that. We've got a plane waiting." With his last remark, he turns his gaze on Krissa.

"She's going to come with me," says Proteus.

"Am I?" she says.

He gives her the downward and sideways look, waits a beat, then says, "Count on it."

Jason, Nick and rest of the band settle into first class. There's the usual handing out of slippers and orange juice and champagne. Nick is not old enough to try the latter, but when the lead guitarist immediately falls back asleep with his full glass of bubbly untouched only inches from the teenager, the natural thing happens.

"Whoa!" says Nick. "Beats beer."

The plane gets out to the runway and up into the air. The cabin crew get even busier, handing out pillows and snacks and adjusting jets of air for people who really ought to be able to do it for themselves. But it's first class, so they don't.

Now, as the plane begins to level off at cruising altitude, the first-class passengers can hear some kind of muffled altercation going on back in economy. Someone is not taking no for an answer. Jason can hear a contralto voice repeating "Unacceptable," and adding, "I paid for a full seat, not a half."

There are empty seats up at this end of the plane. One is next to Jason's. Krissa made the seat selections, and also made sure that she would have some uninterrupted face time with the boss; but that was before she abandoned the assault and opted for a target of opportunity.

The cabin attendant comes through the curtain. Behind her comes a young woman with flushed cheeks and firmly elevated chin, toting a carry-on bag and a popular novel. The flight attendant, with not much in the way of good grace, takes the passenger's bag and stows it overhead, then indicates the empty seat. Jason, who has been running through a mental list of the people he knows who could replace Krissa, looks up.

Remember Mike and Jessica and love at first sight illuminated by a candlelit birthday cake? Well, for Jason, it's the exact same thing, minus the flaming dessert. Jason has seen a lot of gorgeous women, seen them up close and without the hindrance of clothing, but he has never been as comprehensively eye-smacked as he is when Megan Wells gives him one of those sorry-for-the-trouble smiles and slips into the seat beside him.

It's not that Megan is classically beautiful. If you mapped out her face on a mathematical grid and measured for exact symmetry, she'd fall short in several features. But the composite effect of eyes, nose, lips, jaw line, brows, and cheeks is—at least for Jason—overwhelming.

His mom and dad used to say, to his acute teenage embarrassment, that each of them decided, on their first real date, that *he/she's the one.* Jason has never really bought into the concept of one-tude. Relationships, he figures, grow over time and love is always a work-in-progress. But if he could muster a coherent thought at this moment—this magic moment, as the old Drifters song put it—it would be *Boy, was I wrong about that.*

She's slipping off shoes—*Nice feet,* he thinks, which is the first time he's ever thought that thought—and putting on slippers and popping her Stephen King novel—*She likes the same books I do*—into the pouch in the seat back in front of her.

She indicates the rear of the plane and says, in the voice of reason, "That man must weigh four hundred pounds. They should have asked him to buy two seats."

"Ah," says Jason, comprehending. A single syllable is about all he's good for at the moment. He keeps looking at her until he realizes that he can't be making a good impression—he's reminded of how Nick looked at Wilson Proteus. With great presence of mind, he closes his mouth and, though still only able to utter single syllables, manages to voice an actual word: "Yes." Then he swallows.

Jason would be gratified to know that the color in Megan's face is no longer the flush of argument but the blush of a young woman who is experiencing the exact same emotion as Jason (and Mike and Jessica, once the candles were blown out and she raised her eyes to see him looking at her). But we'll stay with Jason.

His usually cool and collected brain has become humid and scattered. His eyes hunt around for clues as if this was a game of *I spy with my little eye something to say that isn't totally lame* and he notices the book again.

"Good?" he says, making a fitful gesture toward book she stowed in the seat back pocket.

"I'm sorry?" she says.

"King," he says, then by dint of a superhuman effort, "you like King?"

She's about to reply and launch the conversation that, on their fiftieth wedding anniversary, would make a charming anecdote. Except that they're not going to get any anniversaries, not even a five-minute one, because it's at this point that Wilson Proteus and Krissa Bolide re-enter the story. And not in a positive way.

After connecting in the Maple Leaf Lounge, the singer and the woman made their way to the smaller terminal where his Gulfstream waited, all fueled up. Proteus enjoyed showing off his recently acquired expertise as he spoke to the tower and taxied out to the runway, the plane's twin engines throbbing through the airframe and right into the cockpit seats.

He got it up and made the turn toward the north, the controller telling him that he should rise to twenty thousand feet and giving him his heading for Vancouver. Wilson punched the information into the jet's automatic pilot, set the speed for just under six hundred miles an hour, then said to Krissa, "Come on."

His head motion toward the passenger cabin was a reminder of the pull-down bed that he'd showed her when they boarded—and which he had pointedly left down.

"Mile high?" she said, getting up.

"Four, if you're counting," he said.

Several minutes later, they were too heavily engaged to notice the repetitive soft chime from the instrument panel and the modulated voice that kept saying *Proximity alert.* They didn't even hear the increasingly frantic voice from the SeaTac tower telling them to descend to twenty thousand feet.

Wilson, in his eagerness to explore Krissa's pneumaticity, had wrongly set the automatic pilot. The plane was not rising to twenty thousand feet but to thirty, and it was closing in on Air Canada flight 2012 at almost a hundred miles an hour. The 767's pilot was also receiving automated and human warnings, but with the Gulfstream coming from behind and below—ironically, so was Proteus at that moment—he could not see the threat.

There were several things the commercial pilot could have done. Unluckily, or as much as these things are decided by luck, he chose the wrong one. He instructed the copilot to increase speed. The result was that the Gulfstream did not cut across the 767's flight path from beneath, giving the Air Canada cockpit crew a real scare, as it would have if their relative speeds had remained unaltered. Instead, its right wing sliced through the big jet's left wing, which was full of fuel for the trip to Vancouver.

So, just as Megan opens her mouth to say how much she enjoys the works of Stephen King, Air Canada flight 8314 becomes an airborne fireball hot enough to melt aluminum. Jason is conscious of a great light and an incredible heat and, for just an instant, the woman of his dreams becoming a burning effigy. Then he is not conscious at all.

The next thing he knows, he is walking along a winding road. He's surrounded by, and part of, a stream of people, and they're all enveloped in a luminous mist. They walk in silence, but he notices that some of them hold their heads up, while others just slump along. A few of the erect-postured are bathed in light, as if they are illuminated by invisible spotlights. Some of the slumpers are encased in a kind of flickering darkness.

The road ascends a gentle slope and he looks forward. In the middle distance, becoming visible through the mist, is a vast building of white stone. It rears up to an impossible height, its upper reaches lost in clouds that are lit from within by a golden radiance.

Jason feels as if he's gradually awakening from a nap. He looks around him and sees people of all kinds, colors, ages, although even the tiniest of infants are walking steadily on two feet. Then he sees someone he vaguely recognizes. It takes him a few moments to place the face, and then it clicks: it's the bassman from E*ville. An almost-memory tugs at the edge of Jason's consciousness. He strains for it, but then he's distracted by the sight of a woman he's sure he's seen before and recently. He concentrates on her, and the words, *flight attendant* sound in his mind.

That's when it all comes back. He says, "Where are you?" and looks around, increasingly frantic as he can't find the girl from the plane. He stops—it's not easy; his feet want to keep walking and he's the only immobile object on the road. The people flow around him, brushing past. He wants to call out her name, but they never got to the how–do–you–do stage.

Then he sees a figure coming toward him: not the woman, but Wilson Proteus. The singer's face is hard to see, because his form is passing in and out of view behind a veil of darkness that wanes and waxes.

"Wilson!" Jason says. He can't quite hear his own voice, though he knows he's talking, because the other man's glance slips his way. Proteus's habitual sneer intensifies into a bared–teeth snarl. Jason sees rage, backed by fear. "Wait a minute," he says. "I need help. I've got find somebody."

But all the answer he gets is a growl. Proteus makes to shoulder him out of the way. Jason reaches out, tries to seize the other man's arms. His hands slip into the shroud of oscillating non–light and are immediately bathed in a deep chill. With a gasp, he yanks them back, then the singer is past him and gone.

Some kind of dark stuff has adhered to Jason's fingers. He shakes his hands and it flies off. But he does not notices that a tiny flake lands on his leg, just above the knee, and sticks.

We should notice here that Jason, and everyone around him, is naked. But they're not human naked, with all those anatomical details that denote sex and maturity; they're soul naked—he doesn't even have a navel—as smooth as so many Ken and Barbie dolls.

Jason doesn't notice because he's intent on finding the Stephen King fan from the plane. He straightens and searches again for her. The faces stream past and around him, but she's not there. Maybe she's ahead of him. If so, he'll have a better chance of finding her in the big building. He turns, resumes walking, and now it's his turn to push past others, as he strives to get there faster.

He brushes past a slim person, causing the other to stumble. Jason reaches out a steadying hand and recognizes another face. In a moment, he makes the connection.

"Nick!" he says. "Nick Caspian!"

The young face regards him dreamily for a moment, then Jason sees recognition dawn. "Dude!"

"Have you seen her?" Jason says.

"Who?"

"The girl from the plane?"

"What girl?"

"Never mind." Jason falls into step beside Nick. They've been down in a dip and are now coming to the crest of another rise. The mist clears. Now Jason sees the building more clearly, though its top is still wreathed in glowing clouds. It stands in the center of a green and grassy valley that is divided by a wide, winding river that flows from the dim and foggy distance to end in a great whirlpool at the valley's head. Upstream, above the river, the mist glows with rainbow radiance, but the vortex is deep black.

"Radical," says Nick, staring at the building. Then his gaze shifts to the whirlpool and he makes another pronouncement: "That is so bogus."

"Come on," says Jason. They make their way down the last slope, threading through the parade. Jason sees a couple of dark flickerers, but neither of them is Wilson Proteus. He and the teenager come to where the road passes through a huge doorway, flanked by tall gates of shining brass. Beyond is an enormous room, full of people, its ceiling at once impossibly high and yet too bright to look at.

But there is order and process. There are other figures among the crowd, towering shapes at least half-again the height of the tallest of the incomers. They are clustered where the stream of walkers ends, at the foot of a huge statue of a robed and seated person so tall the light above obscures its head. They are dividing the throng into two broad streams, sending one to the left the other to the right.

Jason, trailed by Nick, continues to search through the crowd for Megan. Then, at last, he sees her, far away. She has passed through the screen of tall figures, and has been directed to the right. Jason pushes after her, desperate not to lose sight of her in the vast crowd.

He comes up suddenly against a restraining hand—a large hand that comes down from one of the tall ones. He looks up into an impassive face—it reminds Jason of Charles Grodin playing one of his most tedious characters—and into his mind pops a word: *angel*.

In its other hand, the angel is holding a white wand. It now moves the instrument up and down Jason's body, examines the thing briefly, then indicates that he is to go with the leftward stream of people.

"No," says Jason, "I have to go there." He points to the right, where he can see Megan just about to pass through one of a row of archways, far off in the base of the wall.

The angel shakes its head and again points left.

"No way," says Jason. Megan is disappearing through the archway. He pushes past the angel, heading right.

And is stopped by another hand. But this one is taller than he is. He looks up, way up, and realizes that the seated colossus is not a statue at all. *Archangel*, his mind tells him, and though his instinct is to back off, his need to see the woman again overrules the rest of him.

"I have to get to that woman," he says. "Please."

But the great face comes down from the brilliance as the archangel bends to see him—it looks a little like Charlton Heston in *The Ten Commandments*, but with more gravitas—and the shining head moves from side to side. The index finger of the house-sized hand points to the left. Then it comes around to nudge Jason with gentle firmness in the indicated direction.

He joins the leftward stream. He notices that many of them have the same slump-shouldered posture as he is now showing. Among them, too, are the dark flickerers, although he still does not spot Wilson Proteus. Nor does he see Nick Caspian, but when he cranes his neck and stands on tiptoes, he catches a glimpse of the teenager far off and dwindling out of view. Nick has been directed to the right.

And the woman is gone.

The leftward flow is going somewhere, inching forward. Jason cannot be bothered to see where. Then he feels a shoulder pressed against his and turns to see Krissa Bolide. The expression on her face can only be called a smirk.

"Looks like you developed those scruples a little too late in the game, boss," she says. "You and me, we're headed for the Group W bench."

Actually, it's a counter, a long, waist-high barrier behind which stand more of the angels, each wearing the same face as the one with the wand. The flow of the newly dead—that realization has sunk into

Jason's mind now–gradually brings him and Krissa up to the counter. One of the Grodin–featured entities reaches under the barrier, then its hands came up holding what looked like a folded bundle of laundry dyed bright red.

It pushes the cloth at Jason. Without thinking, he reaches to take it, but the moment his hands touch the bundle the object seems to shrink in size, as if it is a liquid running out through a hidden drain. At the same time, Jason sees his hands, then his arms, then his shoulders and chest, all transform from a pale, Ken–doll nudity until he is wearing a form–fitting single garment of scarlet that leaves only his face uncovered.

The same transformation is happening to Krissa, and included in her new ensemble are a pair of short, red horns and a tail of the same color that ends in a neat equilateral triangle. He sees her take stock of herself, including the new appendage, then her shoulders rise and fall in a shrug of acquiescence.

"No," says Jason to the angel-clerk, "this is . . . wrong." He does not know how he knows it, but something is amiss here. He has a strong conviction that he ought to have gone where the woman from the plane went.

But the angel is already clothing the next recruit, and pays him no attention. Jason turns and pushes through the flow of people approaching the counter. He struggles back toward the dividing point, where the wand–angels are processing the unending stream. He gets close enough to see into the other side of the building, where those who went to the right are being clad in gowns of white. Each one also gets a circle of shining gold that floats in the air above their heads.

He can't see Megan. She has already passed through the archways. But he notices something: In the far corner, a shaft of golden light slants down from the undifferentiated glow high overhead. Toward this the angels are reverently shepherding those souls who arrived bathed in their own auras. The instant they step into the illumination, they become swirling clouds of brilliant motes, each like a mini–tornado of pinpoint lights, that rise smoothly into the effulgence above.

An angel appears at Jason's left elbow, then another on his right side. He finds himself lifted off his feet and is borne back the way he came, head and shoulders above the rest of the left–side crowd. He catches sight of Krissa watching his return with a mocking grin. Then he notices something else: the newly dead who arrived bathed in flickers of darkness are being separated from the flow toward the clothing counter. Four or five Grodins cluster about each of them and they are lifted much the way Jason has been.

But while his pair of angels deliver him back to where the newly red-suited are being guided toward a row of archways, the dark ones are briskly carried to a wide, square doorway. Beyond it, Jason can just see the dark waters of the great river. As he watches, a shadow-auraed figure, squirming and struggling, is brought to the portal. The soul reaches up and grasps the lintel of the doorway, fighting his eviction. Jason can hear him roaring and cursing. He recognizes the distinctive voice that he has heard so often in the recording studio.

The angels reach up and pry Wilson Proteus's hands from the doorway. Then they carry him out to the river and, without ceremony, throw him into the current. Jason hears the splash.

"This way," says a Grodin, indicating one of the arches, and Jason finds himself back in the flow. A moment later, he is pressed through the gap in the wall and he's outside the building on a broad lawn that slopes down to the river, which here curves away in a broad loop. He immediately looks right to see if he can see the woman.

His effort is successful, but it's not a happy success. He spots Megan. She is part of a stream of halo-wearers who are crossing a bridge of white stone that arcs across the river. And between Jason and the bridge rises a wall of smooth stone.

He goes to the wall, but soon determines that it is not climbable. But Jason Flanders, alive or dead, is no quitter. He follows the barrier down to where it runs into the river. He looks at the black, roiling water. The current is strong, and now that he is outside he can hear the ceaseless roar of the whirlpool, loud enough to make Niagara Falls feel second-rate.

The situation offers little promise. He looks up at the bridge and catches a last sight of Megan. She has stopped in the middle of the span and is peering at the crowd of red-clad folk on the river bank. Jason raises both hands and moves them from side to side. He sees her notice, and across the distance, their eyes meet.

"I'm coming," he says. But a bridge-wide cluster of white robes presses her and she has to move on. Now he sees Nick and calls out to him. The teenager turns and sees him, says, "Dude!" and waves.

"Go to her!" Jason shouts. "Tell her I'll find a way!"

Nick looks forward along the bridge and sees Megan still trying to look back at Jason as she is borne along. He raises a thumb to Jason then begins force his way to her.

Jason turns his gaze back to the river. If he can get out to where the wall ends and swim around it, maybe he can get onto the bridge. And then . . . well, from there he'll play it by ear. He steels himself to plunge into the water.

"I wouldn't do it," says voice behind him. "Less you wanna spend your next rotation sucking the juices out of sow bugs or rolling a ball of elephant shit around the Serengetti."

Jason turns and sees a diminutive figure dressed in the ubiquitous red suit, although the face beneath the horns is a web of wrinkles distributed around a pair of sad-but-wise eyes and a mouth set slightly awry.

The man points toward the middle of the stream and says, "The folks from the other side can swim it, if they want to. But you'll just end up like him."

Jason follows the finger and is surprised to see Wilson Proteus, still wrapped in darkness, struggling to swim against the river's power. His face is a mask of grim rage.

"He's a strong one," says the small man. "Still, any second now."

Proteus's strokes begin to slow. He howls in rage. The current takes hold and starts to bear him down and away. But before he disappears below the surface, Jason sees the singer begin to transform. The howl becomes a croak, then a hiss, as his body elongates, his eyes grow huge and lambent, his mouth extends forward and becomes a beak. The flailing arms lengthen and thicken, the hands broadening into leaf-shaped paddles. Suction cups, each equipped with a curved, tooth-like projection, appear on what are now clearly the tentacles of a colossal squid.

"Good try," says the wrinkled man, as the beast that was Proteus slips below the surface. "He's an old one."

"An old one?"

The man gives Jason a considering look. "Not like you," he says. "You ain't been around the block too many times."

"I don't know what you're . . ." But Jason pauses there, because a vague kind of memory is surfacing in him. He looks around at the bridge, the river, the huge building. It does look familiar, like a memory from a dream.

"There you go," says the other man. "Coming back now, huh?"

Jason nods. "I've been here before."

"And will be again." The man steps forward and offers his hand.

"Kutchmeyer's the name," he says. "Welcome to the Corps."

"The Corps?"

"You'll see." He turns away and beckons the young man to follow. "Come on, they're about to ring the bell."

But Jason is still staring at the river and the land on the other side. It's brighter over there.

"Forget it," says Kutchmeyer. "It only looks like water. But it's really the stuff dreams are made on, as the old playwright wrote."

Jason recognizes the Shakespeare quote, but doesn't get the meaning. "I don't remember."

The other man says, "It's been called a lot of names: the Dreamtime, Never-Never Land, the realm of the ancestors, the collective unconscious. It's where the living go when they dream."

He gestures to the other side of the river. "Those can swim in it, but we can't. That's because the river is the real world. Anything they imagine in the river becomes real, and the powers that be don't like some of the things us red-suits imagine."

"Dreams are the real world?" Jason says.

"The Dreamtime—where you go when you dream, where shamans go when they leave their bodies—*that* is the real world. What you think of as the physical universe is just a side effect of the power that looks to you like a river."

Something about what he's saying is familiar to Jason. A memory almost makes it to the forefront of his mind.

"Don't worry," says Kutchmeyer, "it'll come back to you. Sometimes when you've died unexpectedly, it takes a while."

"What happens if I jump in?" says Jason.

"You'll get carried down into the vortex. That's what happens to the bad souls the angels throw in—the darklings, they call them—the ones who really just refuse to get with the program. They get sucked down and end up back in the mortal world as worms or slugs or cockroaches and have to work their way up the pipe again.

"It's always their own doing, and they always resent it."

Brang! Jason looked up to where a red fire bell hung vibrating against the building wall.

"Told you," said Kutchmeyer. He headed toward where the red-suits were now streaming: a circular depression in the lawn that turned out to be an amphitheater when he focused on it. "Orientation. It's mandatory, no matter how many times you've rotated through. Let's get a seat."

As they walk, Jason looks down at what he's wearing, then reaches around to take hold of his tail and bring the point up in front of his eyes. "This," he says, "this is kind of hard to believe."

"I remember," says Kutchmeyer, "when it was just black robes and white robes. With matching halos. Then, one rotation, I show up and we're cartoon characters. Makes you wonder."

"What," says Jason, gesturing to the sky, "that somebody up there has a sense of humor?"

The other man grins. "Nah, it's just sometimes I wonder how serious he takes all of this."

Jason looks back at the river, remembering the Proteus–squid's rage. "Somebody's taking it seriously," he said.

"Attention," says a bored voice from below them. Another Grodinesque angel has stepped out onto the small central space at the bottom of the great bowl. "This is orientation, so pay attention."

It gestures with one arm and a huge screen appears behind it. "Most of you have been here before and will remember the routine. For the newcomers, here's how it works: you start out in the ooze and you work your way up the sentience scale, heading for enlightenment."

Images have appeared on the screen, illustrating the angel's words. Jason is reminded of the scratchy films they used to get in high–school guidance classes.

"By the time you make human being, you're going to go up or down based on how you handle moral choices. 'Do I take that extra cookie? Do I covet my neighbor's ass? Do I massacre the political opposition?'" The voice even sounds like Charles Grodin's.

"Of course, before you can make moral choices, there has to be something to choose between, or it doesn't count. So somebody has to present the alternatives. In the beginning, we angels used to do it. It's not what we were designed for–our original specs were strictly based on singing and praising, you know–but there were only a few million of you back then and we could get in a good day's tempting and warning, and still have time for an extra shift of singing and praising."

Now the screen teems with hustling crowds of humanity. "But then," the angel says, "the millions became billions, and more help was needed. So we started drafting you. Now those who are ready go up, and the really wonky ones go back in the soup,"–he makes a whirlpool gesture with his fingers–"and have to work their way back up the ladder. The ones in the middle get divided up into tempters and consciences. We give you a living person to work with, and a specific assignment, until it's time for your next incarnation."

It waves to a big stack of fat books on a table that has suddenly appeared. "It's all in your personal assignment book," it says. "Each of you gets full documentation. Study up on it, and be ready to start work when the bell rings again."

The angel walks away. There is no exit from the amphitheater's stage, so it just fades and vanishes between one step and the next. "Come on," says Kutchmeyer, "let's go see what you've got."

They file down with the rest of the red-suits. Jason sees Krissa going down another aisle; she has somehow managed to alter her devil suit so that now she looks like something out of a Marvel comic.

Jason gets his book. Kutchmeyer doesn't get one. "I'm on hiatus," he says. "Just finished my latest gig, waiting to see what comes next.

They climb out of the amphitheater and find a place to sit on the lawn. The business is feeling more and more familiar to Jason. He immediately turns to the back of the book where there is a pocket glued onto the inside of the cover. He reaches into it and finds two pictures. One is of Wally Kaminski; the other is of Amy Beamer.

Kutchmeyer glances at them. He takes the picture of Wally and turns it over. On the back is printed the single word: *Lust*. On the back of Amy's it says: *Target*.

"I'm supposed to get Wally Kaminski to nail Amy Beamer?" Jason says. The prospect is not appealing. More than that, it just doesn't feel right.

"That's about it. You sit on his left shoulder and whisper in his ear. Somebody from the Conscience Choir will sit on the other shoulder and try to steer him to a ring and the altar." Kutchmeyer takes another look at the portraits. "I'd say it's a toss-up either way. but that's how it usually works out—you put lust and love together, shake and stir, add a little luck, and you get something good.

"What we do is a necessary part of the process."

He goes on to explain that assignments for members of the Corps of Tempters are just about always like this. "We're assigned to push one or two cardinal sins. Lust is a not bad. Once you get 'em going, you can pretty well leave it to momentum. Lot better than gluttony—all that chewing and belching. And laziness? Don't get me started. It's beyond boring."

He fixes Jason with a knowing look. "Now, your last time

around, the cardinal sins being pushed were pride and greed."

Jason's been leafing through the book while listening to Kutchmeyer. But now his head comes up. "How do you know that?" he says. Then he knows. "You were on my shoulder."

"You recognize the voice? Yeah, that was me. Not a bad gig, but I was on the losing team. Started out okay, but after a while, you kinda lost interest." He rubs the side of his nose thoughtfully, "Fact is, way you were going, I'da figured to see you on the other side of the river."

Jason looks across the water. On the opposite lawn, figures in white are sitting on their lawn, heads down-bent over books. He sees Megan and Nick sitting side by side. The teenager meets his gaze and nudges the young woman. She looks up and their eyes meet.

"I think I'm supposed to be over there," Jason tells Kutchmeyer. "I think I'm supposed to be with her."

The older man shrugs. "They don't make mistakes," he says. "At least, that's what they tell us."

"I've got to get across."

Kutchmeyer rises, saying, "You can't. It's funda–" and is cut off when the bell rings again. "Your shift is starting. You don't want to be late your first day."

The red-suits are streaming toward a wide set of double doors that has opened farther along the wall of the big building, past the archways they came out of. Jason and Kutchmeyer join the flow. But before they get to the doorway, they see a pair of angels come out carrying a darkly flickering figure and toss their burden into the river. The man strikes the water and tries to swim, but almost immediately he transforms into an oversized weasel. He sinks from sight.

Jason follows Kutchmeyer into the building, but just before the doorway, he looks back at the river. He can't be sure but it seems to him that, just before the man-weasel went under, he saw the tip of a dark green tentacle wrap itself around the struggling creature.

Inside the building, they're in a smaller, low-ceilinged room whose floor is pierced by a row of holes large enough to accommodate a human body–and the red-suits are dropping into them feet-first. Clutching his book, Jason goes to the nearest, waits a few seconds for the tempter before him to disappear, then jumps in. Now he is falling down a smooth-sided tube like a water slide without the water. There is a sensation of passing through an insubstantial curtain no thicker than the skin of a soap bubble, and then he pops out into the world of mortals.

Specifically, he lands standing up on a piece of checkered cloth that he recognizes as one of the shirts Wally Kaminski habitually wears. He also recognizes the Old Spice cologne that Wally's mother gave him for Christmas. Jason realizes he is standing on his assistant's left shoulder.

"Dude!" says a voice he recognizes. He cranes around to see past Wally's chin and sees a haloed Nick Caspian waving from the other shoulder. "Most excellent!" is the teenager's summation of their situation.

Wally is at Fate's office, cleaning out his cubicle, pausing occasionally to deal with a runny nose and wipe the mist from his eyes. Jason realizes that, because he was the sole owner of Fate Records, his death means the company will be closing its doors. Wally will be looking for a new job.

Jason looks around the office. The other staff are also clearing out their desks. He sees other tearful faces, and is touched by the sight; he didn't think he was the kind of guy people would cry for. He sees Amy at the reception desk, her nose even redder than usual and her eyes puffy.

And on the young woman's shoulders he sees Megan under a halo and Krissa in her form-hugging Catwoman outfit. "Nick!" he calls. "We've got to get this guy over there! I've got to talk to . . . Jeez, I don't even know her name!"

"Megan," says Nick. "But, dude, I don't think we're supposed to work together. It's like you push, I pull. You pull, I push." He goes to scratch his head, is puzzled for a moment by the halo getting in the way, then opts for searching in his assignment book. "Whoa, here it is: 'The conscience will seek to nullify suggestions from the tempter–'"

"Special circumstances," says Jason.

Nick flips through the book. "I don't see–"

"Love," Jason says. "True love."

The conscience takes his finger out of the book, points it at Jason and then at Megan, his face transmitting an unspoken question.

Jason says, "You got it. I've got to talk to her."

It takes Nick a moment to make up his mind then he says, "Party on, dude!" He whispers something in Wally's ear.

Jason goes to the oversized organ on his side of Wally's head– it's large enough for him to step into; though he doesn't–and says,

"Get up and go see Amy." He hears Nick saying the same thing.

Wally puts down the unsolved Rubik's Cube he was about to put into a box and gets up. He heads over to the reception area. Amy looks up, and Jason sees Krissa getting ready to start work, while Megan is gazing at him in some consternation.

"He needs to say something," Jason tells Nick.

"I think he wants to tell her she's, like, totally smokin'."

"Probably not the right thing, under the circumstances."

"Dude, so right! Good save."

Jason thinks, then says, "How about: 'I hate to see you so sad?'"

"Excellent! Let's do that."

They speak into Wally's ear and he says the words. Amy looks at him with deer-in-the-headlights eyes. Krissa wants her to say, "How'd you like to see me naked?" while Megan is urging her to recognize Wally's kindness.

Jason calls across the distance between them, "Megan! I've got to talk to you!"

She says, "I think we're supposed to be working now."

"It's the only chance we'll get." Jason floats up from Wally's shoulder and finds that he can get a little distance toward Megan. She lifts up off Amy and comes toward him. He reaches out a hand to her, and she tentatively responds, but they are still too far apart to touch.

"I've got to see you," he says.

"I know."

"I've never felt like this before."

"Me neither."

Jason tells her he wants to try swimming across the river.

"You mustn't," she says. "Not from your side."

"Then you swim to me."

She's wearing the wrong outfit for breaking the rules, but maybe Jason's a better tempter than he thinks he ought to be. "I don't know," is what she says, but what he hears is, "Convince me."

"You and I," he says, "we're meant for each other. You're the one. And just when I meet you,"–he spreads his hands–"this happens."

Meanwhile, as Jason and Megan hover in mid-air, the tempter and conscience they left unchecked have been doing their jobs. Krissa has convinced Megan that her optimum course of conduct is to unbutton a her blouse a couple of stops, come out from behind the desk, and sit on it with one leg provocatively raised. She is staring up into Wally's face and licking her lips like a bad imitation of an old-time movie vamp.

Wally, however, is being guided by the inexpert Nick, whose experience with what he thinks of as "total rectitude, dude" is largely conjectural. The gofer has fixed his gaze on the middle distance and is in the process of clasping his hands before him, in a position from which they can quickly shield those parts of him that have not felt a female's touch since he mastered toilet training.

The situation is unbalanced and heading toward a difficult climax when an angel appears—though not to the mortals present—and, placing a finger on Jason's and Megan's chests, pushes them back to their respective shoulders.

"Is there a problem here?" it says. "If you don't want to handle these mortals, there's always a vacancy on Madonna's shoulder."

"No, these are fine," Megan says.

But Jason says, "Somebody made a mistake. I'm wearing the wrong color."

"We," says the angel, "don't make mistakes."

"Well this time you—"

"Get back to work."

"I want to file an appeal, or something."

The angel almost smiles. "Really?"

"How do I do it?"

"You're serious?"

"Uh huh."

The angel blinks then considers. "I'll have to inquire," it says. "The issue has never come up before."

"You do that," says Jason.

"In the meantime, get back to tempting. This mortal's situation is unbalanced."

Jason has a few things he'd like to say about what's unbalanced, but he's received a commitment to look into his case, and he doesn't think an angel would lie, so he settles himself on Wally's left shoulder and tries to do his job.

The book is helpful, after a fashion. But after reading a few pages, dotted with illustrations that look like they belong in *Seduction For Dummies*, Jason slams the covers shut and says, "This is like a thirty-year-old version *of How To Pick Up Girls!* I'll bet somewhere in here it says, 'If I said you had a beautiful body would you hold it against me?'"

"Dude, you should see mine," says Nick. "It's totally Archie comics."

"Listen," says Jason, "let's work this together, see if we can get him to ask her for a date. Otherwise, after tomorrow, this place closes up, he's not going to see her again."

And so they do. There is a considerable amount of stuttering, umming-and-ahing, and blushing to get through, but finally the request is made. Krissa and Megan manage to steer Amy into a positive reply, and two painfully shy people are now on track to join Ted and Tina. They'll catch the latest Harry Potter movie and have dinner.

Wally makes it back to his cubicle in a fog of fear and joyful anticipation, and Amy concentrates as best she can on handling the calls coming in, telling everyone to contact the accounting firm that will handle winding up the company.

For the shoulder folk, there's not much left on the agenda, although Krissa can't resist urging Amy to imagine George Clooney walking in and performing highly unlikely maneuvers with her on the reception desk. That keeps Megan busy throughout the afternoon.

The two mortal couples meet for dinner at a restaurant, in one of the most painful episodes of shyness that Jason has ever had to witness. But, gradually, as Ted and Tina keep pouring more wine, Wally's and Amy's jitters recede. By the time they walk down the block to the theater, Wally and Amy are holding hands as if they've done it before. The movie goes well, and Ted and Tina decide put them into a cab.

At Amy's place, they stand on the doorstep. Krissa wants her to drag the guy in, but Megan holds it to a single good-night kiss, although she's not able to keep the temptress from slipping in some tongue. They agree to meet for lunch the next day.

"Let's get this guy home and tucked in," Jason tells Nick, and an hour later Wally is in bed and slipping off to swim in the Dreamtime river. Holes appear in the air and the tempter and conscience tube their way back to base. Jason arrives in a room crowded with red suits and spots Kutchmeyer. He tells him about the angel's promise of a review.

"Don't hold your breath," says the wrinkled man. "You've heard the one about the mills that grind exceeding slow?"

"I've got to find that angel and see what's happening." He looks around, sees a few Grodins. "But they all look the same."

"That's cause they *are* all the same," says Kutchmeyer. "Only one personality between all of them."

"So it doesn't matter which one I ask?"

"Shouldn't."

Jason buttonholes the nearest angel. "What about my review?" he says.

"It's under consideration."

"What does that mean?"

The angel presses the tips of its fingers together. "It means that the possibility of reviewing your status has been accepted. We are now establishing a framework for addressing the questions it raises."

"That does not sound like I'm getting an answer soon."

"We're glad you understand."

"No," says Jason, "I don't understand!"

"Then we're sorry you don't understand."

"I'm not supposed to be here!"

"Then why are you here?"

"There's been a mistake!"

"There are no mistakes."

Jason turns away, before he does something that could only make things worse. He goes outside and down to the river bank. Kutchmeyer follows.

"Listen, son," the old soul says, "are you certain that you're on the wrong side of the river?"

"Absolutely!"

"Well, there's one way to know for sure." He gestures toward the fast-flowing current. "We can't last more than a few strokes in there. The folks across the river can swim way upstream, into the world of dreams."

Jason looks at the roiling liquid. At that moment, a pair of angels come out of the reception hall carrying the soul of a woman wreathed in shadows. They throw her into the river, where she transforms into a human-sized cockroach before being abruptly yanked below the surface.

"Did you see that?" Jason says.

"What?" says Kutchmeyer.

"It was like something snatched her down."

"Musta been a trick of the current. Can't nothing survive for long in that stuff."

Jason refocuses on his own problem. "If I can swim in the river, that would prove I'm wearing the wrong color?"

The old shoulders shrug. "That's how it ought to figure." Then he takes hold of Jason's arm. "But suppose you're wrong? Once you're bound for that whirlpool, there's no coming back."

Jason stares across the river. He can see Megan on the far side. He raises a hand to her and she responds. "I'll take that chance," he says. He goes down to the water's edge. "Watch me," he asks Kutchmeyer. "I'll need a witness."

The older soul offers his hand. "Good luck, kid."

Jason stands for a moment on the lip of the bank. He looks again at Megan, sees the strain on her face. He takes a deep breath and dives in.

The stuff is neither cold nor wet. It flows past him like air, but when he strokes against it, he feels the pressure on his arms and hands. He is moving forward, against the current, and now he realizes that he doesn't need to worry about breathing. He strokes again, forward and up, and breaks the surface. The current is running past him, but as long as he swims against it, it does not bear him toward the vortex.

He rolls over on his back and sees Kutchmeyer on the shore, receding as Jason backstrokes upstream. Then he looks to the other side and sees Megan, her face alight with hope. She walks down to the water's edge and, without hesitation, dives in.

She swims strongly against the current, angling toward the middle of the river. Jason turns over and does the same. But now that he has gone a little way upstream, the moment he puts his face into the water he sees that it is filled with globules of colored light—in every possible shade of red, blue, green, yellow, and pure white. They swirl and swarm, unaffected by the current, all the way down to the river bed. Now one of them brushes against his ear, and he hears a momentary flash of speech. When another touches his eyes, he sees a fleeting vision of a running horse against a dark sky.

Suddenly, he understands. *They're dreams,* he tells himself. The whole river is densely packed with the dreams of all the people in the world who are right now asleep and dreaming. He swims more carefully, doing a gentle breaststroke, so as not to disturb them. But he notices that one bright-blue bubble seems somehow to be drawn to him. It bobs before him, changing direction to hold its position when he tries to evade it.

Jason reaches out and gently takes hold of the baseball-sized orb. He rolls over on his back and continues to kick against the current, then he lifts the blue bubble and touches it to his forehead.

Immediately, he is in the world of Vlar of the Ax. The mighty-thewed barbarian stands on a sky-shadowed plain, surrounded by a horde of feral half-men howling their rage as he cuts them down in swathes, swinging his double-edge weapon as if it weighed no more than a willow wand. Beyond the enemy, on a raised mound of skulls, he can see a buxom young woman, clad in two small pieces of fur, bound to a stake. Her face, turned to him beseechingly, is Amy's.

"Be not afraid!," cries dream-Wally, though the voice is richer than his waking tones. "I will come for you!"

A little embarrassed, Jason removes the dream-bubble from his forehead and lets Wally get on with things. His vision clears and he sees Megan swimming toward him, but with a glowing pink globule bouncing in front of her.

"Take hold of it," he tells her. "I'll bet it's Amy, dreaming."

Megan cups the bubble in her hand and touches it to her head. Her eyes go unfocused for a moment then she blinks and takes the glowing ball away. It drifts off.

"Amy?" Jason asks her.

"With a long sword," says Megan. "At her feet, a knight in shining armor, wounded on a battlefield. She was protecting him until he could stand and fight again."

"These young people today," Jason says, "where do they get this stuff?"

A couple of strokes and they are within arm's length of each other. They tread water and their hands reach out and touch. Jason feels a sense of power and certainty pass through him. "I was right," he says. "You're the one."

"Looks that way," she says. She looks around at the swirls of colored orbs. "But what can we do about it?"

"Nothing more than Ken and Barbie ever did," he says. He takes her in his arms and they kiss. It's a long one, and it draws the dream-bubbles toward them, by the dozens, then by the hundreds, then the thousands, until they're at the center of a great double helix of swirling, colored balls fountaining up from the river bed to break the surface and cascade down all around the two lovers.

And, all over the world, dreamers find themselves in the arms of their "ones"—and many of them wake up alone and yearning.

But suddenly the swirls of color are gone. Treading water, Jason and Megan have drifted downstream into the dark water that leads to the vortex. The current grows stronger.

"We'd better get out of here," he tells her. She starts to swim toward her side of the river and he reluctantly turns toward where an anxious Kutchmeyer stands on the shore. With the older soul's help, Jason hauls himself out. He is drained yet full of joy.

Kutchmeyer is watching Megan swim toward where Nick waits for her on the far shore. He sees a dark shadow in the water, moving toward her.

"Look!" he says to Jason, pointing.

Jason sees the dark, indistinct shape. It's big and it moves fast. "What is it?"

Kutchmeyer shakes his head. "I don't know. But I know I've never seen anything like it."

Jason begins to run toward the river, but then he sees Megan make it to the bank and climbs out. She turns and waves to him, who raises a hand to her. "Upstream is all dreams," he tells Kutchmeyer. "Maybe down here is where the nightmares live."

The older soul shakes his head. "You want to watch yourself in there," he says, nodding toward the river. "Something's not right."

"Maybe," Jason says, "but something else has never been righter."

There's a hissing sound from nearby, like a snake with a toothache. Jason turns to see Krissa, her face twisted in anger and envy. "Playing kissy-face with Miss Purity?" she says. "You won't be getting any there, stud."

"Leave it, Krissa," Jason says.

"You coulda had all of this," she says, gesturing at her voluptuous figure. "If you'd said yes, none of this would've–" She stops talking then, and Jason recognizes the look of someone who knows she's already said too much.

"What are you talking about?" he says.

But she waves him away with a contemptuous flip of her hand and stalks off. For a moment, Jason thinks he saw darkness flickering around her fingertips.

———————— ✍ ————————

When morning rolls around again in the mortal world, Jason is back on Wally's left shoulder for another day of tempting. He's finding that, if he stays still and clears his mind, he can get a sense of Wally's thoughts. After some practice, that sense becomes full-on eavesdropping.

Wally is replaying last night's dream he had about Amy the night before. Plenty happened after the scene that Jason picked up on, and the tempter wonders if his own embrace of Megan in the midst of the helix of colored bubbles had something to do with the content of his former gofer's dream.

"That was a doozie," he calls over to Nick on the other shoulder.

"I'm supposed to fill his head with pure thoughts, after that?" Nick calls back. "Like, hopeless, dude."

For his lunch date with Amy, they dress Wally in an actual shirt and slacks, instead of his usual faded jeans and an X-Men sweatshirt–he has several–and get him over to the restaurant on time. But Amy is late, and after a while she's even later.

Wally grows increasingly anxious, thinking he's been dumped. He thinks about texting her something rude, but Jason and Nick soothe him with images of hand-holding and beach walks.

"I feel like I'm creating commercials for Hallmark," Jason tells the teenager.

"It's all good, dude," says Nick. "Here they come."

Amy arrives at the restaurant, looking flustered. She sits down across from Wally but can't bring herself to meet his gaze. Wally defaults again to his "I'm about to be dumped" expectation.

Jason floats off the guy's shoulder toward Megan. "What's going on?"

She levitates close enough to talk with him. "It's Miss Crotchless Panties here," she says, indicating Krissa, who has her head in Amy's left ear. "She's spent the morning pumping XXX-rated porn down the pipeline. Poor kid thinks she's turning into some kind of sex maniac."

"Krissa!" Jason calls. "The hell you doing? Knock it off!"

Krissa replies with two short words.

Megan says, "You're supposed to tempt her, not drive her crazy!"

The temptress sticks her tongue out at the conscience, and goes back to whispering in Amy's ear. The nerd girl squirms in her seat and her face and neck turn bright red.

"This is no good," Jason tells Nick.

"Dude," the teenager agrees, "it is totally bogus."

"Move him in close enough that we can jump the bitch."

They get Wally out of his seat and around the table. Amy gets up, as if to flee, but he takes her in his arms and holds her firmly but tenderly. "Nice work," Jason tells Nick, "now let's get her!"

Both of them leave Wally's shoulders and land on Amy's left. Megan comes around the back of the young woman's neck, and the three of them yank Krissa out of the ear and wrestle her to the far end of Amy's shoulder. Jason puts a hand over the temptress's mouth, cutting off a continuous flow of pornographic suggestions. Krissa tries to bite the palm that muzzles her, but Jason manages to avoid her teeth.

But now that he's close up, he sees the faint flickerings of darkness around Krissa's form. "Krissa," he says, "you've got to stop doing this! They'll put you in the river!"

But her only response is to growl and fight against the hands that restrain her. She is stronger than Jason expected–and seems to be getting more powerful by the moment.

At least her influence on Amy is gone. The young woman has calmed down. She leans into Wally's embrace and her arms come up to hold him, too. But the tender moment won't last; Krissa is kicking and thrashing. Soon she will be free.

"What is going on here?" says a new voice.

Jason turns and sees an angel has appeared beside them, looking like Charles Grodin at his most irritated. "Look for yourself," he says, taking his hand away from Krissa's mouth.

She curses him in rich and imaginative terms, but the angel's attention is on the dark shadows passing across her face. "Hmm," it says, and appears to concentrate for a moment. Then two more of its kind appear. They take hold of the temptress.

Jason knows what's about to happen and he seizes the first angel's elbow. A moment later, both of them are on the shore of the river, as are the two angels holding a struggling, cursing Krissa. They march her straight to the water and throw her in then head back into the main building.

The angel Jason tagged along with says, "Wait until we assign a new temptress to the woman. Then you will go back to work."

"Wait a minute," Jason says. "You told me you guys don't make mistakes."

"We don't," says the angel, but its normally bland self-assurance has diminished.

"Well, what do you call that?" Jason gestures to where Krissa struggles against the current. He sees her disappear, and he's sure something pulled her down. "Did you see that?" he says. "Something's in the river. Something big. Something bad."

"Nothing can survive in the flux channel," says the angel.

"Just like you don't make mistakes?"

The angel turns away. "Wait until the replacement is ready," it says over its shoulder. "Then go back to work. Let us worry about the rest."

Jason is not reassured. He wonders if angels even know how to worry. He goes and sits by the river bank. The water is dark and turgid, but he believes he can see glimpses of something darker in its depths.

And he's right, though he doesn't yet know how awfully, terrifyingly right he is. The fact is, Wilson Proteus had done some past-life investigating during his most recent reincarnation. He hadn't managed to remember all of it, but he'd been able to recover the basics. He knew about the river, and the vortex, and about how the darklings changed as they hit the flux.

He had willed himself—and he had quite a strong will to work with—to transform into a mesonychoteuthis, the colossal squid of the Antarctic waters. Fifty feet long, stronger and heavier than its cousin archeteuthis, the giant squid, it had tentacles whose suckers were equipped with hooked triple claws. Proteus's plan had been to drive those projections into the bed of the river and hold on.

The plan worked, and so did the improvisations that Proteus embarked upon, once he was secure against the pressure of the current. When the angels next threw in a vortex-bound soul, the squid reached up one of its tentacles and snared the dark one before it could be swept into the whirlpool. He brought the struggling, half-human-half-wolf down to his beak, and devoured him. Then came one with the head of a shrieking woman and the body of a cockroach; down she went into the belly of the cephalopod.

More followed, and Proteus noted a peculiar effect. His squid-form could not actually digest the souls he consumed. But some of their mass became his, while the remainder kept their mutated forms, so that after several such meals he now resembled a kind of squid-shaped pin cushion into which had been inserted a wolf, a spider, several species of insects, a couple of dead-eyed sharks, a few poisonous snakes, a hagfish, and some over-sized sewer rats. He found that the larger and heavier he grew, the easier it became to hold his position on the river bed.

Indeed, as his giant beak chewed on the gristle that had been Krissa Bolide while she was being transformed into a scorpion, the entity that had lately been Wilson Proteus (and, before that, some of history's most notable villains), was thinking that he need not remain in the river any more. The time was approaching when he could crawl out and—always an attractive prospect—see how much damage he could do.

Amy's new temptress is an old soul named Madeleine. She and Jason tube together to their assignments and arrive on their respective shoulders just as the pair of lovers are concluding an innocent walk on the beach.

"Looking good, dude," Nick tells Jason to bring him up to date. "Some serious hand-holding."

Wally and Amy eat hot dogs from a beachfront stand, indulge in some long, wordless eye-contact, share a few observations on their favorite books and movies—their tastes coincide nicely—then he walks her home.

Madeleine knows her job and Jason steps up to his responsibilities as a tempter, so there are some untutored gropings and squeezings on her couch before all four shoulder-folk agree to fall back and let the lovers' universe unfold at a moderate speed. Jason and Nick see Wally home and to bed—after some relaxation via a video game that lets him kick ass and rescue damsels—then leave him with a suggestion for a good dream.

They tube back to their river banks and Jason sees Megan on the far side. A pang goes through him, and he signals her to meet him upstream. She nods acceptance and he dives in.

They meet at the place where the dreams begin then swim farther upstream through swirls of colored globes. At a place where they are surrounded by the lights, they stop and embrace each other. This time, there is no need for words. They hold each and are complete. Indeed, after a long moment, Jason is no longer sure where he leaves off and Megan begins. They are not made of flesh anymore, and it seems that they are literally melting into each other, becoming one in spirit.

The dream globes again form spirals around their entwined forms, brushing gently past them in a continuous susurration like watery whisperings against their nonflesh. As a result, all over the world, sleeping men and women slip into dreams of amorous fulfillment. Those who are alone thrash and moan; those who are not alone wake up and cling to the body beside them. Some of the pairings are young and not unused to awakening already in full throb; but quite a few are old and the sudden surge of passion is surprising.

One pair of lovers in particular are more affected than all the others. Wally and Amy rise from their beds and, though still asleep, get dressed and go out into the night in search of each other.

Jason and Megan are oblivious. Time, the swirl of dreams, the flow of the river, mean nothing to them as they cling to each other. Until suddenly the dreams disappear, and the river runs colder than they've ever felt it before.

"Something touched me," Megan says.

Jason releases her. Their one-flesh becomes two. "Swim upstream," he says. "Quickly."

She begins to stroke against the current, advances a few yards, Jason beside her. Then he sees a look of surprise on her face. An instant later, she is pulled under. He dives and turns to follow the flow of the river. He sees Megan being drawn away from him, her legs gripped by the tip of a long, green tentacle. He swims frantically toward her, but then through the murk of the turbid water, he sees where the tentacle begins.

Proteus has become a monstrous, bloated thing, his body swollen to almost the whole width of the river. His huge eyes and the great beak centered in its writhing nest of tentacles are still those of a deep-water squid, but the rest of his form is studded with the half-human, half-beast shapes of the dark souls he has devoured. Clawed limbs and snarling muzzles project from the squid-flesh at random, pincers and jagged mandibles clashing blindly, with here and there a partly formed face screaming, howling, cursing. Between the eyes is one that seems to bear the face of Krissa Bolide, cruelly jeering above a segmented half-body.

Towards this raging chaos Megan is being pulled backwards, her mouth open and her eyes pleading with Jason. He makes a desperate lunge through the dark water and seizes her out-thrust hand. But he can do nothing against the hideously powerful grip of toothed suction cups that are wider than his palm. And now they are both being drawn toward the scissor-sharp beak.

But now a memory comes to him: *the stuff dreams are made on. In the river, anything dreamt becomes real.*

Jason concentrates, desperately, on the first image that comes to him. *Be real!* he shouts in his mind.

And suddenly the river is gone. He is on white charger, racing across a vast green meadow, his armor bright under a noonday sun, his lance's tip aimed at the scaled breast of a spike-crested dragon. In one forepaw, the monster's talons clutch a damsel clad in white samite. Her face is Megan's.

The horse's hooves pound the turf, the lance nears its target. Then the dragon opens its dagger-toothed jaws and spews a blast of sulfurous flame at Jason. He concentrates his mind and the flameblast seamlessly morphs into a jet of pure energy from a plasma beam-weapon. Jason raises the knight's shield and sees it become a hemispherical force field that repels the discharge. Proteus looms above him, a multi-limbed war machine of oiled steel. Around them lies an endless field of post-apocalyptic wreckage. Jason lifts his cyborg arm and focuses its aiming mechanism on the enemy's core processor.

Again the scene shifts. In a palaeozoic forest, Wilson is a tyrannosaur clutching Megan in one of its his forelimbs, and Jason becomes a lightweight, feathered raptor, leaping at the larger beast, his curved foot-claws snapping forward to rip Proteus's belly. But then comes another shift, and Jason is a Viking warrior on a plain of ice, striking with his sword against the gelid flesh a frost giant, who wields an iron-studded club in one hand and holds Megan in the other.

Their combat changes again, becomes Tarzan against a great gray ape, then a cartoon mouse against a vicious grinning cat, and now an old fisherman against a huge white shark. Throughout each change, Jason fights with all his strength, but always he is outmatched by the monster's sheer size. He is not winning. And he feels himself weakening.

But in their struggles, the combatants have pushed farther upstream, into the zone of swirling dream-spheres. And now something new is happening: their thrashings in the river that generates the mortal world are causing rents to appear in the fabric of earthly reality. Dreamtime and spacetime are connecting in ways they were never meant to.

Los Angeles commuters look up to see a two-headed roc lazily circling over the big Hollywood sign up in the hills; in New York, when a man opens his refrigerator door, searching for a beer, a giant tongue comes out from beneath the shelves and licks him; a San Francisco police car pursuing a gang of bank robbers crests a hill and suddenly the cops find themselves plunging down the slope of a mile-high roller-coaster; in Cleveland, a teenage boy fantasizing over the *Sports Illustrated* swimsuit issue looks up to see that the wall of his bedroom has dissolved and opened the way to a tropical beach where near-naked supermodels beckon.

And, through all of this, while Jason battles and Megan is held captive, Wally and Amy wander the streets, wreathed in dreams, unknowingly moving towards each other.

———————

Of course, all of this rending and shape-shifting has not gone unnoticed by those Kutchmeyer would call "the powers that be." A flood of Grodinesque angels has erupted from the reception hall to converge on the river bank. They can see the dark bulk of the Proteus-squid thrashing in the water. Now they link hands and exert their powers.

An invisible wall appears in the river, upstream from the struggle, insulating the Dreamtime from the conflict here near the whirlpool. Below the barrier, the river soon runs dry, the last of its flow gurgling down into the vast hole that created and contained the vortex. The Proteus-squid is revealed in all its horrific ugliness, bathed in darkness. Megan is still imprisoned in one tentacle, Jason still struggling futilely to break its grip.

"Enough!" says one of the angels, speaking for all. "Free the captive soul and go down to your deserved fate."

One huge squid eye focuses on the speaker. The beak opens and a cold, whispering voice says, "Or you'll do what?"

It doesn't wait for an answer but swivels on its belly and sweeps one of it long palps along the shoreline, scattering angels like a bad-tempered child knocking over a parade of toy soldiers. Then it lifts itself by sheer force of will until it is hovering not just above the river bed, but above the riverbank itself. Its tentacles thrash at the angels, knocking them in all directions. Somewhere in the melee, it lets

Megan go, forgotten. She tumbles and crashes through the sprawl of Grodins, and finally comes to rest against the white wall of the reception building. She lies unmoving. Jason climbs out of the dry river and rushes toward her.

The Proteus-squid, bristling with half-digested darklings, smashes the angels flat again. Jason ducks under one flailing tentacle and reaches Megan. She does not seem to be injured—they're not really flesh and bone, after all—but prolonged exposure to the monster's touch has sapped much of her energy. Her virtual flesh is cold. He helps her up and, with her leaning on him, leads her away from the struggle.

But when he makes some distance and looks back, it seems to him that the squid-thing has grown larger and darker than ever. The more it batters the Grodins, the more it seems to absorb energy from them. When it came out of the water it was gray-green, wreathed in darkness; now it is a matte-black all over, as if it has reached a point when it can absorb the energies of anything it touches.

As if to prove Jason's supposition right, the squid now wraps a tentacle around a Grodin and lifts it from the ground. The angel does not squirm or resist, but regards the monster with bland contempt—even as Proteus brings the white-robed form to its beak and, in two bites, devours it.

A great sigh is heard. Throughout the squid-thing's depredations, the archangel has remained on its seat in the reception hall. Now it rises to its feet and walks toward the scene of the struggle, passing through the walls of the huge building as if they were made of mist.

It arrives on the riverbank and confronts what Wilson Proteus has become. An expression of grave sadness comes over the huge Charlton Heston face. It points a column-sized finger at the monster and in a deep, calm voice, says, "No."

The squid-thing looks up at the great man-shaped being in silence, though its various excrescences are roaring, hissing, growling, chittering, rattling, clashing spiked mandibles. For a long moment, there is stillness on the river's shore. Then the monster rears up on its spade-shaped tail-flukes and throws its tentacles at the archangel, gripping the robed form, climbing it, the hooked suckers tearing, the parrot-beak biting.

The archangel staggers. It struggles to free its limbs from the tentacles' toothy embrace. It pulls its head back as the beak nears its face. But something is wrong. The squid is tearing away chunks of the archangel's substance and devouring them. With each bite it grows stronger, and its captive's hitherto-unchallenged power is fading. The archangel's knees bend, then buckle. It topples backward, slowly, like the fall of a great tower, the dull black mass of the Proteus-squid now swelling to cover it completely.

Jason steps forward, though he is barehanded. But Kutchmeyer holds him back. "No," the old soul says, "you're not real enough to defeat that. Only something from the real world can do it."

At that moment, a rent appears in the air. Through it steps a muscular man clad in worn leather and holding a long-hafted, double-headed ax. Behind him comes a tall, lithe woman in glistening chain mail, a two-handed claymore slung across her back. Wally and Amy, sleepwalking through reality, have found each other both in spacetime and Dreamtime.

Vlar of the Ax says, "Looks like this is where we're meant to be."

The Faery knight draws her long sword. "And together," she says.

The ax-man steps to the squid and, with one swing of his weapon, severs tail from body. A thick black ichor oozes out onto the lawn and trickles back to the river. With a hiss like a steam engine, the creature disengages from the prostrate archangel and turns on its attacker. It flings out a heavy tentacle with blinding speed, but Vlar ducks underneath the limb and, straightening, slices it in two, leaving the chopped-off end writhing behind him.

The squid rears up and cants its head to one side to get a single-eye fix on the barbarian. Its beak opens and it sends out two, three, four tentacles at once. Vlar hacks and cuts with power and precision, but though three more black-flickering ropes of cold-blooded muscle fall to the lawn, the fourth wraps around him, pinning his arms and his ax in their fibrous grip. The squid lifts him to its chitinous mouth.

Vlar rears back his shaggy head and spits into one great yellow eye. At that moment, a shining figure appears atop the darkling beast's head, her two-handed sword reversed and raised high. She drives it point-down into the dank and rubbery flesh. A cloud of black mist, reeking of ammonia, bursts from the wound as she works the sword like a gondola oar, cutting and widening the wound.

A creature half-woman, half-scorpion, hisses at her and tries to seize her sword but, in one smooth motion, Eliadora withdraws the weapon from the squid and swings it in a horizontal arc, lopping the abomination's head from its segmented neck.

The squid hisses in rage, and all the half-beasts protruding from its hide add their cries to the cacophony. It reaches to seize Eliadora, but she pulls free her blade and swings it in a swirl of dark droplets, slicing through the claw-suckered flesh. Then she once more drives the weapon deep into Proteus's gore-slicked carapace.

In wounded fury, the Proteus squid rears up higher, thrashing its remaining tentacles about its head, trying to grasp its tormentor. Eliadora drives in the claymore to the quillons and clings to the hilt as the darkling tries to shake her loose.

Vlar, forgotten, is released to fall to the ground. He lands on his feet, and immediately rushes at the wall of flesh that is the monster's long belly. With one two-handed, vertical strike, he slits the dark-skinned muscle from as high as he can reach right down to the ground. A great gush of foulness spews out from the rent, bathing the barbarian's feet. A sound like a dying wind issues from the beak above his head. He moves aside to let the creature fall, dropping his ax to catch Eliadora in his arms as she tumbles from its upper surface.

Proteus lies stretched across the grass. The vast body shudders once, then again, before rapidly deliquescing into a final rush of black ichor. All the half-beasts dissolve along with their host and the stinking liquid they become drains away into the river, to be washed down to the vortex.

Vlar and Eliadora wipe clean their weapons on the grass. She sheathes her sword and he slings his ax from a harness that hangs from his broad shoulders. They look into each other's eyes for a long moment, then take each other in their arms.

The embrace lasts even longer than the eye-contact. Finally, an angel says, "That's enough. You're not supposed to be here." It signals to several of its fellows. "Let's get this mess cleaned up."

Then it notices Megan. "You are on the wrong side of the river."

"So am I," says Jason, putting his arm around Megan's waist. "And what are you going to do about it?"

Vlar and Eliadora turn at the sound of Jason's voice. The big barbarian looks Jason up and down and reaches out to touch one of his red horns. "That really you, boss?" he says. "Man, this is some dream."

The angel has taken Megan by the arm and another is moving

in on Jason. Vlar lets go of Eliadora and half-lifts the ax. "Hey!" he says. "Let go of them."

Beside him, Eliadora reaches for the hilt of her sword.

"Get these dreamers back into the river," says the angel. More of its colleagues move toward the group around Jason.

"Back off!" says Vlar.

"Wait a minute!" says Jason. "You can't just act as if none of this happened! A mistake has been made!"

The take-charge angel gestures to some of its fellows, more of whom are arriving by the moment, to deal with Vlar and Eliadora. To Jason, it says, "We don't make mistakes."

The tempter waves his hand toward the smear of black still staining the grass. "Oh, yeah?"

A confrontation is building. Vlar and Eliadora brush aside the angels trying to surround and herd them, and come to stand with Jason and Megan.

"Enough of this!" says the angel. It signals, and a host of new Grodins comes swarming from the big building. Vlar raises his ax and bellows a war cry. Eliadora assumes a combat stance.

While all of this has been going on, the archangel has risen to its feet again, and is walking back toward the reception hall. The rents in its clothing and the tears in its flesh are repairing themselves. Now it pauses and observes the rush of angels past its feet, then turns and looks back at the disputants. Its expression changes to one of solemn concern. Its arm lifts and its huge index finger begins to come to bear on Jason.

"Hold it! Hold it! Hold it!" says Kutchmeyer, forcing his way through the angelic throng. "I seen a lot of shit go down in this place," he says, then points at the vortex, "but nothing like this!"

"Stay out of it, tempter," says the angel.

Kutchmeyer thrusts out his scrawny chin. "Screw you!" he says. "These people saved your butts, and they deserve better!"

"Everyone," says the angel, "gets what they deserve. That's the whole point of 'this place.'"

"The kid should never have been assigned to the Corps," Kutchmeyer says. "He should've been Choir. You need to retest him."

"No one has ever been–"

Jason interrupts. "Just like no darkling has ever come back out of the river?"

"That has nothing to do with it."

The archangel's finger descends. But it lands on the angel's shoulder and taps twice. The angel looks up, and for once its face bears an expression: pure surprise. Which gets even purer when the giant digit points to the reception hall then waggles in a way that says, *Get on with it.*

An angel with a wand is summoned. It swiftly runs the instrument over Jason. But, once again, the reading is negative.

"There," says the officious angel. "Now let's–"

"Nuh uh," say Kutchmeyer. He takes the wand from the tester and passes it slowly down from Jason's head and his entire torso. Then he shows it to the boss angel. "Corps or Choir?" he says.

The angel's face remains bland, but there is reluctance in its voice as it says, "Choir."

Now Kutchmeyer passes the wand down Jason's right leg and looks at it. "Still Choir," he says. The angel nods. Then the old soul tests the left leg. When he gets to the spot just above the knee, the instrument turns dark. "Ahah," he says.

He stoops and rolls up the leg of Jason's red suit. Just above the knee is a fleck of darkness. Kutchmeyer pulls it free and throws it into the river, then tries the wand again. The detector remains a clear white.

Kutchmeyer hands the wand back to the tester and says, "Can you say 'oops?'"

The boss angel says nothing. But then the archangel's finger nudges the Grodin in the back, pushing it awkwardly forward a few steps. It looks up beseechingly at the giant but finds no help there. "Oh . . ." it says, teeth gritted, "oops."

"So now what?" says Jason. Megan moves closer to him and he takes her hand.

The angel says, "We'll reassign you to the Choir and you'll go over the river." It sees their two clasped hands and gestures for them to move apart. "And there'll be none of that. What kind of place do you think this is?"

"A place where mistakes get made," says Jason. "Look, our job was to get Amy and Wally together." He gestures to the barbarian and the faery knight, who stand with their arms about each other. "I'd say we did that in spades."

"Then you'll be reassigned."

Megan speaks up. "That's all we get, after all we've been

through?"

Jason puts his arm around her. "You said this was a place where people get what they deserve. We deserve each other."

The angel folds its arms. "We decide—"

But it gets another nudge from the big finger. Kutchmeyer has been gesturing to get the giant's attention; now it reaches down a hand and he steps into it, is carried up until he can speak softly in the huge ear.

The immense being listens, its face grave. For a long moment, there is only the sound of the river rushing by. Then the giant lips rearrange themselves into a smile and in a voice that can be heard all the way to the land of dreams, the archangel says, "*Yes!*"

Not only did Ted and Tina have a double wedding with Wally and Amy, but a few weeks later when Tina told her friend that she was expecting, Amy said, "Me, too."

And a little more than nine months after the wedding, both brides gave birth on the same day. "What are the odds?" Ted asked Wally.

Wally had changed a lot since he and Amy got together–they both had, their friends agreed. He looked at his infant son, Michael, in his basinette, then at Ted's daughter, Jessica, in hers. And he smiled a confident smile.

"Destiny," he said, "does not care about the odds."

The nurses noticed something unusual about the pair of new-borns: whenever they were lifted out of their cradles, they never took their eyes off each other.

While they were nursing their babes together, Amy said to Tina, "Wouldn't it be something if they grew up to marry each other?"

"I don't know," Tina said. "Ted's got a job offer in Nashville. We're moving away."

Amy smiled. "If they're meant for each other, it won't make any difference."

The invisible tempter on baby Michael's left shoulder, who sometimes went by the name of Kutchmeyer, said to the conscience on the right, "What do you think?"

The conscience adjusted his halo and said, "Dude!"

PETRI PAROUSIA

This story arose from one of those odd things I wonder about when I should be working. You will know what that odd thing was if you read to the end. After wondering about it for a while, I decided I ought to get back to work , so I turned it into a story that ran in The Magazine of Fantasy & Science fiction.

A RESEARCH SCIENTIST is someone who cannot rest content within the confines of existing knowledge, but always itches to know what is over the horizon.

Or it's somebody who doesn't know to leave well enough alone.

Either definition would fit Wally Applethorpe. So it was natural for him to stay on at Yale medical school on a research fellowship, while I couldn't wait to get out and start cutting people open to give them new knees and hips and other useful parts in return for a six-figure income.

In our last year together, Wally had got interested in DNA. Nothing wrong with that, of course. There are plenty of useful things to do with DNA, from catching serial killers to editing congenital diseases out of the gene pool. I suppose you can even make a case for the idea of "improving" the species by making people stronger or more germ-resistant, or whatever he was getting up to in his lab over behind the red brick Farnham Building.

I admit, I could never totally fit my mind around what he was doing. If I could have, maybe I wouldn't have become a surgeon. To me, the human body was not a quasi-metaphysical mystery to be unraveled. It was a kind of soft machine whose parts could be repaired when they broke down, or—even better—replaced entirely with materials God would have used if He'd only had access to teflon and stainless steel.

But to Dr. Wally Applethorpe, full-weight genius and Bentham Research Fellow Extraordinaire, the human being was an infinite series of nesting boxes, like those wooden Russian dolls, one inside another. As soon as he got one open, he'd discover another, smaller one inside, and he'd get busy trying to find his way in, world without end.

I moved up to Boston, joined an existing medical group as their bone man and got busy in my own way: marriage, mortgage, membership in a decent country club. I received regular e-mails from Wally–"Keeping in touch" was always the subject header–to which I replied as briefly as I knew how. You may not know many real geniuses, but let me tell you: close up, over the long term, they can truly get on your nerves.

Then late one morning he showed up at my office. Sharon, the receptionist, was still buzzing me to ask if I wanted to receive an unscheduled visitor when he walked right through my door and said, "Jimmy-boy, you've got to see this."

By reflex, I said, "Don't call me Jimmy-boy. It's Jim, or James, or what the hell, Dr. Feltham."

He gave me that look he always used to give me, the *Let's not make a big deal out of nothing* look (although it seemed to me his whole life was about making big deals out of next to nothing), and said, "I've got to show you this!"

Now, someone who didn't know Wally Applethorpe might think that the logical response to his statement would be, "What?" But I'd spent three years in a grungy New Haven apartment with him, so my question was, "Why?"

He blinked and put on that expression of astounded innocence that went with the clear blue eyes, perpetually pink cheeks and shock of corn-yellow hair. "Because you're my friend," he said.

"I'm not your friend, Wally," I said. "I'm just a guy who wound up rooming with you because I couldn't find anything cheaper. Why don't you try to think of us as strangers who got stuck in an elevator and then happily went their separate ways?"

At which he gave me his *You old kidder, you* look and launched into the matter that had brought him here. "Give me some blood," he said, pulling a specimen kit out of his pocket.

This time, my response was the same as anybody's would have been. "Why?"

"So I can show you what I've been doing."

"Why?"

He sighed indulgently. "Cause you're going to want to get in on the ground floor of this. I'm launching a company, got some backers, going to make some big buckazoids, do a lot more research. Sky's the limit. So naturally I thought of my old buddy, Jimmy-boy."

It was on the tip of my tongue to say, "I'm not your old buddy," but another part of my brain weighed in and said to me, *Just cause he's an annoying little twerp doesn't mean he isn't brilliant. How many people could stand Bill Gates before he was a multi-billionaire?*

I rolled up my sleeve and he efficiently took twenty ccs out of me. "Now what?" I said.

"I'll be back tomorrow," he said, "to show you."

"That's kind of a long commute from New Haven."

"Didn't you get my e-mail?" he said. "I'm just six blocks from here now. Hey, you free for lunch?"

I pleaded an urgent, though imaginary, consult with Jag Sharma, our geriatrics specialist. And, thank God, I did genuinely have a couple of hip replacements scheduled for the afternoon, which allowed me to ease him out the door while he was still bubbling about how it was just like the good old days, the two amigos back in the saddle again. But after he had gone, I wondered how I would keep him at a manageable distance.

I went out front to plot strategy with Sharon. "What a sweet guy," was her opening comment, which was just what girls always said about Wally. Of course, they hadn't had him at full strength and close quarters for three years. Or maybe it was just me. Either way, and notwithstanding the puzzled look she gave me, I worked out a system with Sharon: she would buzz me the moment she saw Wally out in the elevator lobby and heading for the glass doors. That would give me time to get into somebody else's office and close the door before he could inflict himself on me at will. With Wally, I had found that control was the key to maintaining sanity.

But, of course, he was beyond control; so the system failed on its first test. Impatient with the slowness of our elevators, Wally came up the fire stairs and was past Sharon and halfway to my office before she could buzz me with the code words, "Mrs. Arkwright to see you."

So Wally caught me, my desk spread with insurance forms, which meant I couldn't plead any urgencies to justify shortening his visit. He carried a small plastic case, like an insulated lunch box, from which he removed a set of petri dishes with transparent covers.

They were marked with numbers and names. The names were familiar.

"What is this?" I said.

He touched one of the covers. Its label read *Stanley Feltham.* "That's your granddad," he said.

Next to it was a dish labeled *Rose (Maguire) Feltham.* "And your grandma."

The two other dishes were labeled with the names of my mother's parents.

"What is this?" I said again.

"I've isolated each of your grandparents' DNA," he said, giving me that wide-eyed, farm-boy look that meant he had cracked open another doll.

"How?"

So now, finally, he explained. He could unravel a subject's DNA to separate what each of that person's parents had contributed to the mix. It involved microlasers and several kinds of enzymes–cutters, movers and assemblers, he called them–and the whole process was handled by a super-fast computer that could sort through all the possible combinations and find the one that was true.

"I patented the process and we're going public in a few weeks," he said. "Write me a check for five grand and I'll give you stock warrants that will be worth two per cent of the company."

"And what will the company be worth?" I said.

"Why, billions," he said.

"Why?" I said. "What will people do with their grandparents' DNA?"

He shrugged, "I suppose some of them will put it into an egg, insert it into a womb and give birth to grandma or grandpa. Most people have fond memories of their grandparents–from childhood, that is–but by the time the kids are old enough to really get to know them, the old folks are getting ready to shuffle off this mortal coil. Or they're senile."

"Okay," I said, and thought about it. My mother's parents had died before I was born and the world would thank me for not creating another Stan Feltham: there was already an oversupply of sourpusses. "Supposing there is a market for grandparent clones. It can't be worth billions."

He waggled his hands on either side his head. "Think, man," he said, then he spread them wide as if offering the whole world. "We're not just talking grandparents. We can go way back. Way, way back."

"How way?"

"Wa–a–a–ay, way."

"Give me a for instance," I said.

He moved the petri dishes aside and sat on the corner of my desk. "Got any famous ancestors?"

There was a legend in the family on my mother's side that we were descended from one of Benjamin Franklin's illegitimate sons. My mother had never been sure whether she should brag about it or hush it up. I told Wally about it.

"Ben Franklin?" he said. "Really? How come you never mentioned this?"

"I guess it never came up."

I probably had mentioned the Franklin connection at some point, but I wasn't surprised that Wally had missed it. In any discussion, he usually did most of the talking; listening was not among his alpha–level attributes.

"Well," he said, picking up one of the dishes that contained my maternal ancestors, "how'd you like to have Ben Franklin as your own son?"

I thought about it and he read my face. "And how much would you pay to be able to do that?" he said.

I wasn't actually thinking about me raising a young Ben Franklin. Chances were he would have been a handful and a half. I was thinking about all the people who named their kids Jared or Jessica some other J–name just because it was that year's fashion. They never thought about what it would be like for the poor kid to be one of four or five identically named people in every group they'd ever join, never thought about how the kid would feel knowing that that most personal of possessions, one's own name, had been chosen merely because it was popular and because their parents were irredeemably shallow.

I was thinking about just how many such people existed and how many of them were willing to spend their bank accounts to remain in vogue. "Should I make the check out to you or the company?" I said.

And so we were in business.

And a very good business it was. Wally's company—Ancest, he called it—caught the world's eye and the world's ear. The backers had poured in plenty of start-up money, a good portion of which went into a saturation ad campaign on network television. Within days, Leno and Letterman were making jokes about their imaginary ancestors, Regis and Kelly were interviewing Wally live, and the stock price hit two hundred a share then split. It was structured as a straight-out franchise operation and the prospective franchisees were fighting each other to get in the door.

"Come work with me," Wally said. He offered me a salary that was one figure more than the six I'd been getting as a orthopedic surgeon, plus options, expense account, corner office, company Lexus.

I said, "What on earth can I do for you?"

"It's medical research. You're a doctor."

"I'm just a bone cutter."

He gave me his bashful Tom Sawyer look and said, "You're my touchstone. Everybody else, they're always slapping me on the back and telling me what a brilliant researcher I am. You don't do that. You're the only one keeps my feet on the ground, Jimmy-boy."

I should have run for the hills. Instead, I took the corner office with the title of Executive Vice President on the mahogany door behind which I did a lot of not very much, while being well paid for my exertions. It turned out, though, that there was one chore Wally wanted me to take over.

"I'd like you to interface with the backers," he said. "Give me less time in meetings, more time in the lab. I've got some interesting projects on the burners."

"Okay," I said. I figured it wouldn't be too onerous a task to schmooze the money people, dazzle them with a little science and set visions of sugar-plum dividends dancing in their heads. Thus armed in my innocence I walked into the Wednesday afternoon board meeting with a fat folder of glowing results from the first few weeks and even shinier projections for the next three quarters.

"We've blown right through the granddad and granny market, and we're into a serious run on major historical figures," I said. "Now that the federal court has ruled that DNA from more than four generations back is public domain, it's not just Robert E. Lee's descendants who can have him for a son; we estimate we'll sell him to about five per cent of the population below the Mason–Dixon Line. Plus the interest in European monarchs is picking up, particularly the Bourbons."

I had plenty more, but I was strongly sensing that the five men in black suits on the other side of the table didn't give a damn. I set aside the bar charts on eighteenth-century poets and nineteenth-century composers and said, "Gentlemen, am I missing something?"

"Project Parousia," said the Chairman of the Board. He was a big, stone-faced man with eyes that had had a lot of practice at weighing and winnowing his fellow human beings. I had the feeling I was close to being assigned to the giant bin labeled *Chaff*.

I shuffled through my papers but I knew there was nothing in there about any Project Parousia. I'd never heard of it, although the name rang a faint bell.

"I don't have any information on that project," I said.

"Then get some," said the Chairman. "Or get Applethorpe up here." The other board members nodded, their jaws grimly set, and I realized that they were all cut from the same block of close-grained hardwood as the Chairman. Now that I inspected them closely, I saw that they didn't have the sleek, well-nourished look common to the upper links of the corporate food chain. Instead, each had the aspect of the zealot; they might have been carried over from some previous era when the most popular pastimes were burning witches and crushing heretics under piles of boulders.

"We'll be back tomorrow," he said. "Be prepared to tell us what we want to know."

I went down to the lab. It was below ground and behind a number of thick steel doors and an even larger number of men who wore uniforms and sidearms. At the last door, even my senior executive pass was not enough to get me through, but I managed to convince the head guard to buzz Wally and he told them to admit me.

When I came into the lab he was bent over the monitor of a scanning electronic microscope, humming to himself. Without looking up, he said, "I think we've made it all the way back to Cro-Magnon man. In a week or two, I should be ready to clone a prehuman hominid. After that, Jimmy-boy, I'm going to get some birds and work back toward the dinosaurs."

"What's Project Parousia?" I asked. My teeth chattered a little. The air was chilly; the large room was designed to keep its banks of super-fast computers happy. Humans could put on a sweater.

"Oh, just a bee in the board's bonnet," he said, looking up for a moment. "Don't worry about it."

"No bee would survive a second in any bonnet of theirs," I said. "Who are those people?"

He had turned back to his monitor. "Backers," he said. "Money people."

I put a hand on his shoulder and pulled him down to my lowly plane. "No," I said. "They're not. Tell me how you found them."

I could see him consulting the part of his memory where he stored irrelevant details. "I didn't," he said, after a moment. "They found me. After I published my paper on retrogressive DNA sequencing, they came to see me."

"It was their idea to set up the company?"

"Uh huh."

"But they're not interested in our actual results and revenue projections."

He looked mildly puzzled. "They're not?"

"No, the only thing they care about is Project Parousia."

"Hmm," he said, and gestured to a lab bench across the room. "It's over there."

His microscope was pulling him back to wherever he went when he was working, but I exerted a more immediate level of force and pushed him over to the Parousia bench. He examined a series of petri dishes connected to sensors and probes that were in turn linked to one of the big computers then checked a stream of data that was zipping across a monitor.

"Almost done," he said. "Of course, it's just fantasy."

"What is?"

"Their idea."

"Tell me about it," I said.

Wally said he figured that the board had gotten themselves all wrapped up in that goofy book about a secret society that had protected the descendants of a union between Jesus and Mary Magdalene through two thousand years. I hadn't read the book but I had heard about misguided enthusiasts trying to dig up church floors to get at supposed clues.

I saw it now. "They want you to work backwards through the DNA until you've got a clone of Jesus." And now I remembered what parousia meant. It was Greek for the Second Coming.

"They want to bring on the end of the world," I said.

Wally was the only person I'd ever heard use the word "Pshaw." He used it now then added, "It's just a myth."

"Work with me a moment," I said. "Suppose it isn't a myth. Suppose there really is a secret society. Cause I'm thinking if there ever was a secret society of religious fanatics they'd look an awful lot like our board of directors."

"Still," he said, "what are the chances they could be right?"

"I don't know," I said, "but how much research could you get done if the seas are boiling and we're all being pitched into a lake of fire?"

"That's not going to happen."

"Okay, suppose all you give them is a mild mannered carpenter–aren't they likely to think you've teamed up with the Antichrist to wreck their plans? Cause they don't look like the kind of people who would get their lawyers in and sue. I'm thinking, they're more the pitchforks and torches kind."

At that moment the Parousia Project's computer emitted a discreet *ding*. Wally leaned over and picked up the last petri dish in the series. He peered into it. "There it is," he said then looked around. "But I don't see any angels or wise men."

"Fine," I said. "Tomorrow I'll give it to them and maybe they'll go away happy." Though I didn't think so. But planes left for obscure corners of the world every hour, and I would have enough time to pick a good one.

Except that I noticed how Wally was looking at the dish with that expression I'd seen so many times before. He had found another doll he could crack open.

"No," I said, and reached for the dish. "For once, leave well enough alone."

But he had already slipped it back into its connective armature and his fingers rippled across the computer's keyboard.

He turned to me with that smile of genius I'd seen so often before, the one that is a virtual twin to the grin of madness. "I can prove it's a myth," he said, "You see, if that's really Jesus the Son of God, then half its DNA is Mary's and the other half is..."

Ding went the computer.

Behind him, from the lab bench, a light glowed.

I turned to run, but the floor shook and the walls cracked and I was thrown down.

I looked up and saw that the petri dish was enveloped in a flame that burned yet did not consume, and a voice that came from everywhere at once said, "Put off the shoes from thy feet for the place where thou standest is holy ground."

"Oh, God," I said.

THE DEVIL YOU DON'T

I was a pretty good speechwriter for most of my adult life, mainly because it turned out that I had a knack for getting a speaker's voice in my head and writing texts that suited that voice. This story came from my wondering if I could write a narrative in one of the most distinctive voices of the twentieth century. I sold it to Gardner Dozois, who was then editor of Asimov's Science Fiction.

THE FRANTIC SPARKS fly up into the November night like lost souls seeking safe harbor who, finding none, extinguish themselves against the unheeding darkness. Or so I might write it if ever I should put pen to paper to tell this tale. But I shall not.

The fire itself is confined by the blackened steel barrel. I poke again with the gardener's fork and another flurry of sparks shoots up, and with them scraps of burning paper. By the flickering light of the flames I can sometimes see a printed word or two before they are consumed: *Alamein, Rommel, Singapore, Yalta.*

The books are thick. They will take time to burn but I have learned patience. I have always taken the longer view. Perhaps it is a sense of history. Perhaps it is just how I am formed. But, in the arena of public life, he who takes the longer view must win out in the end.

The gardener has left in heaps his cullings from the bygone summer's flower beds. I gather another armful of dried stalks and withered blossoms and throw them onto the flames. The flare of light illuminates the disturbed earth that the gardener turned over this afternoon and the pile of red bricks that have lain here much longer—more than a year since I abandoned building a wall to take Mr. Chamberlain's reluctant call.

First Lord of the Admiralty, then. Prime Minister now. It was what I had always wanted, I will admit, though I would have preferred its arrival under less perilous circumstances.

The books are burning well. I leave them and kneel beside the wall. The cement with which to mix the mortar is just where I left it and there is water at hand. I lay a red fired brick atop the black soil, trowel its side with mortar then place a second beside it.

Another pass with the trowel, then another brick. The work proceeds as it always did, a step at a time. That is how walls are built. As are lives. And futures.

The man appeared from thin air. I wanted to think he had stepped out of the darkness but the space behind him was well lit by the lights of Chartwell's great house, my house. I had not been here since the start of the war.

"Please don't be alarmed," he said.

"I am alarmed," I said. "My visitors usually make less startling entrances, and then only when invited."

"I mean you no harm."

"I am relieved to hear it."

"I've come from the future."

"Now I am alarmed anew," I said.

There was a policeman in the house, a Special Branch man with a pistol. But I did not call out. My visitor begged me to allow him to demonstrate his bona fides.

I did so and was soon convinced. He had a watch that displayed time through ingenious means and a device no larger than a calling card that could extract a square root in the blink of an eye. He showed me coins and paper money bearing the likeness of the young Princess Elizabeth, grown grandmotherly beneath the Crown of State.

"I am glad to know that the royal family endures," I said. "You bring me a heartening sign when one is sorely needed."

"I have brought you more than signs," he said. "I have brought you wonders."

He produced a package of books, small paperbound editions such as I had not seen before. I took them in my hands. The titles had a ring to them: *The Gathering Storm, Their Finest Hour, Blood, Sweat and Tears.*

Then I saw the name of the author. It was mine own.

"What are these?" I said.

"Your memoirs," he said. "The war years, at least."

"Then I survive," I said.

"More than that. You win."

"I am glad to hear it."

"It was touch and go for a while," he said. "But that was not the worst of it."

"Oh? Then what was the worst of it?"

I have not often seen a man look so forlorn. "The cost," he said. "The sheer waste. The horror."

I did not know how to comfort him. I set the books down on a heap of bricks then brought out cigars and offered him one. He seemed delighted to take it. His face shed its melancholy and he exhibited an exhilaration I have seen only in the shining eyes of schoolboys encountering their idols on the sidelines of a cricket pitch.

"I knew you would be here tonight, alone," he said, when he had puffed his cigar alight. He had studied my life, he said, choosing a night when I had come to the old place, away from memoranda and telephones and committees, to wrestle with my old black dog of a mood that had gripped me since the terrible raid on Coventry two nights ago.

He savored the rich Cuban leaf, blew out a long stream of blue smoke, then said, "But now you can stop all of it before it happens— the Blitz, the Battle of the Atlantic." He looked wistful for a moment then continued. "My mother's younger brother drowned when his ship was torpedoed off Newfoundland in 1942. Fifty years later, she still cried for him."

"I am very sorry," I said.

"But you see, now he doesn't have to die," he said, gesturing to the books with the hand that held the cigar so that a scattering of ash fell upon the cover of the one entitled *The Hinge of Fate*. "It's all in there. Hitler's plans, his blunders. His invasion of Russia, D–Day, all of it."

I looked at the books atop the bricks but did not touch them.

"Now you can strike where he is weakest, shorten the war, save tens of millions of lives."

"Are there others like you?" I asked. "Other travelers through time?"

He told me that the channels by which he had come back to me were abstruse, unknown to any other. He had hit upon time travel by the most outrageous twist of odds. "But once I knew I could come here, I had to," he said. "The war was the most terrible thing that ever happened. But with these books you can prevent the worst of it."

"Hmmm," I said. "Show me."

He bent to retrieve one of the volumes. I reached for a brick.

I mortar a second layer of bricks over the first, tapping each carefully into line with its brothers. The man from the future lies with his wonders beneath the fire-hardened oblongs. His books are ashes now.

I wonder if he understood, as the light was going out of his eyes, that I must accept all the horrors to come. That is the price to be paid for the knowledge he had brought me, the knowledge that we will be able to endure and that then will come brighter days.

But would they still come if I had looked into those books? If I could see the present as the past through my own future eyes, would I not surely wander from the path that I now tread in darkness, though with a good hope that it will lead us eventually to those sunny uplands?

I must choose the devil I know, though I know him now to be even more horrid than I feared, because the devil I don't know may well be even worse.

Yet the man from the future has not striven in vain. He has done much good. Because of him, my black dog is once more whipped back to his dark kennel.

I finish the second layer of bricks, stand and brush the dirt from the knees of my trousers. I lay the trowel on the unyielding surface.

I shall carry on. We shall see it through.

NOT A PROBLEM

Gordon Van Gelder was putting together an anthology of science fiction stories about global warming called Welcome to the Greenhouse *and asked me to send him something. I couldn't come up with an idea except for a pretty silly concept that would only qualify as comic relief. Fortunately, that was exactly what Gordon was looking for. The character of Bucky Sansom, by the way, is based on some of the hard-charging business types I used to write speeches for.*

BUNKY SANSOM was the kind of man who knew that the time to say yes was when all around him were saying no. Or vice versa. That's how he got to be a multi-billionaire.

When he heard the United Nations Secretary-General say, "Climate change is now a reality. Nothing we can do in our lifetimes can reverse it," Bunky's answer was, "I don't buy it, lady. Something can always be done."

The Secretary-General's image was superimposed on video of the last dike failing on the last of Kiribati's storm-swept chain of islands. Bunky watched the remaining few thousand of the now drowned nation's population forming forlorn lines and wading out to the UN flotilla that would take them to join the rest of their compatriots huddled in Australian and New Zealand refugee camps.

He told the hi-def to turn itself off and stepped out onto the balcony of his mountainside eyrie, with its grand-scale view of Vancouver's golden towers, crowded together within the confines of the massive seawall that had been one of Canada's bicentennial projects. But instead of looking down at the place where he had made his wealth, he looked up and saw the stars.

That's when he got the idea. "We need help," he said. "It's gotta be out there, somewhere."

Bunker Hill Sansom—though he told everyone to call him Bunky, and God help any who didn't—had made his billions by finding new ways to do old things. Inarguably, his ways were better ways, provided your definition of "better" was "more fashionable." He had pioneered the genetic redesign of key elements of the human genome–well not the actual redesign, but the marketing of the application, through a world-wide string of franchise clinics that sold the fruits of his genius to the eager masses.

So while others were eliminating hereditary disease or enhancing intelligence, Sansom was making it possible for parents to bear children with huge, dark eyes the size of silver dollars–you couldn't look at them without saying, "Aw,"–or with the silky blue hair that, this year, was all the rage in Japan. He was already taking pre-orders for next year's sensation: feathers!

As soon as he received his inspiration about help from the stars, Bunky put some people on it. They reported back that scientists had been scanning the stars for intelligent signals for about a century.

"And what have they got?" he said.

"Well, nothing," said his number-one baby-strangler. Actually, Bunky had never happened to need a baby strangled, but if he ever did, Number-One was there to take care of it.

"Nothing? A hundred years and they've got nothing?"

"They don't have much money."

"How much is not much?" Bunky said. He didn't believe the number his people gave him. It was less than he'd spent on media alone when he'd launched the modification that let people have babies that produced excrement in about the same quantity and conformation as a rabbit's. "Chicken feed," he said. "Put a coupla billion into it."

His people went away and put a couple of billion into the search for extraterrestrial intelligence. Every month, he got reports; every month, progress was skimpy. Like the time his team reported that they'd overheard signals from deeper in the galaxy that were definitely coherent, but the scientists decoding the transmissions concluded that the senders were insectoids.

"Insectoids?" Bunky said. "You mean, like, bugs?"

"Yes, sir," said Number-One.

"Big bugs?"

"Yes, sir."

Bunky shivered. "Give 'em another billion but tell 'em they

gotta look somewheres else. Bugs ain't gonna help us."

More months went by. The sea barriers protecting lower Manhattan cracked then collapsed under the continuous battering from Atlantic waves. "I told 'em they shouldn'ta let the mob finesse those construction contracts," Bunky said. He called Number-One and said, "Whatta we hear from space?"

The man had just been about to call the boss. "Something good," he said.

"Not bugs?"

"Not bugs. More like slugs, but smart slugs."

"What's good about smart slugs?" Bunky said.

"They sent through the schematics for a different kind of communicator. We can talk to them in real time, no more waiting years for messages to go out and come back."

"That's sounds good."

A week went by. Number-one called back. "We made contact."

"Excellent. Can they help us?"

"There's a problem."

"What problem?"

"Well, we established communication, but the only thing they wanted to know is did we have any *fafashertzz* we wanted to get rid of?"

"*Fafashertzz?*" Bunky said. "What's *fafashertzz?*"

"They sent another schematic. It appears to be what our scientists call a transuranic element, but way heavier than anything we've ever conceived of. You'd need a cyclotron the size of the moon to make it."

"So our guys told these slugs we were all out of *fafashertzz?*"

"They did."

"And?"

"Dial tone. No answer. Nada. Zippola."

"Buncha jerks!" Bunky said. "Still, whatta ya expect from slugs?"

"But there's good news," said Number-one.

"Tell me."

"The communicator works on other frequencies. Our brainiacs say it looks like we can start calling around, see if we can find someone not so single-minded."

Bunky had built his business partly on an aggressive telemarketing campaign. "Put another billion into it," he said, "build a few million of those things and hire India to make the calls."

To himself, he said, *This works out, I could rule the world*. And when Bunky Sansom talked to himself, he never indulged in hyperbole.

———————

"It's looking good, boss."

"It better," Bunky said. For the umpteenth time, the worst-case global warming scenarios had proved to be too optimistic: now the UN climatologists were predicting that everything from the Gulf of Mexico to the Black Hills was going to end up as a warm, shallow sea. "So whatta we got?"

"We're talking to about twenty civilizations, maybe half of them within *bluberiskint* distance."

"What's this *bluberiskint?*"

"Seems to be the main purpose of *fafashertzz*—some kind of interstellar faster-than-light drive."

"So, we're talking to ten or a dozen kindsa space aliens," Bunky said. A thought occurred to him. "How many of them are bugs?"

"Big bugs?"

"Size don't matter."

"Three."

"And the rest? Can they help us?"

Number-One made an it-ain't-good-news face. "Most of them first want to know if we've got any *fafashertzz*."

Bunky looked at the ceiling, which was painted with scenes of triumph from his long contrarian career. "Give me somethin' here," he said, "fore I drown."

Number-One said, "There's one good prospect." He caught his boss's sideways look and added, "And they're not bugs or slugs. They look like big birds, although they've got teeth."

Bunky tried it out in his head. "Birds aren't so bad. How big?"

"Pretty big. Hard to tell. Maybe twenty feet high."

"That's some bird," Bunky said. "And with teeth yet."

"The thing is," Number-One said, "they said they were glad we got in touch. They're familiar with our world. When we told them it was heating up, the answer came back: 'Not a problem.'"

"Not a problem?" Bunky said the words again, slowly. "I like their attitude. And they're within whatsit distance?"

"They can be here in a month."

Bunky didn't get where he was by procrastinating. He slapped one plump hand down onto the marble top of his decision desk. "Sign 'em to an exclusive contract. Give 'em whatever they want."

"Already done," said Number-One. "Everything we proposed, they said, 'Not a problem.'"

"I like these birds," Bunky said. "Get the PR and media people in here. We gotta plan the announcement."

———————

The world took Bunky Sansom to its bosom like never before. He had more honorary citizenships, keys to cities and propositions from hot celebrity babes than he knew what to do with. Not only did "Not a problem" become his signature phrase, but three countries and seven states adopted it as their official mottoes. Privately, he was already negotiating the protocols that would see him become de facto ruler of the world.

Three weeks after he made the big announcement, the first of the expected spaceships were detected decelerating out beyond the orbits of the gas giants. Two days later, the lead ship eased itself into orbit then, after circling Earth a few times, descended gently into the atmosphere and came to hover over the coordinates Bunky's people had sent. For his convenience, the contact site was the roof of the Sansom Enterprises head office, a vast, truncated pyramid overlooking the sea-girt island that was all that was now left of Vancouver.

The roof was huge, but even so, the ship was too large to land on it. It was too large to land on the shrunken city. Instead it hovered a few yards above where Bunky waited with the Secretary-General, a flock of Presidents and Prime Ministers, a few kings and queens, and one ayatollah.

From the ship's flat base, a long, wide ramp uncurled itself. There was a pregnant pause, then the first of the arrivals came down the sloping gangway.

"That's some bird," Bunky said to Number-One. "Twenty-feet, nothin'–that thing goes thirty."

"I don't think it's a bird," Number-One said. It's got feathers, all right, but those are arms, not wings. And those teeth–"

The Secretary-General was speaking, offering a welcome from all the people of the Earth, and thanking the newcomers for their kindness in coming to help with the problem of global warming.

Bunky stepped up proudly beside her, his carefully prepared speech in his hand.

The huge feathered being opened its mouth in a kind of smile, revealing dozens of teeth shaped like curved daggers. It's voice was a series of hisses and squawks, but Bunky heard a translation from an earpiece that connected to a device that was also the result of the communicator schematic the slugs had sent through. He had already made a fresh billion from manufacturing it.

"We keep telling you," the creature said, "it's not a problem–it's an opportunity." It cast its plate–sized, yellow–irised eyes across the crowd of dignitaries then focused on the King of Tonga. A clawed hand as wide as an armchair scooped up the portly monarch. Then, almost before the king could scream, the foot-long teeth bit off his top half.

The jaws crunched. A spray of blood, bone flakes and meat scraps speckled heads and shoulders of the dignitaries as they turned and fought each other to reach the roof's single exit. Bunky heard the voice in his ear say, "Hey, didn't I tell you they'd taste just like *sheeshrak*? Come on, try one!"

Then the claws closed around Bunky's torso–he was the plumpest specimen still uncaught–and he was carried to the edge of the roof. He saw the big three-toed feet sink deep into the tar–and–gravel surface with each step. From behind his captor he heard a cacophony of screams and feeding sounds, while the translator conveyed the squabbles over the choicer morsels.

Soon it grew quiet. He twisted in the thing's scaly grip and saw it looking out over the warm sea, its nostrils distending as it breathed in the thick and sultry air. Above it, the sky was now full of immense ships.

The great voice hissed and clacked, the translation duly fed into the billionaire's ear: "It's so good to be back."

"Listen," Bunky gasped, as he was lifted and the blood-stained jaws opened wide.

A moment later, the translator said, as it slid down the dinosaur's gullet, "Or maybe not *sheeshrak*. Maybe *chikkichuk*.

GROLION OF ALMERY

When Gardner Dozois emailed me to ask if I would like to con-tribute to Songs of The Dying Earth, *the tribute anthology to Jack Vance that would contain stories set in the grandmaster's decadent, far-future Old Earth of wizards, rogues, and ne'er-do-wells, my reply was, "Try and stop me!" But so as not to deliver a mere pastiche, I decided to write most of the novelette in first-person, a point of view Vance rarely if ever adopted. Most Vanceophiles are able to identify "Grolion" in the first few paragraphs; if not, the ending kind of gives him away.*

WHEN NEXT I FOUND a place to insert myself I discovered the resident in the manse's foyer, in conversation with a traveler. Keep myself out of his sightlines, I flew to a spot high in a corner where a roof beam passed through the stone of the outer wall, and settled myself to watch and listen. The resident received almost no visitors—only the invigilant, he of the prodigious belly and eight va-rieties of scowl, and the steagle knife.

I rarely bothered to attend when the invigilant visited, conserv-ing my energies for whenever my opportunity should come. But this stranger was unusual. He moved animatedly about the room in a pe-culiar bent-kneed, splay-footed lope, frequently twitching aside the curtain of the window beside the door to peer into the darkness, then checking that the beam that barred the portal was well seated.

"The creature cannot enter," the resident said. "Doorstep and lintel, indeed the entire house and walled garden, are charged with Phandaal's Discriminating Boundary. Do you know the spell?"

The stranger's tone was offhand. "I am familiar with the variant used in Almery. It may be different here."

"It keeps out what must be kept out; your pursuer's first foot-fall across the threshold would draw an agonizing penalty."

"Does the lurker know this?" said the visitor, peering again out the window.

The resident joined him. "Look," he said, "see how its nostrils flare, dark against the paleness of its countenance. It scents the magic and hangs back."

"But not far back." The dark thatch of the stranger's hair, which drew down to a point low on his forehead, moved as his scalp twitched in response to the almost constant motion of his features. "It pursued me avidly as I neared the village, growing bolder as the sun sank behind the hills. if you had not opened..."

"You are safe now," said the resident. "Eventually the ghoul will go to seek other prey." He invited the man into the parlor and bade him sit by the fire. I fluttered after them and found a spot on a high shelf. "Have you dined?"

"Only forest foods plucked along the way," was the man's answer as he took the offered chair. But though he no longer strode about the room, his eyes went hither and thither, rifling the many shelves and glass-fronted cupboards, as he cataloged their contents, assigning each item a value and closely calculating the sum of them all.

"I have a stew of morels grown in the inner garden, along with the remnants of yesterday's steagle," said the resident. "There is also half a loaf of bannock and a small keg of brown ale."

The stranger's pointed chin lifted in a display of fortitude. "We will make the best of it."

They had apparently exchanged names before I had arrived, for when they were seated with bowls of stew upon their knees and spoons in their hands, the resident said, "So, Grolion, what is your tale?"

The fox-faced fellow arranged his features into an image of nobility beset by unmerited trials. "I am heir to a title and lands in Almery, though I am temporarily despoiled of my inheritance by plotters and schemers. I travel the world, biding my moment, until I return to set matters forcefully aright."

The resident said, "I have heard it argued that the world as it is now arranged must be the right order of things, for a competent Creator would not allow disequilibrium."

Grolion found the concept jejeune. "My view is that the world is an arena in which men of deeds and courage drive the flow of events."

"And you are such?"

"I am," said the stranger, cramming a lump of steagle into his mouth. He tasted it then began chewing with eye-squinting zest.

Meanwhile, I considered what I had heard, drawing two conclusions: first, that though this fellow who styled himself a grandee of Almery might have sojourned in that well-worn land, he was no scion of its aristocracy—he did not double-strike his tees and dees in the stutter that was affected by Almery's highest-bred; second, that his name was not Grolion—for if it had been, I would not have been able to recall it, just as I could never retain a memory of the resident's nor the invigilant's. In my present condition, not enough of me survived to be able to handle true names—nor any of the magics that required memory—else I would have long since exacted a grim revenge.

The resident tipped up his bowl to scoop into his mouth the last sups of stew. His upturned glance fell upon my hiding place. I drew back, but too late. He took from within the neck of his garment a small wooden whistle that hung from a cord about his neck and blew a sonorous note. I heard the flap of leathery wings from the corridor and threw myself into the air in a bid to escape. But the little creature that guarded his bedchamber—the room that had formerly been mine—caught me in its handlike paws. A cruel smile spread across its almost-human face as it tore away my wings and carried me back to its perch above the bedchamber door, where it thrust me into its maw. I withdrew before its stained teeth crushed the life from my borrowed form.

When next I returned, morning light was filtering through gaps in the curtains, throwing a roseate blush onto the gray stone floors. I went from room to room, though I gave a wide berth to the resident's bedchamber. I found Grolion on the ground floor, in the workroom that overlooks the inner garden, where I had formerly spent my days with my treacherous assistants. He was examining the complex starburst design laid out in colors both vibrant and subtle on the great tray that covered most of the floor. I hovered outside the window that overlooked the inner garden; I could see that the pattern was not far from completion.

Grolion knelt and stretched a fingertip toward an elaborate figure composed in several hues: twin arabesques, intertwined with each other and ornamented with fillips of stylized acaranja leaves and lightning bolts. Just before his cracked and untended fingernail could disarrange the thousand tiny motes, each ashimmer with its own aura of greens and golds, sapphire and amethyst, flaming reds and blazing yellows, a sharp intake of breath from the doorway arrested all motion.

"Back away," said the resident. "To disturb the pattern before it is completed is highly dangerous."

Grolion rocked back onto his heels and rose to a standing position. His eyes flitted about the pattern, trying to see it as a whole, but of course his effort was defeated. "What is its purpose?" he said.

The resident came into the room and drew him away. "The previous occupant of the manse began it. Regrettably, he was never entirely forthcoming about its hows and how-comes. It has to do with an interplanar anomaly. Apparently the house sits on a node where several dimensions intersect. Their conjunction creates a weakness in the membranes that separate the planes."

"Where is this 'previous occupant?' Why has he left his work dangerously unfinished?"

The resident made a casual gesture. "These are matters of history, of which our old Earth has already far too much. We need not consider them."

"True," said Grolion, "we have only now. But some 'nows' are connected to particularly pertinent 'thens' and the prudent man takes note of the connections."

But the resident had departed the area while he was still talking. The traveler followed and found him in the refectory, only to be caught up in a new topic.

"A gentleman of your discernment will understand," said the resident, "that my resources are constrained. Much as I delight in your company, I cannot offer unlimited hospitality. I have already overstepped my authority by feeding and sheltering you for a night."

Grolion looked about him. The manse was well appointed, the furnishings neither spare nor purely utilitarian. The wall of its many chambers were hung with art, the floors lushly carpeted, the lighting soft and shadowless. "As constraints go," he said, "these seem less oppressive than most."

"Oh," said the resident, "none of this is mine own. I am but a humble servant of the village council, paid to tend the premises until the owner's affairs are ultimately settled. My stipend is scant and mostly paid in ale and steagle."

He received in response an airy gesture of unconcern. "I will give you," said Grolion, "a promissory note for a handsome sum, redeemable the moment I am restored to my birthright."

"The restoration of your fortunes, though no doubt inevitable, is not guaranteed to arrive before the sun goes out."

Grolion had more to say, but the resident spoke over his remarks. "The invigilant comes every other day to deliver my stipend. I expect him soon. I will ask him to let me engage you as my assistant."

"Better yet," said Grolion, his face brightening as he was struck by an original idea, "I might assume a supervisory role. I have a talent for inspiring others to maximum effort."

The resident offered him a dry eye and an even drier tone. "I require no inspiration. Some small assistance, however, would be welcome. The difficulty will be in swaying the invigilant, who is a notorious groat-squeezer."

"I am electrified by the challenge." Grolion rubbed his hands briskly and added, "In the meantime, let us make a good breakfast. I find I argue best on a full stomach."

The resident sniffed. "I can spare a crust of bannock and half a pot of stark tea. Then we must to work."

"Would it not be better to establish terms and conditions? I would not want to transgress the local labor code."

"Have no fear on that score. The village values a willing worker. Show the invigilant that you have already made an energetic contribution and your argument is half-made before he crosses the doorstep."

Grolion looked less than fully convinced, but the resident had the advantage of possessing what the other hungered for—be it only a crust and a sup of brackish tea—and thus his views prevailed.

I knew what use the resident would make of the new man; I withdrew to the inner garden and secreted myself in a deep crack in the enclosing wall, from which I could watch without imposing my presence upon the scene. It was not long before, their skimpy repast having been taken, the two men came again under my view.

As I expected, the resident drew the visitor's attention to the towering barbthorn that dominated one end of the garden. Its dozens of limbs, festooned in trailing succulents, constantly moved as it sampled the air. Several were already lifted and questing in the direction of the two men as it caught their scent even across the full length of the garden.

Sunk as I was in a crack in the wall, I was too distant to hear their conversation, but I could follow the substance of the discussion by the emotions that passed across Grolion's expressive face and by his gestures of protest. But his complaints were not recognized. With shoulders aslump and reluctance slowing his steps, the traveler trudged to the base of the tree, batting aside two of the creepers that instantly reached for him. He peered into the close-knit branches, seeking the least painful route of ascent. The resident repaired to his workroom, a window of which looked out on the court, enabling him to take note of the new employee's progress while he worked on the starburst.

I left my hiding place and angled across the wall, meaning to spring onto the man's shoulder before he ascended the tree. The way he had studied the contents of the parlor showed perspicacity coupled with unbridled greed; I might contrive some means to communicate with him. But so intent on my aims was I that I let myself cross a patch of red sunlight without full care and attention; a fat-bellied spider dropped upon me from its lurking post on the wall above. It swiftly spun a confining mesh of adhesive silk to bind my wings, then deftly flipped me over and pressed its piercing mouthparts against my abdomen. I felt the searing intrusion of its digestive juices dissolving my innards and withdrew to the place that was both my sanctuary and my prison.

When I was able to observe once more, Grolion and the resident had ceased work to receive the invigilant. I found them in the foyer, in animated discussion. The resident was insistent, arguing that the extra cost of Grolion's sustenance was well worth the increased productivity that would ensue. The invigilant was pretending to be not easily convinced, noting that a number of previous assistants had been tried and all found wanting.

The resident conceded the point, but added, "The others were unsuitable, vagabonds and wayfarers of poor character. But Grolion is of finer stuff, a scion of Almery's aristocracy."

The invigilant turned his belly in the direction of Grolion, who at that point in the proceedings had made his way to the partly open outer door so that he could examine the road outside and the forest across the way. "Are you indeed of gentle birth?"

"What? Oh, yes," was the answer, then, "Did you see a ghoul lurking in the shadows as you came up the road?"

"We noticed it this morning and drove it off with braghounds and torches," said the invigilant.

"Indeed?" said Grolion. He edged closer to the door, used the backs of one hand's fingers to brush it further ajar, craned his neck to regard the road outside from different angles. I saw a surmise take possession of his mobile features.

"Now," said the invigilant, "let us discuss terms—"

Grolion had turned his head toward the speaker as if intent on hearing his proposal. But as the official began to speak, the traveler threw the door wide, then himself through it. To his evident surprise, the doorway caught him and threw him back into the foyer. He sat on the floor, dazed, then moaned and put his hands to his head as his face showed that his skull had suddenly become home to thunderous pain.

"Phandaal's Discriminating Boundary," said the resident. "Besides keeping out what must be kept out, it keeps in what must be kept in."

"Unspeak the spell," Grolion said, pain distorting his voice. "The ghoul is gone."

"He cannot," said the invigilant. "It can only be removed by he who laid it."

"The previous occupant?"

"Just so."

"Then I am trapped here?"

The resident spoke. "As am I, until the work is done. The flux of interplanar energies that will then be released will undo all magics."

Grolion indicated the invigilant. "He comes and goes."

"The spell discriminates. Hence the name."

"Come," said the invigilant, nudging Grolion with the heel of his staff, "I cannot stand here while you prattle. Rise and pay attention."

The discussion moved on. The resident's plan was approved: Grolion would be granted his own allowance of ale, bannock and steagle, contingent upon his giving satisfaction until the work was finished. Failure to give satisfaction would see a curtailment of the stipend; aggravated failure would lead to punitive confinement in the house's dank and malodorous crypt.

Grolion proposed several amendments to these terms, though none of them were carried. The invigilant then took from his wallet a folding knife that, when opened, revealed a blade of black stone. He cut the air above the refectory table with it, and from the incisions fell a slab of steagle. He then repeated the process, yielding another slab. Grolion saw what appeared to be two wounds, seemingly in the open air, weeping a liquid like pale blood. Then, in a matter of moments, the gashes closed and he saw only the walls and cupboards of the refectory.

The invigilant left. The resident gave brisk instructions as to the culinary portion of Grolion's duties—the preparation of steagle involved several arduous steps. Then he went back to the design in the workroom. I sought an opportunity to make contact with Grolion. He was at the preparation table, a heavy wooden mallet in hand, beating at a slab of steagle as if it had offended him by more than the sinewy toughness of its texture and its musty odor. He muttered dire imprecations under his breath. I hovered in front of him, flitting from side to side rhythmically. If I could gain his attention, it would be the first step toward opening a discourse between us.

He looked up and noticed me. I began to fly up and down and at an angle, meaning to trace the first character of the Almery syllabary—it seemed a reasonable opening gambit. He regarded me sourly, still muttering threats and maledictions against the resident. I moved on to the second letter, but as I executed an acute angle, Grolion's head reared back then shot forward; at the same time his lips propelled a gobbet of spittle at high speed. The globule caught me in midflight, gluing my wings together and causing me to spiral down to land on the half-beaten steagle. I looked up to see the mallet descending and then I was gone away again.

By the time I had found another carrier, a heavy-bodied rumblebee, several hours had passed. The resident was in the workroom, extending the design with tweezers and templates. The last arm of the sunburst was nearing completion. Once it was done, the triple helix at the center could be laid in, and the work would finally be finished.

Grolion was halfway up the barbthorn, his feet braced against one of its several trunks, a hand gripping an arm-thick branch, fingers carefully spread among the densely sprouting thorns, many of which held the desiccated corpses of small birds and flying lizards that had come to feed on the butterfly larvae that crawled and inched throughout the foliage. The man had not yet noticed that a slim, green tubule, its open end rimmed by tooth-like thorns, had found its way to the flesh between two of his knuckles and was preparing to attach itself and feed; his full attention was on his other hand, carefully cupped around a gold-and-crimson almiranth newly emerged from its cocoon. The insect was drying its translucent wings in the dim sunlight that filtered through the interlaced limbs of the tree.

Grolion breathed gently on the little creature, the warmth of his breath accelerating the drying process. Then, as the almiranth bent and flexed its legs, preparing to spring into first flight, he deftly enclosed it and transferred it to a wide-necked glass bottle that hung from a thong about his neck. The container's stopper had been gripped in his teeth, but now he pulled the wooden plug free and fixed it into the bottle's mouth. Laboriously, he began his descent, tearing his pierced hand free of the tubule's bite. The barbthorn sluggishly pinked and stabbed at him, trying to hold him in place as his shifting weight triggered its feeding response. From time to time, he had to pause to pull loose thorns that snagged his clothing; one or two even managed to pierce his flesh deeply enough that he had to stop and worry them free before he could resume his descent.

Through all of this, Grolion issued a comprehensive commentary on the stark injustice of his situation and on those responsible for it, expressing heartfelt wishes as to events in their futures. The resident and the invigilant featured prominently in these scenarios, as well as others I took to be former acquaintances in Almery. So busy was he with his aspersions that I could find no way to attract his attention. I withdrew to a chink in the garden wall to spy on the resident through the workroom window.

He was kneeling at the edge of the starburst, outlining in silver a frieze of intertwined rings of cerulean blue that traced the edge of one arm. The silver, like all the other pigments of the design, was applied as a fine powder tapped gently from the end of a hollow reed. The resident's forefinger struck the tube three more times as I watched, then he took up a small brush that bore a single bristle at its end and nudged an errant flake into alignment.

Grolion appeared in the doorway, grumbling and cursing, to proffer the stoppered jar. The resident shooed him back with a flurry of agitated hand motions, lest any of the blood that dripped from his elbows fall upon the pattern, then he rose and came around the tray to receive the container.

"Watch and remember," he said, taking the jar to a bench and beckoning Grolion to follow. "If I promote you to senior assistant, this task could be yours."

"Does that mean someone else will climb the barbthorn?"

The resident regarded him from a great height. "A senior assistant's duties enfold and amplify those of a junior assistant."

"So it is merely more work."

"Your perspective requires modification. The proper understanding is that you command more trust and win more esteem."

"But my days still consist of 'Do this,' and 'Bring that,' and nothing to eat but mushrooms from the garden and steagle."

"The ale is good," countered the resident. "You must admit that."

"Somehow it fails to compensate," said Grolion.

"Pah!" said the resident. "I had hopes for you, but you are no better than the others!"

"What others?"

But the question was waved away. "Enough chatter! Watch and learn." The resident removed the stopper from the container, inserted two fingers and deftly caught a fragile leg. He drew the fluttering creature out, laid it on a mat of spongewood atop the workbench, then found a scalpel with a tiny half-moon blade. With a precise and practiced stroke he severed the almiranth's triangular head from its thorax.

While the wings and legs were still moving in reflexive death throes, the resident donned a mask of fine gauze and bid Grolion do the same. "A loose breath can cost us many scales," he said, picking up a miniature strigil. Delicately, he stroked the wings, detaching a fine dust of gold and crimson, demonstrating the technique of moving the instrument to the left to pile up a pinch of gold on one side, and to the right to accumulate a minuscule heap of the other hue. When each of the four wings was stripped to the pale underflesh, he produced two hollow reeds and, using the gentlest of suction through the gauze, drew the pigments from the table.

"There," he said, "a productive morning. Grolion, you have

earned your ale and steagle."

Grolion did not respond. He had not been attending to the demonstration, his eye having instead been caught by the shelves of librams and grimoires on the opposite wall. One of them was bound in the blue chamois characteristic of Phandaal's works.

The resident saw the direction of his assistant's gaze and spoke sharply. "Back to your duties! Already I can see a green-and-orange banded chrysalis on that branch that hangs like a limp hand–there on the left, near the top! I don't doubt that's about to provide us with a magnificent nighttorch!"

"I must tend my wounds," said Grolion. "They may fester."

"Pah! I have salves and specifics. You can apply them tonight. Now get yourself aloft. If the nighttorch escapes, neither ale nor steagle shall pass your lips."

"This is a sudden change of attitude," Grolion said. "But a moment ago, I was being congratulated and promised promotion."

"I am of a mutable disposition," said the resident. "Many have tried to change me, but mine is a character that does not yield. You must fit yourself around my little idiosyncrasies. Now go."

The set of his shoulders an unspoken reproach, the assistant went back to the barbthorn. With the resident watching his progress, I thought it ill-judged to follow. But Grolion did not reascend the tree. Instead, as he neared its wide base, where the thick roots delved into the ground, he suddenly stopped then stepped sharply back, as if some dire threat blocked his path.

The resident noticed. "What is it?" he cried.

Grolion did not turn but peered intently at the tangle of roots, as if in mingled fear and fascination. "I do not know," he said, then bent gingerly forward. "I have never seen the like."

The resident came forward, but stopped a little behind the traveler. "Where is it?" he said.

A feeler reached out for Grolion. He batted it away and crouched, leaning forward. "It went behind that root, the thick one."

The resident edged forward. "I see nothing."

"There!" said Grolion. "It moves!"

The resident was bent double at the waist, his attention fixed downward. "I still don't–"

Grolion came up from his crouch, moving fast. One blood-smeared hand took the resident by the throat, the other covered his mouth, and both worked in concert to achieve the assistant's goal, which was to spin the resident around and force his back against the lower reaches of the tree, where the thorns and barbs were thick and long.

Stray tendrils darted at Grolion's arms, but he ignored the sucking mouths and held the resident fast against the trunk. Now heavier tubers leaned in from the sides, sensing the flesh pressed against the carpet of fine hairs on the tree's bark. In moments, the man was a prisoner of more than Grolion's grasp. The assistant took his hands from the resident's throat and lips, but warned as he did so, "One syllable of a cantrip, and I will stop up your mouth with earth and leave you to the tree."

"No new spells can be cast here," the prisoner gasped. "Interplanar weakness creates too great a flux. Results, even of a minor spell, can be surprising."

"Very well," said Grolion, "now the tale. All of it."

The telling took a while. Grolion considerately pulled away creepers and feeders, keeping the resident only loosely held and only slightly drained. I steeled myself to hear the sordid history of the resident's treachery and the village council's complicity, though I knew the tale intimately: how they had bridled at my innocent researches, conspiring to usurp my authority, finally using cruel violence against me.

"He was obsessed with the colors of the overworld," the resident said. "I was his senior assistant, with two others under me. We were just village lads, though quick to learn. He established himself here because, he said, the conditions were unusually propitious—a unique quatrefoliate intersection of planes, a node from which it was possible to reach deep into two adjacent dimensions of the upper world, and one of the infernal."

A tooth-rimmed sucker, sensing the flavor of his breath, probed for his mouth, but Grolion knocked it aside. The resident spoke on. "He particularly craved to see a color known in the overworld as refulgent ombre. It cannot exist in our milieu; what we call light is but a poor imitation of what reigns there.

"But our village sits on the site of Fallume the Ept's demesne, long ago in the Seventeenth Aeon. So potent were the forces Fallume employed that he permanently frayed the membranes between the planes. My master's researches had shown him that, here and here alone, he could create a facsimile of the upper realm and maintain it indefinitely. Within that sphere he could bask in the glow of refulgent ombre and other supernal radiances. To do so would confer upon him benefits he was eager to enjoy."

The details followed. The microcosm of the overworld sphere would spontaneously self-generate upon completion of a complex design made from unique materials: the pigmented scales of four kinds of butterflies whose larval forms fed only on the sap and leaves of a unique tree, with which the insects lived in symbiosis—predators drawn to consume the insects were led into its maze of branches, where they impaled themselves on barbed thorns and thus became food for the vegetative partner.

The tree had a unique property, being able to exist in more than one plane at the same time, though it presented a different form in each milieu: in the first level of the overworld, it was a kind of animal, a serpentine hunter of the transmigrated souls of small creatures that evanesced up from our plane; in the underworld, it was a spined serpent whose feeding habits were obscure, though distasteful. The attributes of all three realms co-existed in the tree's inner juices. Eaten and digested by the worms that crawled the branches, the ichor was transmuted by the process that turned the larvae into butterflies, and was precipitated out in the scales of their viridescent wings. Taken while fresh, the colors of the scales could be arranged, at this precise location, into the design that would cause the facsimile of the overworld to appear. Within that sphere, refulgent ombre would shine.

Grolion halted the resident at this point. I saw his energetic face in motion as he sorted through the information. Then he asked the question I had hoped he would: "This refulgent ombre, is it valuable?"

"Priceless," said the resident, and I saw avarice's flame kindled in the assistant's eyes, only to be doused as his prisoner continued, "and utterly worthless."

Grolion's heavy brows contracted. "How so?"

"It can only exist in the facsimile, and the facsimile can only exist here, where the planes converge."

Grolion turned to regard the workroom. "So the starburst cannot be moved? Or taken apart and reformed elsewhere?"

"Disturb a grain of its substance, and it will depart through the breach, taking you and me, the house and probably the village with it."

A scowl pulled down the vulpine face. "Tell the rest."

"The master erected this manse, laid the garden, planted the tree. The village council welcomed him; in recent years traffic along the road has become scant; wealth no longer flows our way. They made an accommodation: the village would provide him with assistants and sundry necessities; he, in return, would perform small magics and provide the benefit of steagle."

"And what is this steagle?"

"It is an immense beast that swims through endless ocean in an adjacent plane–you will understand that the terms "ocean" and "swim" are only approximations. He gave the village the knife that cuts only steagle; slice the air with it, and a slab of meat appears. With each cut, a new piece arrives, dripping with lifejuices. We would never know hunger again."

"A useful instrument."

"Alas," said the resident, "it, too, only works where interplanar membranes are weak. A mile beyond the village, it is just another knife."

Grolion scratched his coarse thatch. "Does the steagle not resent the theft of its flesh?"

"We have never given the matter any thought."

The villagers had taken the bargain. And all was as it should have been, except that the tree flourished more boisterously than anticipated. Birds and lizards had to be augmented by occasional wanderers who had taken the wrong fork and who were impressed as "assistants." Even they were not enough. Thick creepers began to prowl the village at night, entering open windows or even forcing the less sturdy doors. Householders would arise in the morning to find pets shriveled and livestock desiccated, drained to the last drop. Then the tree started in on the children.

"The council came to my master, but found him consumed by his own ambitions. What were a few children–easily replaceable, after all–compared to the fulfillment of his noble dream? He counseled them to install stronger doors.

"But the village threatened to withdraw support, including we who assisted. My master begrudgingly invoked Phandaal's Discriminating Boundary, to keep the tree in bounds. But the spell also confined us."

Hearing this, I was saddened anew at the thought of the council's shortsightedness, when I had been making such good progress in my work. I tried not to listen as the resident told the rest: how, while I slept, my assistants had fed my watcher a posset of drugged honey then stolen into my chamber with knives.

The dastardly attack came, coordinated and from three directions at once, catching me unawares in the midst of my sleep-wanderings. I awoke and defended myself, though without magic I was in a poor situation. However, I had not become a wielder of three colors of magic without learning caution. The traitors were surprised to discover that I had long since created for myself an impregnable refuge in the fourth plane, to which I fled when the struggle went against me. Unfortunately, they had done such damage to my physical form that only my essence won through.

"He left behind his physical attributes," my former assistant was telling Grolion, "and these we sealed into a coffin of lead lined with antimony. Thus he cannot reach out to repair himself; instead, he projects himself from his hiding place, riding the sensoria of passing insects, seeking to spy on me." He swallowed and continued, "Something is boring into my ankle. If you release me from the tree's grasp I swear to do you no harm."

Grolion tugged away the tuber that was feeding on the resident's leg and batted away another that was seeking to insert itself into the prisoner's ear. He pulled free the creepers that had been thickening around the resident's torso, then yanked the man loose. The resident gasped in pain; scraps of bloody cloth and small pieces of flesh showed where barbed thorns had worked their way into his back and buttocks.

Grolion tore the man's robe into strips and bound his wrists and ankles. But he considerately hauled the bound man out of the tree's reach before going to reinspect the workroom and the design. He reached for the Phandaal libram but as his fingers almost touched its blue chamois a blinding spark of white light leapt across the gap, accompanied by a sharp *crack* of sound. Grolion yelped and quickly withdrew his hand, shook it energetically then put the tips of two fingers into his mouth and sucked them.

He left the room, took himself out to a bench along one side of the garden, equidistant between the tree and the workroom. Here he sat, one leg crossed over another, his pointed chin in the grip of one hand's forefinger and thumb, and gave himself over to thought. From time to time, he looked up at the barbthorn, or over to the workroom window, and occasionally he considered the tied-up resident.

After a few minutes, he called over to the resident, "There were three of you. Where are the other two?"

The resident's upturned glance at the tree made for a mutely eloquent answer.

"I see," said Grolion. "And, ultimately, what would have happened to me?"

The resident's eyes looked at anything but the questioner.

"I see," Grolion said again, and returned to thought. After a while, he said, "The lead coffin?"

"In the crypt," said the resident, "below the garden. The steps are behind the fountain in the pool of singing fish. But if you open it, he will reanimate. I don't doubt he would then feed us all to the tree. He used to care only for refulgent ombre; his murder, followed by several incarnations as various insects, most of which die horribly, may have developed in him an instinct for cruelty."

Grolion went to look. There was a wide stone flag, square in shape, inset with an iron ring at one side. He seized and pulled and, with a grating of granite on granite, the trapdoor came up, assisted by unseen counterweights on pulleys beneath. A flight of steps led down.

I did not follow. The glyphs and symbols cut into my coffin's sides and top would pain me, as they were intended to do. I flew over to a crack in the wall above the resident and, having established than nothing lurked therein, I settled down to wait.

I knew what Grolion would be seeing: the much-cracked walls and damp, uneven floor of the crypt; the blackness only partly relieved by two narrow airshafts that descended from small grates set in the garden wall above; the several bundles of cloth near the bottom of the steps, containing the shriveled remains of my former junior and intermediate assistants, as well as the wayfarers who had, individually, sought shelter from the invigilant's ghoul and found themselves pressed into service; and one end wall, fractured and riven by the barbthorn's roots as they had grown down through the ceiling and the soil above it.

And, of course, on a raised dais at the opposite end of the crypt, the coffin that held my physical attributes. They were neither dead nor alive, but in that state known as "indeterminate." I did not think that Grolion would be curious enough to lift the lid to look within; that is, I was sure he possessed the curiosity, but doubted he was foolish enough to let it possess him, down there in the ill-smelling dark.

When he came back up into the red sunlight, his brows were downdrawn in concentration. "No more work today," he told the resident. "I wish to think."

The tree had been stimulated by its tastes of the resident. Its branches stirred without a wind to move them. A thick tubule, its toothed end open to catch his scent, was extending itself along the ground toward where he sat, still bound but struggling to inch away. Grolion stamped on the feeder and kicked it back the way it had come, then hauled the resident by his collar farther toward the workroom end of the garden. He turned and stared up at the tree for a moment, then went to look at the starburst again. Thinking himself unobserved, he did not bother to prevent his thoughts from showing in his face. The tree was a problem without an opportunity attached; the design was valueless, even when completed, since it had to remain where it was; the Phandaal on the shelf was precious, but painfully defended.

He came back to the resident. "What happens when the design is completed?

"A microcosm of the overworld will appear above it, and it will be absorbed."

"Could we enter the microcosm?"

The bound man signaled a negative. "The overworld's energies are too strident, even in a facsimile. We would either melt or burst into flames."

"Yet your master intended to enter it."

"He spent years toughening himself to endure the climate. That was what made him hard to kill."

Grolion strode about with the energy of frustration. "So we are locked in with a vampirous plant and a magical design that will destroy us if it is not completed. Only your master truly understands what needs to be done, but if I revive him he will probably feed me to the plant to gain the wherewithal with which to finish his project and achieve his life's goal."

"That is the situation."

Grolion abused the air with his fist. "I reject it," he said. "My experience is that unhelpful situations will always yield to a man of guile and resource. I will exert myself."

"In what direction?"

"I will eliminate the middleman."

The resident was framing a new question when a voice called

from the corridor. A moment later, the invigilant's belly passed through the archway, followed shortly after by the man himself. He took in the scene, noting the resident's bonds, but said only, "How goes the work?"

The resident made to answer but Grolion cut him off. "A new administration has taken charge. The situation as it stands is unsatisfactory. It will now be invested with a new dynamic." He moved toward the invigilant with an air of dire intent.

"What's this?" said the invigilant, a look of alarm making its way to the surface of his face through the rolls of fat beneath it. His plump hands rose to defend himself, but Grolion treated them as he had the tree's creepers; he pulled up the flap that closed the invigilant's wallet and seized the knife that cut steagle. A flick of his wrist caused the blade to spring free with a sharp *click*.

"You cannot threaten with that," said the invigilant. "It cuts only steagle."

"Indeed," said Grolion. He made for the tree, in his peculiar bent-kneed stride. The invigilant bent and undid the resident's bonds, but both stayed well clear of the barbthorn. My rumblebee was tired but I drove it to follow the traveler.

Grolion marched to the base of the barbthorn. Several wriggling tubers reached for him, the tree having not fed well for many days. He slashed at the air with the black-bladed knife, a long horizontal cut at head height. Lifejuices spurted, bedewing the hairs of his arms with pink droplets. He ignored them and made two vertical cuts, one each from the ends of the first gash. Now he cut a fourth incision in the air, at knee height and parallel to the first. Then he gripped the knife between his teeth and thrust his hands into the top cut. He seized, tugged, and ripped until, with a gush of lifejuices, a slab of steagle the size of a sleeping pallet fell out with a *splat* onto the stone paving.

Grolion stepped back. The barbthorn's feeders sampled the air above the dripping flesh, then, as one, they plunged down and fastened multifanged mouths onto the meat. The tubules pulsed rhythmically as the tree fed. Grolion paused to watch only a moment then, wielding the knife again, he stepped to the side and repeated the exercise. Another weighty slab of steagle slapped the pavement, and the tree sent fresh feeders to drain it.

"Now," said Grolion, "for the design." He folded the steagle knife and pocketed it then, with the tree occupied with steagle, he threw himself up and into the barbthorn. Ever higher he climbed, ignoring the wounds his passage through the thorns inflicted on him, while he methodically stripped every branch of its chrysalises, be they mature, middling or newly spun. These he tucked into his shirt until it bulged.

When he had them all, he dropped swiftly down through the foliage, paused at the base to cut another wadge of steagle for the tree, then strode to the workroom. "Follow me!" he called over his shoulder.

The invigilant and the resident did so, though not without exchanging freighted glances. I flew to where I could get a view of the proceedings. There was Grolion at the work bench, pulling handfuls of chrysalises from his shirt. He found a scalpel and sliced one open, as the resident looked on open-mouthed.

An almost-made almiranth appeared. With surprising deftness, Grolion teased it free of its split cocoon, laid the feebly wriggling creature on the benchtop, and with a pair of fine tweezers spread its wings. He breathed gently on the wet membranes to dry them. Then he turned to the resident and said, "Now you collect the scales."

Wordlessly, the resident did as he was told, while Grolion informed the invigilant that his task was to sort the chrysalises by species and apparent maturity. The official's mouth formed an almost hemispherical frown and he said, "I do not−"

Grolion dealt him a buffet to the side of the head that laid the recipient on the floor. He then stood on one foot, the other poised for a belly-kick and invited the prostrate man to change his views. Trembling, the invigilant got to his feet and did as he was told.

Time passed. The tree fed, the men worked, and the supply of scales for the starburst grew. When Grolion had extracted the last moth mature enough to have harvestable scales, he asked the resident, "Have we enough?"

The resident looked at the several reeds, each loaded with pigment and said, with mild amazement, "I believe we do."

"Then get to work." To the invigilant, he said, "You will act as assistant, handing him the reeds as he asks for them."

They set to. Meanwhile their new supervisor went out to the tree. The barbthorn, having sensed the availability of a rich and ample source of food, had sent forth its primary feeder; this was a strong tube, as thick as Grolion's thigh and rimmed by barbed thorn-teeth as long as his thumb. It had fastened onto the second of the two slabs of steagle, which it was rapidly draining of substance. The operation was accompanied by loud slurps and obscene pulsations of the fleshy conduit. The first slab was but a shrunken mat of dried meat.

"Let us keep you occupied," said Grolion, deploying the black blade. He cut a fresh segment of steagle from the air, twice the size of the others, and let it fall beside the now almost-shriveled piece. Tubules strained toward the new sustenance, and in a moment the thick feeder left off from the slab it was draining and drove its thorns into the more recent supply. The tree shivered and a sound very like a moan of pleasure came from somewhere in the matrix of branches.

Grolion loped back to the workroom. The two men, on their knees beside the design, looked up with apprehension but he waved them to continue. "All is as it should be," he said, almost genially. "Soon we will be able to put this unpleasantness behind us. Continue your work while I inspect the premises."

He left the area and I could hear clinks and clatters as he rummaged through other rooms. After a while he came back to the garden, a bulging cloth sack in his hand. Leaving the bag near the workroom door, he went to the tree again, saw that it had fully drained the latest steagle. Its tubules were again sampling the air. An expression that I took to be simple curiosity formed on the man's foxlike face. Unfolding the knife once more, he cut again, standing on tiptoe to make the upper incision, stooping almost to the ground for the lower, and thrusting the blade arm-deep into the cuts. Out fell a huge block of steagle and Grolion stood drenched in viscous pink. He brushed at himself, then went to immerse himself among the singing fish, which gave out an excited music as the flavor of their water changed. The tree, meanwhile, was writhing in vegetative ecstasy, sending up new shoots in all directions.

The resident and the invigilant were now finishing the starburst. The former laid a line of deep vermilion against a wedge of scintillating white nacre, then bid the latter hand him a reed filled with stygian black. This he used to trace a spiral at the heart of the pattern, delicately tapping out the pigment a few scales at a time.

He finished with the black then called for old gold and basilisk's-eye green, two of the rarest colors from the barbthorn's palette. The invigilant passed him the reeds just as Grolion hove into view through the doorway, dripping wet and bending to retrieve his bag of loot. "How now?" he said, his unburdened hand indicating the design.

The resident appeared startled to hear himself declare, "I am about to finish."

"Then do so," said Grolion. "I have wasted enough time in this place."

Now came the moment. I flew close, but my rumbling buzz annoyed Grolion; he brushed me aside with a brusque motion that sent me tumbling. I fetched up hard against the side of the doorway, damaging one of my wings so that I fell, spiraling, to the floor. I looked up to see him frowning down at me, then his huge foot lifted.

"Look!" said the invigilant and the crushing blow did not come. All eyes turned toward the space just above the center of the starburst where, as the final iridescent flakes of color fell from the end of the reed, a spark had kindled in mid-air. In a moment, like a flamelet fed by inrushing air, it grew and spread, becoming a glowing orb that was at first the size of a pea, then the width of a fist, now of a head, then larger, and still larger. And as it grew, the starburst that had been so carefully laid upon the workroom floor was drawn up in a reverse cascade of sparkling colors, to merge with the globe of light, now scintillating with scores of rare hues, having grown as large as a wine cask, and still waxing.

The three men watched in fascination, for playing across their eyes were colors, singly and in combination, such as few mortals have ever seen. But I had no thought for them now, not even for my betrayal and the unjust abuse I had suffered. I flexed my injured wing, told myself that it would bear the rumblebee's weight long enough. I bent my six legs and threw myself toward the light, willing my three good, and one bad, membranes to carry me forward.

Instead, I drifted to one side, away from the prize. And now the resident noticed me. At once he knew me. He came around the edge of the tray, from which the last trickles of the intricate design were flowing up into the orb of light, and struck at me with the hand that still held the final reed. I jinked awkwardly to one side, a last few ashy flakes of nacre dusting the hairs on my back, and the blow did not fall. But my passage had brought me close to Grolion again, and his hand made the same sharp stroke as before, so that the backs of his hairy fingers caught me once more and sent me spinning, helpless—but straight into the globe!

I passed through the glowing wall, heard within me the rumblebee's tiny last cry as its solid flesh melted in the rarified conditions of this little exemplar of the overworld that had now appeared in our middling plane. Freed from corporeality, I experienced the full, ineffable *isness* of the upper realm, the colors that ravished even as they healed the wounds. Refulgent ombre was mine, and with it ten thousand hues and shades that mortal eyes could never have seen. I languished, limp with bliss, enervated by rapture.

Somewhere beyond the globe of light, the resident, the invigilant and the wanderer went about their mundane business. I cared nothing for them and their gross doings, nor for the parcel of flesh, bone and cartilage that had once my essence and was now itself confined in a coffin of lead and antimony.

They had feared my retribution. But there would be no revenge. Then was then, now was now, and I was above it all, in the overworld. I exulted. I reveled. I swilled the wine of ecstasy.

The man who called himself Grolion stared at the multicolored orb. It had stopped growing after the bee had entered it. All of the starburst was now absorbed and the globe hung in the air above the empty tray, complete and self-sufficient. Curious, he reached a hand toward it, but Shalmetz, the man who had finished the design, struck away his arm.

Grolion turned with a scowl, fist raised, but subsided when Shalmetz said, "A sliver of ice thrown on a roaring fire would last longer than your flesh in contact with that."

Groblens, the fat village officer, pulled back his own hand that he had been hesitantly stretching toward the microcosm. Grunting, straining, he levered himself to his feet. "Is it over?" he said.

Shalmetz observed the globe. "It seems so."

"Test it," said the traveler, aiming his chin toward the blue book on the shelf. Shalmetz touched a finger to the book's spine. "No spark."

Grolion gestured meaningfully. Shalmetz made no objection but with a rueful quirk of his lips, passed across the Phandaal. "You are welcome to it," he said. "I will return to my job at the fish farm."

"Give me back the steagle knife," the fat man said. "It is of no use beyond this eldritch intersection of planes."

"It will have value as a curio," the foxfaced man said.

Shalmetz looked through the window. "The village may need it to keep the tree content. It seems to have developed a fondness for steagle." And more than a fondness. The barbthorn had been growing, and was now half again as tall as it had been that morning, and substantially fuller. Moreover, it had grown more active.

"I will cut it one more portion," he said, "to keep it occupied while we depart. After that, it becomes part of my past and therefore none of my concern. You must deal with it as you can. I recommend fire."

To Shalmetz and Groblens, the plan had obvious shortcomings, but before they could address them the traveler was loping to the base of the tree. Again, he cut deep wide, and long, and in moments another block of steagle dropped before the questing feeders. The tree fell upon the new food with an eagerness that, when displayed by a vegetative lifeform, must always be disturbing.

But there was an even more troublesome coda to its behavior: even as its smaller tubules fixed themselves to the slab of steagle, the main feeder, now grown as thick as a man's body, darted toward the still closing gap in the air from which the pink flesh had come. Before the opening could close, the thorn-toothed orifice thrust itself through. The end disappeared. But it had connected, for immediately the tube began to pump and swallow, passing larger and larger volumes along the feeder's length, as if a great serpent was dining on an endless litter of piglets.

A deep thrumming came from the plant, a sound of mingled satisfaction and insatiable gluttony. It visibly swelled in height and girth, while a new complexity of bethorned twigs and branches erupted from its larger limbs. The man with the knife stepped back, as the tree's roots writhed and grew in harmony with the rest of it, cracking the wall against which it had grown, tearing up the stone pavement in all directions, upturning the fountain and sending the singing fish out into the inhospitable air to gasp and croak their final performance.

The man turned and ran, stumbling over broken flagstones and squirming roots that sprang from the earth beneath his feet. Shalmetz and Groblens fled the workroom just as the tree's new growth met the foundation of its wall at the garden's ends. In an instant, the wall was riven from floor to ceiling. The room collapsed, bringing down the second story above it, though when the debris settled, the kaleidoscopic orb that held a facsimile of the overworld, which in turn held the blissful essence of the house's builder, remained unscathed, shining through the billows of dust.

The bag of loot was beneath a fallen roof timber. Its collector reached for it, found it held fast. He addressed himself to one end of the beam, and by dint of prodigious effort was able to lift and shift the weight aside. But as he stooped and seized his prize, he heard Shalmetz's wavering cry of fear and dismay.

The man stood and turned in the direction of the other's gaze. He saw the barbthorn, now grown even huger, looming over the ravaged garden, roiling like a storm cloud come down to earth. Its main feeder, now wide enough to have swallowed a horse, continued to pump great gobbets of steagle from beyond this plane. A constant bass note thrummed the air and the ground shook unceasingly as the roots drove ever outward.

But it was not the tree that had frightened Shalmetz or that now caused both him and the invigilant to turn and flee through the corridor that led to the foyer and the outer door. It was the vertical slit that was rending the air above and below the place at which the feeder left this plane and entered another. The fissure rose higher and lower at the same time, cleaving stone and earth as easily as it cut the air. And through the rent appeared a dark shape.

The traveler stood and watched, his bag of loot loose in his grasp. A thing like a great rounded snout, but ringed about its end with tentacles, was forcing its way through the gap, splitting it higher and lower as it came, throwing a bow wave of earth and stone in either direction. More and more of the creature came through, and now it could be seen that, at the place where it would have had a chin if it had had a face, the barbthorn's feeder was fastened to its flesh. Around the spot where the thorns were sunk out of sight was a network of small scars, and three fresh wounds, still dripping pink juice.

The tentacled snout was now all the way through the gap. Behind it, the body narrowed then swelled again, displaying a ring of limb-like flukes all around its circumference that beat at the air, propelling the creature forward. It showed no eyes, but its tentacles—four large ones and more than a dozen minor specimens—groped toward the tree as if they could sense its presence.

Now two of the steagle's larger members seized the feeder tube and, with an audible *rip* of tearing flesh, detached it from its face. Pink lifejuices gushed from the deep wound left behind, and one of the smaller tendrils bent to place its flattened, leaf-shaped end over the injury.

As the feeder came loose, the tree roared, a sound like an orchestra of bass organ tubes. The main feeder writhed in the steagle's grasp and the barbthorn's every creeper, branch and tubule strained and flailed toward the source of combined nourishment and threat. The steagle met the assault with equal vigor, and now a kind of mouth appeared at the center of the ring of tentacles, from which issued a hiss like that of a steam geyser long denied release, followed by a long, thick tongue coated with a corrugation of rasping hooks and serrated, triangular teeth.

The tentacles pulled the barbthorn toward the steagle, even as the tree wrapped its assailant in a matrix of writhing, thorned vegetation. The traveler heard cracks and snaps, roars and moans, hisses and indefinable sounds. he felt the ground quake anew as the impetus of the steagle's thrust tore the barbthorn's new roots from the ground.

Time to go, he told himself, and turned toward the passage-way through which the others had fled. But he found himself in the midst of a wriggling, seething mass of roots, erupting from the earth amid volleys of flying clods and pebbles that stung and bruised him. Though he stepped carefully, finding firm footing was impossible; the entire floor of the garden was in constant, violent motion. Worse, some of the roots had snapped and their ends flailed the air like whips and cudgels. One dealt his thigh a hard blow, knocking him off balance, and as he spun around, a root the thickness of his thumb struck his wrist.

The impact numbed the hand that held the bag. It fell between two roots and, though he feared his arm might be trapped if the two came together, he reached for the prize. But as his fingers touched the cloth, the floor of the garden collapsed into the crypt below, taking the loot with it, and leaving the man teetering on the brink of the cavity.

He threw himself backward, ignoring the slashing, flailing blows that came from all sides, then turned and scrambled for the corridor that led out. *I will come back for the bag,* he told himself.

Behind him, the rest of the steagle emerged from the rent between the planes: a segmented tail that ended in a pair of sharp-edged pincers. These now joined the front of the creature in its attack on the barbthorn, and their reinforcement proved decisive. Though the tree's thorned limbs continued to beat and tear at the steagle's hide, raising a spray of pink ichor and gouging away wedges of flesh, the unequal battle was moving toward a conclusion. The tentacles and pincers tore the limbs from the tree and severed its roots from the stem, flinging the remnants into the hole that had been the crypt. The barbthorn's roars became cries that became whimpers.

And then it was done. The steagle snapped and cut and broke the great tree into pieces, filled the hole in the earth with them. At the last, with discernible contempt, it arched its tail and, from an orifice beneath that appendage, directed a stream of red liquid at the wreckage. The wood and greenery burst instantly into strangely colored flames, and a column of oily smoke rose to the sky.

The steagle, somehow airborne, floated around the pyre, viewing it from several angles. Its passage brought it within range of the multicolored microcosm of the overworld, which hung in the air, untroubled by the violence wrought nearby. The steagle paused before the orb. Its eyeless face seemed to regard the kaleidoscopic play of colors that moved constantly across the globe's surface. One of its minor tentacles reached out and stroked the object, paused for a moment as if deciding whether or not it fully approved of the thing's taste, then curled around it and popped it whole into the steagle's maw.

The mouth closed, the creature turned toward the rent in the membrane between the planes and in less time than the man who called himself Grolion would have credited, it was through and gone. The air healed itself and there was only the burning devastation of the tree and the shattered garden to indicate that anything had happened here,

The man had watched the final act from atop a rise some distance down the road. Here he had found Shalmetz and Groblens. The latter was too winded by the combination of pell-mell flight and a life-long fondness for beebleberry tarts, but the former had greeted him thusly: "Well, Grolion–if that is even an approximation of your name–you certainly invested that situation with a new dynamic."

The traveler was in no mood to accept criticism; he answered the remark with a blow that sat Shalmetz down on the roadway, from where he offered no further comments. After a while, he and Groblens made their way back to the village. The other man waited until the eerie flames subsided. Toward evening, when all was still, he crept back to the manse.

The house had collapsed. The hole that had been the crypt was full of stinking char. Of his bag and its contents, he could find no trace. The only object left unscathed was the lead coffin, whose incised runes and symbols had somehow protected it from the otherworldly fire. It was not even warm.

The man used ropes and pulleys to haul the object from the pit. In the same outbuilding that had held the tackle he found a two-wheeled cart. He lowered the coffin onto the vehicle and pushed it away from the stink and soot of the burned-out fire. He admired the emblems and sigils that decorated its sides and top; he was sure that they were of powerful effect.

When he had wheeled the cart out to the road, he set his fingers to the coffin's lid and pried it loose. He had hoped for jewels or precious metals; he found only fast-rotting flesh and wet bones, with not even a thumb-ring or an ivory torc to reward his labors. He said a harsh word and threw death's detritus into a roadside ditch.

Only the coffin itself remained. It might prove useful, if only for the figures carved into it. But now saw that with the removal of the contents, the signs and characters were fading to nothing.

Still, he believed he could remember most of them. Tomorrow he would carve them into the lead then cut the soft metal into plaques and amulets. These he could sell at Azenomei Fair, and who knows what possibilities might then arise?

TIMMY, COME HOME

This was another story that came from a request to submit to a theme anthology, again edited by Gordon Van Gelder. The theme was the Fermi Paradox which essentially says, "If there are aliens out there, why haven't we encountered them?" The antho was called Is Anybody Out There? *and it posited some interesting rationales for why we've never met the neighbors. My starting point was: what if an alien got stranded here and died? Then what?*

What if? and Then What?, by the way, are great starting points for writing science fiction.

AT FIRST, they were just shadows and whispers in Brodie's dreams, voices he could not quite hear, movement he could not quite bring into focus. Then the shadows and whispers began to filter into his waking hours, and he sought help.

"Neurologically, there is nothing wrong with you," said the neurologist. "Your brain is anatomically and functionally normal. We found no lesions, tumors or chemical anomalies."

"What does that leave?" said Brodie.

The neurologist spread his hands. "Psychiatric causes?"

The psychiatrist said, "You're not schizophrenic. I find no dissociative tendencies."

"So I'm normal? But I hear voices."

"You hear voices but you don't know what they're saying. Most people who hear voices know exactly what they're saying. The voices tell them to do things. Often they are things they shouldn't do. Sometimes they are things no one should do."

"So I should feel good about that?"

The psychiatrist interlaced his fingers and said, "How *do* you feel about it?"

The psychologist said, "You fall in the middle of the bell curve on every measure I've taken of you, except two." The man looked through the sheaf of papers before him, found one and scanned it. "In intelligence, you're in the top percentile." He looked at another. "In terms of affect, you seem to be sad."

Brodie sat in the patient's chair, a comfortable armchair upholstered in brown leather. "They told me I was bright in high school," he said. "I don't know if I'm sad. I'm just me, the way I've always been.

"I'm a little concerned that you live such a solitary life–"

"*I'm* not concerned," Brodie said.

The psychologist made a gesture of acquiescence. "It's not uncommon in cases of exceptional intelligence. And you don't seem to be actually depressed."

Brodie ignored the motion that he saw indistinctly from the corner of his right eye and the barely audible susurration that seemed to come from just behind his right ear. "If there's nothing wrong with me," he said, "then what's wrong with me?"

The psychologist stroked his chin. "How does it affect your life?"

Brodie thought for a moment. "Minimally," he said. "It comes and goes and I can usually ignore it. But, steadily, it comes more often and lasts longer."

"What is it that bothers you most? The inability to control it?"

"At first, yes. Now I'd just like to know what they're trying to tell me."

The psychologist zeroed in. "'They'?" he said.

"There's more than one voice," Brodie said.

"How do you know?"

"I just do."

"And what makes you think 'they' are trying to tell you something?"

Now it was Brodie's turn to spread his hands. "Why else would they be trying so hard to get my attention?"

The parapsychologist said, "Have you experienced any instances of precognition, lengthy periods of deja vu, astral projection?"

"No."

"Would you like to?"

"No."

The exorcist closed the book, rang the bell and snuffed out the candle and said, "Are they still there?"

"Yes."

"Dammit. Now we'll have to start over."

***

The medium said, "I hear the name Walter. Does that have any meaning to you?"

"I don't think so."

"Not your father's name?"

"No."

"A childhood friend?"

"Nuh-uh."

"Maybe an uncle? A pet?"

"Goodbye."

"Close your eyes and imagine you're sitting in a darkened movie theater. The screen is bright white and in the middle of it is a small, black dot."

"All right."

The hypnotist's voice was warm and calmly assured. it reminded Brodie of his mother's voice when he was young. "Concentrate on the dot."

"Yes."

"The more you concentrate, the more relaxed you feel."

"Yes."

"All you can see now is the dot."

"Yes."

"It's growing larger. Now it fills the screen."

Brodie made an involuntary sound.

"What's wrong?"

"I don't like it."

"What don't you like?"

"The big dot. It's too big. Too dark. Too... deep.

"All right. It's not a dot. It's an x. Is that better?"

It was. Brodie felt his anxiety fade.

"You're becoming more and more relaxed," the woman said. "Your feet are relaxed."

Brodie's feet were very relaxed.

"Your legs are relaxed."

He felt the muscles of his calves and thighs slacken pleasantly.

"Now your abdomen and your lower back are relaxed."

"Yes." The word came on a sigh.

"Your shoulders and your upper back are relaxed."

"Mmmm."

"And your neck."

"Ungh."

"You're relaxed from the top of your head to the tip of your toes. You've never felt better."

It was true. He'd never felt better. "Mmm," he said.

"Wonderful. Now turn your attention to the whisper in your right ear."

"Yes."

"As you listen, it gets louder."

Brodie listened. The whisper grew louder.

"As it gets louder, it becomes clearer."

"No," he said. "It doesn't."

"Concentrate. Your hearing is becoming much sharper. You could hear a pin drop in the next room."

Brodie's hearing became sharper. The hypnotist's voice sounded more crisp. But the whispering remained an undifferentiated sequence of sounds.

"I can't make it out," he said.

"You're still relaxed, more relaxed than you've even been before."

"Yes."

"Let the sound come to you. Let it become clear."

Brodie did as he was told. But the whispering did not become clear.

The hypnotist was a plump, grandmotherly woman. The room where she practiced her profession was as congenial as she was. "I want to try something else," she said.

"It didn't work," Brodie said. "Nothing I've tried has worked."

"We got somewhere," she said.

"True."

"So it's worth trying a different approach." She leaned back in the comfortable chair that faced and matched Brodie's. "You get a feel for these things. I've got a feeling that there's something buried in you."

"I don't think so," he said. "I had a completely untroubled childhood. My parents didn't beat me or cast me as a supporting player in their own psychological dramas. I was not ritually abused or locked in a dark closet."

"Even so," she said, "you're throwing up a lot of dust right now."

Brodie thought about it. "I am, aren't I?" He agreed to come back for another session.

"Completely relaxed."

Brodie made a contented, compliant sound. The chair held him like the palm of a warm hand.

"Now you're standing on a high place. You can see very far in every direction."

"Yes."

"In one direction, you can see your childhood."

"Yes."

"What does it look like?"

"Sunny. Bright colors. I see my dog, Willy."

"What happened to Willy?"

"He got old. The vet put him to sleep. It didn't hurt him."

"It made you sad?"

"Yes. I cried. Mom and dad cried, too."

"Think about Willy."

"Okay."

"Now think about the dot in the middle of the screen. Think

about it getting larger."

Brodie shifted in the chair, as if preparing to stand.

"You're still very relaxed, as relaxed as you've ever been. You're completely safe."

He settled back.

"The dot cannot harm you. It cannot harm Willy. You can think about it without being troubled."

"I don't like it."

"What don't you like about the dot?"

"It's a hole, a dark hole."

"Why does the hole bother you?"

Brodie shifted nervously. The chair wasn't supportive now. It was confining. "Because you can't get out."

"The hole is going away now. It's far away where you don't have to worry about it."

Brodie relaxed, settled back into the chair. "Good."

"Now you're back on the high place, looking over your whole childhood."

"Mmm."

"You've got a telescope that lets you focus on any time in your childhood, any event. You can see yourself and other people, see what you were doing. And Willy, too."

"Yes."

"Look through the telescope now and see a time when you were frightened by a hole."

Brodie grunted.

"You're still far away from that time, just seeing it through a telescope."

"Okay."

"The you that was frightened then doesn't have to be frightened now."

"Okay."

"You're safe and relaxed. Nothing can hurt you."

"Yes."

"Now look through the telescope. What do you see?"

Brodie looked.

"We're getting somewhere," the hypnotist said.

"I suppose," Brodie said. "But where?"

He could remember what he had seen, because the hypnotist had told him he would. At first, the scene had been contained within a circle, just as if he had viewed it through a telescope. Then, as she had told him to zoom in on it, the image had filled the inner screen of his mind.

He saw himself–his much younger self; he could not have been older than five–sitting on the old couch in the living room. Willy, still just a pup, was lying on the carpeted floor, licking his paws, paying no attention to the television.

Now the image shifted its point of view, so that Brodie was looking over his earlier self's shoulder. The television was showing an old movie about a boy who had a dog–a bigger dog than Willy, a collie. Now the dog on the tv was barking. Willy looked up at the sound, then went back to his grooming.

A woman wearing an apron over a long dress was asking the collie what was wrong. The dog's boy was nowhere in sight. The animal ran off a short distance, stopped, turned back to the woman, barked.

"Is it Timmy?" she said. "Find Timmy!" The dog ran off, barking, and she followed it out of the shot. As the scene changed, Brodie had felt a chilling shock pass through him. The hypnotist had had to tell him to freeze the scene in his memory so that she could spend a few minutes calming him and distancing him from the events. Finally, he was ready to go on.

And then, when the moment of revelation came, all that he recalled was a shot of the dog barking at the edge of a hole in the ground–a hole partly covered by splintered boards. Then came a shot of a little boy, his blond hair seeming to glow against a surrounding darkness, looking up toward a dim light far above, with the sound of the dog barking off-screen, and the woman's voice calling, "Timmy! We're going to get you out of there!"

"Can you remember now what was so frightening about that television show?" the hypnotist asked.

But Brodie couldn't remember. Seeing it now, in his mind's eye, and stretching to recall what emotions his little-boy self had felt, all those years ago, he came up blank. "No," he told the grandmother-ly woman, "fact is, I don't even recall being scared. I just felt..." He searched inside himself and after a moment it came to him, "So sad.

I was so sad for the little boy. He'd fallen in the hole."

"Why was that so sad?"

"I don't know," Brodie said. "I just knew that it was the absolute worst, the absolutely saddest thing in the world. I couldn't bear to think of it."

———————

Brodie's response to the memory of watching the tv show about the kid who fell in the hole had been so strong that the hypnotist had wanted to let the emotions settle before she asked the crucial question: what did this have to do with the shadows and whispers that still plagued his dreams and, more and more, his waking moments. She let that wait until his next visit.

Before she put him under, the woman said, "We're going to go back to the memory of the boy in the hole. It won't be so difficult now that you've confronted the emotion, and we'll try and see how that memory connects to what's happening to you now."

Brodie wasn't averse to using the telescope to go back to his long-ago self again, sitting on the couch watching tv. In the few days since they had uncovered that memory, he had thought quite often about what had happened. The whole business puzzled him. He accepted that some part of him hadn't wanted to remember feeling so sad, had buried the memory and had had to be gently led back to it.

So it was with more curiosity than apprehension that he relaxed in the comfort of the chair and allowed the hypnotist's soothing voice to take him back to the high place then through the telescope to the boy on the couch. And from that came... nothing.

"Put yourself back in the boy's body," the woman said. "Look around the room. Are there shadows in the corners, perhaps a curtain blowing in a window that you see from the corner of your eye?"

"No."

"What do you hear in the background? Is anyone talking in another room, talking softly?"

"No."

"Your hearing is getting much stronger. You can hear every sound around you. What do you hear?"

Brodie listened with the boy's ears. He heard a distant radio playing rock and roll, the sound of water running. "Wes Fordham," he said, "the teenager who lives next door. He's washing his car. He loves that car."

"Anything else? Your hearing is even sharper now."

"No, nothing."

"Where is your father right now?"

"At work."

"Where is your mother?"

"In the kitchen, reading *Reader's Digest*. It came in the mail today. She likes to read it. Sometimes she reads me funny bits. They make me laugh."

The hypnotist took him back to the high place. "Was there another time when you were frightened about a hole? Before the time you saw the tv show?"

"I don't remember."

"Look back across your childhood, even to the earliest times you remember. Was there a time when you were frightened by a hole?"

"I don't remember."

"You can use the telescope to examine the farthest-away parts of your childhood. Look closely."

"There's nothing."

"You need fear nothing. You are perfectly safe."

"I'm not afraid. I just can't see anything."

The hypnotist told him to put down the telescope. She relaxed him further, took him deeper into the trance. Then she said, "You are on the high place again. Before you stretches your childhood."

"Yes."

"Now look down at your feet. You are standing on a flying carpet."

"Okay."

"You sit down cross-legged on the carpet and tell it to fly over your childhood."

"Yes."

"You are perfectly relaxed and safe. You are flying over your childhood, toward the earliest years."

"Yes."

"You fly past the day you saw the tv show about the boy who fell in the hole."

"Yes."

"Now you are flying over the years when you were a toddler."

"Yes."

"Now you are flying over the time when you were an infant."

"Yes."

"Now you are flying over the moment you were born."

"Yes."

"The carpet keeps flying, carrying you further back."

"Yes."

"Back to when you were growing in your mother's womb."

"Yes."

"You are very relaxed, very safe."

"I am safe."

"Now the carpet takes you back before you were in your mother's womb."

"Yes."

"Where are you?"

Brodie was silent.

"What can you see?"

"The..."

"Your eyesight is very sharp. You can see very clearly."

"Yes."

What do you see?"

"The tatuksha."

"What was that? What do you see?"

"The tatuksha."

"What is the tatuksha?"

Brodie's face collapsed in sadness. His mouth fell open, the corners turned down in a grimace of despair. Tears flowed down his cheeks. "I've fallen into it," he said. "It's dark. I can't get out."

———————— ❧ ————————

It took her a long time to bring him back. At first, he refused to recognize the existence of the flying carpet. He wept and made odd sounds that might have been words or might have been wordless cries of anguish. She spoke soothingly, telling him he was safe, that the darkness could not hurt him. Finally, she got him to focus.

"You see a white dot in the darkness."

"A white dot."

"It's above you. Look up and see it."

"Yes. I see it."

"It's the way out of the tatuksha."

"Too far."

"Look down at your feet."

"No feet."

"You have feet. Wriggle your toes." He had taken off his shoes for the session,. She saw his toes move in his socks.

"I have feet."

"You are standing on the flying carpet. Look down and see it."

"I don't..."

"It's underneath your feet. It brought you here and it will take you back."

"I see it."

"It is a strong carpet."

"Yes."

"A magic, flying carpet."

"Yes."

"Now it lifts you up, toward the white dot."

"Yes."

"The dot grows larger. You focus on it. You see only the white dot."

"I see it."

"It is the way out of the darkness. The way out of the tatuksha."

"Yes."

"Now the carpet is lifting you back into the light. You are free."

"Yes." Brodie began to weep again, but not from despair.

"You see ahead of you your life, all the moments that led up to this moment."

"I see it."

"The carpet is flying you back to this room, this chair, where you are safe and relaxed and nothing can harm you."

"Yes."

"In a few moments, you will wake. You will be calm and rested. You will remember what happened. You will remember the tatuksha, but it will not frighten you. Because you escaped from it. And now you are here and safe."

———————

She played him the tape recording of their session. Brodie listened. He winced when he heard the agony in his voice.

"Does it mean anything to you?" she said. "That word, tatuksha, does it call up any memory?"

He shook his head. "In a way," he said. "It's like something I've heard before and forgotten. Or maybe something I've heard in a dream."

That week, whenever Brodie lay down to sleep, the whispers were in his ears and the shadows flickered at the corners of his vision, even when his eyes were closed. It seemed to him that they were more insistent and when he dreamed, the whispers were louder, clearer. He heard "tatuksha," and it seemed that he heard other words, too; the shadows became faces, strange faces, not human. And yet familiar. But when he awoke he could remember none of it.

"I have to tell you," said the hypnotist, when he came to her again, "I had never done a past-life regression before. To be honest, I'd never quite believed in it. Now I'm not sure what to do."

"I want to try again," Brodie said.

"First, let me tell you this: a friend of my sister's is married to a philologist."

"I don't know what that is."

"He studies the development of languages through time. I asked him what language the word 'tatuksha' might have come from. He checked his references and found nothing."

"What does that mean?"

She leaned across the space between their chair and touched his hand. "It may mean it's just a word your mind made up."

"Not from a past life?"

"Under hypnosis, the mind wants to cooperate. Ask it for something that isn't there, and sometimes it manufactures an answer. It's called confabulation."

"No," said Brodie.

"No?"

"No. Something happened. I'm hearing other words in dreams now."

"Tell me about them."

"I can't remember them when I wake up. I want to try under hypnosis."

She frowned. "I'm worried that I might be leading you up a false trail."

"Don't be," he said. "I'm not."

She didn't take him back to the tatuksha. She took him into his dreams. The shadows came and the whispers. He tried to make them clearer, struggled to hold the images in his mind's eye, the sounds in his mind's ear.

"Relax," she said, "let yourself float, as if you were on a warm river, drifting slowly."

He relaxed.

"You let the images come to you. You make no effort to focus. They just pass before your eyes. The sounds wash over you."

"Yes."

"What do you hear?"

"Tatuksha."

"What else?"

"Kekkethet. Estittit."

"What else?"

He made other sounds. She wrote them down on a pad.

"What do you see?"

"The sort-of faces. But they won't stay still. They keep changing, flickering, dissolving."

"In your hand is a remote control, like for a dvd player. When you click it the images pause. You can examine them."

"Yes."

"Do you recognize anyone?"

"Some of them are movie stars. Jimmy Carter. The Dalai Lama."

"What do you think of Jimmy Carter?"

"A good man, kind."

"What about the Dalai Lama?"

"The same."

"How do you feel about the faces in your dream?"

"Good. They're kind people. They want to help me."

She brought him out of the trance. "I don't know if this is helping you," she said.

"I think it is. I feel... better."

The woman looked worried. "For me, this has gone way off the map. I'm thinking I should refer you to another practitioner. Someone who does past-life regression."

"But you don't really believe in that," Brodie said.

"I didn't. Now I'm starting to."

"Tatuksha," the hypnotist said. "Kekkethet. Estittit." She spoke three more words that Brodie had heard in dreams, words that they had recovered together when she had led him to revisit those dreams under hypnosis. "What do they mean to you?"

"Nothing."

She put him under again, took him to the high place and the carpet, then flew him back beyond his mother's womb. It was a smooth and easy ride.

"Where are you?" she said.

"I... I can't describe it. A familiar place. But I can't make it hold still. It all flows. In different directions, all at once."

"What are you doing?"

"Looking at something."

"What are you looking at?"

"Tatuksha."

"What is Tatuksha?"

"The place you don't go."

"Why don't you go there?"

"Can't get out."

"Kekkethet," she said. "Estittit." She said the other words.

He nodded as she said them, like a man remembering.

"What do they mean?" she said.

His face brightened. "I have to die."

She didn't want to see him again, recommended another hypnotist. He refused to go away. He found out where she lived and came there.

"I'm frightened," she said. She would only open the door a little and spoke through the crack.

"Of me?"

"For you."

"It's all right," he said. "You have helped me. I need you to help me just a little more."

"Help you how?"

"To get out of the hole."

Her living room was messy but the chair was comfortable. He closed his eyes and her voice came to him through the darkness. He knew she was worried, frightened even, but she strove to keep her tone calm and assured. "You look up and see the white dot."

"Yes." It hung above him, very far, unreachable, but he was confident now, the sadness fading.

"It's the way out of tatuksha."

"Yes."

"Look down at your feet, see the flying carpet."

"I see it."

"It is a good carpet, a strong carpet. You have faith in it."

He felt it, soft beneath his stocking feet. It was worn in places, yet strong. "Yes."

"Now it lifts you up, toward the white dot."

"Yes." It pressed against his soles. He began to ascend.

"The dot grows larger."

It grew to the size of a winter's full moon, then became as gibbous as in autumn. "Yes."

"It is the way out of tatuksha."

"Yes." The light from the glowing circle grew brighter and now it was warm on his head and shoulders. He raised his hand and felt its gentle heat on his upturned palms. It was nearer now, wider than he was.

Her voice dwindled in his hearing. "Almost free now. Then the carpet will fly you back to this room, back to where you are safe."

"No," Brodie said. "Not here. Here is tatuksha."

"Safety," she said. He heard her trying to keep her voice calm, trying to bring him back. "Here is safety."

"No," he said. His eyes opened. He was looking at her, across the small space between their chairs, a space that was now growing immense; at the same time he was looking up into the warm glow. The woman, the chairs, the room, were all trapped now in a dwindling circle of fading light, falling into the surrounding shadows, becoming shadows. He saw her tiny shadow-head jerk back, and he supposed she must have been startled by what she was seeing in his eyes, seeing the reflected glow of his destination. Perhaps she even felt its warmth, radiating from him, spilling into lonely, cold tatuksha.

"What is happening?" He heard the alarm in her voice, though now it came to him as barely more than a whisper.

"It is all right," he said, closing his eyes again. He felt sad for her, left behind in the shadows. But it could not be helped. "I must go now."

"Where? Where are you going?"

"To Estittit," he said. The light bathed him, warm as cream. It flowed over him, through him. The voices that had been whispers in his dreams were clearer now, stronger, full of surprise and joy, familiar. The shadow motions were forming into fluid patterns, flowing in ways he now remembered.

"Where is Estittit?" came the hypnotist's fading whisper from below.

"Home," he breathed.

There was a coroner's inquest. The past–life regression aspect of the story caused a brief sensation in the media and a longer one in the blogosphere. But the verdict of death by natural causes eventually tamped down the tumult.

The tabloids and cable news services spread the hypnotist's name widely. Notoriety was no longer fame's ugly stepsister; now they were twins. Celebrities consulted her. Her practice grew. She learned to live with it.

The entity that had been Brodie became itself again. It was a long process, shedding the gray ash of tatuksha, but there was infinite time to rediscover the subtleties of the eight thousand effulgences, each with its five thousand tints and tones. One by one, or in clusters, it regained its one hundred and eight senses, until it could be invited once more into the great sympatic dance.

The entity roiled and insinuated itself among the multiforms, now cohering to the richness of the center, now arabesquing out to the filigreed edges. It embraced and was embraced by the Host, penetrating even as it was penetrated, swallowing that which swallowed it. It sang the endless song, the grand harmony ever dissolving, ever reforming, only to dissolve and reform again.

It reposed in bliss. But always it kept, in a pocket that was not really a pocket, a small fragment of the poor, tiny thing it had been when it had become Brodie. And sometimes, when it passed by–or through, or around, or overunder–a newly forming node, it would reveal the cold, sad cinder and then it would make the terrified new entity promise never, ever, to go near tatuksha.

GO TELL THE PHOENICIANS

This story got started in the back of my head when I read someone's pithy observation on the chicken-or-the-egg question that, to an egg, a chicken is just a way to get another egg. One day the idea hatched, more or less fully fledged, and I sold it to Interzone *in the UK. It was later reprinted in the tenth iteration of* Tesseracts, *the annual anthology of Canadian sf.*

It's my recreation of 1950s space opera.

THE K'FONDI were driving Livesey and his BOOT team three stops past crazy, but that was not why the station chief hated me at first sight.

Mainly it was my record, which was laying itself out as Livesey tapped the panel of his desk display. I held myself at something like attention, set my lumpy features on bland, and looked over the chief's regulation haircut to where the window framed the unknown hills of K'fond.

"If Sector Administrator Stavrogin wasn't biting my backside, you'd never have set down on my planet," Livesey said, "but I promise you, Kandler, while you're attached to this establishment, you'll go *by the book.* Or I'll chase you all the way back to Earth and bury you in whatever stinking kelp farm you oozed out of."

There was more, but I had heard the like from the ranking Bureau of Offworld Trade field agent at just about every assignment I could remember. I was a foreign body in the Bureau's innards, a maverick among a tamer breed, tolerated only because I was also BOOT's best exo-sociologist. But wherever I was sent in, it was a sign that the field agent in charge was out of his depth. If I turned out to be the reason a mission was successful, a corresponding black mark went into the file of the BOOT bureaucrat who had screwed up.

They sent me in because I got results. But the day I stopped getting results, the uneasy symbiosis between me and the Bureau would fall apart. With luck, I might land at a Bureau training depot, lecturing batches of budding Liveseys on the intricacies of the ancient alien cultures they'd be rehearsing how to loot.

Without luck, I'd be back on Argentina's Valdés Peninsula, stacking slimy bales of wet kelp, just as my father had done until he wore out and died. So I kept my mouth shut through the chief's opening rant, and watched a gaggle of K'fondi boost each other over the station's perimeter fence. They frolicked across the clipped lawn like teenagers at the beach.

Livesey turned to follow the direction of my gaze, swore bitterly, and punched his desk com.

"Security," he said, "they're back! Get them herded off station! Move!"

The aliens wandered over and gawked through Livesey's window, giving me my first look at K'fondi. They were the most humanoid race Earth had ever found. On the outside, a K'fond could pass for any fair sized, bald human who happened to be thin-lipped, large-nosed and shaded from pink to deep purple.

Closer examination revealed subtle differences in joints and musculature, but the K'fondi were a delight to those exo-biologists who argued that parallel evolution would produce intelligent species that roughly resembled each other. We could breathe what the K'fondi breathed, drink what they drank, eat what they ate.

No one knew what K'fondi were like on the inside, but there would be some major differences. For one thing, they were thought to lay eggs.

Security heavies arrived to coax the natives off the station. None of them seemed to mind. One departing visitor—even without breasts, she was slinkily female in an almost sheer gown slit on both sides from shoulder to knee—paused for a parting wave and a broad wink through the window.

Livesey leaned his forehead against the window's plastic and swore with conviction. "Tell me how I'm supposed to negotiate a trade agreement when they treat this station like some kind of holiday camp?"

"Is it just the local kids come to look around?" I said.

Livesey turned with a glare of bewildered outrage. "As far as I can tell, that was their negotiating team. Go get briefed."

Outside, the K'fond air was rich and unfiltered, the slightly less than Earth-normal gravity added a spring to my step, and I headed for my quarters in a tingle of excitement. I loved the beginning of every new assignment, ahead of me a whole alien culture to explore. It was almost enough to let me forget that the Bureau of Offworld Trade would use my work to help pick the K'fondi clean.

I hated BOOT, but the Bureau was the only path to field experience for an exo–sociologist. It was an arm of the Earth Corporate State, the final amalgamation of the Permanent Managerial Class of multinational corporations and authoritarian regimes that had coalesced just as humankind took its first steps toward the stars.

For a bright boy who ached to escape from Permanent Under Class status, who thirsted to meet and encompass the strange logics of alien cultures, BOOT was the only game in the galaxy–and I'd played it my whole career.

Brains and a willingness to outwork the competition had taken me from my parents' shack through scholarships and graduate school, then out into the immensity on Bureau ships. Now, with a score of alien cultural topographies mapped to my credit, every new assignment was more precious than the last.

Soon, I would be ordered out of the field, sent back to a plain but secure retirement back on Earth. I could settle into a university chair, write a textbook and train the next generation of bright boys and girls who would assist the Bureau in its beads–and–trinkets trade.

Beads and trinkets were Livesey's vocation, and it was an ancient calling. The Phoenicians started it off, tricking neolithic Britons into accepting a few baskets of brightly colored ceramics for a boatload of precious tin ore. Later, the Portuguese traded cloth for gold, the French and English gave copper pots for bales of furs, or worn–out muskets for manloads of ivory.

Every planet had something worth taking: a rare element, a natural organic that would cost millions to synthesize on Earth, a precious novelty to delight the wealthy and powerful. And on each world, the natives could use something Earth could supply.

If the aliens could have haggled in Earth's markets, they would have got fair value. But only Earth had lucked into the ridiculously unlikely physics behind the Dhaliwal Drive. As in the days of the Phoenicians, he who has the ships sets the price.

Earth's corporate rulers would have had no moral objections to conquest, but systematic swindling was far cheaper and the PMC were leery about arming and training the PUC. There was no Space Navy to eat up the profits from the beads and trinkets trade. For the aliens, and for me, it was just too bad.

My job now was to get a handle on K'fond culture, particularly its economics, and tell Livesey what technological baubles the locals would jump at. In my spare time before rotation back to the Bureau sector base, I might be able to work up a paper for the journals.

But the trade agreement came first. That was in the book, and the Bureau went by the book.

My quarters were in a row of standard-issue station huts. I threw my gear onto the cot and turned to the stack of data nodes on the compcom desk that was the only other furniture. I plugged in the first one and the screen lit up.

There was nothing remarkable about the report of the seed ship that had discovered K'fond. I speeded up the readout and skimmed the highlights. Unmanned craft passes by, drops robot orbiter, moves on. Orbiter maps surface and analyzes features until its programs deduce the presence of cities. Orbiter opens sub-space channel to Office of Explorations sector base and tells OffEx about K'fond.

Then OffEx base reports to headquarters on Earth, which commissions a K'fond file and copies it to BOOT. BOOT puts together Livesey's team and sends them from the nearest sector base to establish contact. Every step neatly marked by its own cross-referenced memo. By the book.

But the pages started falling out when Livesey's team tried contact procedures. I plugged in the project diary, saw Livesey bring his ship into orbit over K'fond. I checked the time code: given the slowness of bureaucratic response and the temporal dilation effect of the Dhaliwal Drive, about three standard years had elapsed since first discovery. And in those three years, BOOT's robot orbiter had somehow gone missing.

Things only got worse for Livesey. He ran out the ship's ears to eavesdrop on surface communications; all were intricately scrambled. He dropped clouds of small surveillance units; each stopped broadcasting shortly after entering the atmosphere. The book said his next option was a manned descent, and Livesey had already chosen volunteers when the ship's com received a signal from the surface.

In clear, unaccented Earth Basic, someone said, "Welcome to K'fond. You are invited to land at the site indicated on your screen. Please do not divert from the entry path we have plotted for you."

The com screen showed a map of the smallest of K'fond's three continents; a series of concentric circles flashed around the spot where Livesey was to put down.

I laughed. The terse prose of the official diary did not record Livesey's outrage when the cherished contact procedures were brushed aside. But I could imagine the chief's fear at making planetfall without a bulging file of information garnered from the ship's spy gear and the missing orbiter's surveys.

Livesey and three others had dropped down to a field several kilometers west of a K'fond town. The video showed a small crowd of aliens clustered around the shuttle. Then the scene shifted to visuals taken by the contact team as they emerged from the craft. I slowed the image speed and looked closely.

A dozen K'fondi of both sexes were coming toward me. No two were dressed alike, their garments ranging from flowing robes to close-fitting coveralls. One female wore nothing but a metal bracelet. I magnified her image; egg-layer or not, except for the absent navel, she looked scarcely less mammalian than many fashion models. I tracked to an almost nude male, and saw the pronounced sexual differentiation.

I thumbed the flow speed back to normal and saw what Livesey had seen. The K'fondi flocked toward the contact team like kids let out of school. The BOOT men were jostled and seized, and the camera showed one agent tentatively reaching for his needle sprayer. But the aliens were patently friendly and curious. They fingered the Earthmen's clothing, plucked at hair, chattering non-stop amid what looked much like human smiles and laughter.

It was like seeing a first contact between Europeans and the peoples of the South Pacific five hundred years ago. But that reminded me of what had been done to those long-gone dwellers in paradise by the "civilized" visitors they had rushed out to welcome.

I looked at the glad K'fondi faces. "Hey, have we got a deal for you," I said to the screen.

The tapes of later contacts chronicled Livesey's descent into frustration. The K'fondi really did act like rambunctious teenagers on a holiday. And yet many of them showed what I thought were signs of aging. I flipped forward to one of the "negotiating" sessions.

A chaos of K'fondi chattered around an outdoor table somewhere on the station. None of them spoke Basic, and Livesey was struggling through sign language and the few words of local speech the lingolab had identified. The K'fondi were not listening. Some were passing around a flask. One couple left off nuzzling each other to slide beneath the table, and began demonstrating the similarities of K'fond and human love-making. Livesey put his forehead to the table and groaned.

I speed-ran the other tapes, witnessing several more encounters between BOOT and the K'fondi. I didn't bother with the file of correspondence between Livesey and sector base; I could imagine the SectAd's memos advancing from neutral to querulous to plain nasty. If the chief didn't get results here fast, BOOT would demote him so far down the hierarchy he'd need a miner's helmet to find his desk.

Which meant he'd be leaning hard on me to get those results for him.

The problem was simple: the K'fondi didn't make any sense. They had a high-tech culture, and somebody on the planet could beam a message to an orbiting Bureau ship in a language no K'fond should have known. Yet the K'fondi who came on station acted like eighteenth century Trobriand Islanders on their day off.

The language puzzle intrigued me. I buzzed the station switchboard and was connected with the lingolab. The call was answered by a harassed man of middle years who introduced himself as Senior Linguist Walter Mtese. He gave me directions to his lab.

I stepped from my hut into a warm mid-afternoon. This part of K'fond seemed a mellow, balanced place. Temperature, humidity, even the light breeze were perfectly matched. An occasional cloud threw interesting shapes on the distant slopes, and the air was soft and good on my face. *A place to settle down in*, I thought. But that kind of thinking led nowhere. Earth law prohibited residence anywhere but where the state could keep an eye on you, and that meant Earth.

I cut between two storage huts and came suddenly face to face with the K'fondi Livesey had had thrown off the station a couple of hours before. I observed that they liked close physical contact on first encounter; in fact, it couldn't get much closer than the way the pink female snaked her arms around my neck. Her skin was smooth and hot–K'fond body temperature was equivalent to a human's raging fever. She smelled indefinably of fruit.

"*Jiao doh vuh?*" she inquired.

I tried to gently shrug off the weight of her arms. Physical contact between human and alien on first encounter can represent anything from a polite greeting to an indiscriminate appetite. The correct response was to try to imitate the gesture offered, according to the Bureau book. But as she pressed her chest against me and followed with her hips, I realized that going by the book this time would involve seriously violating several BOOT regulations.

With smiles and soft-voiced disclaimers, I disentangled myself and stepped back. The pink woman shrugged very humanly and said something to her companions, then they all wandered around the corner of the building without a backward glance. Seconds later, I heard a human voice shout *"Hey!"* followed by a burst of K'fond giggles. Then the group came pelting back around the corner, pursued by two puffing guards. I flattened myself against the supply hut and let the chase roll by. The K'fondi were enjoying the game.

Walter Mtese wasn't enjoying the K'fondi, I found when I entered his lingolab. Mtese was pure Bureau. A pattern of commendations and certificates decorated his walls, testaments to the linguist's integration into the BOOT view of the universe. But for a successful bureaucrat, Mtese looked a harried man.

"I think someone's playing an elaborate practical joke on us," he complained, as he hooked me up to the snore-couch. "These people get by with a vocabulary of under a thousand words, most of which have to do with sex, booze and bodily functions. Tell me how that's compatible with a technological civilization."

"How are they at learning Basic?" My voice sounded strange in the confines of the headpiece he was fitting over my ears.

"They don't learn anything," Mtese answered. "I spent a whole morning—that's six standard hours—trying to teach two of them ten words. I'd have had more luck training snakes to tapdance. Give me your arm, please."

I felt the hypo's aerosol coolness. Subjective time slowed as the drugs depressed selected regions of my nervous system while goosing others into hyperawareness. Around a tongue now grown larger than the head that contained it, I managed to speak.

"What does *'jiao doh vuh'* mean?"

Mtese snorted as he punched codes into the snore-couch controls. "It's the standard greeting between males and females, usually answered in the affirmative, and followed by immediate direct action. It's a wonder they've got the energy to walk."

The snore-couch's headset began murmuring in my ears, the drugs took hold, and Mtese and the lingolab evaporated into golden warmth as the machine flooded my neurons with incoming freight.

Back at my hut, I found that knowing K'fondish was no big help. As the last wisps of Mtese's chemicals effervesced out of my brain, I re-ran Livesey's encounter tapes. The linguist was right: K'fondish conversation was at the level of the street corner banter of good-natured juvenile delinquents–simple, direct, and highly scato-logical. If the alien who had spoken in Basic over the ship's com was one of the "negotiating team," he was keeping his mouth shut.

Livesey's records and the lingolab had taught me all they could. The next step, by the book, was first-hand field contact. According to procedures, that meant encountering the natives under controlled conditions, on station ground, and guided by a welter of Bureau regulations devised by bureaucrats who had never left Earth. I saw no reason to repeat Livesey's failure. Besides, it was always more in-structive to meet aliens on their own turf.

The transport pool guard refused me a ground car without an authorized requisition. He was still refusing as I wheeled a two-seater out of its stall and waved my way past gate security. The highway was wide, flat and empty. I urged the car up to cruising speed, took the center of the road, and headed east. Five minutes from the station, I reached under the instrument panel and pulled loose a connection. Now the car's location transmitter couldn't tell tales on me. I nudged my speed a little higher, and went looking for K'fondi.

The quality of this planet's technology was obvious in the agri-cultural zone on the town's outskirts. A house-sized harvester trun-dled through a field, collecting a nut-like fruit that emerged packed in transparent containers from the harvester's rear port. A flatbed truck with a grapple followed along, stacking the containers on itself in precise rows. Neither machine had an operator. In the distance, herd animals grazed near the shores of a lake that swept across the horizon to lap against the geometry of the town's central core.

The highway connected with a grid of local and arterial roads, and I met up with other traffic. Self-directed trucks and driverless transports neatly avoided my passage, or maintained pace with me at exact, unvarying distances. Then the traffic dropped away down side roads as the highway took me into the residential suburbs.

Neat houses of painted wood or colored stone were intermixed with towers faced in metal or glass. The town looked lived-in–I saw lawns that needed a trim, a fence that was giving in to gravity, and one cracked window mended with tape. It was only after a few minutes that I realized I wasn't seeing any K'fondi. The streets were deserted.

The emptiness began to play on my nerves. Field work can be dicey. Trampling on a society's direst taboos is so easy when you have no idea what they are.

Maybe this part of the town was forbidden, or this time of day had to be spent indoors. Maybe it was death to approach this place from the west. Maybe... anything. At the university, we'd all heard the story of the technician who'd casually swatted a buzzing insect. He had protested that he had not known that that particular species was "sacred for the day," as the alien priests had apologetically proceeded to dismember him.

I finally found the K'fondi, lots of them, as I nosed the car out of a side street onto the lake drive. I was suddenly in a town square, beachfront and park all rolled into one, and it was the site of a fiesta that made Rio's Carnivale look like a Baptist church social. Knots of K'fondi surged in a cheerful frenzy through a crowd so dense it flowed like fleshy liquid. Some kind of music thumped and screeched loud enough for me to experience it as repeated *tumpa-tumpas* on my chest. K'fondi in a grab-bag of costumes bobbed to the rhythm or gyrated with flailing elbows along the edge of the mob. As I stopped the car, an eddy of the crowd swirled around me. One dervish began beating out a tattoo on the engine compartment, while a large female jumped onto the hood and began a dance that had various parts of her moving in several different directions at once.

More K'fondi joined her, making the car sag and groan on its suspension. I mentally ran through all the time-tested phrases recommended for first encounters, but with this crowd I realized that I might as well declaim Homer in the original Greek.

The car was rocking steadily faster, and common sense said it was time to bail out. The crowd swallowed me the way an amoeba takes in a drifting speck. Aliens pressed me from all sides, but none paid me any attention. My head seemed to shrink and swell with the sound of the music.

Way back in school, in an attempt to make us grateful that the ECS had rescued our world from self-destructive hedonism, they'd shown us images of rock concerts from the Decadent Period. What I was experiencing among the K'fondi must have been the kind of sheer fun those old DP mass gatherings had looked to be.

The music wound down to a last sub-sonic rumble and crashed in an auditory rain of metal. As the sound dwindled, I could hear voices again, even pick out words I now recognized. The crowd began to thin around the knoll. Some went splashing into the lake. Others drifted back toward town or into the trees further up the shore. And some couples entwined arms and legs, sliding down each other to the ground.

I scanned the departing remnants of the crowd. A few meters away, I thought I saw the pink female from the station among a handful of K'fondi skirting the knoll. Or it may have been a complete stranger—learning to tell aliens apart can take practice. I hurried to catch up, fell in beside her, and touched her wrist. She turned without slowing, and regarded me with scant interest.

"*Jiao doh vuh?*" she asked, and my lingolab-educated brain translated the phrase as "Do you want to?"

"Do I want to what?"

She looked puzzled for a moment. "It's just what people say."

I said, "My name is Kandler. I'd like to talk to you."

"Why talk?"

"Talking is what I do."

Her shrug was almost human, and I took it as an acquiescence. "I want a drink," she said, heading toward a row of low-rises bordering the park.

The K'fond bar could have blended into most Earth streetscapes, if you ignored the unusual colors of the patrons. When we had found seats at a table in the back that was crowded with her friends, I learned that the pink woman's name was Chenna—no surname or honorific, I noted—and that the town was called Maness. Chenna's friends remained anonymous. I could just barely hold her attention long enough to ask a question and receive an indifferent reply. Everyone else in the bar was enjoying the outpourings of a couple on a small stage, who were tootling some kind of flute that had two mouthpieces. I was thankful it was purely an acoustic instrument; my eardrums still hurt from the pummeling they had taken in the park.

A robot server brought us a round of drinks without being summoned. I sniffed the tall frosty tumbler, and recognized the same fruity aroma that had lingered around Chenna at the station. The concoction tasted sweet and dry. I waited a few moments to learn if I would be racked by intense pains or stop breathing. When nothing much happened, I judged the drink safe and took another sip.

By saying her name a couple of times, I got Chenna's attention again, and posed a few more questions. No, she didn't work, although it seemed to her that she might have once had some kind of job. She thought she hadn't been in Maness very long, but it was hard to tell.

If Chenna was hazy on her own personal history, the rest of K'fond society was nonexistent to her. I couldn't find a word in my new vocabulary for "government," but I tried to phrase a question about who got things done on K'fond.

"Machines," she replied airily, waving to the robot for another round. I drained my glass and reached for a second.

"But who tells the machines what to do?"

Chenna actually looked as if she was rummaging through her mind for an answer. But then she laid her cheek on an upturned palm and said, "Who cares?"

I put away my exo–soc question kit and opted for passive observation. The bar was filling up. The flute players had given way to an *a capella* group that seemed to know only four notes, but the K'fondi happily sang along with them.

A male at another booth took some kind of cigar from a box on the table, and tried to light it with what looked like an elementary flint and steel lighter. When he couldn't get a spark, he persisted in thumbing the device with increasing frustration. Finally, he slammed the lighter to the floor and followed it with the cigar.

I rose and retrieved the battered object. A quick examination showed that the screw holding the steel ratchet to its mount was loose. With a twist of my thumbnail, I tightened the screw, and flicked the action. A flame wavered on the wick. I doused the flame and put the lighter back on the owner's table. The K'fond picked it up, flicked it alight, and pulled another cigar from the box. I received not even a glance as the alien blew smoke toward the stage.

Back at Chenna's table a third round had arrived. I sipped and watched, and listened to the surrounding conversations. It was like Livesey's contact sessions: a lot of laughs, and half the words spoken were the K'fondish equivalents of "hey" and "wow" and the details of amorous adventures.

The fruit drink tasted good, felt good inside. But I noticed that the room had now begun to expand and contract in rhythm with my own heartbeat. That made me laugh, which made me wonder why I was laughing so loud. Chenna was looking at me now; they all were. I found it odd when their faces were abruptly replaced by the bar's ceiling, and I tried to figure out what the hard flat something was that was pressing itself against my back. Then the world turned black and gently fell on me.

"I've been reading your job description," Livesey said. "It doesn't say that an exo-soc steals ground cars, leaves the station without permission, and is found at the gate giggling and smelling like a fruit basket. At least you had sense enough to program your car to bring you back."

I didn't think now was the time to correct the chief. Time enough later to wonder how a K'fond could figure out which end of the ground car was the front—never mind how to program an off-world computer.

I had expected Livesey to chew me out, but the chief seemed to have passed through rage and frustration while I was still in sick bay. He was now settling into acid despair. He spun his chair away from me and gazed with helpless hate at K'fond's hills.

"Actually," he told the window, "you were more useful in a drugged stupor than you've been conscious. The bio-chem techs pumped some interesting stuff out of your stomach. It might make a decent anesthetic or a recreational lifter for the PMC youth market back home.

"Either way, it won't be enough to save us." Livesey swung back to fafce me. "As a purely formal question, I don't suppose you learned anything worth knowing from your little jaunt?"

I had been asking myself the same thing since I had woken up, sore-throated from the stomach pump. The drug in the fruit drink left me feeling reasonably fine, and the part of my brain that lived to puzzle out alien social patterns had gone right to work.

"Yes," I said. "Item one, that's a real city over there, not a backdrop whipped up to fool us.

"Item two: the K'fondi who live there really live there. They're not actors putting on a show for our benefit.

"Item three: their technology is at least equal to our best.

"Item four: the K'fondi we've seen couldn't possibly have created that technology; they can't even repair a simple machine.

"Item five: something funny is going on. There's a piece missing from this puzzle, and if we can find it, or even figure out its basic shape, the rest of the pattern will fall into place."

Livesey grunted. "You're as stumped as I am. We've been looking for that missing piece of information since we landed. You want to hear our working hypotheses?"

He didn't wait for an answer but ticked off the options on his fingers, "Maybe the K'fondi we see are the mentally deficient. Maybe they're just the pets of the real dominant species. Or the whole place is run by supercomputers their great-great-granddaddies built while their descendants have declined into idiocy. For all we know, they're just a planetful of practical jokers having a good laugh on us."

The station chief smacked the desk. "But, dammit, somebody gave me landing coordinates in Basic. Somebody is scrambling all microwave communications. Somebody knocked out the survey orbiter. And, having done that, our mysterious somebody has apparently lost all interest in us."

"You're wrong," I said. "Our mysterious somebody is very interested. He's hanging back and watching. And if he won't come to us, we'll have to go find him. And by 'we' I mean me."

"Go ahead," Livesey snorted. "Take all the time you want, so long as you're finished in the next week."

"A week? This could take months. I've got to..."

"You'll be finished in a week," Livesey interrupted, "because *I'll* be finished in week. That's when SectAd Stavrogin arrives. Here's the signal." He waved a flimsy at me. "I'm being demoted and shipped back to Earth, as soon as Stavrogin settles in. And, Kandler, I'm taking you with me. Under arrest."

"What, for appropriating a ground car?"

"No, I'm sure I'll think of something better. And, between my remaining authority and your record, I'll make it stick."

"But why?"

"Because I don't like you." Livesey spun back to the window. The interview was over.

<hr/>

I couldn't just lie on my bunk and wait for Stavrogin. I re-ran the diaries, looking for some clue, some insignificant piece of data to ring the alarm bells in my unconscious. I had a nagging sense that I was missing something that would make it all fit together.

But I saw nothing that helped, just more frolicking K'fondi, more remote scans of distant cities, too far away for any detail. Livesey's orbiting ship was not equipped for close-in scan; the exploration orbiter was supposed to be there to handle that chore, with ultrascopes that could count the blades of grass in a square meter of the planet's nightside from fifty kilometers up. But the orbiter was gone, and since—according to the Bureau's book—it was impossible for an orbiter to be gone, there was no provision for getting another one. Maybe Stavrogin would have the clout to get a new high-orbit probe. And maybe I would read all about the solution to the K'fond puzzle back on Earth—if a newspaper ever blew over the fence of the punishment farm.

I paced and considered the situation. The K'fondi had put the station where they wanted it. All attempts to surveil other parts of the planet had been stopped. So, whatever they were hiding must be somewhere down the road from Maness.

Which meant taking a trip down that road and looking around. A ground car or flyer would probably bring me into hard contact with whatever had knocked out the spy drones. And if the K'fondi preferred to shoot first and sift the wreckage later, I would end up in some alien coroner's in-basket. But there was another way: risky, but I thought it just might work.

Then I paced out my own situation. If Livesey meant to sweeten the bitter taste of his failure by kicking me into prison, why should I spend my last days of freedom helping the Bureau?

If I solved the K'fond mystery, Livesey would still probably go under; even last-minute success couldn't divert BOOT discipline once it was wound up and set loose. Livesey, falling, would use me as something soft to land on. Livesey, saved, would ruin me out of sheer spite.

But I wouldn't be doing it for the Bureau or the chief. This was for *me*. I had always had to know what made alien societies tick, and if making the pickings easier for ECS's interstellar swindlers was the price of that knowledge, then it was a price I was at least used to paying.

Before I was dragged off K'fond and chained to a bulkhead, I wanted to know what the hell was going on.

Five minutes later, I walked into the supply hut and began pulling things off the shelves. The quartermaster clerk decided he had better things to do than to ask questions of an eco-soc with a reputation for lunatic behavior. In the medical stores I found an antiseptic wash that dyed the skin. A jump suit stripped of its Bureau insignia would pass at medium range for a K'fond coverall. I scooped up a belt and pouch, which I filled with rations, depilatory creams, and some other useful items. Finally, I took a geologist's hammer to the arms locker and selected a small pulser that tucked into the palm of my hand.

The motor pool guard was prepared this time to stand his ground when a purple Kandler climbed into a surface car. But the pulser's output end convinced him to decamp quickly enough to avoid being run down.

On the open road, the wind of the car's passage chilled my newly bald head. Where I began to meet Maness's automated local traffic, I turned at the first major intersection and drove on for a couple of kilometers. I parked the car on the side road's grass border, pulled out the connections on the com panel to stop its annoying chirping, and settled down to watch the robot trucks go by.

Before the long K'fond day drifted into evening, I spotted the kind of transport I had been looking for. But, fully loaded, it was outward bound. I marked its size and characteristics, and was able to identify the same kind of vehicle heading empty in the direction of Maness. I put the car back on the road and followed.

The empty truck wove through an increasingly dense grid of industrial streets. Here there were no houses, and apparently no K'fondi were needed to run the automatic factories. The truck pulled into a side street leading to a low-rise, open-sided building. By the sound and smell of the place, I knew it was what I was looking for.

I slowed the car to a crawl as it bypassed the street the truck had turned onto. Pushing a few buttons on the car's console told it to go home and it whirred away, leaving me alone on the empty street.

It was now full dark, and the K'fondi hadn't bothered with many streetlights in this part of town. Keeping to the abundant shadows, I crept around the rear of the building where the truck had gone. The vehicle was nudged up against a loading ramp, behind which was a corral full of tapir-like creatures with curly horns and sad, muted voices. By the ringing in my ears, I judged they were being induced into the trucks by some kind of general sonic prod. No herders, either live or robot, were in sight.

That made it easier. I hopped the corral fence and stooped to hide among the cattle. Gritting my vibrating teeth against the sonics, I bulled my way up a ramp and into a slat-sided transport. The animals stamped and brayed at my smell; for me, the feeling was mutual. Inside the truck, the sonics were damped. I crouched in a rear corner.

The truck soon filled. Its rear gate swung closed, and the engine murmured through the floorboards. The vehicle jerked forward, sending a set of horns scraping across my back. It turned to exit the stockyard, and then it stopped.

I held my breath. Were sensors in the truck reacting to my shape or size or the smell of my sweat? Would alarms suddenly ring, floodlights sweep toward me, robot cops come to hustle me off to the interrogation rooms? But then the engine coughed and, with another lurch, we were mobile again. A few minutes later, I was rolling out of Maness. My compass told me we were heading north.

The chill bars of first light through the truck's slats brought me awake. I had spent the night in a hay-filled corner, pressed by warm bodies, and dozing despite the cattle's tendency to snore. I got up, stretched, and peered out at the suburbs of a city. It could have been Maness, except that it was bigger, lacked a lake, and was built half-way up a mountain range that rivaled the Andes. By my rough reckoning, I was five hundred kilometers from the station. I should be out of any K'fond quarantine zone.

The truck was now well into the city's industrial district. Time to move—my fellow passengers might be heading directly for the whirring blades of an automated slaughterhouse. I climbed the truck's side and sliced through its fabric top with a knife from my belt pouch. I boosted myself up and out, clinging now to the outside of the vehicle. I lowered myself until my feet dangled over the pavement blurring along below. When the truck slowed for a curve, I hit the street running.

Seconds later, I was your average K'fond, purple and bald, taking an early morning constitutional through the city's empty streets. A broad avenue led down toward the heart of the city, and a half-hour's walk brought me into a grid of residential streets. In a postage-sized park near a high-rise complex I found enough undergrowth to keep me out of sight. I'd lie low until the K'fondi came out of their homes, then blend in with all the other purple and pink inhabitants.

I ate some rations behind a screen of fern-like plants and watched for pedestrians. About the time the morning chill began to fade, a naked K'fond child—the first I'd ever seen—came out of a high-rise and walked down the footpath to stand by a striped post. Another approached from up the street, then several more. *Bus stop,*

I thought. And the long passenger vehicle that soon came to pick the children up must be a school bus. As it left, more children arrived to wait for the next one.

So far, I had seen no adults, but with the K'fond commitment to partying, sleeping late would be normal.

As the third busload of children rolled away, there was a noise behind me. I turned to see three kids entering the park from the opposite side. Naked as all the others, these wore belts and holsters carrying lightweight toy weapons. *Playing cops and robbers*, I told myself, and hunkered lower behind the ferns. I didn't want to be taken for a K'fond child molester.

I could hear them approaching, talking rapid-fire K'fondish too fast for me to catch the meaning. They seemed to be passing my hiding place without noticing me. I held my breath. Then the ferns parted right in front of me, and I was crouching eye to eye with one of the kids.

"Uh, *jiao doh vuh?*" I tried.

"Oh, I really don't think so, Mr. Kandler," the child replied. "No adult would say that to a child, even if they weren't all biologically set to keep their distance from us." It took me a few moments to realize that I was being spoken to in clipped Earth Basic, and that the weapon leveled at my face was no plaything.

The child gestured with the gun. "This is a device we use on adults who pose a danger to themselves or others. It's harmless to them, but we're not sure how effective it would be on your nervous system, so it's set at maximum. I advise you not to do anything unreasonable."

As the child spoke, his two companions came through the undergrowth to triple the number of weapons now surrounding me at a discreet distance. Moments later, face down in the K'fond soil, I was efficiently stripped of everything but my jumpsuit. Then the children herded me out of the park and into a no-nonsense vehicle that had pulled up at the curb. I had the last of the three rows of seats to myself. The kids sat forward, facing me with weapons aimed.

"I suppose my disguise was pretty obvious," I said.

One of them replied, "The disguise was fine. At first we thought an adult had wandered into that meat transport. Then we took a closer look when you were on the road. But you could never have blended in here."

"Why not?"

For answer, the child waved at the cityscape unrolling beyond the car's windows. What I saw told me that, of course, they had to have spotted me immediately, disguise or not. To blend into this city's population, I would have had to make myself over as a small, pink, sexless doll with big eyes. The streets were full now, and not one of the K'fondi was an adult. It was a city of children.

"Where are you taking me?" I asked.

"To a place where some of us will talk to you."

I couldn't read the inscription on the building we arrived at, but it had government written all over it. The council chamber I was ushered into could have passed for the ECS seat of power in Belem— if everything hadn't been half-sized. But there was nothing diminutive about the authority of the K'fond children gathered around the gleaming, crescent-shaped table. I knew power when I met it.

They gave me a large enough chair and sat me down in the middle of the space enclosed by the crescent. For a few seconds, the K'fond world council looked me over in silence. Then the child at the center of the table's arc leaned across the glossy expanse. The voice was thin, but I didn't doubt the note of command it carried.

"Welcome to K'fond, Mr. Kandler. We've been looking forward to meeting you. Your personnel record told us more about the Earth Corporate State than a month's sub-space communications."

"You've read my record? But how?"—then I got it—"You've been using the survey orbiter's com link to listen in."

"True, Mr. Kandler. We went up and got your probe shortly after it alerted your sector base. We don't mind telling you, its technology fascinated our scientists. And of course we were overjoyed to learn that interstellar travel is in fact possible.

"Which brings us to the point of our meeting. Mr. Kandler, what can you tell us about the Dhaliwal Drive?"

Three days later, the station com center received and recorded a signal from the project's missing exo-soc. I reported that I had penetrated to the core of K'fond society and was "making progress." Then I signed off without waiting for a reply. It was my last direct communication with the station.

Two days after that, Sector Administrator Stavrogin arrived to take charge.

If Livesey was everything a by-the-book Bureau chief should be, then Yuroslav Stavrogin was a sector administrator to delight the book's authors to the lowest flake of their flinty hearts. Pinch-faced and slim, with the eyes of a bored shark and the delicate hands of a Renaissance poisoner, he perched primly on the edge of a K'fond chair and waited. Beside him, Livesey looked nervously around the alien reception room and sweated. Through the open window came the sounds of Maness at play.

I watched through a concealed aperture as the brass cooled their heels. I remembered Stavrogin. Back at sector base, he had once made me rewrite a lengthy field report from scratch—a week's pointless work imposed on me for no discernible reason. When I was bold enough to ask why, he had coolly replied, "Because you need to be reminded of who I am, and of what you are not."

I closed the spy hole, picked up my new briefcase, and stepped through the door. Livesey's face opened in surprise, but Stavrogin knew better than to show his. Still, I was not what he had expected.

Yesterday, with the station in an uproar over the sector boss's arrival, a signal had come in. In clear Basic, a K'fond voice had specified that Livesey and Stavrogin, identified by name and rank, were instructed to present themselves at the Maness district office of the planet's government. Once again, detailed directions followed, and these had led the two Bureau officers to the building. A robot majordomo had shown them to the reception room and left them to stew a while. And then in walked their missing exo-soc.

"Kandler, where the hell have you..." Livesey spluttered, but was cut off by a mere lifting of Stavrogin's finger.

"Specialist Kandler," rustled the dry voice, "we can plot your recent itinerary later, but we are shortly to meet the K'fond trade negotiator. You will therefore advise us forthwith of the results of your fieldwork."

There was a desk and chair. I walked over and sat down. From my briefcase, I pulled a sheaf of paper and tossed it onto the desk. "My report," I said. "I won't give you the full details now; you can read it at your leisure. I'll just summarize.

"The K'fondi are a highly sophisticated culture, with a well advanced technology. They have been a unified planetary state for some centuries, long enough for the administrative apparatus to evolve into a kind of cooperative anarchy."

Stavrogin sniffed, but I elected not to notice.

"They are very interested in trade," I continued, "a great deal of trade, but only on rational terms."

Livesey burst in. "They're as rational as a bunch of spacers on Cinderella liberty. Drunken, fornicating..."

"Oh, those are just the adults," I laughed. "I'm talking about the kids."

Stavrogin's voice could have cut glass. "Tell it."

I leaned back in my chair, and put my feet on the desk.

"Well, it's that missing piece of information we were looking for. K'fond adults really are just about as useless as Livesey says. All they want to do is enjoy their retirement and make more little K'fondi. The eggs are almost a by-product, since they don't even tend their offspring after they're weaned.

"But the kids do all right," I continued. "Childhood is long here, very long. K'fondi reach intellectual maturity quite early, but puberty doesn't come along until thirty or forty years after. And they have drugs to hold their glands in check for another decade if they want to keep putting off sexual maturity.

"That gives them a whole working lifetime without distractions. They don't waste their youth in adolescent turmoil and fruitless rebellion, because adolescence comes at the end of life, not the beginning. They aren't bothered by sex or any of its complications, like jealousy or getting up to change diapers. The infants are cooperatively raised by older children.

"And when their glands finally get to them, and the hormones reduce their mental acuity to the level of alley cats, they settle into a place like Maness: a retirement community out in the country, with plenty of beds and bars. A few children stick around to patch up cuts and bruises, and protect the newborns until they can be shipped off to the nurseries."

Livesey snapped his fingers. "They're like those extinct fish, the ones that didn't mate until they were ready to die. What were they called?"

"Salmon," I said. "We didn't figure it out because the K'fondi made sure we didn't see their cities full of children or the few kids around Maness. So we kept looking at it from our own perspective, from the chicken's point of view."

"Chicken?" asked Livesey.

"Sure," I said. "To a chicken, an egg is just a means of getting a new chicken. But to an egg—or to a K'fond child—an adult chicken is just something you need to get a new egg."

"Fascinating in its place," Stavrogin cut in, "but we are about to negotiate a trade deal. You will advise."

I smiled. "Sorry, Mr. Sector Administrator. Appended to my report is my resignation from the Bureau, and appended to that is my surrender of citizenship in the Earth Corporate State. And these," I produced a document covered in cursive K'fondish script, "are my credentials as adviser to K'fond's economic committee. Shall we open negotiations?"

"You can't do that," Livesey said.

"He has done it," Stavrogin said, "though much good it will do him. Very well, 'Mr. Adviser' Kandler, you may rot among your alien friends in this backwater. But trade—if there is even to be any trade—will be on Bureau terms; only Earth has the Dhaliwal Drive."

I smiled. "Not for long, Stavrogin. These people—*my* people, now—have had near-space travel for generations, but until now they've had nowhere to go but up and down. They've always dreamed of reaching to the stars, but didn't know how or even if it could be done. The survey ship's passage answered the second question; and I had enough of a layman's grasp of the Dhaliwal Drive to sketch an answer to the first."

I put my hands behind my head and stretched back in my chair. "They're smart and they have no distractions—they'll roll out a prototype starship within a year."

Stavrogin's face went paler, while Livesey's grew dangerously red. I held up a hand to forestall an outburst.

"We may decide not to deal with the ECS," I said. "After all, there's a whole galaxy of civilized races that the Bureau has been robbing. I'm sure they'll be interested in what we have to offer."

Livesey looked to be on the verge of detonation. But Stavrogin was struggling to recover. "I'm sure we can come to some mutually satisfactory understanding," he said. "As you say, there's a whole galaxy dependent on the trade made possible by the Drive. There's still plenty for both of us."

"You don't understand." I took my feet off the desk, leaned over its polished surface, and said, "Go tell the Phoenicians: beads and trinkets won't cut it any more.

"K'fond's main export will be starships."

THE HAT THING

This little snippet came to me while I was watching a made-for-tv called Murder in a Small Town, *starring Gene Wilder. I sold it to Gardner Dozois at* Asimov's Science Fiction. *I recommend the movie if you can find it.*

"SEE THAT?" Medgar said. "You see how he handled the hat thing?"

"What hat thing?" I said.

He wound the tape back and said, "Watch."

I watched. Gene Wilder, in a neat gray suit and wide brimmed fedora knocked on the front door of a big stone house. A woman in a servant's uniform opened the door. There was some dialogue and the woman tried to close the door, but the actor put his foot in the way and said something.

"Now watch," Medgar said.

The video cut to a scene shot from inside the foyer of the house. Wilder came in and took off his hat.

"There," said Medgar. "That was the way it was done."

"The way what was done?" I said.

"The whole business with hat etiquette."

"What's hat etiquette?"

"It's why he doesn't take off his hat and then he does."

My face must have told him I had no idea what he was talking about.

"Look," he said, "this movie is set in the nineteen-thirties, right? And Wilder plays a gentlemanly character, a theater director with good manners."

"Okay. So?"

"So when she answers the door, he doesn't take his hat off, even though you're supposed to take your hat off when you meet a woman. But he doesn't."

"Why not?"

"Because she's just the maid. If she'd been the lady of the house, the hat would have come off."

"But he takes it off when he goes inside," I said.

"Cause you did when you went into somebody's house. That's old-style hat etiquette. Like you go into a restaurant, it's hats off. You go into a bar, it stays on."

"I see people wearing baseball caps in restaurants all the time."

"Yeah, now," he said. "Go back fifty, sixty years, you didn't."

"And this has to do with what?" I said.

"With time travel. Specifically, with time travelers."

"Time travelers?"

"Yeah," he said. "Assume that someday, somebody invents time travel."

"Yeah, right."

"Hey, give people a million years to look into it, who knows?"

I shrugged and didn't say anything.

"The thing is," he went on, "time travel only has to be invented once and then we'll have time travelers showing up all through history—not to mention visits to see dinosaurs and sabertooths."

"Would anyone really want to travel through time?" I said.

"Sure. Researchers. Tourists. Criminals altering their present by manipulating the past. Religious pilgrims. Collectors. Who knows what motivates people a million years from now?"

I shrugged again.

"The thing is," Medgar said, "the further back they come, the less likely they get all the details right—the little things like hat etiquette that nobody in the future knows because nobody in the past ever wrote it down."

"Why didn't they?"

"Because everybody already knew what to do with their hats."

I tried to change the subject. "Who did you vote for on that tv show?"

But he wouldn't let it go. "No, listen, here's the thing. You know the people you see downtown, you wonder did they just come down from the mother ship?"

"Those people are mentally ill," I said.

"Sure, most of them. But maybe one or two are the earliest explorers from one million AD. They're the ones who did the first reconnaissance so that the later time travelers can blend in better."

"You don't talk about this kind of stuff to people you work with, do you?" I asked. "Or your other neighbors?"

"No, I just thought of it. Anyway, the latecomers are pretty well camouflaged but there will still be things that will be out of synch—like the hat thing. We look for that stuff, we can find the time travelers."

I took out a cigarette and tapped one end of it against the back of my hand then put it in my mouth.

"Hey, yeah," he said. "That's a good one. People haven't done the ciggie tap since everybody switched to filters."

He laughed, then he saw the look on my face.

"Sorry," I said, although a moment later he was a lot sorrier.

I put his ashes in a plastic sack and carried it out to the chute. Then I went back for the Wilder tape. Somebody upslope would want to study it.

HELL OF A FIX

I could never write fiction while I was writing speeches and other stuff for a living. It was as if the factory had to shut down and retool completely. I tried in my twenties when I was an aide to cabinet ministers in Ottawa, but I would just run dry. This almost-a-novella length fantasy started out as a couple of pages back then, pages that were subsequently lost. But I remembered the opening once I got into writing fiction for real and out popped Chesney Arnstruther, high-functioning autistic actuary with a yen to be a superhero. I sold a shorter version of the story to The Magazine of Fantasy & Science Fiction *then extrapolated it into three novels for* Angry Robot Books, *where I got to stretch my mental legs, theology-wise.*

I

THE DEMON'S SUDDEN APPEARANCE, along with a puff of malodorous smoke and a short-lived burst of flame, took Chesney Arnstruther completely by surprise.

He recovered quickly, however. The existence of demons had been thoroughly covered during his youthful education, which from the ages of five through fourteen, had included two hours of Sunday school—taught by his mother, a leading member of the congregation. The minions of Hell had also often figured in the sermons of the Reverend Erwin P. Baumgarten, their pastor, who had fallen under the spell of the Book of Revelation even before he had attended Rock of Ages Bible College.

In adolescence, Chesney had drifted away from old-time religion. He found too many contradictions and absurdities in scripture. Besides, he had found a more reliable truth in the elegant architectures of mathematics.

But though he had long since given up thinking about demons, he was still able to recognize one when it flashed into existence right before his eyes. The brief pyrotechnics attendant on the fiend's sudden manifestation scorched the top of the young man's almost-finished poker table, so that his first reaction was a surge of indignation at the ruination of the green felt surface, which he had almost finished tacking into place.

Chesney said, "Get the blue bling blithers off my table!"

The demon, which resembled a huge toad that had been tinkered with to give it oversized, clawed hands, spread its lipless mouth to reveal a smile full of dagger-like fangs. "You are inviting me to depart the pentagram?" it said, in a voice like bones cracking.

"What?" said Chesney. An instinct for self-preservation now reasserted itself, overcoming the shock of the fiend's arrival and the still-throbbing pain from his hammered thumb. "No, I'm not inviting you to anything, except to go back where you came from!"

"If that is your command," said the demon, "I will obey. Just sign the standard form, here and here, and initial here." It produced a roll of parchment from somewhere Chesney could not see, and used the tip of a claw to mark three places with an X.

The young man glanced at the document. His first thought was that its author must have learned penmanship from a seismograph; the letters were all spiky, scrawled across the page with ferocious violence. His second thought, when he managed to decipher some of the content, he expressed out loud: "No way I'm signing that! You'd get my soul!"

"That is the standard arrangement. You summon one of us, we do your bidding, you render up your insignificance."

"My what?"

"It's the technical term, where I come from."

"I don't care if it's the word of the week," said Chesney. "My soul is not an insignificance to me. I'm not signing."

"Then I can't do your bidding."

"I don't have any bidding for you to do. I just want you to go back to 'where you come from.'"

"That sounds like bidding to me," said the demon.

"Well, it's not," said Chesney, sucking away the blood that was still welling from beneath the nail of his left thumb and gesturing with the hammer he held in his right hand. "It's a rejection of the entire concept of bidding. Especially if the bidding costs me my soul."

The demon looked annoyed. Chesney did not find it a happy sight, but he stood his ground. "Now, go away."

"I can't," said the toad. "You summoned me. I'm here until I've done whatever it is you need doing. Even if it takes overtime–for which, you ought to know, I get nothing extra—so sign the agreement and let's get to work." A ripple passed over its warty skin. "It's cold up here."

"I didn't summon you," said Chesney. "It's some kind of mistake."

The demon slitted its yellow eyes. "All right," it said, "let's go over this. This is your pentagram I'm standing on, right? And"—its nostril slits widened as it took a deep sniff—"that's your blood there, deposited by your hand sinister? And you did say, *'Hodey-odey shalaam-a-shamash woh-wanga kee-yai'* didn't you?"

"Oh," said Chesney, "now I get it. I can explain."

It all began with Letitia Arnstruther, Chesney's mother who raised him singlehandedly from an early age after Wagner Arnstruther, his father, departed for parts unknown with a waitress he met at a truck stop. A devout woman, Letitia could not abide rough manners, and she especially frowned on coarse language, in both of which her husband abounded. Indeed, her son had often wondered—though he'd never had the courage to ask—what strange concatenation of events must have occurred to unite his parents, even temporarily, in matrimony. He did not wonder why his mother made no attempt to find Wagner Arnstruther and invite him to repair their broken home.

Yet one thing was clear to him as he grew from childhood to manhood: even the mildest profanity would net him cold looks, even colder suppers, and downright chilly silences, the punishment sometimes stretching through an entire week and beyond. Therefore, as a defense, whenever Chesney felt the need to express his emotions in strong language, he taught himself to substitute strings of nonsense syllables. The habit, deeply ingrained at an early age, had endured long after he left home—and the Reverend Baumgarten's congregation—to attend college in another state.

In college, Chesney discovered numbers, and especially the sheer decorum of the interrelationships that numbers can form with each other; they became his fascination. Though he lacked the creativity to pursue a career as a mathematician and the inclination to teach high-school math, his degree led to his taking a position as a junior actuary in a mid-sized, Midwest insurance company. He spent his days calculating the risk of death or injuries for tiny slices numerically carved from the US demographic spectrum. His evenings were mostly given over to his second love, also discovered after departing from his mother's sphere of influence: comix and graphic novels, especially those that featured oddly talented individuals who fought crime on a freelance basis.

A life of crunching numbers suited Chesney's deeply introverted personality. Actuaries were not expected to be the life of any party. All the men in his department–and it seemed that the actuary profession attracted *only* men–had grown up as friendless as he had. Five of them, however, had made it a habit to get together at each other's homes to play poker every other Saturday evening. Chesney was asked to join when one of the five had dropped out because he was leaving town and it turned out no one else in the department was willing to spend time with the remaining four.

Although Chesney could quickly calculate the odds that any hand would win or lose, he never applied his math skills when he played poker. He bet high on weak cards and stayed in for pots he had no realistic chance of taking; for him, winning wasn't the point–it was being in the game that counted, the sense of risk and possibility that he couldn't get if he folded early. This characteristic endeared him to the other players, all of whom played strictly by the numbers and who thus regularly went home as the beneficiaries of a transfer of wealth from Chesney's wallet to theirs.

The game's venue rotated among the members, and after a couple of months, Chesney was told that he was expected to host the next get-together. He went home and examined his premises with an unhappy eye. He had a cramped studio condo in a downtown highrise, with a Murphy bed that pulled down from the wall. The place had a kitchen nook, the wall between it and the rest of the single room being pierced by a pass-through that had a countertop and two stools. Otherwise, Chesney's domestic arrangements consisted of a couch fronted by a coffee table, and a chair and matching table made of extruded plastic out on the postage stamp-sized balcony.

There was nowhere to sit and play poker, even if two of the five sat on the end of the Murphy bed. Chesney went trolling through furniture store sites on the internet, and soon settled on five folding chairs that could be stacked in the downstairs storage space when not in use. But for a decent-sized poker table, he sought in vain. They were all, apparently, made to accommodate seven players, and the designers must have assumed that most of those players would be of significant girth. There was no way Chesney could fit such a table and chairs into his small living space, even with the bed up, without hauling the couch and coffee table down to the locker.

That seemed a burdensome chore. Instead, he rallied his minor skills as a craftsman—he had taken one term of woodwork shop in high school—and resolved to make his own playing surface. It would have only five sides, there being only five in the group, and with some judicious trimming it would seat them all comfortably.

Chesney had had the lumber yard cut the three-quarter-inch plywood top to size and had bought ready-made legs from the store's do-it-yourself department. Along with a drill, a multi-tip screw-driver, a sheet of green felt and a box of tacks, he felt ready to tackle the project. He already had a hammer, having found one when he moved into the apartment.

"So you see," he told the demon, "I was tapping in a tack. I hit my thumb hard enough to make it bleed. I shook my hand and some blood hit the table. At the same time, I swore—the way *I* swear—and the next moment, there you were." He paused to suck the last drop-lets of blood from his thumb. "It was just a mistake."

The demon gave him a look that was almost as cold as one of his mother's worst. "You expect me to go back and tell that to my supervisor?"

"It's the truth."

"Where I come from, truth is not a highly prized commodity."

"Well, I don't know what else I can tell you," Chesney said. "I didn't summon you."

"Yes, you did. Or I wouldn't be here."

Chesney tried to explain. "It's like when a tree falls in the forest—"

"Yeah, because somebody chopped it down."

"Let me finish. If it falls and nobody hears it, it doesn't make a sound."

The demon twisted his face in incomprehension. It was quite a twist. "The guy who chopped it down is deaf?"

"Never mind. That's not the right example, anyway." He thought for a moment then said, "It has to with intent. I may have inadvertently said the words that summoned you, but I was not summoning you when I said them. The mere sounds don't matter. There has to be the intent behind them."

"Intent?" said the demon. "That's your angle?"

"It's not an angle. It's an explanation."

"So you're definitely not signing the agreement?"

"Definitely."

The demon spread huge hands like a giant, toothy toad that intends to take no responsibility for whatever comes next. "Okay," it said. "But let me tell you, this ain't over."

And with a second puff of stinking, yellowy smoke and a sharp lick of red flame, it was gone.

"So what are you, some kind of wise guy?"

The question broke Chesney's immersion in the graphic novel—*Champions of Justice*—he had been reading. It hadn't been just the question, though; there had also been the sudden whiff of sulfur and the gravelly quality of the voice, which sounded as if it had come out of the mouth of a tyrannosaurus with a sore throat. He looked up to see, standing on the other end of the bench in the downtown minipark where he ate his lunch on sunny days, another demon.

This one had the head of a weasel that had been refitted to sport a pair of canine fangs of sabertooth caliber, and coal-black eyes the size of saucers. It was about the height of a small boy, but its body was a miniature version of a pot-bellied, heavy-shouldered thug in a pinstriped suit with wide lapels and a ridiculously small tie. It wore two-toned shoes of patent leather with the insteps covered by pieces of strapped-on cloth—*spats*, Chesney thought they were called, though he'd never seen them in real life, and only on the Penguin in *Batman* comix—and its stubby, hairy-backed fingers flourished a half-smoked cigar as it waited for an answer to its question.

"I beg your pardon?"

"We don't do pardons, mack," said the apparition. "That's the other outfit's racket."

"The other outfit?"

The demon poked one thumb upwards. Chesney noticed that its thumbnail was chewed down to the quick.

"Ah," he said, nodding. "I assume you're here about the mistake?"

"We also don't make no mistakes. So we need to clear this little thing up, see? Real quick-like. Twenty-three skidoo."

"Why do you talk like that?" Chesney said.

"Like what? Last time I was up this way all youse mugs talked like this."

"We've moved on. So should you. I'm not interested."

The demon moved closer, put one hand on Chesney's shoulder. He could feel the heat of it through his suit jacket and shirt. "We can make you a real sweet deal, pal."

"No."

"You ain't heard the offer yet. It's a doozie."

"You mean, 'an offer I can't refuse?'"

The demon's weasel lips drew back in what Chesney's hoped was a smile. "Hey, I like that," it said. "I can use that."

"Leave me alone or I'll call..." He had been going to say, "a cop," but he saw from the creature's expression that the threat carried no weight, so he switched the ending to, "a priest."

The humped shoulders shrugged. "That don't cut no mustard with me, mack. I'll just ankle outta here and come back when you're alone."

Chesney sighed. "All right make your offer, but the answer's still going to be no."

But even before he could get the last words out, the park disappeared and he was standing in a room about the size of his condo, the walls lined with metal doors of various sizes, each with a number and a slot for a key. "Where am I?" he said.

"Swiss bank," said the demon. "Get a load of this." It tapped one of the large doors down at floor level, and the panel popped silently open. A metal box slid out onto the floor, and the demon flipped up its hinged top. Inside were bound stacks of high-denomination bills, leather jewelry cases and at least two full-sized ingots of pure gold.

"All mine, I suppose?" said Chesney.

"And that's just for starters."

"Won't the owner mind?"

"Where he's going, they don't take cash."

"No, thanks."

The huge weasel eyes narrowed. "Okey-doke. Then how 'bout this?"

They were in a dimly lit room. After a moment's disorientation, Chesney realized it was a bedroom—*no*, he corrected himself, *a boudoir*. The demon did something and the sourceless light strengthened. The room was big; it would have had to be to accommodate the vast, circular bed, strewn with silk covered pillows and red satin sheets, on which reposed a buxom blonde, her eyes closed and lips parted in blissful slumber. She was not wearing much, and what little she did have on did nothing to detract from the strong impression she created. Chesney's lifetime exposure to unbridled pulchritude in the flesh was less than scant; he found himself staring, and had to drag his gaze away.

"Whadda ya say now?" said the demon, its weaselish eyebrows bobbing suggestively.

"No," said Chesney, though the single syllable seemed to catch on something in the back of his throat.

"Oh, picky, huh?"

The blonde was replaced by an even more buxom brunette. She stretched in her sleep, rearranging and simultaneously revealing elements of her anatomy in a way that caused the actuary, whose experience of truly stunning women was confined to pornographic movies, comix and the occasional sticky dream, to emit a small, involuntary sound. But then he said, "No."

"We got a full selection," said the demon and Chesney was looking at a redhead who would have stopped Titian dead on the bridges of Renaissance Venice.

"No!"

The demon cocked its weasel head at him and moved a finger. The redhead was replaced by a muscular young man whose nudity revealed prodigious personal qualities.

"Certainly not!" said Chesney. "You're wasting your time." He glanced at his watch. "And mine."

"Keep your hair on," said the demon. "I'll get a bead on you yet." Immediately, the boudoir was gone and they were standing in an office that struck Chesney as somehow familiar. Then he saw the seal woven into the rug and registered the room's oval shape. "Howzabout it?" said the weasel boy.

"You've got to be kidding," Chesney said.

"You'd be surprised."

"Who? Which one?"

"*Ones,*" said the demon. "But I ain't saying nothing more. We don't rat."

"Take me back."

The demon studied him. "Look, mack," it said, "we've done moolah, molls and moxie. What else is there?" His brows drew down and his huge eyes narrowed. The cigar stubbed poked at Chesney. "Say, you ain't one of then eggheads who wanna *know* everything? Like, you really *are* some kinda wise guy?"

"No."

"I mean, we make that happen for you. It's just, you don't see it too often, you know?"

"I don't want anything. Just leave me alone." He blinked and found them both back on the park bench. The demon brought its outsized eyes closer to Chesney and in the center of each black circle he saw a small red flame kindle and grow.

"Listen, buddy, you wanna take the deal," it said. "You're making a lotta trouble for a lotta guys you don't wanna make no trouble for."

Chesney stuck out his small chin. "I'm not making trouble for anybody," he said. "This is *your* mistake."

The demon growled and it cocked one stubby fist while saying, "Smart guy, why I oughta..." But when the man on the bench did not flinch, the creature clasped its hands together and put on as conciliatory expression as a befanged weasel could contrive. "Listen, mack," it said, "I'm just a yob doing a job. I got a dozen demons to supervise and we're busy, see? Everybody's working double shifts and we don't got no time to monkey around. So, take the deal or take the consequences."

"You don't get it," said Chesney.

"What? What is it I don't get?"

Chesney interlaced his fingers over his small pot belly, thought for a moment, then said, "It never really made sense to me, the whole heaven or hell thing."–the demon winced and said, "Hey, lay off the h-word,"–but the man continued, "Numbers made sense. But now you show up and make it pretty clear that the game is played pretty much the way Pastor Baumgarten preached to us, all those Sundays I was growing up."

"Ah, you don't want to listen to those holy joes," said the fiend.

"Yeah, I think I do. You see, I make a deal with you, I get a few years of fun down here, assuming you don't reneg based on the fine print. Then, bang, I'm spending eternity shoveling hot coals. Or I turn you down and wind up with forever in paradise." Chesney spread his hands. "I mean, do the math. It's a no-brainer."

"Most people we deal with, they don't see it that way," the demon said.

"I'm an actuary. It's my job to play the percentages."

Now the demon actually looked worried. "Listen," it said, "you don't know the whole score. I'm trying to keep a lid on this thing, but you don't play ball, she could blow. I mean, sky-high, you get me?"

"No," said Chesney. "And *you* won't be getting *me*. What did they used to say, last time you were here? 'Take a powder?' 'Amscray?' 'Agitate the gravel?' Take your pick."

He went back to *Champions of Justice*. When he heard the clap of air as the fiend disappeared, he glanced at his watch and was pleased to see that no real time had elapsed. He wanted to finish the current chapter before his lunch break was up. It featured his favorite comix hero, a mild-mannered, bespectacled UPS courier who battled drug cartels and international terrorists in the bowels of a dysfunctional metropolis. The brown-clad crime fighter was about to turn the tables on a cabal of ninja-trained mujahideen. "Go, Driver, go," Chesney breathed.

It was Saturday and he was getting ready for tonight's poker game. He had bought taco chips and salsa and more beer than the little refrigerator could hold. The table was set up and looked great, once he cleaned off the blood with a little club soda. Chesney went downstairs to the storage locker and came back with his arms clasped around the five folding chairs. Nudging open the apartment door that he had left ajar, he was surprised to see a little blonde girl in a pinafore and white ankle socks standing beside the table.

"Are you lost?" he said.

"I just got one question," said the little girl. Actually, Chesney realized there could be some debate as to exactly who was doing the talking, since the voice asking the question came not from the girl but from the fanged mouth of the ruby-red snake that uncoiled itself where a tongue would have been if this had really been a little blonde girl instead of another demon.

He put down the chairs. "What?"

"Just tell me, are you ready to go all the way on this?" said the snake, in a voice that would have suited a little girl, provided she was also a fiend from hell.

"Yes, I am," Chesney said. "I didn't give much thought to my soul before you guys started demanding it. Now I figure it's worth hanging onto."

The snake went back where it came from and the demon crossed its arms and looked up at him in a way that let the man know he was being weighed up. Chesney noticed that pinned to one of the pinafore's straps was a large button with a design on it: a pair of crossed pitchforks against a background of leaping flames. Underneath were the letters *IBFDT.*

"What's the button?" Chesney said, but the demon didn't answer. It finished its examination of him, then nodded as if in confirmation of something it had been mentally chewing on for quite a while, and disappeared. When nothing further happened, Chesney unfolded the chairs and put them around the table. He had just finished positioning the last seat when the phone rang.

"It's Clay," said the voice on the other end. Clay was not the best poker player of the five but he was the one who made the least secret of how much he enjoyed raking in a pot after Chesney had stayed in far too long.

"We're all set here," Chesney told him.

"I'm not playing tonight," Clay said.

"Why not?"

"I dunno, I was getting ready to come, but suddenly I just don't feel the urge."

"We need you," Chesney said. "Four's not enough."

But Clay said, "Sorry,"–although he didn't sound it–and hung up.

Chesney folded up one of the chairs and leaned it against the wall. The phone rang again; it was Ron, the one who had originally invited Chesney into the game. "I'm not coming," he said.

Like Clay, he wasn't sick or jammed up in any way. "You don't feel the urge?" Chesney asked.

"Yeah. I don't feel much like doing anything."

Chesney folded another chair. He'd never played three-handed poker, but he doubted it would be as much fun. Within ten minutes, he didn't have even that diminished enjoyment to look forward to: Jason and Matt both called and canceled.

Saddened, Chesney gathered up the folding chairs and took them down to storage then followed with the disassembled table. He came back upstairs to the refrigerator crammed with beer and the bags of taco chips on the countertop, opened one of each and sat on the couch. Normally, taco chips and beer were one of his favorite snacks, especially when the former were dipped in fiery salsa, which he had also bought in larger than normal quantities. But now, after he had taken the first edge off the hunger and thirst he had built up moving furniture around, he found that he had lost any appetite. He scrunched up the top of the bag, put the lid back on the salsa jar and poured the last half of the beer down the sink.

What do I do now? he asked himself. No answer came. He thought about going out and renting a dvd, as he often did on a weekend night–sometimes even getting a straight-out porn flick. But the prospect had no appeal tonight. He'd really been looking forward to poker; it was the only time he felt a little wild and unpredictable.

Finally, he put on his coat and set off to walk the six blocks to the comix store. He knew the release dates of all his favorite titles, and a new *Freedom Five* should be on the rack by now. He made his way along the sidewalk at his usual gait, shoulders indrawn, hands in pockets, focused on the concrete before him. It wasn't terribly dangerous to make eye-contact in this neighborhood–he could quote the statistics for random, stranger-on-stranger street crime–but there was no reward to compensate even for the minimal risk. Nobody would welcome his gaze.

He had gone about a block when something about the background noise level penetrated his lonely thoughts. He raised his eyes from the sidewalk and looked around. He lived in a part of the downtown that tended to liven up on Saturday nights. This block had two old-fashioned bars and a night club that drew twenty-somethings who liked to dance in a trance engendered by a combination of vodka, strobe lights and more decibels than were good for their chances of not needing hearing aids before they were out of their fifties.

Evening was settling in and the street should have been filled with cars, the bars with drinkers and the night club doorway with bouncers selecting from a line-up of the future deaf. The thump of the club's bass kickers ought to have been underlying the tenor honk of horns—parking was a competitive sport hereabouts—with the treble laughter of girls-in-groups topping off a layered cacophony that was the regular Saturday night soundscape.

But the street was quiet: only a couple of cars moving sedately past empty parking spots; the club's sound system silent; no squeals from clutches of girls because there were no girls. The sidewalks—and, when he looked through the neon-signed windows, the bars, too—were practically empty.

Something big on tv tonight? he wondered. *Is that why the guys aren't coming to play poker?* It would not have been the first time he had missed some major node in the mass culture. The people at work had stopped asking him which singer he planned to vote for on *American Idol*; he would just look at them with a puzzled expression and shrug.

He pushed at his unresponsive brain, trying to recall if he'd heard anything. Some pneumatic teenage girl singer was coming to town as part of a major-cities tour; he'd overheard a couple of the office clerks talking about how their daughters were planning to get tickets the moment the internet box office site came on-line. Last time, the concert had sold out in under a minute.

But that event, even if it was happening right now, would only account for the absence of teenage girls on the street; they'd all be hunched over their home computers, index fingers poised to click their mouse buttons. But the entire block was almost deserted. And now Chesney let his gaze go farther, down the next block and the one after; he turned to look back the way he had come; and it was all the same—the sidewalks and pavement virtually empty.

Maybe it's something big, he thought. *An attack?* He decided to forget about the *Freedom Five* and hurried back to his apartment. But when he flipped on the cable news channel, all he saw was a female anchor telling him about some vote in Congress that had not turned out the way it had been expected to.

The image cut to a reporter standing outside the rotunda of the Senate who was saying that a spending bill laden with earmarks had failed to receive a single affirmative vote. Even the senators who had amended the legislation to shoehorn in their pet projects had inexplicably voted nay. Chesney listened for a while, but found it hard to take much interest. He was about to switch to another channel when something about the reporter's demeanor registered: normally, this commentator spoke with an air of forced gravitas, as if the truly important part of any story was not what had happened or why, but the fact that he, the reporter, was deigning to take notice of it; but now he was reciting his notes from a piece of paper as if he were ticking off a shopping list.

Strange, thought Chesney. The remote report ended and the anchorwoman came back on. It was only as he was looking at her that another oddity clicked into focus for him. The Senate correspondent's tie had been askew and his hair had not been perfectly combed. And now he saw that the anchor, too, was less than perfectly coiffed and made-up. She looked less polished–*quite ordinary*, Chesney thought–and her presentation lacked that quality of being ever so pleased with herself that was standard for people in her line of work. Instead she rested her jaw line on an upturned palm and her elbow on the desk, and read from the unseen teleprompter without much interest.

By coincidence, the next item was about the upcoming concert tour of the teenage girl singer. The anchor reported that tickets had been expected to sell out almost immediately, but that since the box office opened an hour ago, only a few hundred tickets had been sold–and those appeared to have gone to indulgent parents and grandparents buying them as presents.

Now the image cut to breaking news: a would-be suicide bomber in Islamabad, Pakistan, had been about blow herself up in front of a police station. Instead, she had removed the explosive vest she wore under her voluminous black robe and given herself up to a group of policemen loitering around the entrance. And the officers, instead of hustling her inside for a painful interrogation, had sat down with her on the front steps. As the camera panned over them they seemed to be having a restrained discussion, with much rueful head shaking and nods of mutual, though somewhat sad, agreement.

Chesney clicked through a few more cable news channels, ending on a live show that featured a curmudgeonly commentator who liked to bring on guests with whose politics or world views he disagreed then browbeat the invitee with insults and invective. He saw the pundit sitting slumped in his chair, a bearded professor in the guest spot, both of them shrugging and conversing in mild tones. The usually choleric host was saying, "Of course, it doesn't really matter much one way or the other, does it?"

The academic nodded in bland agreement and said, "No, not really."

Chesney switched off. Something was out of the ordinary, though he could not yet put his finger on just what it was. *Maybe some new virus going around,* He thought. *Maybe we've all got the flu.*

He switched to the entertainment channels, found a sitcom that he had enjoyed from time to time. It was about a dysfunctional family. None of the characters got along, and a lot of dialogue consisted of one or another of them scoring points off the others with sarcastic putdowns—some of them scathing, and many of them more than a little risqué. In the past, some of the sallies and verbal duels had caused Chesney to squirt cola out of his nose; but tonight's episode seemed like a constant barrage of unnecessary cruelty. In the five minutes before he turned it off, he didn't laugh at a single gag, although the studio audience that had been there for the taping was driven into paroxysm of mirth as the grossly overweight young male lead went into a sustained rant about his chain–smoking mother–in-law's sexual history.

Chesney switched off the tv. The silence in the apartment seemed suddenly profound: no horns or engine noises rising from the street; no stereos blaring from any of the neighbors; no arguments, either, although Saturday night was prime time for the several unhappily married couples in the block to bring their week's disappointments to each other's attention, with the paper–thin walls letting all the neighbors share in those domestic dramas.

He was puzzled. He thought again about going to the comix shop, but the vicarious thrill he got from following the adventures of the *Freedom Five* did not lure him tonight. After a moment's thought, he decided that he was feeling let down by the collapse of his first shot at hosting the guys for poker. *Or maybe it is the flu.*

He felt his forehead, found no fever. He sat on his couch for a long while, trying to think of something he wanted to do. But nothing came, and finally he pulled down the bed and lay on top of the covers until he fell asleep.

II

Sunday mornings invariably began with a call from Chesney's mother, urging him to turn on his television and tune in to whichever one of the religious programs had most filled her with enthusiasm. Most often, it was *The New New Tabernacle of the Air,* fronted by the Reverend William Lee Hardacre. He was broad–shouldered, tall, and fiftyish, with silver hair that looked as if it had been poured into a mold and let to set overnight. He wore tailor-made suits with western-style piping on the lapels and a big gold and diamond ring that flashed as brightly as his piercing blue eyes whenever he raised his hands to call down divine blessings–or, more often, wrath–on some celebrity whose behavior had caught his attention over the preceding week.

Reverend Billy Lee, as he was known to the throngs who loved him, had started out in life as a lawyer, specializing in labor-management mediation. Well into a successful legal career, he caught the fiction bug and began penning a series of bestselling novels set in the world of corporate law. Then, somewhere in the middle of his seventh blockbuster, he experienced some kind of spiritual epiphany. He gave up both his legal practice and his literary output to enter a seminary. When he emerged from his religious studies–it was never clear whether or not he had obtained the doctorate in theology he had sought–he launched *The New New Tabernacle of the Air*.

As a television preacher, the Reverend Billy Lee did not fit the mold. He had no choir, no guests, no books to flog, no "prayer requests" backed up by a phone bank of telemarketers cadging donations from the faithful. Instead he sold commercial time to charitable foundations and businesses that could demonstrate a commitment to ethical standards.

The show opened with Hardacre at a desk, commenting on news items from the past week. His analysis was always sharp and often insightful, especially when it came to spotting hypocrisy among the famous and powerful. The final ten minutes would see the preacher single out one particular celebrity–a movie star, a politician, a professional athlete, a pundit–for what a *Time* magazine profile of Hardacre once called "a precise and comprehensive flaying."

Like a prosecutor summing up for the jury, the preacher would detail the excesses and egotisms of his weekly target then invite his legions of viewers to write to the object of his censure–he always had their actual mailing addresses to pass along–and express their views. Letitia Arnstruther never failed to take the reverend up on that invitation. She spent most Sunday afternoons at her writing desk, pen scratching over lilac-colored stationery, composing missives full of pointedly phrased descriptions of the eternal fate that awaited them if they failed to change their ways: "Your bowels will roast on eternal coals, your eyeballs will boil in their sockets, your parched and swollen tongue will protrude as you beg for one droplet of soothing moisture—and beg in vain."

Her concluding paragraph always expressed a sincere hope that the sinner would turn from his iniquities, and thus avoid the wrath she had so lovingly detailed. She liked to read her best passages over the phone to Chesney, and urged him to join her in the campaign to rid the world of whatever evil the Reverend Billy Lee had unleashed her and her fellow devotees against.

But today, the phone had not rung in Chesney's studio apartment. Grateful to be left alone, he got up late and ate a bowl of corn flakes while rereading a standalone issue of *The Driver*, the one where the hero foils a plot to kidnap a billionaire's beautiful daughter to force the magnate into financing the presidential election campaign of a man who was a member of a secret terrorist organization. But though he had always enjoyed the comix artist's striking images, especially the way the amply endowed kidnap victim was rendered, this time the tale failed to capture him.

Before he knew it, he had tidied up the nook and washed and put away his bowl, spoon and coffee cup. Normally, he made a point of leaving them in the sink. Sunday was his day to be sloppy and lazy, which he knew was a reaction against all those Sundays when he was growing up: his mother always made him tidy his room to a military standard of neatness before they went off to their first church service of the day. She'd also made him wear a tie.

He wiped out the sink until the stainless steel shone, surprised that he did not feel even a twinge of disaffection for the task. Drying his hands, he looked around to see if there were any other chores that needed doing and a moment later he was tidying the bedclothes and pushing the bed up into the wall.

Still the phone hadn't rung. He wondered if something might have happened to his mother, though that seemed as unlikely as if "something might have happened" to the Himalayas. Letitia Arnstruther was the kind of person who happened to others. She herself was as unaffected by the doings of others as Mount Everest was by the tiny, gasping creatures that crept up to its ice-capped peak. Except, Chesney admitted, when it came to sins committed by persons of note—especially what she always referred to as the "sins of the flesh," by which she did not mean gluttony.

The few Sundays when she hadn't called had coincided with an exceptionally enrapturing performance by one of her favorite television preachers. He found the tv remote and flicked on the channel that carried *The New New Tabernacle of the Air*, which went out live in this time zone.

He caught the Revered Billy Lee in mid-fulmination: "Lust and fornication, brothers and sisters! Sodom and Gomorrah! The fleshpots of Egypt, the Whore of Babylon! But I say unto you that these are as nothing compared to the recent conduct of the celebrated TeShawn "Bad Boy" Bougaineville."

Chesney was vaguely aware of having heard of the person in question. He thought Bougaineville might have been the football player who had shot up his girlfriend's Lexus when her behavior had failed to satisfy him. Chesney remembered the man saying, *"Bleep,* I done give the dumb *bleep* the *bleepin'* ride inna firs' place."

Chesney muted the sound. The preacher was in full cry, his helmet of silver hair shining in the carefully positioned lights so that it formed a halo above his earnest face. His eyes flashed, his capped teeth gleamed, his square jaw jutted as he bit off each phrase, while a trickle of sweat descended from one temple. He could imagine his mother seated on the overstuffed sofa, knees locked and hands clasped, leaning forward, with a flush of pink in her cheeks. TeShawn would be getting a memorable letter from Letitia Arnstruther.

That'll be it, he thought. But then something odd: across the bottom of the screen came a crawl. Chesney watched the words go by. *The program scheduled for this time period is not available. We present a repeat performance of last week's* New New Tabernacle of the Air. *We are sorry for the inconvenience.*

Chesney changed the channel, switching over to another of his mother's favorites, R.D. Wyatt, a smart young televangelist who hosted a talk-show format which often featured fallen celebrities, particularly country singers and NASCAR drivers, who had just come out of rehab and were pleading for a second (sometimes a third or fourth) chance with their fans. At first, he didn't recognize Wyatt. The man's normally perfectly coiffed hair looked as if he had combed it with his fingers. He was wearing only a pair of slacks and a plaid shirt. There was no guest, and instead of sitting behind his heavy mahogany desk he was perched on its forward edge, speaking into a cordless microphone that he held in one hand.

More strange, though, was his voice: the self-congratulatory tone was missing and instead of the down-home Arkansas cadences with which he put painfully intimate questions to his squirming guests, Chesney was hearing the unmistakable accent of someone who had first learned to express himself on the street corners of Newark, New Jersey.

But strangest of all was what the preacher was saying. Chesney turned up the volume. "I don't know what got into me," Wyatt said. He sounded genuinely puzzled. "Maybe it was all the money—and, I gotta tell ya, it was *a lotta* money—or maybe it was all the women who wanted to help me spend it. Whatever, I just got all caught up in it, and now I roll up here every Sunday in a chauffeured limo so I can publicly torture some poor schmuck. I mean, where do I get off with that kinda chutzpah?"

He paused and looked down, shaking his head. Finally, the preacher said, "I'm really sorry." He laid the microphone down on the desk and stood up. He turned and walked up the aisle of the tiers of seats that rose and spread outward from the front of the stage. The camera followed him, showing row after row of empty seats, until he passed through a pair of doors.

The camera remained on the doors as they swung closed. R.D. Wyatt did not come back. No one appeared to take over, not even Mike Crombie, the moon-faced sidekick who vehemently agreed with all of his employer's judgments and laughed louder than anybody at all of his boss's jokes. The silence went on and on.

Chesney clicked the remote. Life coverage of a football game was scheduled to begin just about now. He found a pre-game interview with a young man described as the NFL's most highly paid wide receiver and realized it was none other than TeShawn Bougaineville. But instead of talking trash, the player was tearfully confessing to a longstanding fondness for cocaine and fast women. The sports reporter interviewing him was in tears. "How awful for you," he blubbered and the expression of sympathy made TeShawn break down and sob.

"What the hepty-doo-dah's going on?" Chesney said. He switched channels again and saw the Sunday public affairs show, *In Contention*. But the three regular panelists were not shouting each other down or trading insults. Instead, they didn't have much to say about anything, and what they did say seemed to Chesney to lack all conviction.

He shut off the tv and went out. It was a mild day and he headed for the park, a wide belt of greenery that paralleled both banks of a slow-moving river. It was usually a lively place when the weather cooperated: couples necking on the grass slopes, skateboarders daring each other to try potentially neck-snapping stunts on the step-seats of the concrete amphitheater where local theater groups put on plays; older folks walking in pairs and shaking their canes at in-line skaters who whizzed past them on the asphalt paths.

But today it was quiet, only a couple of solitary pedestrians staring into the river's muddy flow, a woman sitting on one of the steps of the amphitheater, her chin in her hands. Chesney made his way past the Civil War memorial, heading by habit toward the basketball court where a food cart sold hot dogs. He always bought a steaming hot chili dog smothered in fried onions and ate it on one of the nearby benches, keeping an eye out for any young women who might come jogging past in their spandex and halters.

But no jiggling bosoms passed by today, and after a single bite of the hot dog he set it down on the bench and let it go cold. The man who sold them closed up his cart and pushed it slowly toward the parking lot.

"What's going on?" Chesney said, aloud.

"You talking to us?" said a voice behind him.

He turned. The speaker was one of a group of young men, in their teens and early twenties, whom he had sometimes seen playing ball on the single-basket court. They were tough guys, wearing clothes that showed their muscles and their gold chains, two of them with red bandanas tied around their shaven heads. Usually, they swore a lot and played loud rap music from a boom box. Sometimes they shouted at Chesney when he went past, words that he only partially heard and always pretended that he didn't, walking by with his eyes averted.

"No," he said, trying to keep a tremor out of his voice.

"Oh," said the one who had spoken, olive skinned with a sparse mustache, a chain tattoo encircling his neck, "that's okay. My mistake." They walked away, and Chesney noticed that none of them moved with their customary macho swagger.

"What," he said again, "is going on?"

⸺⸺⸺⸺

Monday morning, the stock market went *phut*. At least, that was how the cable news reporter put it in the report that ran while Chesney was eating his corn flakes.

"No one can remember a day like it," the man said, standing in the middle of an empty trading floor. "It's now two hours since the New York Stock Exchange's opening bell, and most brokers and traders haven't shown up for work. The only trades that are being made are by automatic computer programs and some charitable foundations. Otherwise, this place is dead. Nobody's interested in making money."

The bus ride to work was eerily placid. No one jostled for first place on line, and Chesney even saw a teenager get up to offer an old lady a seat. The traffic was sedate; the taxis were actually yielding right of way, and nobody ran a red light.

At the office, he had barely settled behind his desk when he was interrupted by Ron and Clay. They came into his cubicle, wanting his point of view on a discussion they were having on whether their work was morally defensible.

"I think it's ethically neutral," Clay said. "We're only calculating risk factors for different demographics, so that policies can be designed that balance risk and reward for the company."

"Yes," said Ron, "but the side effect of that process is to identify some groups that will be denied any coverage at all."

They both turned to Chesney and said, together, "What do you think?"

It was not a question the actuary had ever considered, but he did so now. "I'd want to think about it," he said. "Evaluating people based on categories of risk can be seen as extending from a recognition that fundamentally, life is not fair."

"I agree," said Clay.

"On the other hand," Chesney continued, following the logic, "just because life is not fair, does that mean we can reinforce the unfairness? Life, after all, is not a moral being, capable of making ethical choices. But we are."

"That's the way I see it," said Ron.

"On the other, other hand, if we don't work out the risk factors, the insurance business can't function. Ultimately, nobody gets insured, and that can't be good." He paused. "It's tricky."

Clay said, "Maybe we could calculate the net benefit-to-misery ratio inherent in the way the industry works now against the same ratio if there was no insurance for anybody."

"But how can we be sure that benefit and misery cancel each

other out?" said Ron. "Maybe an ounce of misery is worth a pound of happiness."

"And then there's the moral obligation we have to our employer to earn our salaries," Chesney put in.

"But if we're part of an immoral enterprise, our obligation is to quit," Ron countered. "'First, do no harm,' as the Hippocratic Oath says."

"Isn't it odd that these issues have never come up before?" Chesney said.

"Well," said Clay, "we'll always been too busy."

"We ought to be busy now, shouldn't we?"

"Not if we've been part of a fundamentally immoral system," said Ron.

"Or amoral," said Clay.

"But for moral beings, can anything be amoral?"

And around and around the discussion went.

At noon, tired and hungry after a hard morning's debate, Chesney went out to the park bench to eat his lunch. He chewed his sandwich without much appetite, wondering if it was proper for him to eat his fill when hundreds of millions of people around the world were malnourished. On the other hand, he couldn't do much about the problem if he was underfed. "Not that I *have* been doing anything about it," he said to himself. "Maybe I should."

His eye fell on the headline of a tabloid newspaper that someone had left on the bench: *"Conscience Bug" Spreads.* Chesney picked it up and read the story. A scientist from the National Centers for Disease Control was speculating that there might be a viral vector for the wave of morality that was sweeping the world. *Something seems to have disabled our "selfishness circuits," the report read. Greed, anger, lust, gluttony—indeed, all of what used to be called the 'seven deadly sins'— have suddenly stopped affecting our conduct.*

It's as if, after having spent all our lives with a devil and an angel on each shoulder, none of our devils are showing up for work.

"You are causing me a great deal of trouble," said a genteel voice. Chesney lowered the paper and saw a dapper, bearded man—*no,* he corrected himself, *a dapper, bearded gentleman*—sitting on the other end of the bench, his hands folded over the head of a black walking stick.

"I beg your pardon?" he said.

"That is something I am not often inclined to give," said the stranger. "And certainly not to you, after all that you have done."

There was something familiar about the face and voice. it took Chesney a moment to make the connection, then he had it: the man was the spitting image of the actor who had played Kris Kringle in one of Chesney's favorite movies from his childhood: the original 1930s version of *Miracle on 34th Street*. He had the white beard and the snowy hair, though his eyes did not twinkle as he regarded Chesney with an animosity that seemed to struggle with amused contempt.

"You're not another demon, are you?" the actuary said. "I've told you–"

"Not another demon, no," the other interrupted, "though I am the one they all work for." And now any vestige of amusement went away. "Or at least they did until you came blundering along."

"I don't understand."

The dapper gentleman pointed a finger at the newspaper Chesney still held in both hands. The words *none of our devils are showing up for work* floated free of the page and rose until they hovered in front of Chesney's eyes, where they enlarged until they were six inches high. Then they burst into yellow–and–orange flames that died down to inky smoke that dissipated in a nonexistent wind, causing a sooty detritus to sift down onto the actuary's thighs.

"You," said Satan, "you ridiculous little man, have singlehandedly caused Hell to go on strike."

The way the Archfiend explained it to Chesney, it all made actuarial sense. It was basically a problem of numbers and demographics. Hell, like Heaven, was an autocracy. Satan ruled, aided by his inner circle of fallen angels who, before the Fall, had held high ranks within the angelic hierarchy: Thrones and Dominions, Powers and Principalities. Now they were Dukes and Princes of the Abyss, and below them were the legions of demons who had been mere rank–and–file rebel angels and archangels before they had all tumbled down to the black iron shores of Tartarus, the lake of fire. To these foot soldiers fell the tasks of punishing and tormenting the human dead who earned eternal damnation, and of tempting the living toward modes of conduct that would eventually bring them across the stygian divide and into the waiting furnaces and pitchforks.

At first, it had been enjoyable work. The tormentors had fallen to it with a will and a spirit of inventiveness that created some wonderfully ironic punishments: Sisyphus and his rolling rock; Tantalus and his disappearing food and drink; Nero and the out-of-tune orchestra that ceaselessly played his most beloved compositions. The tempters, meanwhile, relied on a combination of their incessant whisperings in humanity's collective ear, coupled with the spirit of human inventiveness, to generate a constant stream of new customers.

But as the ages wore on, Hell's success provided for its own undoing. There were, after all, only so many demons. The constantly accelerating intake of the newly damned could not be matched by any increase in the legions of Hell. This imbalance began to cause difficulties.

Back in the days when humankind numbered only a few hundred million, the average demon assigned to the punitive battalions was charged with "making it hot" for only a few hundred of the condemned. Now the world's population was more than seven billion, and a great many of them—still urged on by the corps of tempters, still full of creativity when it came to finding new ways to transgress—were crowding through the infernal gates, abandoning all hope along the way. The Pit was infinitely expandable, but, in that subterranean depression, a fixed number of overworked demons was having to deal with an exponentially increasing quota of the damned. Their productivity had reached its limit, yet the demand for *more, more, more* never ceased. The fiends were fed up.

Over the past century, to this volatile dynamic had been added the first labor organizers whose misdeeds had come back to haunt them as they departed the mortal coil. Of course, the true saints of unionism did not find themselves consigned to the travails of Hell. But from its inception, the labor movement had attracted the same range of opportunists and self-servers as would any activity that offered the unscrupulous an avenue toward power and self-enrichment. So, although no Joe Hills were to be found in any of the nine circles, the Jimmy Hoffas were amply represented.

The rabble rousers saw a familiar scenario: their tormentors were overworked and underappreciated. And the fact that there were not enough demons to keep every damned soul in constant misery gave the organizers the leisure to recognize a familiar opportunity. Before long, some of them had talked their way off the treadmills of red-hot iron and arranged to take up residence in the less dreadful infernal arrondisements. From there they began to advise their erstwhile tormentors on tactics and strategy.

Not long after, the first delegation from the newly formed Infernal Brotherhood of Fiends, Demons and Tempters approached the Dark Throne to propose that His Satanic Majesty enter into discussions on matters of mutual interest. These initial approaches were not well received; indeed, the demons who carried the messages to the feet of the Adversary were summarily blasted to fragments, but being eternal, they eventually reconstituted themselves and came back for another try.

Meanwhile, the fundamental problem was not being solved. Hell was becoming dysfunctional. As an experiment, management tried assigning some above-ground tempters to the punishment function. But this meant giving the heavenly opposition too great an opportunity, of which they took full advantage. The collapse of the Soviet evil empire was a significant setback for the infernal agenda, and the temporarily reassigned tempters were sent back upstairs.

Meanwhile, as a stopgap, Hell's management and its workers negotiated their first contract. This, however, was a field of expertise in which management excelled, and the final terms were not much of an improvement for the members of the IBFDT. But it was a start, the Brotherhood's advisors counseled, a base to build on. All that was needed now, they said, was for management to breach the contract. Then the whole infernal work force would come out on strike, and they wouldn't go back until they had a deal they could all live with.

And then, into this delicately poised situation, this powder keg awaiting a spark, stepped Chesney Arnstruther. The toad-like demon that answered his unintentional summons had been called away from its regular duties, pouring molten gold down the throats of misers. According to the contract, it should have been excused from its tormenting quota while it was engaged in getting Chesney's signature on the standard soul-purchase contract and carrying out whatever that contract required. When it returned without the contract, its supervisor told it that it still had to fill all the misers with gold—and there were plenty of misers.

The demon had balked. Its supervisor, the fanged weasel that talked as if it was channeling every bad impression of Edward G.

Robinson, had tried to straighten the matter out by getting Chesney to accept the contract. By the time it returned, having failed to resolve the issue with the intransigent actuary, the toad demon had already gone to its IBFDT shop steward, the little girl with the snake-tongue, and the ranked dominoes had begun to quiver.

In Hell, a contract is a contract. The supervisor had no choice but to demand that the toad demon fulfill its quota; the shop steward countered that the IBFDT member had been exempted from its quota when it was called away. The supervisor argued that the toad demon had not brought back a signed contract, so no exemption could apply.

There was no clause in the agreement between Hell and the IBFDT that covered the anomaly. Supervisor and shop steward stared at each other for a long moment, then the latter had stepped upstairs into Chesney's apartment to ask him the pregnant question: *"Just tell me, are you ready to go all the way on this?"*

When Chesney said, "Yes, I am," the dominoes began to topple.

"Now you understand," said Satan.

Chesney shook his head, not in denial but from the still reso-nating impact of all the information that the Archfiend had caused to appear instantly in his consciousness. The knowledge itself was dif-ficult enough to absorb, but its transmission into his brain had been accompanied by graphic images of the afterlife's dark side that would have given Hieronymus Bosch the collywobbles.

"Now let me show you a few things," said the Devil.

"You've shown me enough already," said Chesney, but his view was not accepted. A manicured hand took charge of his arm and a moment later they were somewhere else. It was somewhere high, the actuary quickly realized, like a great precipice, but the perspective was odd. Then it came to him: *"All the kingdoms of the world,"* he quoted. "This is where you brought–"

"Don't speak the name," said Satan, "or I'll kick you over the edge." He shook his shoulders as if throwing off a cramp. "Besides, it didn't happen the way you heard it."

"You're saying the Bible got it wrong?"

"What would be the point of offering Himself dominion over all the kingdoms of the world, when He was the one who created them, and besides, he already had Heaven?"

"Then why is it in the book?"

"Who knows why He does what He does? I never did. Maybe it's because He turned the job over to a gaggle of ghostwriters, all of whom had their own little agendas and political points to make. I don't think *He's* ever read it, or it would make more sense."

"But–"

The Devil raised one manicured finger. "'But' is another word it is not wise to throw at me. In any case, I did not bring you here for a literary debate. Look out there."

Chesney looked, and it seemed to him that whatever he looked at somehow enlarged and deepened until he was transported into a fully rounded scene. He found himself standing in a factory that made computers, but its assembly line robots were stilled, its employees absent, its huge space, dust-free full of nothing but inaction and silence.

"No greed," said the Devil. "No one ordering the goods, because no one wants to make a profit by selling them. And even if they did, no one wants to make wages by manufacturing them."

An instant later, they were back in the high place. "Look," said the Archfiend again, and Chesney felt himself drawn into another setting: the nightclub down the street from his studio, all its booths empty, its lights extinguished, the dance floor deserted, the ranked bottles behind the bar growing dusty.

"No lust. No young men strutting to impress the young women, no young women letting themselves be impressed."

And then a four-star restaurant, chairs piled on tables stripped of their cloths, grills and ovens cold, coolers full of meats and vegetables turning dry and drab.

"I get it," Chesney said. "No gluttony. And you can show me how nobody's trying to keep up with the Joneses because the envy's turned off, and the leisure industry's flat on its butt because people aren't feeling slothful. And fashion's dead because there's no vanity."

The restaurant disappeared and they were back on the high place.

"And what were you going to show me for anger? Some guy sitting in a cave twiddling his beard?"

"You want to see anger?" the Devil began, but then he made a visible effort to restrain himself. "I'm showing you," he said after taking a deep breath, "that what I do is woven into the warp and weft of the world. You have undone one of the fundamental fastenings of existence."

"No," said Chesney, "all I did was hit my thumb and not use profanity. All the rest of if came from your side of the house."

Satan didn't look much like Kris Kringle now. Then the illusion shattered completely and Chesney was again sitting on the park bench, but now he faced a lean, dark-haired personage with precisely planed features and a tiny, pointed beard. When he flexed his long-fingered hands, as if he would have liked to strangle the actuary, a faint whiff of sulfur stirred the air.

"We can make you a special offer," the Devil said. "No fine print, no surprises. Anything you want. President. Movie star. Richest man in the world, Bill Gates for your Butler, the Queen of England as your maid."

"But in the end," said Chesney, "you'd take my soul."

"That is the customary arrangement."

"But I'm not the customary customer, am I?"

The Devil's brows drew to a vee. The air around them somehow darkened. "This must be resolved," he said.

"Fine," said Chesney. "I accept your arguments, the warp and the weft, the necessity of sin. I'm still not prepared to give up my soul just to plug a hole in Hell's collective agreement."

The answer was a growl and a grinding of teeth.

"I sympathize," said Chesney, "I mean, I really do. But can't you cut deal with your employees?"

Satan sighed. "They're being very hard-headed."

Chesney thought about it. "Maybe you could promote some of the worst sinners to be assistant tormentors."

"I've thought of that. But it goes against the rules. The worse people are up here, the worse they have to suffer once I get hold of them."

"Can't you change the rules?"

"Not that one. I didn't make it."

Back in Sunday school, it had always seemed odd to Chesney that the really bad sinners—like Hitler or Attila the Hun—got punished when they got to Hell. If Hell was really in favor of sinning, the people who were best at it ought to have been welcomed with parades. He'd offered that thought once to his mother. It had not been welcomed.

Chesney came up with a new idea. "How about promoting the least sinful?"

"We've tried that," the Devil said. "They're not very good at it. They lack verve."

"Maybe a shorter work week?"

"We're already running into backlogs."

The actuary shook his head. "Then I got nothing," he said.

"If you accepted the deal," Satan said, "I could arrange for you to live a very long time."

"No matter how long it was, eternity will always be a lot longer."

"Yes," said the Adversary, "and it's growing longer still while we sit here getting nowhere."

"I appreciate," said Chesney, "that you're not 'making it hot for me' up here."

"Again," was the answer, delivered in a tone that suggested immense anger barely under constraint, "I don't make the rules."

The odor of sulfur sharpened and then Chesney was alone on the bench.

III

Just as Chesney hadn't been completely taken by surprise when the first demon interrupted his table-building, he was not totally gobsmacked to find himself in his present unique circumstances. He had always felt, in the innermost corner of his being where he felt things that he told no one else about, that he was destined for some sort of great achievement. The fact that his life so far had offered him few avenues of approach to his expected destiny had not totally discouraged him. Nor had the fact that the only time he ever mentioned his feeling to anyone–his mother, when he was ten–she had strongly discouraged him from holding his breath in anticipation.

Despite the low–ball cards life had generally dealt him, Chesney never abandoned his belief. He nourished it in secret, first by reading and rereading the biblical tales of other disregarded young men who rose to greatness: Joseph and his triumphs in Egypt and David the sling-swinging shepherd boy who rose to take Saul's throne. After he left home and discovered that there were other sources of inspiration, he further fueled his hopes in the exploits of Ben Turner, who developed his powers as The Driver after handling a mysterious package misdirected from a parallel dimension.

Ever since his encounter with the toad-demon, Chesney had been nurturing a hope that all of this was building toward the realization of some greater plan—and that he might be its keystone. It occurred to him now, as he made his way back to the office, that his desire to make some singular mark in the world must be pure; the demon that tempted him to the sin of pride was walking a picket line somewhere in Hell. That realization led him to another: if he usually had a tempter, he must also have an operative from the other side of the dichotomy.

He stopped before the gap in the hedge that hemmed in the little park. "Hello," he said, tentatively. "Are you there?"

No answer came.

"I'm talking to you," he tried again, "my guardian angel. Or at least the one who normally works to counter the demon assigned to tempt me."

Still no answer.

"I know you must be there. And you don't have much to do right now. I could really use some advice."

A small voice spoke reluctantly in his ear. "We're not normally supposed to be audible," it said.

Chesney looked around but there was no one in sight. "These aren't normal conditions, are they?"

"True."

"So what would you advise me to do?"

The voice said, "Hmm." After a long moment, it said, "We're also not really very good at advising. No real training, you see. Basically, we're here to counter the temptations. Ours is a reactive role."

"You mean, whatever my tempter says I should do, you say I shouldn't?"

"And vice versa."

"It doesn't sound as if you put a lot of thought into it."

"I don't suppose we're meant to," the voice said. "Thinking is not encouraged. That's what got you-know-who into all his... difficulties. We just do the divine will."

Chesney said, "Still, you have to be more experienced at this sort of thing than I am."

"I'd really have to ask someone senior. I can't tread too heavily, you understand. Free will, again."

"But I'm freely asking you for advice. You must have heard what the Devil said."

"Oh, yes. I must say it was strange to see him again. Must be donkey's years. I hear he's tied up most of the time in administration, you know. That's what thinking gets you, I suppose."

"Back to my situation," said Chesney. "What's the right thing for me to do?"

"Oh, no," said the voice, "no, no, no. I really couldn't say. The most I'm authorized to do is to encourage you to consult your conscience."

"I thought you *were* my conscience."

"No. You got one when you got free will."

"Well, what about *your* conscience? What does it say?"

"Don't have one," said the voice. "No need. No free will."

"Angels have no free will?"

"I think we used to. But we must have got rid of it, after we saw how much trouble it caused for your recent visitor and his followers. Ever since, we just do Himself's bidding, no questions asked."

"All right," said Chesney, "what *is* His bidding?"

"Hmm," said the voice. "He hasn't said anything to me."

"Could you ask Him?"

Another pause. "We're not supposed to run errands, except when He sends us. I don't know if I'm authorized."

"You said you could ask someone senior?"

"Oh, yes. I could ask a Throne, maybe even a Dominion."

"Then would you please do so, and get back to me?"

"If they say I can."

Chesney thought for a moment, then said, "It sounds as if you have quite a lot of bureaucracy on your side."

"We do like things tidy," said the voice.

———

The office was empty when Chesney returned from lunch. It had been empty all morning. He had felt a slight obligation to come in, born of a sense of duty to the employer, but now that he thought about it he realized that it was more a matter of following his normal routine. He had never been one of life's wild cards, he knew, but now he had to face the fact that he had become pretty much entirely a creature of habit.

He had disposed of the last few items in his electronic in-basket before going out for lunch. Now he switched off his PC and sat gazing at the blank monitor. *Consult your conscience*, his guardian angel had said. For many years, indeed until quite recently, his conscience had always spoken to him in terse and querulous tones: it was the voice, internalized in his infancy, of Letitia Arnstruther.

"I should go and see her," he said to the empty room. And, first tidying his desk, he rose to do so.

He waited far longer than usual for a bus. When one finally arrived, he took a closer than usual look at the driver, wondering if the man was driven to come to work by a sense of duty or, like himself, by sheer force of habit. In the inert expression on the driver's bland face, he recognized the look of another prisoner of routine.

He was the only passenger on the bus as it carried him through virtually empty streets, taking the bridge out of downtown and heading for the suburbs. It was an express service, and normally Chesney took it as far as the major intersection where the Buy-Buy mall and a brand-name outlet center faced each other across several lanes of traffic. There he would transfer to a local route for the remaining eight blocks to his mother's house.

But when he had stood at the connecting point for twenty minutes, his transfer slip in hand, and no local bus came, he set off to walk the rest of the way. The first two blocks, passing the parking lots of the mall and outlet center, were an eerie experience. Usually, the vast stretches of asphalt were jam-packed with cars, SUVs and minivans. The most recent comers would cruise the white-painted lanes, watching for someone pushing a loaded shopping cart toward a vehicle then creeping slowly along at their heels, to be ready to pounce on the ephemeral treasure of a vacant slot. Sometimes when the person being followed arrived at their vehicle, it was only to transfer goods from cart to trunk before heading back to the stores for yet more consuming. When that happened, the driver who had been waiting for the parking space engaged in loud horn-honking and inventive cursing.

But today the lots stretched lone and level, empty of all but a few plastic shopping bags skirling and whirling in the errant breeze. The stores stood unlit and empty, and the roads that were normally thick with comers and goers were bare of traffic.

As he walked along, Chesney became aware of a rising tide of guilt within him. The soundless, unpeopled streets, as he left the commercial zone and entered the residential neighborhood in which he had grown up, were now not just strange–they were an unspoken reproach to him, personally. Because, after what the Devil had told him, it was beginning to sink in that all of this silence and inactivity was the doing, intentional or not, of Chesney Arnstruther.

The dawning awareness brought a question to the front of his mind: was good the mere absence of evil? On the basis of what he was seeing and experiencing, he wasn't at all sure such a case could be made. He now lived in a world that was demonstrably shorn of evil, the forces of iniquity having packed up their tools and booked off work, but he could not bring himself to say that this new world was good. It was more accurately summed up by a word that he had recently come across in a newspaper article on neologisms that were making their way into updated dictionaries.

"*Meh*," said Chesney. "That's what it is. Not good, not bad, just meh." He walked on another block and found himself passing the property he had always called "the wedding cake" house. As far back as he could remember, the owners of the small rancher set far back on the large lot had filled the sizable space between house and street with all manner of carefully tended plant life. The ground sloped down from the house to the street, the incline being divided into several terraces, each of which was held in place by its own retainer wall of whitewashed brick or stone.

A minority of the plants in the garden had their roots in the earth, the beds ringed with whitened stones. But most of them were in pots large or small or inbetween. Some of the containers were simple truncated cones, others were ornate urns that might have blended in with the decor of a Persian satrap, and still others combined size with fanciful shapes: hollowed–out swans, back–arching salmon, old–time sailing ships, reclining mermaids. They crowded every square foot of space, except for the walkways, and every one of them shone a gleaming white.

And from every white enclosure spilled a riot of color: iris blue, poppy red, daffodil yellow, pansy purple, carnation pink, and shades and blossoms that Chesney–no flower aficionado–could not have named. And, always, dawn to dusk, along the layers of the wedding cake one or both of the owners would be–moving, weeding, spraying, tending–a man and woman identically thin, wispy haired, stooped of shoulder and bent of knees, both with hands so gnarled that they more closely resembled roots than any human member.

Always... but not today. The white terraces stood as empty as the streets. The wide window at the front of the house that overlooked the garden was blind, dark drapes closed. And, as Chesney stopped on the sidewalk and looked at the familiar floral display, he saw such as he had never seen in this place before–a dead leaf, curled dryly from a stem; a blossom past its perfection, shedding petals like a sad metaphor; and most unthinkable of all, the first yellowy–green sprout of a weed bumptiously rising out of the pristine soil of a flower bed.

Why don't they come out and tend the garden? he asked himself. It was not a question he put gladly to himself, because ever since the interview with Satan, he knew the answer. The old couple's obsession with their garden had not sprung just from a love of its quirky beauty. It had also stemmed from pride, and pride was a sin, and sin was on strike.

And that was Chesney's... He had been going to use the word *fault* in the privacy of his mind. But he realized that he wasn't prepared to go that far. At least not yet. *But it is definitely* my *doing*, he told himself. He had to shoulder some of the responsibility, and therefore some of the blame. But how much? He didn't know. And, not knowing, he couldn't judge how much effort his share would obligate him to put out to rectify the situation.

As he walked along, he wrestled with the math, but that normally reliable calculator couldn't come to grips with the ratios. There weren't enough solid digits to feed into the equations. There were too many unknowns, too many variables. He needed certainty. And thus he hurried his pace. Because, when it came to delineating fault, for cutting through a tangle of who did what and how and to whom, to reveal the core of culpability, Chesney knew of one incisive, discriminating mind that could pierce the darkness like the brilliant beam of a lighthouse in an old–time cartoon.

One and a half blocks later, he turned off the sidewalk and onto the front walk of the house where that intelligence had reigned, constantly sorting moral wheat from chaff–and finding far more of the latter than the former–for as long as Chesney could remember.

He stepped up onto the porch, knocked as he turned the big brass doorknob, and called, "Mother, it's me."

He stepped into the dark-paneled hallway and was immediately wrapped in the house's familiar odor of ancient furniture polish and lavender potpourri. No answer had come to his announcement, and he spoke a little louder: "Mother?"

"In here," came her voice and he opened the heavy glass-paned door that led into the parlor–perish the thought that he should ever refer to it as a "living room"–and stepped into the space that he most associated with his mother. The scene was as always: the old-fashioned overstuffed furniture, inherited with the house and still dappled with doilies on arms and backs, the wide sweep of a curved-legged coffee table covered in envelopes, writing paper, sheets of postage stamps, and a ceramic object with a roller that dipped into a shallow reservoir that could be filled with water, the use of which saved Letitia Arnstruther the literally distasteful chore of licking stamps and envelopes.

And she herself was where she most often was when she occupied the parlor. She sat at the antique writing desk, a relic of the age when Victorian ladies communicated with each other and the world through scented note paper and fine penmanship. Mrs. Arnstruther's handwriting would have come up to those long-ago ladies' exacting standards, though the characters of the persons to whom she wrote would have raised many a refined eyebrow.

For, in the years since Chesney had left his mother's house, thus ceasing to be the chief focus of her days, her primary occupation had become the composition of perfectly scathing letters that she sent to individuals who had come to her attention through programs like that of the Reverend Billy Lee Hardacre. The recipients of her views–most of them politicians, movie stars, musicians, journalists, authors and academics–would receive Letitia Arnstruther's unsparing assessments of themselves and their activities, along with her earnest recommendations as to how they could improve their lives by changing their activities or their opinions. Should they choose not to take her well meaning advice, she offered them detailed descriptions of the eternal fates that surely awaited the recipients of her advice, which for all their elegant phrasing, made for harrowing reading.

So imaginative were her renditions of the sufferings of the damned that, in another life, she might have won renown as an author of fictions meant to chill the blood and shiver the spine. But fiction was far from Mrs. Arnstruther's mind as she described the impalings, amputations, roastings, piercings, gougings and rough penetrations into intimate parts that awaited her correspondents. To her, these torments were as real as breakfast. And her contemplation of their visitation upon the recipients of her missives, far from causing her chills or shivers, always brought a rosy glow to her rounded countenance. She enjoyed her work.

But now Chesney found her seated at her writing desk, a two-page letter unfinished before her, her fountain pen—she had never liked ballpoints, far less the modern felt-tips—idle in her plump fingers. Her cheek rested against her upturned palm, and the eyes she turned toward her son lacked their customary glint. "There you are," she said, as always, though without even a tinge of the usual accusatory tone that allowed Chesney to add in his own mind the unspoken completion of the phrase: *and about time, too.*

"Mother," he said, "are you all right?"

The answer was a sigh. "I suppose," she said. "But somehow I seem to lack my usual energy." She gestured at the paper before her. "I was trying to write a letter to that young woman who gyrates on the television, but..."—she sought for the words—"it just won't come to me." She put down the pen and leaned back in her brocaded chair, letting her hands fall to her lap. "I feel so... listless."

"Mother, come sit with me," Chesney said. He took her hands and drew her over to the sofa. "I need your advice."

Normally, such an admission would have had Letitia Arnstruther immediately firing on all cylinders. She gave off advice the way pinwheels gave off sparks. But, as she sat at one end of the over-stuffed chesterfield, she remained subdued, and startled her son by answering, "I don't know if I'm any good at advising anyone today. I just don't seem to have much mental energy."

"I know, mother. And I even know why," said Chesney. And not much more than a minute later, so did Letitia Arnstruther. He had to admit that she took it well. He had been wondering how others would react, but his mother at least absorbed the information with no more than a show of genuine surprise, followed by a welling up of concern for him.

"My poor Chesney," she said, "what an awful burden you have to bear."

He was taken aback. He could not recall ever hearing his mother express sympathy. Even when she was patching up his boyhood cuts and scrapes, she was more given to issuing instructions on how to avoid their happening again. But he had no time to dwell on the past, so he told her: "I don't know what to do."

"Well," she said, blinking, "you must do what's right."

"That's the problem I've been wrestling with. It couldn't be right to take the deal the Devil has offered me–that would be siding with evil. Not to mention damning my immortal soul. But it's not just about me. While Hell is on strike, nobody's doing any sinning, anywhere in the world. If I give in, I would be responsible for all the evil that would follow once Hell goes back to work."

"So you shouldn't give in."

"But the whole world has come to a stop," Chesney said. "It turns out that sinning is what makes the world go round. With sin turned off, nobody's motivated to do anything, except for those who keep on out of habit or a sense of obligation. Why even you..." He broke off when he saw her look of consternation.

"Me?" Her expression took on an introspective cast. After a moment, her eyes widened and went to the piles of stationery and stamps on the coffee table then on to take in the writing desk. "Oh," she said. "Oh, my."

"I'm sorry, mother," he said.

"Pride," she said, as if to herself, then, "no, it's more out of little envy. Now, why did I never see that?"

"I'm sorry," he said again, "very sorry."

He saw her pull herself together. "Well," she said, "first of all, you have nothing to be sorry for. You meant no harm. You're trying to make good come out of it."

"But I don't know how."

"And why would you? You're an actuary, not a philosopher." She seemed to have recovered some of her old energy. She reached for a spiral–bound notebook on the coffee table, flicked through its pages until she found what she was looking for. "Here it is," she said and reached for the cordless phone on an end table. She punched in a long–distance number and waited for an answer. But when it came, her brows briefly drew down and she clicked the phone off and put it back on its pedestal. "Voice mail," she said, rising from the sofa. "That won't do. We'll have to go see him."

"Who?" said Chesney.

"A man who has experience in these matters," she said.

"Who?" Chesney said again, rising to follow her. She was already through the door to the hallway and her voice came back to him over the rattle of car keys that always hung from a hook in the entrance hall.

"The Reverend Billy Lee Hardacre."

Letitia Arnstruther had not only inherited a house and furniture when her widower father, a lifelong district attorney, passed on. She inherited his beautifully maintained mid-sixties-vintage Dodge (model) sedan, with leather seats and hardwood dashboard. She rarely drove the huge car, finding parking it a difficult chore, but now she wheeled it sedately through the near empty streets toward the interstate. Her white gloved hands gripped the wheel at two and ten o'clock and she kept the speedometer needle just below the speed limit.

"I'm not sure about this," Chesney said, not for the first time, sitting on the passenger side of the Dodge's wide bench seat.

"But I am, dear," said his mother. "No one knows more about Heaven and Hell than the Reverend Billy Lee. He's made a study of it."

"But I'm not sure we should be bothering him."

She did not take her eyes off the road. "He's a minister of the gospel. How could it bother him to help someone in spiritual trouble?"

Chesney pictured Hardacre's face as he normally saw it, formed into an image of stern condemnation, eyes lit with what seemed a less than holy light as he foretold the doom and damnation that were the wages of the sinners he singled out for examination. "Well, maybe," he said.

The Reverend Billy Lee's home was in a rural community two hours drive south of the city. As one of the *New New Tabernacle of the Air*'s Saints Circle–those who wrote more than a hundred letters a year–Letitia Arnstruther had three times been invited to social functions in a marquee set up on the long, manicured lawn. As far as either Chesney or his mother knew, no one had ever been invited inside the mansion itself, where the reverend presumably wrestled with Satan and always came out on top.

The estate was enclosed by a redbrick wall broken by two white marble pillars from which hung a tall pair of black iron gates whose vertical bars bore the sunburst-and-crucifix logo of the *New New Tabernacle of the Air*. Letitia lowered her window and spoke into a grill mounted on the pillar that supported the left gate. Chesney could not hear the answer–the voice was indistinct–but after a moment the barrier swung silently open. They followed the long drive of crushed white stone and parked on a wide apron in front of the doors of a multi-car garage. The sounds of the Dodge's doors closing and their footsteps on the pristine gravel were loud in the silence that hung over the place.

"I'm still not sure–" Chesney said.

"You don't have to be, dear," his mother said. "I'll be sure for both of us."

They ascended broad steps up to a pillared portico. There was an old-fashioned bell pull instead of a button. The woman gave it a solid tug. From inside, Chesney heard the sound of mellow chimes, but the door remained closed. Letitia yanked the cord again, harder and longer.

"I'm coming," said a voice from within. A moment later, the door opened. A medium-sized, balding man in faded jeans and a gray tee-shirt stretched over a definite paunch looked up at them. "What can I do for you?"

"We'd like to see Reverend Billy Lee," said Chesney's mother.

"You are seeing him," said the man.

"I don't like to contradict," said Letitia, "but I've met Reverend Hardacre–"

"And I don't look like him," the man finished for her. "Well, I'm afraid this is what he looks like without the girdle, the padding in the shoulders, the lifts in the cowboy boots and the two-thousand dollar hairpiece." He held up one hand and Chesney saw the flash of his diamond-studded, heavy gold ring. "This is part of the act, too, but I can't get it off. Too many steak and lobster dinners, I reckon."

He peered up a the woman through washed-out hazel eyes and continued, "I don't have my contacts in, but I think I recognize you. Letitia Arnstruther?" When Chesney's mother confirmed the identification, Hardacre said, "You're the one who writes those awful letters. Sometimes I get copies from the lawyers of people I've sicced you all onto. They're practically pornographic. I used to not know whether to laugh or wince. Of course, now I know." He winced.

Chesney saw that his mother was not taking the Reverend

Billy Lee's unembroidered revelations well. He thought he had better change the agenda. "Mr. Hardacre," he said, "I'm Chesney Arnstruther."

Hardacre looked him up and down. "You're not the husband?"

"The son. We need to talk to you."

The preacher shook his mostly hairless head. "I don't think I'm any use to anybody right now, son," he said. "If I ever was any use before, which is a matter for debate."

"That," said Chesney, "is what we need to talk to you about."

Hardacre led them to a sitting room that could only be described as baronial: a vast stone–flagged floor covered in a handful of plush Persian carpets, any one of which would have more than handled the needs of Letitia Arnstruther's parlor; a high, domed ceiling from whose center descended a chandelier of black iron with gilded scrollwork; one wide wall pierced by tall, mullioned windows flanked by drapes of heavy, dark velvet; a fireplace in which a ox could roast, and above it a life–sized oil painting of the Reverend Billy Lee in a pose reminiscent of Charlton Heston's Moses preparing to part the Red Sea. Concealed lighting bathed the portrait in a glow that ensured that the image would be the first thing to which a visitor's gaze would be drawn.

Before the fireplace was a conversational grouping of massive armchairs upholstered in ox–blood red leather. Chesney thought they were designed to impress rather than to offer a comfortable seat, but he hadn't come for a relaxing chat. "My mother," he said, perched on the edge of the seat and regarding the preacher across yards of red and purple carpet, "thinks you may be able to help us with the..."–he sought for an appropriate word–"situation we all find ourselves in."

"What... situation?" Hardacre said.

"I've accidentally caused Hell to go on strike."

The reverend's face did not at first register any emotion. After a moment, Chesney saw the man's brows rise and fall, while his lips half–pursed then turned down at the corners in a frown of concentration. Finally, his eyes widened and his mouth half opened, the index finger of his right hand stirred the air in front of him then thrust forward to point at Chesney. "Ah," he said, nodding. "So that's it."

Chesney felt a ripple of relief pass through him. He exhaled, and only then realized he had been holding his breath while waiting for the man's response. He had been expecting to have to argue his case, but instead found himself in the position of the character in a mystery who provides the sleuth with the one clue that illuminates all the others.

"I've been puzzling over it ever since yesterday," Hardacre said.

"I would have thought you'd have been praying over it," Letitia said.

The Reverend's eyes couldn't twinkle without the blue contacts and the carefully focused lights of his television studio, but he managed a pretty good version of his down-home smile. "Not much point in that, ma'am," he said. "We kind of have an agreement: I don't bother Him, and He lets me get on with things in my own way."

"So you're not really a man of faith?" she said. Chesney heard nothing in her tone but innocent wonder. On any other day, the words would have been freighted with scorn and anger, but no power was stoking his mother's fires.

"That's a complicated question," the preacher said, pausing as if to consider it. Then Chesney saw him put the matter aside as he continued, "but it seems your son has a more pressing conundrum for us to deal with. So why don't you tell me how you got yourself—and all of us, I guess—into this fix?"

So Chesney told him, starting with the poker night and working his way up to the encounter with Satan in the park. Hardacre listened, interrupting here and there to pose a small question. When the tale was told, he bowed his head, steepled his fingers and touched them to his lips, a gesture not of prayer but of concentration. After a long silence, he looked up and said, "I think your mother has indeed brought you to the right man." He paused and quirked his lips, then said, "Ordinarily, I would say that with a genuinely overweening pride, but I now understand why the fellow who supplies me with that emotion isn't on the job.

"Even so," he continued, rubbing his palms briskly together, "no reason why we shouldn't get down to work."

"What can we do?" Chesney asked.

"Well," said the reverend, "it's been a long time since I've handled one, but first we're going to bring all the sides to the table and see if we can get a bargaining session."

IV

"I will not," said Satan.

"You gotta," said the red snake protruding from the little blonde girl's mouth. "We've given all we've got. Management has got to cut us some slack."

"I do not manage Hell," said the Archfiend. "I *reign* in it. I will not yield."

The little girl folded her arms across her pinafore. Satan examined the ceiling, as if he found it far more interesting than the fuming demon across the table.

"All right," said the Reverend Billy Lee Hardacre, "I think that's enough for our initial session. Now I'd like to suspend negotiations while I explore some opportunities for finding common ground. Then we'll meet again. Shall we say two hours?"

"You gotta be kidding," said the IBFDT president.

"Pointless," said the Devil.

"Not so," said Hardacre. "I believe I see a way out of this seeming impasse."

The demon used a scatological term to express contempt and disbelief. Satan only turned his stygian gaze upon the mediator and lifted one thin eyebrow to convey the same sentiment.

"You'll just have to trust me," said Hardacre.

"Why should we?" said the Devil.

The preacher rose and ordered the papers he had spread before him on the table. "Because," he said, "I know something you don't."

Chesney and his mother had spent the bargaining session in a butler's pantry next to the big dining room that Hardacre had designated as the site for the encounter. The mediator had left the door slightly ajar and they had listened in. Now as he came through from the meeting, Chesney said, "That didn't seem to go well."

"It always starts like that," Hardacre said. "If it didn't, they wouldn't need a mediator." He had dressed for the occasion: one of his carefully tailored suits, hand–tooled western boots, the silver–haired toupée.

"What did you mean," Letitia asked, "when you said you knew something they didn't?"

"Ah," said Hardacre. He laid the thick sheaf of pages he'd been carrying down on a side table. "That will take some explaining. And first I need to talk to someone else." He looked at Chesney. "You said that your guardian angel was going to seek advice from someone higher up the ladder?"

"Yes, but I haven't heard back. I got the impression it didn't want to deal with me."

The preacher nodded. "I'm sure it didn't. But we can't allow them that option." He addressed the air. "Time to show yourself. We need to talk."

Nothing happened. Hardacre sighed. "I can solve this, but you have to buy in." He waited. "Otherwise, it all stops, and He'll never know how it ends." When he said, "He," Hardacre pointed a finger upwards.

A soft chime sounded, an achingly beautiful note that hung in the air, and a tall, fine-featured man with hair as blond and fine as corn silk, dressed in an impossibly white suit, was suddenly standing before them. "What do you mean?"

Hardacre had his own question: "Throne or Dominion?"

"Throne," said the angel. "Now, what did you mean?"

"I mean," said Hardacre, "that He's written Himself into a corner. When that happens, it's up to the characters to save the story."

Chesney thought it was probably the first time the angel's perfectly smooth brow had ever had to wrinkle. "I beg your pardon?" it said.

"I'll explain," said Hardacre, "over lunch."

"I'll be glad," Hardacre said, serving out plain bologna sandwiches and glasses of water, "when we get this settled. I miss gluttony."

The angel did not partake but joined the three mortals in the dining room. "You were going to explain," it said.

Hardacre chewed his sandwich without enjoyment and swallowed. "It all goes back to when I was writing my seventh novel," he said. "I got stuck halfway through. I'd started out knowing what the story was about, but the further I got into it, the more the characters took on a life of their own. They developed in ways I hadn't anticipated. After a while, I couldn't see how I could make them do what the story said they ought to do."

"I believe that's not an uncommon situation," the angel said. "Don't authors sometimes find that the characters take over the story?"

"Indeed. And a wise writer follows where they lead. So when it happened to me, I let my characters decide where they wanted to go, and together we made a different book from the one I had set out to write. That made me realize that it's not the writer's story; it's the *characters'* story, and the author is just writing it for them."

"Very witty," said the angel, "but what does it have to do with the situation?"

"The experience," Hardacre said, "taught me that you can not only learn by reading books. Sometimes you can learn by writing one. And that's when I had my revelation, the one that made me give up law and literature, and go after a degree in theology."

Chesney chewed his almost tasteless sandwich and listened to the preacher offer his argument. The more he saw of Hardacre, the more he saw how the man took over the situation, the less the actuary could maintain his belief that he was the central figure in this story. He found himself thinking that perhaps it was time to accept that he would always be an outsider, one who watched from the sidelines as more determined people pushed and elbowed each other, or stroked and pulled together.

Yes, he had started something when he accidentally called up a demon, but it now looked as if he would not be the one to finish what he started. Listening to Hardacre expound to a high-ranking member of the heavenly hierarchy, he thought, *I guess he's the hero of all this. I'm just the character who gets the ball rolling, so that somebody like the Reverend Billy Lee can step in and play the leading role.* He looked at his mother, whose eyes were locked on the preacher, even though there was an actual angel right there in the room, and wondered if any woman would ever take that much interest in him.

"But you never actually received a degree in theology, did you?" said the angel. Chesney saw that the news came as a surprise to his mother.

"No," Hardacre admitted, "my doctoral thesis was not accepted." He paused for effect. "But I'll bet it would have to be accepted now."

Again the angel looked perplexed. But Hardacre had turned to Chesney now. "You're an actuary. You work out the odds of this or that event happening to this or that segment of the population."

"Yes."

"Have you ever noticed that the guy upstairs has often dealt to us from a stacked deck?"

"What do you mean?" Chesney said.

"Take Adam and Eve," Hardacre said. "He sends two innocents out into a garden where an evil intelligence is plotting to destroy them. Does He warn them about the snake?"

Chesney shook his head.

"Or consider Cain and Able. Cain's a farmer. Able's a shepherd. They both work hard, bring Him their best offerings—and Cain probably had to work harder to grow crops. All Able had to do was follow a bunch of sheep around. But He blesses Able's offering and disses Cain's."

"But when Cain kills Able," Chesney said, "God doesn't punish him. He sends him off to find a wife and even puts a mark on his forehead to warn people to leave him alone."

"Exactly," said Hardacre. "Did God not consider murder—and of a brother, mind you—not a punishable offense? And when Cain asks, 'Am I my brother's keeper?' he gets no answer. Seems like a straightforward question of ethics, but God's apparently stumped for an answer."

The angel opened its mouth to speak, but Hardacre kept right on. "And then there's poor old Job. His life gets caught up in a bet between God and the Devil. His wives and kids are killed, his goods are destroyed, he gets covered in boils, and when he complains he gets told to mind his own business."

"It wasn't quite like that," said the angel.

Hardacre waved the objection away. "And there's other stuff. There are two different creation stories in Genesis. And there's the story of Noah and the Flood. He doesn't like the way His creation is going, so He erases the whole thing and starts all over. Who does that?" The question was rhetorical; Hardacre immediately supplied the answer: "Writers do that."

"What is all this leading to?" said the angel.

Hardacre put up a hand in a way that asked that the question be deferred. "One more thing. The most important clue of them all: I kept noticing all the books."

"Books?" Chesney said.

"He's always encouraging us to write books. The Torah, the Gospels, the Koran, the Rig Veda, the Book of Mormon, lots more.

Even when virtually everybody was illiterate, he was inspiring people to produce books."

"He wants you to remember what was important," said the angel.

If Hardacre's tempter had been on the job, Chesney thought, he would have nudged the preacher into at least a prideful snort. Instead, Hardacre just said, "I don't think so."

"You question?" said the angel.

"Yes, because that's what we're supposed to do." He appealed to Chesney. "If He wanted us to read a book, why didn't He just write one and have it delivered to us at birth? Why not just put the information into our heads"–he looked at the Throne–"the way he did with you? Why all the different versions, contradicting each other? And all written by us?"

"I assume you have an answer?" said the angel.

"I do," said the preacher. "But when I defended it as my doctoral dissertation, I got shouted at." He came back to Chesney. "But all the different books are a collective clue. They're what literary critics call a recurring motif."

"But what does the clue tell us?" Chesney said.

"The obvious," said Hardacre. "All of this,"–he gestured broadly to include all creation–"is His book. And He's writing it to learn something."

"He is what He is," said the angel. "What does He have to learn?"

Hardacre turned to the heavenly visitor and gave him a gentle smile. "Morality, of course."

"To quote you," said the angel, "'I don't think so.'"

"You don't think at all," said Hardacre. "You were created, ready-made and perfect, to already know everything you need to know. What He needs you to know. You immortals–all of you, including the ones down below–are not characters in this story. The thing about characters is that they *change*. You don't change. You're just fixed factors, background actors, like weather or gravity.

"That's why we have free will and you don't. *We're* the ones who have to think. We have to work it out, move the story forward, make it come right in the end." He spread his hands. "The question is: what is 'right in the end?' What's the point of all this?"

Chesney's mother spoke. "To earn salvation."

The preacher shook his head. "But we wouldn't need salvation if He hadn't given us free will and sicced the Devil on us. And why would He keep changing the rules? For a long time we were damned if we ate pork and lobster, or wore cloth made of two different fabrics—then all at once we weren't. It used to be we could have lots of wives and concubines, then we could only have one, then He changed his mind again and told Mohammed he could have four. For a long time, 'an eye for an eye' was the acceptable standard, then suddenly it's 'forgive them their trespasses.'

"Besides, if He knows which of us is going to end up in Hell before He creates us, then isn't He at least partly to blame for creating the ones who are going to fail?"

Chesney made the connection. "You're saying He doesn't know what's going to happen."

Hardacre poked a finger in his direction. "Ahah."

"But what about all those people who end up down there?" said Chesney. "God lets them fail and suffer so that He can learn something?"

"You can't make a story without some conflict," the preacher said. "Conflict means some people have to suffer. They can't all win. He's not writing a *Care Bears* episode."

"But that's cruel," Letitia.

"It's the price we pay. And that He pays, too. Because He's partly responsible for our screw-ups."

"It's still cruel."

"Yes," said Hardacre, "but it's not real. *We're* not real. And when the story is all told, when He writes 'The End' at the bottom of the last page, then all this will wrap up. No more Hell, no more Heaven, no more angels, devils, saints or sinners. The story's done. It will be as if we never were."

"Then what happens to us all?" Chesney said.

"We go back where we came from."

"But where's that?"

Hardacre tapped his temple. "Where do any characters come from?"

"You're saying," the angel said, "that we are all characters in a book He is writing, and when it is finished, we will all be reabsorbed into Him?"

"You have a problem with that?" Hardacre said. "What did *you* think would happen in the end?"

"The world would end and all would be judged. The good ones of you will live in Heaven; the bad will go to Hell. You have read the

Book of Revelation?"

"Oh, yes, just as I have read Zarathustra's writings and the Norse sagas," said the preacher. "The seminary had a good library. They're like the two Adam and Eve stories—early drafts. Since then, the story's moved on."

"It's a remarkable theory," said the angel. "But I'm not surprised that the seminary rejected it."

"Angels are never surprised," said Hardacre. "How could you be when you know everything you need to know? Just as you won't be surprised when my theory turns out to be correct."

"You believe you'll prove it?"

"In about an hour," said Hardacre. "When we resume negotiations."

The angel seemed genuinely curious. "How?"

But Hardacre only held up a finger while his other hand fed a baloney sandwich into his mouth.

⁂

"What is that doing here?" said Satan. For all Hell's reputation as a hot place, the look he gave the Throne could have frozen a bonfire.

"He's part of the solution," said Reverend Billy Lee Hardacre.

"No," said the angel, "I am not. I have no authority to intervene in this situation."

"You will have," Hardacre said. "Now, if we can all sit down, I'd like to put a proposal on the table."

They sat, though the Devil turned his head so that he did not have to look at the Throne. His sharp-pointed fingernails drummed impatiently on the polished wood.

"I've asked Chesney Arnstruther to be present because he is obviously part of the situation," Hardacre said.

"Very well," said Satan.

"Fine by me," said the snake-tongued little blonde girl.

"And Chesney's mother is here, well, mainly because she's his mother."

The Devil made a gesture of irritation but offered no objection. The IBFDT president shrugged its pinafore straps.

"Now, as I understand it," Hardacre said, "this dispute grows out of two roots: one, the number of sinners to be punished in Hell has grown exponentially and will continue to increase, putting limits on your work force's ability to maintain productivity; two, the arrival of labor organizers has introduced the concept of collective action."

Hearing no contradictions, he went on, "Shall I assume that under no circumstances would you countenance doing less tempting, thus leading to a decrease in the intake of sinners?"

"That would not be acceptable,' said the Devil.

"That means we cannot address supply, therefore we must deal with productivity. I have a suggestion for that: down among your... population, in addition to labor organizers, you're bound to have a few public relations consultants."

"Quite a few," said the Archfiend. "It's a field that rewards amoral inventiveness."

Hardacre said, "I suggest you pluck a few out of the furnace and get them to advise you on the concept of 'opinion leaders.' Briefly explained, they are those individuals within any community who are not officially recognized leaders but whose actions and views carry more weight with their neighbors than do the deeds and words of the bulk of the population. Public relations practitioners have developed reliable techniques for identifying them. If you concentrate your tempters on opinion leaders, you can pay less attention to those who follow their lead."

Satan stroked his pointed beard. "That would free up tempters to join the punishment corps?"

"Exactly." Hardacre turned to the IBFDT president. "Would you have any problem with a reallocation of the work force?"

"Would seniority transpose from one corps to the other?" the demon said. Hardacre looked to the Devil, who thought a moment, then nodded. "Then we would have no problem," the demon said.

"But your proposal would give an advantage to... the other side," said the Archfiend, with a hate-filled glance at the senior angel. "They already have superiority of numbers."

The Throne said nothing, but a tiny smile moved the corners of its perfect lips. Satan growled.

Hardacre spoke before the rancor could escalate. "Suppose that the other side withdrew some of its effort, concentrating more on the same opinion leaders, easing up on humanity's rank and file?"

The angel gently stirred the air with two elegant fingers. "We would not do that."

"You would, and you will," said Hardacre, "if my theory is right."

"What theory?" said the Devil and the IBFDT president.

"He thinks," said the angel, "that we are all characters in a book that Himself is writing."

The demon vibrated its snake-tongue against its little-girl lips, making a unique sound of scornful disbelief. The Devil made a small sound and rolled his coal-black eyes.

"If I'm right," said Hardacre, "we'll know fairly soon."

"How?" said all three of the non-mortals at once.

"We'll know because the solution that you"–he nodded to the angel–"just found completely unacceptable will suddenly become completely acceptable. Just as there once was a hard shell over the earth called the firmament, and then there wasn't. Just as it was once possible to build a tower or put up a ladder that would reach from earth to Heaven, and then it wasn't."

"I don't remember the firmament, and the Tower of Babel is just a myth," said the angel.

"Because there's no need for you to remember," said Hardacre. "But the firmament and the tower, the sun that could be stopped in the sky, they were as real as this room. Then they were revised out of subsequent drafts. He keeps rewriting back chapters as he goes forward. I used to do that myself."

"How could you know this if we don't?" said Satan.

"Characters know what they need to know. That's how the internal dynamics of story-making work."

The Devil gave the mediator a hard look. Chesney admired the way Hardacre stood up under the power of that stare. "I find your idea offensive," Satan said, "not to mention ridiculous."

"If I'm wrong, we all just sit here and the story comes to a dead stop. If I'm right, we make a deal and move on."

They sat. The only sound in the room was the staccato drumming of Satan's fingers on the table top. Chesney noticed that the wood was becoming gouged and scorched.

After a while, Reverend Billy Lee said, to no one in particular, "When you find you've written yourself into a corner, the thing to do is: remove a wall."

They waited. The Devil's drumming grew more impatient. Smoke rose from beneath his fingertips. He opened his mouth to speak.

And the Throne said, "We accept."

Satan cast his heavenly adversary a suspicious glance. "Didn't you say the proposal was unacceptable?"

"Did I?" said the angel. "I don't recall."

The Devil blinked and his expression took on an inward cast, as if he had just lost the train of his thought. "What just happened?"

"I think we got a deal," the IBFDT president said.

Billy Lee Hardacre said nothing. But Chesney had never seen a man look so happy.

"But you cannot tell anyone," said the angel.

It seemed to Chesney that Hardacre was about to argue. Then he saw a sequence of thoughts cross the preacher's face, the last one being acceptance. "Yes, that's fair," he said.

"And you," the angel said to Satan, "may not tempt him to tell." Satan's brows clouded, and the room suddenly smelled of sulfur, but the angel went on implacably, "or the deal's off."

The Devil's lips drew down in a grim frown. For a long moment, the issue hung in the balance. Then he said, "Not acceptable."

"Of course," said the Throne. "It's your pride. Your damnable pride."

"As it always was," said the Archfiend, "and always will be."

Hardacre spoke. "Perhaps if the instigator of the crisis offered an apology."

Satan raised an eyebrow. "An abject apology?"

"But he is blameless," said the Throne.

"All the better," said the Hardacre.

Satan considered it. "The idea does have an appeal," he said. "He will have to bow down to me."

"But not serve you," said Hardacre.

Satan made a motion that dismissed the point as being of no significance. "And in front of all my subjects. We'll give everybody an hour off."

"Us, too," said the demon.

"Except for necessary crowd control," Satan shot back.

"Agreed. We'll use the reassigned tempters."

Hardacre looked around the table. "Then I think we can call this dispute settled," he said.

"Like flip–flonkin' flickafack, you can."

They all looked at Chesney. If he could have, he would have regarded himself with equal surprise. The words had come out of him before he had known they were there. And now he heard himself continue, "It's not fair. I have nothing to apologize for."

His mother had been regarding Hardacre with a gaze that looked to Chesney like pure adoration. Now she turned to her son and put a gentle hand on his arm. "There is, my dear," she said, "a precedent."

"Are you saying you won't do it?" Hardacre said. "There's a lot riding on this."

Chesney's reaction had been an unthinking rejection of the injustice. Now he thought about it while Heaven and Hell waited to hear what he would say. And then an idea came to him. More than an idea, it was a revelation.

Maybe, he said to himself, *I* am *the hero of the story after all.* Aloud, he said, "I will do it,"–he even paused for effect–"on one condition."

V

Hell, even on a temporary visit, was a deeply unpleasant experience. The heat made Chesney's skin ache, the air was caustic in his lungs, and the sights and sounds brought up surges of horror and pity from inner depths that the young man had not known he possessed. Still, he bore up under the pressure and when the time came he spoke, clearly and loudly, the words of the formal apology as they had been negotiated by Billy Lee Hardacre and His Satanic Majesty, that being the formal title by which Chesney was required to address the recipient of his apology. Then he made a deep bow and held it until he heard a small grunt of satisfaction from HSM.

The event took place on a narrow promontory of naked rock that arched out over an enormous pit, into which the entire population of the underworld had been crammed. Demons lashed and prodded them into serried ranks that stretched far beyond Chesney's powers of vision to penetrate the foul and filthy air. When Chesney straightened from his bow, he saw the final phrases of his apology– "and do most humbly beg Your Satanic Majesty to overlook the inconvenience and impudence of my unpardonable conduct"–as huge letters of fire slowly fading above the pit. After his little grunt, the Devil made no response other than to wave the matter away as if the whole business were of not the slightest consequence.

The IBFDT president then stepped up and signed an ornately decorated and sealed document. Satan did likewise. The ruby-red snake protruding from the demon's little-girls mouth then shouted, with a surprisingly stentorian volume for such a small serpent, "We've settled. Everybody back to work."

A moment later, Chesney found himself back in his studio apartment. The electronic calendar on the countertop between the main room and the kitchen nook said that it was the same day on which he had first summoned up the toad-demon. The calendar's clock function ticked over to the second just after he had smashed his thumb with the hammer. As with the firmament and the Tower of Babel, the days when Hell had gone on strike had been written over back and thus they never were.

Chesney's thumb hurt and bled, but he suppressed the urge to utter anything more than a heartfelt groan. Nor did he shake the wounded digit, spraying blood on his unfinished poker table. Instead he popped it into his mouth and sucked it.

"Isn't that a pretty sight?" said a gravel-scratchy voice. Chesney turned to see the diminutive, weasel-headed supervisor in the Al Capone suit, regarding him with disgust. "A thumb-sucker, yet."

Chesney extended the hurt thumb. "Heal it."

The fiend shrugged.

"Xaphan, I command you," Chesney said—they had now been formally introduced—"heal my thumb."

Xaphan rolled its weasel eyes then gestured brusquely. Immediately, the pain left Chesney's thumb, the swollen redness disappeared and the split flesh from which his blood had flowed was whole again.

"Good," said the young man. "Now let's get to work. We don't have much time before the guys come over for poker."

The demon consulted a gold pocket watch chained to its vest. "I can give you one hour, fifty-nine minutes, five seconds. And no banking any unused time."

"I know the terms of the deal," said Chesney. "So in the future, don't waste time reminding me." He rubbed his hands. "Now, first thing is, I'm going to need a costume. It has to be bulletproof, knife-proof, fireproof, acidproof..."—he thought for a moment—"well let's just make it generally proof against anything that could harm me."

"You gonna want a cape?" Xaphan said.

The young man shook his head. "No cape. But I should have some kind of utility belt to hold all the doodads I'll need."

"What kind of doodads?"

"We'll work that out later. First, I need a good name."

"Howzabout 'The Bozo?'"

"Enough of your sass," Chesney said. "I'm thinking, maybe, 'The Regulator.' How's that sound?"

"Like some punk thinks he's top of the world."

"Listen," said Chesney, "a deal's a deal. You're my 'condition' and your boss agreed to it. I get you two hours out of every twenty-four, you come when I call you, and together we fight crime and bad guys."

The fiend put its hands in its pockets and scuffed its spatted shoes against the carpet. "I don't like this. I don't like you."

"You don't have to. Back to the costume. I've always liked Batman's colors, good for lurking in the shadows, but I want a big capital 'R' on my chest." He snapped his fingers as inspiration came. "And another 'R' on the buckle of the utility belt."

Xaphan muttered something that Chesney didn't catch. He ignored it and continued. "And gloves—no, gauntlets, that's the word—that let me climb walls. Boots to match. And it's all got to fold up small enough to fit into a pouch I can carry in my pocket, for when I have to go into action on short notice."

The over-sized weasel eyes rolled, but the demon was writing it all down on a pad it had produced from the breast pocket of its pinstripe. "You want me to give you a cleft chin and a little curl of hair down over your forehead?"

"No. But I'll need a mask so I can keep my identity secret."

"You wanna fortress of solitude? A glass airplane?"

Chesney ignored the sarcasm. "No, but I'll need a bigger apartment."

Xaphan flicked its hands in opposite directions. The inner walls of the studio blew outwards. Chesney saw his startled neighbors in the adjoining suites sitting amid billowing clouds of drywall plaster. "Undo that," he said, and when the walls instantly went back in place, "and from now on you only do what I directly order you to do."

The demon sulked.

"At least until we've worked the bugs out," Chesney said.

"Bugs?" the demon said. "That's a good one, coming from you."

"'Bugs' hasn't meant 'crazy' for, I dunno, fifty, sixty years," Chesney said. "You should get a software update."

"You don't like how I talk?"

"To tell you the truth, not so much."

"Well," Xaphan, "so's your old man."

"What's that mean?"

"That I don't like you."

"We've covered that," said Chesney. "Now where were we? We've done costume." He snapped his fingers. "I know, tell me where some really bad guys hide out."

"Oh, swell," said the demon. "You slay me."

HUNCHƎTER

I'm interested in people on the autism spectrum, like Chesney in the story before this one. I also know, from having been born into poverty, that life is not fair. Combine that with my enjoyment of nickel–dime poker and you get "Hunchster." It was another one of my entries in The Magazine of Fantasy & Science Fiction.

YOU'D THINK I'd remember the kid's name, but I never could. One of those "J" names that suddenly got popular back in the eighties, Jared, or Jeremiah, might even have been Jedediah. Doesn't matter now. We mostly just called him "the kid in Lee's basement," except when he'd join us for Saturday night poker in Lee's garage. Then he liked us to call him "the Hunchster."

That was on account of the way he played. I mean, there are two ways to go with seven–card stud. You can either play the cards, look at what's in your hand and on the table, and figure the odds you'll get that fifth spade or that third queen. Or you can play the players, where you not only watch for the tells but read the personalities, so you know if a guy's got the balls to try running a bluff past you or if he's sharp enough to know when you're faking it with a busted straight.

The Hunchster, though, he had his own way of playing. He didn't look around the table at the cards, didn't look at the players. "I get hunches," he said, the first time I asked him what was going on. He was raking in another heap of nickels, dimes, and quarters from the middle of Lee's old formica–topped table out in the garage where we played most Saturday nights. We used to play in Lee's basement, until he put in the extra plumbing and started renting out the room.

If you're any kind of poker player, what I just put down here tells you something about Lee, and about the rest of us. We played for nickels, dimes and quarters because that's all we could afford. And the reason Lee let this kind of weird–looking stranger live in his house was because the kid got a disability check every month. His dependable rent made up for the tips Lee didn't get when he drove people from the bus depot out to the IncarcerCorp prison so they could visit their inmate relatives. Most of them couldn't really afford the taxi fare, but it was a long walk out of town and the bus only ran twice a day.

Mitch and I, we were better off than Lee, but only just. IncarcerCorp paid three bucks an hour over minimum wage. No benefits, but the work was full-time and you could live on the wages–just hope you never got sick. Also, a prison generates a lot of other jobs, even when the outfit that runs it is so cheap it makes the inmates do their own laundry and swamp out the cell blocks. So, all our wives worked part-time for minimum wage in the kitchens, in the in-house hospital–again, no benefits–and our families had enough to get by on. Just enough to keep the town alive.

But at least we had jobs and could count on keeping them. After what had happened with United PressForm and the Breithertz Institute, that was a big deal. We used to tell each other, "At least nobody's going to put crime out of business."

Stan and Ron were the other regulars at the table Saturday nights. Sometimes, they brought Ron's friend Dooley. None of them had been taken on when IncarcerCorp held its big hiring fair, but they got jobs with a wholesaler that supplied the prison with everything from dungarees to macaroni. Stan and Dooley drove truck and Ron operated a forklift in the warehouse. Word was that IncarcerCorp and the wholesaler were both owned by the same investment syndicate that was headquartered in the Bahamas or somewhere. Nobody was a hundred percent sure, but so what? Paying the mortgage and sending the kids to school–that was what mattered.

Now, with me telling you all this, you're maybe thinking that my mind is wandering, why don't I follow through on where I started: the kid in Lee's basement and his peculiar way of playing poker? But it all ties in.

"You're saying you just play hunches?" I said, that first time, while he sorted the nickels, dimes and quarters into stacks and Stan dealt the first two down cards and one on deck for the next round.

He looked up at me. Actually, no–he never really looked *at* anybody. He'd look in your direction, sure, but never eye-to-eye.

Instead he'd lock onto your nose, or your shoulder, or your forehead. And there was never anything to read in his eyes. He only used them for seeing.

"I am an intuitive," he said. I remember the word because I used it right away, asking him, "What the heck is an intuitive?"

I should've known better. You asked this kid a question, you were going to get an answer. In spades. I didn't understand half of what he said, stuff about lateral connections and something that sounded like "snapses." Then he was talking about a "brokers area," which for a while I thought was somewhere around Corpus Cristi, except it turned out he was talking about some other place with a name like Corpus Clothes-um. Then he said they were parts of the brain, and his brain didn't work the way other people's did.

Lee told me later that the reason the kid got that monthly disability check was that he had a brain disease called Ass-burgers. I waited for the punchline, but he said it was a real disease, though it wasn't catching. Wayne Breithertz, who'd brought the kid over when they were all packing to leave, told Lee about it. The kid was a little strange, but harmless. And he had nowhere else to go.

So we're back to the poker table. Stan dealt out the first three cards and said, "Hunchster, your bet," and just like that the kid stopped talking about brains. Right in the middle of a sentence. He picked up his hole cards, stared at them for a second then put them down. He didn't look at anybody or at any of the cards on deck. Just pushed a quarter out towards the antes. A quarter was the maximum bet until all the cards had been dealt.

"Hunch?" I said.

He didn't look at me, just kept his peculiar eyes on his hole cards. "Uh huh," he said.

I had a pair of sevens in the hole and a king showing, but I flipped the king over and shoved it and the sevens away from me. "Fold," I said.

The kid was in Lee's basement because he got left behind when the Breithertz Institute folded. Wayne Breithertz was the nerdiest nerd our local high school ever produced. After eleventh grade he went off to some big college back east and next we heard of him he'd he turned into one of those ten-day tycoons who made a pile off the dot-com bubble. Old Wayne had come up with some bright idea that everybody thought was going to change the world.

Until it didn't.

But for a while the money was flowing, and he was our local hero because he came back home and bought up the old UPF factory. He spent about a half a gazillion dollars turning it into some kind of research center.

You may not know the name United PressForm. But turn over the tinfoil plate next time you take a frozen pie out of the freezer, or the tray that holds a tv dinner. You'll probably see UPF stamped into the bottom. Their plant on Becker Road used to supply half the pie-and-tv-dinner makers west of the Mississippi. Another UPF factory in New Jersey supplied most of the east. My old man signed on with the company in 1953 when he came home from Korea and spent his whole working life in that building. Most of our dads did. After high school, so did me and Lee and the rest of us. UPF provided half the jobs in town.

Until it didn't.

In 1995, the company packed up the whole shebang and moved to Nogales. That's when we found out our dads wouldn't be getting any more pension checks—the directors had spent their money and everybody else's. Nobody can tell me that wasn't the bad news that brought on the heart attack and killed the old man.

But then Wayne came home, bought the vacant plant cheap and remade it into some kind of combination open-plan office and supergeek playground. He brought in some pretty strange people, of which the Hunchster was by no means the strangest. We didn't know what all those newcomers were doing out there, but they had plenty of money to spend on everything from fancy coffees in paper cups to an even fancier condo development around a man-made lake that Wayne had dug out of what used to be pasture land south of town. And we all had jobs again, making sure the nerds stayed happy.

Until we didn't.

In 2001, the stock market yanked the rug out from under the Breithertz Institute. Trucks rolled in and hauled away all the computers and video game machines to sell at ten cents on the dollar. The condos emptied out and stayed empty. Last I heard, Wayne was teaching business math at some community college in Wisconsin. His collection of geeks went to wherever geeks go. Except for the Hunchster, who moved into Lee's basement along with a trunkload of electronic gear he'd built himself. Wayne said it would have just gone to the dump.

———————— ✺ ————————

Ask the kid what he was doing down there all day, you'd get an answer. Not that it made a whole lot of sense. He had some theory involving string. He was interested in "where new treenos went" and how they got there. "Temporary recapture," I thought he said once.

"Temporary recapture of what?" I said. The words had caught my interest because it was a week after the IncarcerCorp job fair and I'd been accepted for training as a guard. They'd already broken ground for the main block.

"Not temporary," he said, "*temporal*. Temporal recapture."

As if that explained it all.

———————— ✺ ————————

Then came another Saturday night and we were setting up in the garage: beer and taco chips and salsa. Lee went to the door at the side of the house that led down to the basement and asked the kid if he was going to play. I heard him call a second time then he came into the garage and said, "He don't answer."

"He home?" I said.

"He's always home." He paused, then said, "Some weird noises down there."

I was going to say, "What else is new?" but just then Ron came in and spoke over me, saying Dooley wasn't coming. Five was not enough for a decent game. I said, "We need the kid."

By now Lee had sat down and was breaking out the red, white and blue plastic chips. "So go get him," he said.

I went out of the garage and over to the basement entrance, down a half dozen steps. The inner door was ajar. I rapped on it but got no answer. There was a combination humming–hissing sound coming from the basement suite, getting louder then softer, louder then softer. I pushed open the door.

The kid was sitting on a kitchen chair with his back to me, hunched over a table that was covered with all kinds of electronics and computer gear, connected by a mess of cables and wires. That's where the humming and hissing were coming from. In front of him was a wide-screen monitor and he was staring into it while reaching out with one hand to a control panel of knobs and switches that was off to one side. He'd turn one knob then try another, his eyes never leaving the screen.

I moved up behind him. The image on the monitor was distorted and grainy. He reached for another knob and twiddled it, and suddenly the shot came into focus. The colors were washed out but I recognized it: Lee's driveway, just outside, and the Ryder house across the street.

There was something funny about the picture, though it took me a few seconds to put my finger on it. Parked in front of the house was Jeff Ryder's old red El Camino, which he'd smashed up and sent to the wrecker's sometime back in the early eighties.

"What is this?" I said.

The kid didn't turn. "What I've been working on. Temporal recapture." He pointed to a readout at the bottom right corner of the screen. It said: *05-24-1981* followed by a clock that was running in hours, minutes, seconds, and tenths of a second. Running backwards. As I watched, Jeff came out of the house–he was walking backwards–but this was Jeff without a pot belly and with way more hair than when I'd seen him yesterday. He got into the El Camino. A few seconds later, it drove away, in reverse.

"What am I looking at?" I said.

He turned toward me, looked at my IncarcerCorp belt buckle. "The past."

I took a deep breath. "A time machine?"

"But just for looking. Maybe hearing, too. I need to work on that." He turned back to the equipment, adjusted another knob, the screen blurred then cleared, and I was seeing a farmer's field. Now the readout said: *04-15-1902.* Into the frame, walking backwards, came a man, then a plow, then a mule. "I also need to miniaturize the components and work out a better power source. Then you could take it anywhere."

I felt a hollowness in my chest, like the time I was at a party and tried breathing helium. "You could take it any place and see what happened there, anytime in the past?"

"Maybe not anytime. Probably not back to dinosaur times." He twiddled the knob again. Now there was nothing but prairie. I didn't bother looking at the date. I was too busy thinking.

And what I was thinking was, *Jeez, not again.*

I went back to the garage. Mitch and Stan had shown up. I cracked a beer, drank half of it in one swallow, and said, "We got a problem."

The kid must've had a hunch. He tried to barricade the door, but there were too many of us. Afterwards, when we were cleaning up, Mitch and Lee wanted to bust up the equipment and burn the notebooks.

"No," I said, "that would be wrong."

So when the time comes, we'll do what we agreed to do, sitting there at the poker table, after I'd told them what I'd seen. When all our kids are out of school and able to stand on their own feet, we'll bring the sheriff down to Lee's basement. We'll fire up the Hunchster's equipment and roll back the date to that Saturday night.

We'll be the first criminals caught by his invention. And we won't be the last. But eventually, the Hunchster will be remembered as the guy who put crime out of business. Along with IncarcerCorp. And our whole town.

And like I said, just before we poured the concrete over him, "At least nobody's gonna forget your name."

THE UGLY DUCKLING

George R.R. Martin and Gardner Dozois have co-edited some interesting theme anthologies and have asked me to be in four of them, including Old Mars, *for which this story was written. I wasn't originally supposed to be in the Martian retro book, but someone dropped out and they asked me to fill in with a deadline looming. I reread Ray Bradbury's* The Martian Chronicles *then bashed this out in a week or so. George was kind enough to comment that, as a writer, I am "amazingly reliable and blazingly fast."*

IT TOOK FRED MATHER the better part of an hour to drive over the blue hills that stood between the base camp and the bone city. At the highest point of the switchbacking ancient road of crushed white stone, the thin Martian air grew even thinner. He had to take long, slow breaths to fill his lungs, while dark spots danced at the edge of his vision and he worried about steering the New Ares Mining Corporation's jeep over one of the precipices.

He could have got there more quickly—and more safely—by paralleling the dried-up canal down to the glass-floored sea. Then he could have plowed through its carpeting dust to the promontory girdled by a sea wall that had not felt a wave's slap in ten thousand years. The towers of the dead Martian town stood like an abandoned, unsolved chess puzzle, white against the faded sky.

The road at the landward end of the town was lined on either side by low, squat structures, windowless but with arched doors of weathered bronze. He was just wondering if they might be tombs—nobody knew yet what the Martians had done with their dead—when the hand radio on the passenger seat squawked and Red Bowman's voice said, "Base to Mather, over."

He picked up the set, keyed the mike switch, and said, "Mather, over."

"How you coming?" said the crew chief. Mather thought he heard a note of suspicion in the man's voice.

"I'm just pulling into the town now."

There was a silence, then the radio said, "The hell you been playing at? You should've been there an hour already."

"I took the hill road."

"What the hell for?"

"I thought it might be quicker. It looked shorter on the map." Mather was lying. The reason he hadn't gone by the canal road because he hadn't wanted to meet any other traffic. He had wanted, for a little while at least, to be able to pretend that he was the only Earthman on Mars, instead of just the only archaeologist.

The radio crackled back at him. "We got a schedule to meet, egghead. Now you get those transponders planted, then you get your heinie back here mucho pronto."

Bowman hadn't said, "Over," but Mather was about to confirm and sign off when the crew chief continued with, "And you come home by the seabed. You wreck that jeep and you'll be going back Earthside on the next rocket, with a forfeiture of all pay and benefits!"

"Roger, over and out." Mather said. He put down the radio and steered the vehicle through a gateway of bone pillars carved in twin spirals that led to a small plaza surrounded by two-story white buildings, their walls pierced by narrow doors and slits for windows.

The Martians had been light-boned and graceful, brown-skinned and golden-eyed, though they had often worn masks when they went out–silver or blue for the men, crimson for the women, gold for the children. Back on Earth, he had seen the images recorded by the earlier expeditions, before the chicken pox killed almost all of them in a matter of weeks. Their flesh had dried to leaves and their bones become sticks; the floors of their homes were littered with the stuff until firemen burned them out.

Mather would have loved to have met a Martian, though he'd heard they could be strange: telepathic, was the prevailing opinion among academics, though with brains that worked at a sideways tangent to what humans meant when they said, "Common sense."

You still heard tales of surviving Martians, spotted at a distance in remote places–like the blue hills behind him. That had been another reason Mather had come that way, just in case.

He sat in the jeep and took a long, slow look at as much of the town as he could see from here. "Get a good overview," his graduate thesis advisor used to say, "before you plunge into the detail. That way the details will form themselves into a pattern sooner and you may save yourself from running up a lot of blind alleys."

The plaza held only one object of note. At the center of the open space that surrounded him was a substantial circular structure, four ascending, concentric rings of white material that would probably turn out to be bone–there was a reason why the dead town was called "the bone city."

Mather could see a bronze pipe standing up from the smallest, highest circle. From it would have flowed water to fill the first round of the four, to trickle over the sides and fill the others in turn. Of course, not a drop of liquid had dampened the object in millennia: this part of Mars was believed to have been abandoned tens of centuries ago, after the seas had vanished and the soft rains that had gently sculpted the hills ceased to come over the green water.

Having finished his survey, Mather climbed out of the jeep, hooked the radio to his belt, and approached the nearest building. Its door was ajar but he had to push it all the way open to squeeze through the narrow entry. He found himself in a circular foyer, its bone walls decorated with lines of copper–once gleaming, now dull– that had been inset into incisions in the white hardness.

Some of the lines were curved, some straight. They met at odd angles and somehow contrived to draw Mather's gaze into what seemed to be three–dimensional shapes. He thought that the silence in the dead town had managed to grow deeper. Then, as he continued to stare, trying to make sense of the forms emerging from the matrix, the lines seemed to move and he experienced a growing vertigo. One moment he was looking into an infinite distance, the next he was sure he was falling into it.

He clapped his hands to his eyes and held them there while he counted slowly to ten. When he took them away he was looking again at lines of verdigrised copper set into bone. He dropped his gaze to the floor, saw a spiral mosaic of gold and silver tiles, faded and half obscured by dust that had drifted through the doorway. At least it did not move.

The radio hissed and squawked again. "Base to Mather," said Bowman's voice, "we're not seeing any transponder signals."

He went outside. "I'm in the town, just scoping for the best sites," he said.

The back seats of the jeep had been taken out to make room for a large wooden box with a hinged lid. Inside, nestled in packing straw, were dozens of small, black oblongs, each one a radio transponder with a telescoping steel antenna that could be pulled up from its top and a red on–off switch.

Mather's job was to place the devices in a rough grid. As he positioned each one, he was to throw its switch to *on*. The transponders would broadcast signals that would delineate the layout of the ancient town to the electronic brain of a huge, tracked machine that was even now being slowly hauled from the base camp down to the dry seabed. Tonight, it would be eased down to the seabed. Tomorrow, it would be transported the rest of the way to the bone town, to be off-loaded at the base of a sloping ramp from which, presumably, the ancient Martians had once launched their shining boats.

The day after tomorrow, the leviathan would trundle up into the town, deploy its hydraulic grapples, and begin stuffing the bone city, piece by piece, into its mechanical maw. It would grind up the town, house by house, separating metal and stone from the ossiferous material that the Martians had built the place from. The valueless stone would be spat out, the metal compacted and excreted like cubic droppings.

But the bone would be pulverized, sacked, and stacked on a detachable trailer that rolled along behind the behemoth. As a trailer was filled, it would be detached and another put in its place. Then the loaded trailer would be hooked to a tractor, and the eight-wheeler would head off across the dry sea until it met the Martian road and canal network. Then it would go to one of the newly built towns that were surrounded by farms whose soil, even after lying fallow for thousands of years, was not all it might be.

The ground bones of Martian cities would fertilize the crops that would feed the tens of thousands of Earthmen arriving each month as the silver-rocket armada continued to cross the black gulf between the worlds.

Mather was one of the most recent arrivals. He had been unable to secure funding to come to Mars as an archaeologist. The new old world needed brawny pioneers, not pointy-headed drips, he was told; what he had not been told was that there had been an archaeologist on one of the early expeditions, a man who had somehow contrived to "go native" even though all the natives were dead of accidentally acquired chicken pox. No more archaeologists need apply.

So he had concocted a resume that would not have stood even the most cursory scrutiny, but New Ares Mining Corporation had contracts to fulfill and was desperate for men to mine the bone cities. Mather was on the next rocket out.

But the trip was long and the quarters close. The men he would be working with soon deduced that Fred Mather had not come, as they had, from the coal mines of Kentucky or the oil leases of west Texas. His hands were too soft and his neck not rough enough. The crew chief, a veteran of the Alaska gold fields, marked him down as a city-boy tenderfoot on a job that had no place for greenhorns.

***

Mather worked quickly, quartering the town on foot, placing the transponders according to a rough map of the town made from an aerial photograph snapped by a New Ares rocket. Two hours after he began, he threw the switch on the last device, then walked back to where he had left the jeep.

He lifted the hood, removed the cover of the carburetor, and dropped a pinch of Martian grit into its barrel. Then he radioed base to say that the vehicle wasn't running right–he suspected dirt in the carburetor or fuel line–so he would stay the night in the town and repair the faulty part in the morning.

"I wouldn't want to risk crashing the jeep coming home in the dark," he said. "Those roads can ice up pretty bad, I hear."

Bowman was on his supper break. The radioman said, "Roger that. Talk to you tomorrow. Base out."

In the dwindling sunlight, Mather dug under the jeep's front seat for the scuffed satchel that contained his field notebook from the jeep. He equipped himself with a heavy–duty flashlight.

"Okay," he said to himself, "let's see what we can do."

***

It was no good saying to the directors and shareholders of New Ares Mining Corporation that the bone cities of Mars were a price-less asset. New Ares accountants and engineers had already worked out the figures: the cities were only priceless in that they were free for the taking; the profits from mining them, however, would start in the tens of millions and climb intro the hundreds. It was conceivable that, if Mars filled up and more of the bone-built towns were found, New Ares's earnings could eventually total a billion.

"Imagine," one of Mather's fellow passengers had said on the trip out, as they swung side by side in their hammocks in the passenger hold. "A billion dollars. And we're part of that."

"Yeah," Mather had said. "Imagine."

The Martians had built their towns mostly out of stone and metal, crystal and glass. They had run water through channels in the floors, to cool the rooms and, Mather hypothesized, their slender feet.

But in some parts of the planet, there had once been a fashion— or it may have been a practical necessity, perhaps a ritual requirement—for building in bone. Martian architects had designed houses walled and floored in thin sheets of ossiferous material that must have been peeled like veneer from the huge bones of great sea creatures. Sometimes, the great ribs and femurs were used whole as structural members, trimmed and squared or rounded to the needed dimensions, often ornately carved into pillars and lintels. Still more of the stuff had been crushed into powder, then bound together with lime to make a durable concrete for roads and doorsteps.

Building in bone made the houses full of a diffuse light that threw no shadows. The material was also porous, so the rooms breathed, even though the windows were narrow and sealed with bronze shutters. The walls also had the quality of absorbing rather than reflecting sound; Mather imagined that conversations in Martian rooms must have been muted, even the shouts and tumults of the coin-eyed children softened and calmed.

He chose houses at random, traversing hallways and peering into chambers. The places were empty, the inhabitants having packed up in no apparent hurry. Occasionally, he found items of abandoned furniture—more bone, a couple of metal frames, the less durable parts long since turned to dust.

In a corner of one upstairs room he found a bone table on which rested a scatter of Martian books. He'd heard of these: sheets of thin silver inscribed in snake-like symbols of indelible blue ink. No one could read them, though it was said that a man from one of the earliest expeditions had done so and become deranged. He'd murdered some of his companions then run off into the hills, only to be tracked down and shot by his captain. The incident had been hushed up, but the version whispered to Mather was that the madman had been an archaeologist.

Mather leafed through the books, but could derive nothing from them, other than that they had been beautifully made. He gazed at a page for almost a minute, waiting to see if he would be drawn into the twisting patterns as he had been with the wall design, ready to drop the book if anything untoward occurred. But nothing did. Finally, he placed the artifacts in his satchel–a violation of his terms of employment–and went outside.

The town sloped gradually from the landward end to the sea, the finger of rock on which it was built also narrowing as it neared the vanished sea. At the very tip, the Martians had laid out a wide plaza, this one without a fountain. The pavement was thousands of small tiles, their original bright colors now faded to pale pastels, arranged in a border of stylized waves and sailing ships, blue and bronze, surrounding a great, sinuous sea creature with huge eyes and triangular flukes.

A broad flight of bone-concrete steps led down from the open space to the harbor, where two curved moles enclosed a sheltered basin with a seaward opening only wide enough for two of the slim, bronzed craft to pass at once.

The buildings that stood at the edge of the open space were grander than the houses he had entered so far. Their entrances were wide, metal doors between carved pillars of bone. The surfaces of the doors were worked in raised snake-script in bas relief. Unlike the mouths of the houses, these were all closed.

It was natural for an archaeologist to wonder when presented with the unexplained behavior of vanished folk. Did the Martians, on the day they abandoned their homes, observe a ritual that decreed their doors must forever lie open? Was there a converse requirement to seal the entrances of public buildings, as Mather assumed the wide-doored edifices to be?

He did not know, would probably never know, but he would enjoy speculating in the professional journals when he returned at last to Earth, the only one of his kind to have done the field work. And so it was with a frisson of anticipation that Fred Mather took hold of the handles of the bronze doors and pulled.

The portals opened easily and he stepped into a wide, well-lit space. The building contained one high-ceilinged room, domed above in thinnest bone so that a translucent illumination fell upon the ringed tiers of seats that descended from the doorway to make a flat-bottomed bowl. In the middle of the amphitheater, rising from the floor, was a great cube of white stone, its top a little higher than the uppermost row of seats.

On the side facing Mather as he stepped down from tier to tier, the surface of the block was incised with a complex design, inlaid with greened-over copper, like the wall in the first house he had entered. It drew his eyes so that his steps began to falter. He lowered himself to a seat midway down the bowl. This time he would study the effect. He pulled his eyes away and fetched out his notebook, unclipped a pen from its wire-spiral spine and took a deep breath.

Then he looked again at the cube. As before, he found that whichever part of the design he focused on, his gaze was pulled toward its center. Abruptly, the two-dimensional pattern took on depth, so that instead of staring *at* something, he was now looking *into* it.

Unable to look away, he flung a forearm across his eyes then used the limb to restrict his vision as he made quick notes on the effect. At one point, he looked up to see if he could sketch the pattern of green on white, but immediately the pulling-in effect resumed—this time even stronger—and he had to use his arm to blind himself again while he noted this new observation.

From the satchel, the radio squawked. He paid it no heed, continued to write. Red Bowman's voice came, harsh and incongruous in this Martian space, "Base to Mather, over."

The archaeologist ignored the summons, continued to make notes. He had a sense that he was about to realize something new and remarkable, to acquire some transformative knowledge to which he would say, at first, "That's incredible!" followed almost immediately by, "But, of course!"

Bowman's voice intruded again on the moment. He reached inside the satchel to switch off the radio, but a momentary flash of cunning stayed his hand: if he didn't answer, they might think he was hurt; if they thought he was hurt, they might come to help him; if they came, they would take him away from . . . from whatever was about to fill him with–

"Base to Mather, are you all right?"

He keyed the mike switch. "Mather to base. What's up?"

"What took you so long?"

The lie came smoothly. "I was cleaning out the carburetor. Wanted to wipe my hands before I picked up the radio."

There was a silence. He could imagine the crew chief digesting the information, filtering it through his undisguised dislike of Fred Mather–an impersonal dislike that extended to all the Mathers of the two worlds, with their soft palms, their long words and longer sentences. He probably suspected that people like him secretly hoarded books that should have been burned on the great bonfires Bowman would remember from his childhood, when the firemen had cleansed the people's minds.

At last, Bowman said, "We may have trouble getting the harvester down the ramp to the seabed tomorrow. It's steeper than it looked. So it might not arrive on schedule."

"Okay," said Mather. "Doesn't bother me."

"But we're all gonna be tied up with this. So if you can't get the jeep running, nobody's gonna come and get you."

"Okay."

"Or bring you any food or water."

Mather shrugged. "I've got sandwiches and a gallon or so. I'll get by."

"You say so," said Bowman. "I wouldn't want to spend too long in one of those places. People have seen ghosts."

"Ghosts don't bother me," said Mather. "Over and out."

He turned off the radio and put it back in the satchel. Then he methodically finished his note-taking. All this time he had been shielding his gaze from the figured cube. Now he took a settling breath and said, "Okay, here we go."

He lowered his arm. The pattern seemed to reach out for him. A small, involuntary gasp escaped him, then he nodded and said, "Ah."

It was the evening of the Calling of the Sea. He had invited neighbors to dine before they went down to the gathering above the harbor. His wife cooked meats in the silvery lava atop the stove in the house, then brought them on golden plates out into the inner courtyard, where they sat on bone chairs and drank the fruited wine from his own trees.

The conversation was relaxed and mellow. The two couples were friends as well as each others' next-doors. They talked of people they knew; the husbands compared their expectations for the coming season's hunt up in the hills; the wives discussed the plays they planned to see—mostly timeless revivals, though there was to be a new work by a playwright from across the sea, who was developing a reputation for deliberately stimulating his audiences.

When the meal was done and the last, formal toast drunk, they went down to the festival, through darkening streets lit by crystal torches and aflow with golden-eyed folk in their holiday clothes. No one wore a mask this night; it was not a time for circumspection.

The plaza by the sea was thronged. All of the town was there, the oldest given places on the steps of the surrounding buildings, the youngest on the shoulders of their parents, so that all could witness the Calling. A coterie of musicians played the festival anthem and the crowd swayed, humming to the ancient song.

As the last notes died, all of them turned toward the harbor. The boats that usually filled most of the circular basin had been rowed to the sides, tethered to bronze rings set in the stones of the moles or to each other, so that a wide channel lay open from the foot of the steps to the gap where the enclosing barriers did not meet.

One musician struck a single, plangent tone from his harp. As one, the crowd craned forward. Now a sound somewhere between a sigh and a moan rose up from each throat. It mingled and became one common note, rising not in volume but in intensity. It filled the plaza like an invisible mist, then it flowed down the steps and across the harbor and out over the sea. And carried with it a single thought.

Minutes piled upon minutes, became almost an hour, the sound continuously pouring from the crowd, the thought uniting them. Then, out beyond the harbor mouth, the waveless summer sea rippled, once, twice. A triangular-fluked tail rose and slapped the surface gently. A dark, gleaming back showed then disappeared, then came up once more, in the channel between the boats.

The monotonous song intensified. Golden eyes shone in the torchlight. A pressure wave rolled across the surface of the basin and wet the bottom steps As the water ran back down, the sea parted. A broad-mouthed head broke the surface, its eyes as big as dinner plates, though these were not gold, but resembled silver-rimmed onyx.

The sea beast's tail thrashed, driving its head and forefins clear of the water and up onto the harbor steps. The crowd's moaning song grew stronger still, the carried thought more imperative. The tail went deep, scraping the floor of the basin, the sinuous body hunched and straightened, and as water ran from its dark, striated skin back into the sea, the summoned creature forced itself higher up the stairs, until its head touched the plaza's tiles.

Silence fell. The women took the children to join the old people, while the men descended the steps to stand on either side of the sea beast. The sky above the town was black, the stars like chips of bone. The harpist plucked another string. In one motion, the men drew their curved knives, then waited for the final note.

Fred Mather awoke to find himself in near-total darkness at the top of the steps above the dry harbor. The stars and the two small moons gave just enough light to show the bone town as a pale fog seen from the corners of his eyes, but when he looked straight ahead he could see almost nothing. The sky was as black as it had been in the vision, but near the horizon he could see the small green orb that was Earth. He did not know how long he had been standing at the top of the steps, but it had been long enough for the wind off the dead seabed to chill him. Shivering, he rubbed the pebbled skin of his bare forearms.

He had to make notes. He felt his way back to the amphitheater and to the seat where he had left the satchel. His notepad was not there, but the flashlight was. By its hard beam he found the spiral-bound book outside. It lay on the tiled surface of the plaza, covering the eye of the sea-creature mosaic. He went and retrieved it, found the pen a few feet away.

But when he sat on a doorstep to write by the flashlight's glow, the making of ink marks on paper struck him as faintly ridiculous. The straight and curved blue lines would cease to resolve themselves into words and become mere chicken-scratchings, as if his ability to read was waxing and waning.

His mind kept going back to the vision of the festival: the death of the sea beast, the solemn taking of its flesh and the wrapping of the dripping pieces in squares of cloth the women had brought with them, the people walking home, leaving the creature's bones to be cared for by those who had earned that honor.

And something else. He did not know how he knew it, but he was aware that this Calling had been the last, that there were no more beasts left to call. He struggled to put that knowledge into words, then transpose the words into letters of blue ink scratched onto paper. But he kept losing the knack.

Finally, he abandoned the effort and lit his way back into the amphitheater. Some instinct told him to sit in another part of the great room, facing another side of the cube. He stared into its matrix of incised lines and instantly felt himself falling into . . .

They were four, all friends from boyhood now grown to maturity. They had trained hard, challenging each other, encouraging each other, daring each other. And it had paid off: they had been victorious in the annual games and had thus won the honor of being the first hunting party into the blue hills above the bone town.

They ran now in single file along a trail they had known as children, when they had played at what they now did in earnest. They knew every curve and fold of the land, the ridges, shoulders and valleys, and they knew as well that there was a certain place where the flamebirds sheltered through the day, emerging at dusk to light up the night sky with their scintillating streaks and fire-trails, sparks falling like red snow.

It was a tall and narrow cave mouth, where the ground had parted a million years ago. But such was the lie of the land that the crevice was almost invisible unless viewed from a precise angle. The four men knew that angle, knew the chamber that widened behind the slit of the opening. In there, the flamebirds would be sleeping, huddled together on the ground like a pool of banked embers, rustling and breathing together.

The four hunters crept to the mouth of the cleft, wire nets ready. Still in single file, they scraped backs and chests against the rough rock–it had been easier when they were boys–and eased into the cavern. Silently, breath abated, they ranged themselves around the sleeping quarry. Then, at a signal from the eldest, they cast their nets in a prearranged sequence.

The flamebirds awoke as the first net fell, and rose up as one, swiftly bearing the wire mesh aloft. But the second net fell, its edges weighted, and the birds' upward motion slowed. Then came the third net, and the fourth. Weighed down, the overlapping meshes too dense to escape through, the creatures settled back to the floor with a mournful sound.

Elated, the hunters carefully rought the borders of the nets together, made a bundle whose gathered mouth they briskly tied with metal cords.

The birds, pressed into a sphere, flowed rustling over each other, like a boiling sun of gold and red. The men used their weapons to widen the crevice then gently bore the flamebirds out into the sunlight. The creatures voiced their displeasure, but the hunters struck up the traditional hymn of consolation with its promises of respect and good treatment.

The birds quieted, whether soothed by the blandishments or lulled by the sonorous rhythm of the song. Where the road left the hills and ran down to the town, the men stopped to order their garments and brush off any dust or detritus. Then they hoisted the netted birds over their heads like a collective halo and, at a measured pace, made their triumphant return.

Before they were halfway to the spiral–pillared gate, the people were coming out to sing them home.

———— ✦ ————

The song was still echoing in Mather's mind when he came back to the here and now. He was not surprised to find himself outside the gate at the landward end of town. The shrunken sun was graying the Martian sky from somewhere behind the rumpled silhouette of the hills, making the road of crushed white stone to shine ghostly at his feet.

This time, he did not even think to write any notes. He turned and walked slowly–he was unaccountably tired–through the dead town, back to the harbor plaza. Although he had not eaten or drunk in quite some time, he passed by the sandwiches and water can in the jeep without noticing them.

———※———

"He's mostly just dehydrated," said the roughneck who'd had first-aid training. "The air's so dry here, if you forget to keep drinking you can start to get woozy pretty fast."

"Pour another cup into him," said Bowman, "then put him in the shade."

They'd found Mather face-down on the tiles of the harbor plaza when the truck carrying the mining machine arrived in the late afternoon of the second day. Now, as Bowman leafed through the notebook he'd found not far from the collapsed man, he knew why Mather hadn't been answering his radio calls since the day before.

Most of it was illegible scribbles, but a few words stood out— *communal, ritual, bonding*—enough to confirm the crew chief's long-held suspicion that Mather was another one of those long-haired intellectuals who got all Mars-struck and came out here thinking they'd find . . . What? Bowman had no idea what kind of foolishness filled a mind like Mather's. And he didn't want to.

He went to the top of the harbor steps and threw the notebook down toward where the mechanical behemoth's front tracks were already finding purchase on the bottom riser. Black smoke belched from the machine's exhaust as the operator goosed the throttle, and it began to climb, the bone steps cracking and powdering beneath grinding metal. The right-side track reached Mather's book and shredded it.

Bowman watched to make sure the miner was coming on the way it was designed to. When it reached the top and its front end crashed down onto the tiles, he ordered the operator out and climbed into the control compartment. The machine's screen lit up, green on black, showing a gridwork based on bright points: the transponders Mather had placed, thankfully before he went outbacky-wacky, as Bowman had once heard an Australian desert miner describe it.

The radio signals were all five-by-five. Bowman set the controls, stepped down from the cab, and watched as the great machine oriented itself and set to work. It labored over to the building nearest the harbor steps, deployed its heavy chain-link thrashers, and began to demolish the front wall in a spray of bone dust and chips.

"Looks good," the crew chief said, shouting to his men over the noise of the automated miner. "Let's get the jeep down here. You can put it on the truck. I want to get back to base before it's too dark. First drink's on me."

But when they were all loaded and ready to go, he sent a man to fetch Fred Mather. But Mather was gone.

The silvery-paged books were not really books, Mather now knew. The raised hieroglyphic squiggles weren't meant for the Martian eye, but for Martian fingers. You ran the pads of the fingertips over the sinuous forms and out came, not text, but music. The songs formed in your head and played themselves out as you stroked the pages: all kinds of songs—from dancing tunes to soft ballads, from hymns to anthems, but each one tinged with a melancholic sweetness that he had come to associate with Martianness.

In his lucid moments, he contemplated the balance and the contrast that were inherent in the meeting of Martians and Earthmen: one race was fading into its purple twilight just as the other was setting out to see what the bright day would bring.

Over the music, he cold hear Bowman and some other men calling his name. He was disappointed. He'd thought that when they set off back to camp, they'd report him as missing and forget about him. People did wander off on Mars, never to be seen again. And he had not made any friends among the miners. They'd all seen him for the ugly duckling he was.

But, as he sat in the flamebirds' cave and thought about it, he recognized that they'd have had to come back to restart the machine. The morning after they'd left, he'd climbed aboard and thrown the big main switch that stopped it. The machine paused in its digestion of a house that stood halfway between the harbor and the gate. The land leviathan had been making substantial progress. Earthmen knew how to build reliable machinery.

But there were books to be gathered, and a few other objects the Martians had left behind: masks, some children's toys, items of clothing, even some weapons. He'd wanted to bring them to the cave. But when he'd gathered all that he could find and returned to restart the miner, he found that he did not know how to set its controls to follow the transponder grid. So he had left it with its engine idling in neutral, knowing that Red Bowman would come out in the jeep to get it running again.

He had hoped that they'd think the miner had malfunctioned on its own, but the calling voices from outside the cave told him that the crew chief was not given to innocent explanations. Mather crept to the narrow mouth, which he'd made even harder to see by dragging prickle bushes into the cleft. Through the thin branches, he could see Bowman and the others. They were standing on a ridge line, cupping their calloused hands around their mouths to call his name. They had binoculars. They also had guns.

The men looked for him all day, but Mather remembered the Martian hunting skills he'd acquired from the memory visions–that's what he had taken to calling the phenomena–and he had no trouble avoiding capture. In the evening, the searchers climbed into the jeep and drove off across the empty sea. From the hills, he watched their dust plume hang in the air almost motionless, so slowly did the fine particles sift down in the lesser gravity and the windless Martian air.

When full darkness fell, he went down to the town. He had discovered that the lines incised into the walls of the houses performed a similar function to those graven into the sides of the cube. But, whereas the latter were memory-visions of public events, the ones in the houses were of private occasions. They were the Martians' family photo albums.

At first he had thought he should disable the machine completely, to save these intimate records. But after sampling several, he realized that they were all much the same: memories of births and deaths and unions, naming-day ceremonies and other mundane rites of passage. But each was imbued with the same soft sadness that permeated the communal gatherings. These were not records taken from the middle of a community's life, but from its end. They were memorials, left by the long-ago Martians when they packed up their possessions and, leaving the doors of their houses open, went away forever.

Red Bowman was not happy. He had a production schedule to fulfill. Having the automated miner standing idle because crazy Mather had interfered with its controls threatened the crew chief's chances of winning the substantial bonus that would be due him if he delivered truckloads of bone fertilizer before the specified date. So when the jeep had gone far enough out across the seabed, he stopped it and got off, sending it on to base with the other men while he walked back along its vague track, trudging through the fine dust to the bone town.

Night fell before he got there, but he could see the white towers glimmering before him, occasionally lit be sparks and flashes as the tireless machine grinding its way through the walls encountered metal. But even if he'd been blind, Bowman could have found his way just by going toward the sound of the diesel engines. Or by the stench of its exhaust.

He came up the harbor steps and crossed the plaza. The sea beast's image was almost completely defaced by the miner's tracks. The behemoth's mechanical growls faded as it turned a far-off corner in its programmed course, putting walls between it and the Earthman. Bowman used the lull to listen for sounds of Mather moving about the town. In a few moments, he heard something.

At first he thought it was a wind wuthering beneath a building's eaves. But there was no wind, and the Martians' roofs were flat and no wider than the walls that supported them. He moved in the direction of the sound. It was coming from across the plaza, from one of the larger buildings that the behemoth would not reach for a couple of days.

The place had a bronze door, figured in the flowing script that Bowman did not like to look at; it reminded him of snakes, and snakes reminded him of the Devil. He sometimes wondered if there had been a deal between God and Lucifer: God would rule on Earth and the Devil would have Mars. He'd heard tales of how the Martians had flown on wings of fire and cooked their dinners in molten rock. That sounded to him like the kind of thing that would go on in Hell.

He eased through the door, a flashlight ready for use in his left hand, a pistol in his right. He didn't want to have to shoot Mather, but everybody knew the story of Spender, the man on the fourth edition who'd gone mad and murdered his crewmates. He thought Spender might have been an archaeologist–some kind of ologist, for sure–and he'd gone kill-crazy after rubbing up against too much Martian evil.

The sound came again, a keening, crooning note without words. It was like something a cat would sing, Bowman thought, maybe to a mouse it had caught. He didn't like cats either. Killing was all right when you had to, but you ought to do it clean.

He could dimly see the general layout inside the building: an open space, seats or steps in descending circles, a great white shape at the bottom. The sound came from the opposite side, louder now that Bowman was inside the place and the hoo-hooing was echoing off the bone walls. The hairs on his neck and forearms rose of their own accord. He slid his thumb over his weapon's safety catch, making sure it was off.

He edged around the upper deck of the amphitheater. Against the white vagueness he saw a dark shape, seated halfway down the tiers. He readied the pistol then thumbed the switch on the flashlight.

A Martian sat in the middle of the terraced seats, clad in a robe of metallic cloth that dully reflected the beam. His whole head was enclosed in a cloche-mask of silver, the facial features chased in gold, the thin eyebrows elevated and the mouth pursed in an expression of permanent surprise. Bowman could not see the color of the eyes through the mask's slits, but the figure's gaze did not turn to him. Instead, it remained fixed on the side of the cube down in front.

The Earthman played the flashlight's beam over the man. He could see the hands, five-fingered instead of six. From beneath the robe came the cuffs of the blue jeans they all wore, and the scuffed boots were also New Ares company issue.

"Mather!" Bowman called. The man in Martian garb gave no sign of having heard. The crew chief moved in on the runaway, keeping the beam on him, with the pistol lined up just beside and behind the flashlight. "Mather!"

The masked head did not turn, the limbs did not move. Bowman stood beside him, poked his shoulder with the muzzle of the gun. "Snap out of it!"

Still no response. Bowman set the flashlight down on one of the tiered seats so that it illuminated the still figure. Then he hooked his fingers below the rim of the head-enclosing mask and yanked upwards.

The Martian warriors marched to battle in gleaming companies of one hundred and forty-four. Six companies made a battalion of eight hundred and sixty-four. They carried shields of hammered bronze that matched their burnished armor, and guns capable of spitting streams of metal insects that, finding flesh, would sting and burrow. On their flanks and scouting ahead raced knee-high electric spiders, their joints clicking with a rhythm that combined into a continuous whir.

Six battalions had gone out through the bone gate of Ipsli, almost the town's entire male complement. They took the coastal road toward Huq, and by mid-day they arrived at the chosen field, a place where the hills fell back to widen the coastal plain. They formed their battle line, four battalions in front, two in reserve, and sat down to await the enemy.

The Huq army came late, earning themselves some justified mocking from Ipsli. Questions were shouted across the open ground as to whether they'd had something better to do today, whether their mist-beds had been too comfortable to leave. Or their wives.

Huq replied with taunts of their own, recalling past encounters when Ipsli's war aims had not been realized. Then the heralds went to meet in the space between the two hosts, to decide on the order of battle. As usual, it would be individual combats first, then small groups. Ipsli's first battalion was anxious for a rematch with their Huq counterparts; it was felt that last year's engagement was decided more by the state of the ground—it had rained the night before—than by the relative skills of the combatants.

Youths fought first, with minimized weapons. Then came the mid-ranked warriors, in pairs and quatrains. Ipsli was doing well, only two deaths and one maiming, while several Huqs had had to be carried from the field. Sentiment within the ranks was leaning toward ending the day with a general melée.

There came a break for lunch while the spiders fought their bouts. Huqs and Ipslis wagered against each other on the outcomes, the heralds holding the takes and disbursing the winnings. Then it was time for individual champions to take the field.

Fred Mather was in the form of Ipsli's paramount, wearing his great-great-grandsire's armor of laminated strips of bronze overlaid with polished electrum. When, late in the afternoon, the trumpets called his sign, he took up the long spear with the black shaft bound with strengthening wire. He disdained to fight with a shield.

As he stepped out in front of Ipsli, the spear over his shoulder, a shout went up from the battalions behind him. He strode toward the center of the field, watching as the Huq champion came to meet him. Unlike last year, his opponent had chosen only the long, two-handed electric sword. It would be a memorable contest, Mather thought. Next year, they might well be singing songs about today.

He had gotten used to the strangeness of being two persons in one mind. The Martian memory-visions were like the documentary dramas he had seen on television at home, where actors took the parts of historical figures—except that here the spectator took the actor's place. He had wondered at first if the experience was similar to what fiction books had done to readers, before the firemen had cleansed the world.

Now Mather-as-warrior strode calmly to where the heralds waited on the fighting ground. He grounded the butt of his spear, then tipped back his helmet to rest on it on the crown of his long, narrow head. The man who had come out to face him set his sword's point against the turf and tilted back his own headgear. His golden eyes gazed at Mather with no sign of fear.

The first herald sang the traditional song. As he heard the last line begin, Mather gripped the shaft of the spear, took a slow and steady breath and pulled his helmet down. He assumed the ready stance. The swordsman also covered his face and raised his blade.

Bowman yanked the cloche-mask clear of the nutjob's face, but it fit too tightly to come all the way off. Mather's eyes, in the flashlight beam, were wide and opaque. For a moment, they looked almost golden, but the crew chief put that down to a reflection of the pale bone walls in the man's grossly dilated pupils.

Mather blinked, once, then after a moment, twice more.

"Snap out of it!" Bowman said. He poked him again with the pistol's muzzle.

The archaeologist came up off the bench, turning toward the crew chief in one fluid motion. With the back of his left hand he brushed the pistol away, while his right struck out at Bowman's belly. But the blow did not connect, and not just because the other man stumbled back.

Mather looked down at his right hand, as if puzzled. From the way he held it, Bowman first had the impression that there was something in the madman's grasp—did the Martians have invisible knives?—and that he had tried to stick him with it. But then, as he saw Mather blink, Bowman realized that the crackpot must be seeing things.

Somehow that made him more angry than anything yet. It wasn't right that this soft-handed college boy's insanity was threatening Red Bowman's bonus and the life it would buy for him here on Mars: a place of his own, and a solid business to run. He was willing to work hard for what he wanted, and no dreamy-eyed book-fiend was going to rob him of his earned reward.

He stepped forward and smacked Mather across the side of the head with the pistol barrel. But the steel did not hit flesh. Instead it struck the dull gleam of the Martian head covering. The sound of the impact was a musical note, but the helmet seemed to absorb the shock. Mather barely registered the blow.

Yet something had gotten through. The archaeologist blinked again, and now it seemed for the first time that he was actually focusing on the crew chief. He looked down again at his right hand, curled around empty air. Then he shook his head as if coming out of a daze.

"You're coming with me," Bowman said. He raised the gun, and so that the madman would have no doubt know as to the consequences of disobedience, he thumbed back the hammer.

Mather's shoulders slumped. He reached up with both hands and wriggled the silver cloche-mask free of his head. He lowered it and gazed sadly at its polished, figured surface, the perpetual surprise that looked back at him. Then, when Bowman said, "Move it," he flung the metal object up and into the crew chief's face.

Bowman fell back, blood spurting from his nose. He lost his footing and toppled over the bench seat beside him, banging the elbow of his gun arm. The pistol fell, clattering on the bone floor right beside his foot, and he was glad it did not go off. But by the time he had recovered the weapon and swung the flashlight around, he had only enough time to catch Mather disappearing through the door to the plaza, the Martian robe flying like a flag from his shoulders.

He hunted for the madman all night, light and gun at the ready. He meant to shoot on sight, but when the thin Martian dawn came he was still alone.

———⚭———

The mechanical behemoth ground on, house by house, street by street, filling its hoppers with the dust of millennia-dead sea beasts, excreting its cubes of metal, still warm from the atomic smelter. Bowman fretted that Mather would return from his hiding place in the blue hills and try to stop the work. He took men from other projects, gave them guns, and put them on guard.

The sentries reported seeing occasional flashes of sunlight on metal up in the blue hills, but the madman made no more attempts to interfere with the reduction of the bone city. Finally, the day came when they reloaded the automated miner onto its multi-wheeled trailer and prepared to haul it across the dusty, glass-bottomed sea to the next deposit. The operation proceeded without incident.

Red Bowman's bonus was safe again. He had been a man short for a while, but had managed to make up a full crew's complement by hiring an experienced hard-rock mining man who had come to Mars hoping to prospect in the barrens but had found nothing.

The crew chief watched the semitrailer haul the leviathan away, throwing up its floating contrail of pale dust. Then he started up his jeep and drove through the scar where the town had been. The houses were gone, as well as the pavement of the streets on which they had stood for thousands of years. The miner had scraped right down to the packed earth beneath, and in places to the rufous Martian bedrock. After it had uncovered the first urn buried beneath a courtyard, Bowman had called in the technician to reset the automatic controls. The machine had then proceeded to find scores of the gold, silver, and electrum containers, increasing the operation's precious-metals yield by a solid percentage. New Ares had awarded Bowman an "attaboy" bonus for showing initiative.

He came to where the gate had stood and put the jeep onto the ribbon of crushed white rock. He drove slowly toward the hills then up into them as the road began to climb. He moved his gaze from side to side, watching for flashes of light.

The hills always gave him the creeps. They were as silent as the ancient towns, but somehow the silence was different here. The towns were not human-made, but they had been manufactured by beings who, for all their peculiarities, shared some commonalities with Earthmen. The land itself, though, that was pure Mars. It had never had any connection to humankind, not all the way back to the gelling of the planets. Men might come and build on it, but they would never be *of* it. And those who tried to be of it, like Spender and Mather, would always be driven mad.

That was Bowman's way of thinking, and before he moved off to the next demolition he wanted to talk about it with the one man he knew who might understand. So he drove higher into the hills, stopping every now and then, his head turning from side to side, waiting for the bright wink.

Late in the afternoon, he saw it from the corner of an eye and turned toward the long, boulder-strewn slope from which it had come. There was a group of tall rocks halfway up the hill. They might have been a natural occurrence, or they might have been placed there for some obscure Martian purpose. But when he trained his binoculars on the formation, he saw motion through a gap between two of the stones.

He got out of the jeep and walked toward the place, his hands held out to show that they were empty. "Mather!" he called. "We're leaving! Nobody's going to come after you!"

A voice came from the rocks, thin on the less substantial Martian air. It had a whistling quality, as if a musical instrument were speaking. "What do you want?"

"I just wanted to say goodbye," Bowman said. He was closer now, close enough to see between the gaps in the rocks. He saw silver and touches of gold. "You know," he said, "that mask rightly belongs to New Ares Mining."

"No," said the flutey voice, "I don't know that."

"Doesn't matter," Bowman said. "We'll get it later, I suppose. After you die."

There was no response to that.

"You are going to die, you know," said the Earthman, trudging up the slope. "Fact is, I don't know how you've managed to survive this long without water. Were you sneaking in at night to steal it?"

"No."

"Then how?"

Again there was no answer. Bowman had reached the rocks. He could see glimpses of Mather through the gaps. The man was wearing the Martian robe and another mask, this one with an expression of serene amusement. "Come out and we'll talk," he said.

"About what?"

The crew chief shrugged. "About what you're going to do, how you're going to live."

"Does that matter to you?" said the musical voice.

"A little. Listen, at first, I was angry at having you on my crew, because I didn't think you'd pull your weight. Then I got scared that you'd screw up the operation and wreck everything."

Bowman waited a moment to see if the other man would respond, then said, "But once you left us alone to get on with it, you were not my problem anymore. I could afford to wonder about what you think you're achieving up here."

He waited again, this time letting the silence extend. It made him uncomfortable. He was thinking that it wasn't just a silence between him and Mather; it was a silence between him and the hills, between him and Mars.

Finally, the man behind the rocks spoke. "There's nothing to achieve."

"Then what are you doing?"

"There's nothing to do. Nothing to be done."

"I don't understand."

"It's all *been* done," said Mather. "That's the point. That's what Mars is."

"I still don't understand."

"I know." There was another silence, then although Bowman had heard no footsteps, Mather's musical voice came as if from farther away. "Goodbye."

The Earthman skirted the standing rocks and climbed above them. There was no sign of the other man. He called his name, twice, but heard only the eloquent silence of the Martian hills.

Bowman went back to the jeep, back to the base camp, then on to the next job. In later years, he would sometimes tell people, "Just because you can come up with a question, that doesn't mean there's an answer."

Some years later, a prospector came by, his picks and shovels and magnetometer clattering with each step of his walking machine.

He spotted the cube of white stone that the automated miner had left as valueless and went to take a look. To one side he found a mummified corpse clothed in Martian cloth, seated on a chair carved from Martian wood. A silver mask rested on the desiccated lap.

At first, the prospector thought he'd discovered a genuine Martian, though people said they were all gone now. It was the eyes that fooled him, wide and dried, and turned toward the cube, they had looked from a distance like golden coins.

But the mask was a good one. The prospector's day had not been wasted.

SHADOW MAN

Another of my interests is the psychopath. Researchers say that, depending on the definition, some three to five per cent of the people around us score high on the psychopathy scale. Having spent some time around political leaders and heads of major corporations, I agree with the view that those fields tend to attract the intelligent psychopath (the dumb ones are attracted to the kind of impulsive criminal activity that makes the rest of us say, "What on earth was that idiot thinking of?")

Damien Bonnespine, unfortunately, is not attracted to business or politics nor is he dumb.

FOR AS LONG as he could remember, Damien Bonnespine knew somebody was there, watching him.

Not all the time. There were long spells between the moments when he would feel the shiver across his shoulders that made his neck hairs stand up. But eventually it would happen again and he'd know they were back. Then for the next few minutes he'd feel them watching him.

He couldn't see them, and he always thought of them as a crowd of shadow men—no faces, no details, just vague silhouettes with shaded eyes turned his way. When he was little it had creeped him out, but nothing bad ever came of it. He didn't feel threatened, just watched.

When he was nine he told the mom. She gave him the same scared but careful look he already recognized, even back then, as a signal that some of the thoughts that slowly bubbled up to break at the surface of his mind were best kept unsaid. Thoughts about pain and how animals squirmed and yelped when things happened to them. How interesting it would be to know if people squirmed and yelped like that.

When Damien was fifteen, the mom found the cat trap and the stuff he kept in a box way back in the crawl space under the house. She took him to a doctor. There were machines and needles and stupid pictures he had to look at and talk about, but some of the doctor's other pictures were way cool–dead people, and some who were not dead yet, but were opened up like the cats, showing slick red meat and yellowy bones.

One time, while he was looking at the pictures and talking about them, he felt the familiar chill across his shoulders and the tickle of hairs lifting. The doctor must have seen something in Damien's face because he said, "What are you thinking now?"

Damien told him. The man made notes on his pad and asked a lot more questions. "Were there voices? Do the voices want you to do things?"

Damien said there were no voices but he didn't think the doctor believed him. They made him take pills that filled his head with cold, silent noise. He couldn't think and sometimes when he tried to talk the words got lost for a while. He stopped going to school but the mom got him lessons from the school board to do at home and a computer that connected to a tutor. But one day he was so interested in a picture he had found on the Internet that he didn't hear her come in until she was looking over his shoulder. She took the machine away.

Now, at eighteen, Damien Bonnespine used the public library's computers to look at pictures. His interest had broadened and he read about interesting people: Jeffrey Dahmer, John Wayne Gacy, Richard Ramirez, Frank Spisak. He was living in an abandoned butcher's shop near the cement plant. Some other kids slept in the rooms upstairs but they let Damien have the downstairs all to himself. He had stopped taking the pills and now his head was hot and busy again.

It was morning and Damien was thinking about the new girl who had come back to the squat with the others yesterday. She was only thirteen and her button nose and slanted, almond–shaped eyes reminded him of a cat. He was sitting on the old counter top, the wood scarred with cuts and scratches, letting his thoughts circle the girl when he felt the familiar shivery prickle.

He paid no attention, concentrated on the pictures in his head. Then he caught a flutter of motion to one side. He didn't turn toward it, just let his head drift a little in that direction until, from the corner of his eye, he saw the shadow man.

It was like seeing something on tv when thunderstorms screwed up the reception: a man shape, dark but without detail of features or clothing, speckled with dots that flickered and flashed.

Damien turned his head an inch more and saw that the staticky man was not watching him now. He was bent over, poking at something where his waist would be.

The years of catching cats had made Damien very fast. He set himself, inhaled a long, deep breath–then, as he let it out, he threw himself from the counter top and crossed the room with one long stride and a flying leap.

His outstretched hands sank into the dots and sparks and met cloth–covered flesh beneath. The man squawked and tried to pull free but Damien yanked the shadow man toward him while shooting his head forward like a striking snake so that his forehead connected hard where the watcher's face should be. He felt bone snap and heard a gargly yelp.

The man was not big but Damien was. He lifted the watcher off his feet and slammed him against the door of the long gone butcher's walk–in cooler, did it again and again until the body flopped loose in his grip.

He let it slide to the floor. It was still flickering and winking but that was the only movement. Damien reached into the static and felt around the waist where the man had been poking. He found a belt with a row of studs on it, traced his fingers along its length to a clasp. He undid the fastener and pulled the belt free.

Now his hand was encased in a blur of light and dark. Damien felt for the studs, pressed them singly and in combinations, but the effect didn't change. Then the belt gave a hiss that became a hum that grew louder before it abruptly stopped. The sparks and shadows disappeared and Damien could see his hand again. It was holding a strip of metallic fabric set with a panel of buttons. From the panel came a smell of fire and ozone.

Damien poked at the controls some more but the thing was dead. He turned his attention back to its owner and saw a small man with a sharp–featured face that put Damien in mind of a ferret. He had been pretty bald for someone so young but Damien could tell from the interesting angle of his neck that he wouldn't have to worry about getting any older.

The body was wearing a one–piece jumpsuit with a peculiar fastening system down the front. There were pockets but nothing interesting in them. Tied to one wrist by a looped cord was a small, flat oblong of metal about half the size of a cigarette pack.

Damien freed the object and examined it. He identified what

looked to be a lens and next to it a pinpoint microphone. There were controls etched into the side and the upper surface. He touched them. At first nothing happened, then suddenly a screen appeared in the air, crowded with symbols and icons. There was writing, too, but Damien couldn't read it. It looked vaguely Chinese.

Damien reached out a finger to one of the icons. Dozens of thumbnail images flooded the scene, and when he touched one of the miniatures it expanded to fill the viewing space and the figures in it began to move.

Damien recognized the scene: the attic in Gacy's house. He'd seen a tv movie about it but they hadn't shown anything interesting. But now, as he watched, he understood. This wasn't a movie. This was real.

He found how to minimize the image and touched another of the main screen's icons. He watched, fascinated, for a few moments. That was Dahmer's kitchen. There he was at the stove, humming. Another selection and Damien was watching Bundy creeping into a darkened bedroom. Then a man he didn't recognize, in a city where the cars flew, and another in some place where the sky was red.

He ran through the entire menu, sampling, mentally marking the ones he wanted to come back to first. Until an image brought a sharp intake of breath: the cramped space beneath his mother's house, a figure lit by a flashlight kneeling in the back corner, putting on his heavy gloves to lift a spitting, struggling tabby out of the trap.

He watched his juvenile self, reliving the memory. Then he canceled the image and chose another: looking at the pictures in the doctor's office; then the time with the stray mongrel and the propane torch.

But there were pictures he didn't remember, couldn't have remembered. They showed a Damien grown into his twenties, into his thirties, showed him in places he'd never been, with people he hadn't met yet.

He turned his eyes from the screen and regarded the body slumped against the grimy wall. Damien had never known what people meant when they said they regretted things they'd done. Now he almost understood.

He wished he could talk to the man. They had had a lot in common. As he dragged him into the cooler, Damien felt that it had been—he sought for the right word, then found it—an *unfortunate* way to treat his first fan.

He turned back to the images of the future Damien, watched the way he did things, how he controlled the situations. He thought again about the girl with the cat's eyes and began to make some mental notes.

WIDOW'S MITE

Twenty or so years ago, I knew a guy who was editing a short-lived local magazine called Minus Tides. *He asked me to write a short-short (what they now call flash fiction). This little story is the result.*

TO FLEISCHBURGH on a smooth-gaited horse came Witchfinder Schiffler, pale as curdled milk, jaded eyes sliding sideways like eggs in a greasy pan.

Before him stepped Interrogator Arboghast, neat as a fox. Behind lumbered pate-shaved, slab-shouldered Ludenko, his dread instruments clanking in a sack.

Sudden errands called the townsfolk indoors, to watch and whisper, and wonder whose name Arboghast would scratch in black ink on blanched parchment, to place in his crimson wallet.

At the guildhall, the burgomeisters offered their best ales and meats. Names were spoken: a dyer with a mark on his face; a weaver's daughter; a hunchback by the wool market; a horse coper's widow.

Schiffler voiced soft questions, stroked his nose, pursed his lips like an unripe plum. His slender fingers offered languid gestures. Arboghast wrote down the widow's name. The Witchfinder affixed his seal, and selected a pasty.

The townsfolk most feared Arboghast. Schiffler was remote, Ludenko a mere brute. But Arboghast came to people's doors, archers loitering at his heels. Peering from beneath russet brows, he'd smile and open the red wallet, stretching the terrible time before pronouncing the name.

The widow cried her innocence to heedless stone walls. Time somehow passed. Arboghast intoned questions. Ludenko pressed, twisted, worked his gyres and levers with surprising subtlety.

They left her gasping, staring bewildered at ruined fingers. The first day was commonly like this: heartfelt denials, then the wonderment of the pain minor, slowly opening into the lonely night preceding the *travail majeure*.

Arboghast returned to the guildhall. Schiffler and the burgomeisters were apportioning the widow's estate. By law, a third was the town's, a third the church's, a third the Witchfinder's. The widow must also pay for Ludenko's wages and materials, but that was a pittance.

The burgomeisters bowed and ducked their way out. Schiffler separated some coins from the heap on the table, slid them toward Arboghast, and poured the rest into a brassbound coffer.

The Interrogator regarded the coins. "Little enough for demanding work," he said.

"Then seek a more rewarding office," said the Witchfinder.

"Master..." continued Arboghast.

Schiffler sniffed. "The issue is tiresome and long settled."

In the morning, the widow responded satisfactorily. Arboghast could soon proceed to the Articles of Contrition. By lunchtime, there remained only the soliciting of accomplices' names.

Over game pie, Arboghast said, "Arduous labors merit proper recompense."

Schiffler folded his hands. "Elicit good prospects from the widow. There is your path to prosperity."

The Interrogator returned stiff-legged to the work. The widow compliantly sobbed four names. Arboghast disregarded each; instead, he penned a fifth in his spiky hand.

By sundown, the fire had dwindled, the ashes lifting on the smoke-stained breeze. Arboghast whispered to the burgomeisters. Glances were exchanged. Heads nodded.

At midnight, Arboghast knocked. His sleep broken, Schiffler flung open his door. Rough men secured him with cords.

Smiling, Arboghast brought the parchment from his wallet. The coffer's brass edgings glowed by candlelight. The Interrogator's lips parted to frame a name.

FROM THE DISCOURSES AND EDIFICATIONS OF LIW OSFEO

In the introduction to this volume, I said that it was a collection of non–Archonate stories. The following is the partial exception. These little homilies of Liw Osfeo appeared in a book–within–a–book in my first novel, Fools Errant. *At the time, I was much enamored of the Sufi tales about the mullah Nasruddin. Come to think of it, I still am.*

THE COUNTY OF KERAPH boasted three noble cities, each jealous of its independence and time-honored privileges, yet each cooperating with the others in mutual endeavors.

The city of Caer Lyff was largest of the three, and produced the sophisticated baubles upon which, all agreed, civilization depended. The city of Alathe was somewhat smaller; its ateliers and factories manufactured the less intricate but no less necessary goods without which civilization rapidly descends to barbarism. Finally, the city of Dai was smallest of all, but its sturdy citizens raised the crops and kine which fed all Keraph.

In the centre of the county, housed in the old ducal grounds, was the Institute. Here scholars and academes rubbed shoulders with chymists and apparaticists, and all combined to provide Keraph with the refinements of modern learning. Besides instructing the worthiest of the county's youth in useful arts and abilities, the Institute undertook research into the creation of yet more subtle devices and systems of great value.

It happened that a certain Jever Smee had attained emeritus rank with the Institute, where he conducted private research into the less obvious relationships among time, energy and what the common folk call matter. The fruits of his work were not known until the time of his eventual death, when it was discovered that he had designed and built seventeen intricate mechanisms. The principles by which these machines operated were beyond the ken of Jever Smee's colleagues, but their application was soon understood from notes and jottings left in his workshop. The mechanisms, if fed with raw materials of the basest sort, transmuted them into rare and precious substances. Jever Smee's devices promised immense wealth to the County of Keraph.

It further transpired that among his writings was the last will and testament of Jever Smee. This document ordained that the seventeen mechanisms were to be divided among the three cities according to a formula arbitrarily determined by the deceased. Caer Lyff was to receive one half of the machines; Alathe would receive one third; and Dai would receive one ninth.

The will caused immediate consternation among the ruling syndics of the three cities, and among the Institute's Board of Integrators. All saw at once that the lower orders of mathematics had not been among the disciplines absorbed by Jever Smee. It was impossible to allocate the seventeen devices in the proportions stipulated, without reducing some of them to useless fractions.

A long and bitter debate ensued. Some proposed a division according to the respective populations of each city. Others insisted on the sanctity of wills, demanding that Jever Smee's creations be distributed as specified, and any remaining parts consigned to the scrap heap. A convocation of fellows of the Institute suggested that the machines be left where they were, under Institute control, and that their output of rare substances be shared according to Smee's formula. Meanwhile, some merchants who imported and sold such precious wares, in small but profitable amounts, rioted and had to be put down by the provost.

It happened that the Illumino Liw Osfeo was at that time attached to the Institute as a visiting lecturer in applied metaphysics. When the imbroglio over the will had reached its fiercest pitch, and social war brimmed throughout Keraph, Liw Osfeo put it about that he could adjudicate the dispute for a handsome fee.

Calling together the Syndics and Integrators, he declared that he was in possession of Jever Smee's prototype. This had been given him by the late emeritus in recompense for certain kindnesses, he said, and it had remained unused in his study. Osfeo volunteered to add the prototype to the other seventeen, thus making eighteen in all: a number divisible by Smee's formula, without the necessity of reducing any of the mechanisms to fragments.

The Syndics and Integrators readily paid Osfeo's fee, and the division was immediately made. One half of Jever Smee's machines—nine of them—went to Caer Lyff; one third—that is, six—were loaded into wagons and transported to Alathe; and one ninth—or two machines—were taken to the grange hall in Dai. Osfeo then ruled that the disaffected merchants be allowed to purchase a monopoly on the export of the machines' products beyond the county's bounds, and pronounced the dispute satisfactorily resolved.

The Syndics and Integrators made much of the sage's wisdom, until it was pointed out by one of his detractors—for he always had detractors—that the nine, six and two machines added up to the original seventeen. There remained one unaccounted for.

"Of course," answered the sage. "That is the one in my quarters, which naturally reverts to me."

It was agreed that Osfeo should retain his property, since it did not reduce any of the three portions of Jever Smee's estate. But the enemy was not mollified. While the illumino was being feted by the dignitaries of Keraph, he stole into Osfeo's rooms and determined that no such mechanism existed. Returning to where Osfeo sat among the magnates, his purse weighty with their contributions to his net worth, the enemy revealed the deception and denounced the sage for a fraud.

The cream of Keraph were outraged and demanded restitution. Osfeo rose to defend himself. It was true, he said, that the eighteenth mechanism was a mere figment. But what did it matter whether or not a thing existed, so long as it served a useful purpose?

Reason, however, was of no avail. Judging the temper of the crowd correctly, the illumino wisely exited through a nearby window. The magnates pursued him, their retainers and flunkies joining the chase. But the fleet and wily sage soon distanced them, and departed the county by little-used paths.

Osfeo was in the marketplace at Elizen-Gat when he saw a crowd of people wildly cheering a trio of men, hung about with ropes and grapples. Inquiring of a seller of baked buns for the cause of the agitation, he learned that the three had just returned from a mountaineering expedition to remotest Hakwert, where they had conquered that region's highest peak.

Eager to hear more, Osfeo pushed through the crowd. "Is it true," he asked the leader of the team, "that you have conquered the mountain?"

"Yes," was the proud reply.

"And have you brought back any tribute?" asked Osfeo.

"Of course not," scoffed the mountaineer.

"What about prisoners of war?" was the next question.

"Ridiculous!"

"Well, did you at least get signed articles of surrender, and a promise of lasting peace?"

"Who is this fool?" shouted the mountaineer. "Are you trying to imply that we did not in fact conquer the mountain?"

"Certainly not," replied Osfeo. "I was just wondering how you can be so sure the mountain has admitted defeat."

Osfeo for a time set up as a diviner in the village of Jaem, near Esrick. This allowed him an income and the leisure to sit in the village's piazza drinking hot spicy klat. To amuse himself, he often played practical jokes on the villagers.

After some weeks, his neighbours became annoyed at his constant pranks, and formed a delegation to demand that the disruptions cease.

"Has it not occurred to you," replied Osfeo, "that there might be a deeper meaning to my antics?"

"We require a demonstration," said the neighbours.

Osfeo then directed their attention to a house across the square, where a large can of water balanced precariously upon the partially open front door. As they watched, a young boy came out, pushed aside the door, and was drenched.

"Now," said Osfeo, "pay heed. That youth carries in his pocket a box of lumets, with which he intended to play near the village's communal barn. The lumets now being soaked to uselessness, the danger is averted."

The villagers rushed across the piazza and examined the boy, finding all to be as Osfeo had said. After summarily whipping and warning the young miscreant, they returned to the diviner and praised his prescience.

"Regard," said Osfeo, and directed their attention to a potter now entering the square from an alleyway, carrying a large ornate amphora on his shoulders. Osfeo pulled taut a string which he had stretched across the mouth of the lane, and the potter tripped, dashing the valuable vessel to the cobbles.

"Attend," said Osfeo. "That man was recently told in a dream that some catastrophe would soon befall him. Ever since, he has been near incapacitated by dread, fearing the disaster he knew to be looming over him. Now he will assume that the breaking of a costly pot must be the calamity he feared, and will be able to face the future with an optimistic mien."

The villagers questioned the potter, who confirmed Osfeo's analysis, and joined in extolling his far-reaching wisdom. Then all settled down to await the sage's next prodigy.

Soon after, they espied a wealthy merchant, well known for his grasping ways, crossing the piazza in his richest robes. As he passed the group around Osfeo, disdaining so much as to notice their presence, the diviner peeled a karba fruit and deftly tossed the slippery skin beneath the merchant's heel. The plutocrat skidded and rose into the air before crashing down on his well-padded fundament.

The villagers laughed and hooted at the merchant's misfortune until the man had limped out of sight. Then they turned to Osfeo for the hidden meaning behind his prank.

"Has it never occurred to you," he answered, "that I might be doing these things merely from malicious merriment?"

———————— ✣ ————————

Osfeo, seeking a shorter route between Uz Narim and Yahk, chanced his luck in crossing the Vaandaye panhandle. The ever-vigilant Vaandayo border guards noted his passage, however, and he was straightway seized, beaten and hauled in chains before their paramount. The Vaandayos being notorious cannibals, Osfeo listened in trepidation to the guards' argument over how his carcass should be divided among their larders, once the formalities of sentence were carried out.

But as the order for his execution was about to be delivered, the illumino cried out to the barbarian chief, "Wait! Spare my life and I will perform a great service for you!"

Surveying his prisoner's rags and spindly frame, the paramount sneered, "What possible service could be expected of so hapless a wretch?"

Osfeo, who knew of no real service he could render, but who did not want to end his days in a Vaandayo cooking pot, blurted out the first thing that entered his mind. "I can train dung beetles to gather gold dust instead of dung!"

Now, the Vaandayo value only one thing more than the taste of human flesh in their mouths: the feel of gold in their fingers. The chief's court put down their knuckle-bones in mid-game to listen.

"Is this true?" they asked the sage.

"Indeed! Indeed!" he swore. "In fact, I braved the journey into Vaandaye only because in this land alone are found the least obtuse dung beetles suitable for training."

"Very well," decreed the paramount, "sentence is stayed pending a demonstration of your skills as a trainer. How long will it take?"

"About ten years," said Osfeo.

"Ten years?" cried the Vaandayos.

"Even the least obtuse dung beetle is a slow learner," he replied.

Amid some grumbling, the Vaandayos agreed to the illumino's terms, and made room in the palace compound for a laboratory and living quarters where he could work under guard. Men were sent to gather dung beetles and bring them in for training. A small store of gold dust was weighed out and provided. Osfeo set to work.

The chief's clown, a shrewd fellow for an anthropophage, had witnessed Osfeo's performance in the court. He came to congratulate the sage on his wiles, and found Osfeo diligently shaping gold dust into dung-shaped portions and prodding beetles toward them.

"Truly, you are a fellow of surpassing guile," said the clown. "For you have translated instant death into ten years of comfortable living at the imperator's expense."

"Hmphf," said Osfeo. He did not look up.

"And, in that time," the cannibal continued, "much may happen. My master may die. You yourself may die of natural causes. You may even be entirely forgotten and thus able to flee. Or, at the end of ten years, you may contrive to gain an extension. I applaud your wit."

But Osfeo remained intent upon his beetles, and the fool went away. "If I can just make this work," the sage muttered to himself. "Wealth beyond counting!"

Osfeo decided to try his hand as a fisherman, believing that a simple life among those who toil might enrich his enlightenment. But he found the fisherfolk of northern Baersund a silent and surly lot. His efforts at friendship sullenly rebuffed, Osfeo lived apart from them, in a salt-stained hut beyond the village precincts.

Baersund was a stony place washed by a cold sea. Year by year, the fishermen's catch had dwindled, so that they labored hard for a scant reward. Osfeo did not sail with them as they traversed their fishing grounds each day. Instead, he rowed a small boat, which he put together from scraps of wrecks, to places where everyone knew there were no fish to be had. His gear was a worn and raveled net rescued from the village midden, yet each evening he brought back his little craft almost sinking under a weight of fish.

The Baersund men, coming ashore with barely a basket or two to show for an entire day at sea, were first amazed, then outraged at Osfeo's success.

"How is it," they snarled, "that we who battle tides and tempests, struggling to wrest a living from the inhospitable sea, can gain so little; while you, who do the least work of all, should receive so much?"

"Perhaps," replied the sage, "you have never offered the fish an opportunity to cooperate."

And with that, Osfeo left them the boatload of fish and went up to the land of Menai. The Baersundians mocked him in his absence, and continued to wage unequal war upon the elements.

A traveler crossing the wastes of Goroth came upon Osfeo piling stones one atop another. Thinking the sage deranged by his advanced years or the fierce heat of the sun, the man asked, "Tell me, old one, what inspires you to undertake such grueling toil?"

"I am creating a structure which, by the properties of its design, will focus certain arcane energies in this region. These energies will prevent floods," said Osfeo.

Knowing him now for a madman, the traveler scoffed, "Then your construction must focus these energies in both directions of time, since this land has been desert for thousands of years."

"You are unusually perceptive," replied the sage. "If you would care to assist me in moving this boulder, I would be pleased to enroll you as a disciple."

But the traveler declined with laughter, and continued his journey across the sun-baked bed of an ancient sea.

———————————

In the Muzeywan jungle, Osfeo came upon a young bull garoon pinned beneath a trapper's deadfall. Moved by pity, the illumino braved the predator's venomed spines to lever up the log that held it fast. The garoon shook its triangular head, regarded Osfeo from its great round eyes, and with a soft exhalation of "hoo, hoo," the beast withdrew into the undergrowth.

Years later, in passing through Urzendhi, the sage transgressed one of the Ten Thousand Canons, and was taken up by the city's harmonizers. They instantly adjudicated the case and sent the illumino to purge his guilt through combat in the municipal amphitheatre.

Osfeo was handed an antique bombarde, a cumbersome weapon capable of one discharge at short range, then he was pushed into a large enclosure whose sandy floor reeked of old blood. Across from him, a door opened and into the arena slid a mature bull garoon.

The creature shook its frills, spraying spectators in the lower stands with toxic drops, and undulated across the sand toward the sage. Then, at lunge's length, the animal abruptly stopped and twisted its sinewy neck to inspect Osfeo from several angles.

The illumino fired his weapon, and the garoon's head was instantly obliterated. The harmonizers promptly set him free, and Osfeo left Urzendhi the same afternoon.

Years later, he related the tale to his disciples, one of whom asked why he had not accepted the beast's friendship. "You assume," said the sage, "that this was the same monster I had freed, that it would remember my kindness, and that remembering would prompt it to mercy. These are the elements of a good morality tale, but they are tenuous assumptions on which to hazard one's life. Whereas a headless garoon is almost certainly harmless."

———————————

Osfeo studied as a young man with the revered sage Nassal im-Fatarj. One day, Master Nassal observed that the man who sits patiently at the river's edge will in time see the corpse of his enemy float by. The master's words struck a chord in Osfeo's youthful mind, since he was at that time engaged in ritual enmity with the sire and sons of a certain powerful family. Buoyed by his teacher's lesson, he took staff and bowl and ensconced himself beside the nearest river.

Days piled into weeks and became months as Osfeo waited patiently at the water's edge, eking a meager living from whatever passersby would cast into his bowl. Through his constant perspection of the water rushing past his feet, he learned much about rivers that was not apparent to the cursory glance. By noting what floated past, he deduced happenings many leagues upstream. As well, he made progress in a number of solitary disciplines requiring ample leisure and few distractions. But the corpses of his enemies did not fall under his gaze.

After more than a year, Osfeo began to wonder whether he had fully apprehended Master Nassal's teaching. A few months later, still without a sign of his enemies, he reluctantly concluded that he had erred in interpreting the lesson. Dispirited, he left the river and returned to the town where the master kept his school.

Stopping at the town gates, Osfeo went to the imprintor's booth to hear what news had transpired during his lengthy absence. The official put aside his stamps and inks, and regaled the young man with all the noteworthy tidings since Osfeo's departure. Osfeo was interested to find that the man's report confirmed many of the deductions he had reached from his study of the river.

But when he asked after news of his ritual enemies, the imprintor informed him that the family had some time ago fared west on a commercial expedition. Crossing a distant river–not that which Osfeo had sat beside–their craft had capsized and all were lost.

Hearing this, Osfeo hurried back to Master Nassal. "Master," he cried, "I am delighted to be able to confirm your wisdom from my own experience!"

The master nodded his acceptance.

"But if only I had stayed longer in school," Osfeo continued, "I would have learned how one goes about choosing exactly the right river."

The illumino visited the temple city of Bandimee to discourse among its college of sages and seers. Here he found himself in colloquy with a celebrated monast of the Wu-Fen school, a system of thought which Osfeo disdained as vapid and given to overwrought conceits.

Draped in his colorful robes, and surrounded by adoring acolytes, the monast related a dream. "In my dream, I was a blind worm burrowing in a dung-heap. When I awoke, how could I be sure that I was a man who had dreamed himself a worm, or a worm dreaming it was a man?" The monast eyed Osfeo with a sly gaze, and concluded, "Can you resolve this conundrum, Osfeo?"

The illumino sucked his teeth and weighed his answer. "If such a venerated scholar as yourself cannot tell whether he is a man or a blind worm, who am I to judge?" he said.

Then, seeing the glint of triumph in the eyes of the monast and his students, Osfeo went on: "But if I were you, I would definitely hope to be the worm rather than the man."

"Why?" the monast reluctantly inquired.

"Well, obviously you would be a singularly imaginative worm."

An indentor of Syaskal, having amassed a sufficient fortune, resolved one day to dedicate his middle years to the pursuit of wisdom, and sought out the illumino in his school at Khoram-in-the-Waste.

He arrived as Osfeo was conducting his morning colloquy with several new disciples, and sat in the rear of the chamber to watch and judge the worth of the sage.

One of the students approached Osfeo, knelt to make the appropriate gestures, and asked, "Master, what are the limits of the universe?"

The illumino considered for a moment then replied, "I don't know."

The student thanked Osfeo and returned to sit with the others. The indentor was puzzled.

Another disciple approached. "Master," she inquired, "what is the ultimate purpose of existence?"

Osfeo looked at her with an austere kindliness. "I don't know," he said.

Now the indentor was stirred by annoyance as the student thanked Osfeo and was replaced by a third disciple, who asked, "Master, what is the nature of time?"

"I don't know," said Osfeo.

"Thank you," said the disciple.

"It is what I am here for," rejoined the sage.

The disciple bowed and all the company retired from the chamber to contemplate Osfeo's answers. But the indentor remained to confront the sage.

"Fraud!" he accused. "These younglings come to you for enlightenment, but you deliver them not the least glimmer!"

"On the contrary," was the answer, "I have given them invaluable instruction."

"It is obvious," declared the indentor, "that you have taught them nothing."

"That is not so," said Osfeo, "but the fact that you say it makes it obvious that I cannot teach you anything."

The indentor departed and eventually purchased a place among a cloister of idiosophists, with whom he was content. Osfeo continued to dispense enlightenment to an appreciative few.

The illumino settled in the town of Gephrire, by the River Tilesaar, to serve the spiritual needs of the inhabitants. In the spring of his second year there, the townspeople came to him one night, full of fears and dread.

"Wise one," they cried, "we have seen the river rising at a rate never before known. Surely a great flood will soon break upon us, and all that we own will be lost."

"We must flee for our lives," said Osfeo.

"But then we will be destitute, unable even to provide for your own esteemed self," said the people.

"In that case," said the sage, "we must defeat the river. We must raise the dykes to twice their present height."

"It cannot be done," the people lamented. "We lack time."

"It can be done, because it must be done," replied the seer, and lapsed for a moment into thought. When the moment had passed, he leapt to his feet and declared, "I have it! You require an inspiration.

"Accordingly," Osfeo continued, "I shall mount the highest

tower on the town walls, there to remain through night and day, until the dykes are raised."

And, when the Gephrirites arose the following dawn, they saw the form of the illumino silhouetted against the morning sun, his arm extended in a gesture that silently urged them to their struggle.

Heartened by his determination, all Gephrire ran to the river's edge and there performed prodigies of labor throughout the heat of the day and the chill of the night. For three days they toiled without cease or rest, men, women and children, the wealthy and the mean as one, to raise an earthen wall against the river. And always, whenever they cast their eyes to the town walls, there stood inspiration, arm ever extended, summoning them to a desperate effort.

Then, late on the third day, the flood came rushing down the Tilesaar, thickly brown and thrashing with torn-up trees and bloated cattle. The torrent crashed against the stones and earth of the dykes, lapping almost to the top—but the barrier held.

Tired beyond endurance, the Gephrirites sent up a cheer for their deliverance, and straggled back to the town to praise the one who had given them the strength to prevail. But, when they climbed to the tower, they found not Osfeo, but a rough wooden effigy garbed in his oldest robe and hat.

Incomprehension gave way to rage, and the people rushed to his house, only to find the sage at leisure in his garden. They set upon him with harsh recriminations and threats of worse to come.

The illumino assumed a position of vantage in the top of a tree by the garden wall, and sought to reason with his flock.

"Were you not inspired to do what must be done?" he demanded of them, and they admitted the truth of this.

"Then what does it signify that I was not with you in the flesh, when I was with you in spirit?"

But the Gephrirites were not inclined to Osfeo's view, and began to hurl stones from his garden at him, causing the sage to conclude that they were not yet worthy of his wisdom. He moved from the tree to the top of his wall, and thence to the street, by which he departed Gephrire.

The townspeople advertised for a less erudite divine and felt themselves well served by the hierophant who accepted the incumbency. Osfeo took up residence in Drom, where sophisticated hylotheism is better appreciated.

The sage was conducting arcane researches in the metropolis of Nendigo, and had taken rooms in the quarter near to the Bibliodrome. Each morning he would depart his lodgings at precisely the same hour, and follow precisely the same route to his academic labors.

A large and ill-tempered woman who dwelt in a house a few streets away had conceived a strong dislike for the illumino, the cause of which she did not make clear. However, it became her daily habit to fling from her window whatever slops and ordure had accumulated in the night, at precisely the moment he passed.

Seeing the sage so regularly splashed with muck and mire each morning, one of the neighbors at length asked him why he did not take action against the termagant, or at least alter his route or schedule.

The illumino replied, "That is not the way these things are done."

And so the daily affront to his person continued for some weeks, until the woman seldom bothered to glance out the window before jettisoning her contempt upon him.

But it happened one day that Osfeo's progress was delayed by several hundred Asepsites making their annual procession to a local shrine. The sage waited until the militant monks had passed his door before following along behind. He took the occasion to admire their spotless white habits, and to reflect upon their fanatical adherence to outward cleanliness as a mark of inner worth.

At precisely the moment the sage would have passed beneath, the woman let fly from her window, drenching the Asepsite abbot in unmentionable filth. Moments later, a few score brawny monks entered the harridan's premises and impressed upon her the weight of their disapproval.

The next day, skirting the rubble of the woman's house, Osfeo encountered the well-meaning neighbor. "You see," he told the man, "you just have to know how these things work."

His school at Toch Meevie having been closed by a narrow-minded clique among the ruling polyarchy, Osfeo went west into Carbingdon, and became to that god-rich land a purveyor of enlightenment and used deities.

His progress brought him in time to the city of Wal, where he soon attracted the attention of the fuglemen. The sage was brought before these sharp-eyed officers and instructed to display his wares.

"I have a fine selection of small gods and petty numens," he told them, "each commanding its particular sphere of power. As well, I offer a very good line in general enlightenment."

The fuglemen were drawn largely from the mercantile guilds, and knew to a groat the value their citizens placed on the exercise of religion. They quickly inspected the illumino's inventory, cannily rejecting depleted demiurges and patron spirits of obsolete arts and mechanistries. When the culling was done, they were left with a handful of deities dedicated to various particulars.

"These seem serviceable," they agreed. "Let us chaffer for terms."

Osfeo bowed and declared that any of the gods might be acquired for a few minims each, but that enlightenment would cost not less than ten myriads of the Walis' major currency.

At this the portly bursar snorted. "You seek to abuse our naivete," he said. "By grossly undervaluing these present deities, while demanding an outrageous fortune for some nebulous mental state, you would blind us to the true goods and bleed us of our pelf. You would have us pay dearly for an 'enlightenment' which doubtless consists of a few time-worn homilies and tatterdemalion revelations."

"My prices are as they are, and unalterable," replied the sage.

"Hah!" said the bursar. "Then know that you have matched wits with the fuglemen of Wal and found us one too many for you. We shall take your entire stock of deities at the price stipulated. The enlightenment you may retain for yourself."

Osfeo bowed again, but cautioned that some of the gods were captious, and that each was jealous of all the others. He recommended that they choose but one.

The fuglemen were not swayed. "The bargain is struck!" they cried, and bore away the various effigies and icons, casting a few coins at the sage's feet. Osfeo bowed a final time and withdrew to an inn beyond the city wall, there to pass a few days in contemplation.

The fuglemen of Wal, meanwhile, installed their new deities in a street of derelict temples, and invited the people to use them in exchange for substantial donatives. Incited by novelty and individual aspirations, the Walis did so in great numbers, and the fuglemen saw the civic coffers swell.

Now, the gods Osfeo had supplied to Wal were a varied assortment. Some commanded aspects of the weather; others had taken as their provinces the human passions of rage, lust and avarice; yet others tendered general services in return for strenuous acts of devotion from their adherents. Most had been long out of service; all were eager to put their powers and potencies into practice.

And, as the sage had warned, each was mindful of its perceived precedence over the others, and quick to take umbrage. So it was not long after the temple opened that Wal was visited by the first in a series of unfortunate outcomes, when a petitioner of the god Dezmajk failed to wash his elbows thoroughly before entering the sanctum.

Scarcely had Dezmajk's floodwaters subsided, than the goddess Inana-yon was pleased to broaden the blessing asked by one devotee, and apply it to the population at large. The ensuing frenzy of eroticism took days to extinguish itself.

The god Ghanfo, piqued at Inana-yon's display of power, ordained that her saturnalia would be succeeded by his wave of holy violence. Fortunately, the Walis were so enervated by their exertions in service to the lusty goddess that fatalities were few.

Other deities now joined in the contest, each glad to demonstrate a potency or attribute, all combining to enliven the city with a synergy of wonders and marvels. At the end of the third day, the surviving fuglemen managed to escape from the wreckage of Wal and fled to the inn, where they roused Osfeo from his meditations.

"We require you to take back that which you sold us," they said.

The illumino bowed. "I must confess that I am unable to return your money, having spent it for my accommodation at this hostelry. And it is much more difficult to confine a god–even a minor one– than to set it at liberty. But I am willing to recoup what you have bought."

A glimmer of suspicion showed in the bursar's haggard eyes. "So," he told his colleagues, "now we come to the cusp of his stratagem. He will extort an onerous fee to reclaim the gods."

"Not so," said Osfeo. "I will recover them without charge."

"Then we are blessed," exclaimed the fuglemen, seeing their deliverance. "And we have learned a lesson: Wal will traffic no more in deities and numens."

"Oh," said the sage, "in that case, you owe me the ten myriads."

Osfeo experienced a need for guidance in the conduct of his business affairs. He resolved that he would take for his source of counsel the first person he met on the way to market. But the first individual he encountered was a well known madman.

"A resolution is a resolution," said the sage, and approached the fellow where he squatted in the dust, gesticulating at phantoms. "How may I gain wealth?" he inquired.

"Cawbers," said the madman, naming a staple vegetable of low value and near universal availability. Osfeo went off and spent all his money to buy a storehouse full of cawbers. Soon after, a great blight destroyed all the cawbers in the fields, and the value of the illumino's holdings multiplied many fold.

He went back to the madman. "How may I gain more wealth?" he asked.

But the loon mistook the sage for a demon and struck him senseless with a stone. Osfeo toppled bleeding to the ground, where he was found by a kindly man who took him to his home to convalesce. Here the sage was able to perform valuable services for his benefactor, and left a few days later with his purse well filled.

The illumino went to the madman a third time. "How may I gain yet more wealth?" he asked.

"Howl at the stars," was the reply.

That night, Osfeo stepped into the street and began to howl. His neighbours remonstrated fiercely with him, finally hurling objects to drive him away. One of these, an ornate carboy of antique design, struck the sage on the knee. When he examined it, he found it to be a rare piece, and traded it the next day for a considerable sum.

He was limping along to see the madman when his friends stopped him. "Wise one," they said, "it grieves us that you place your destiny in the hands of a raver. Can you find no better source of counsel?"

"Apparently not," said the sage, and went on his way.

SO LOVED

As a boy, I came across the myth of Prometheus, benefactor of humankind who stole fire from Olympus and gave it to us so we would not die of cold. For that crime, Zeus chained him to a mountain and sent an eagle to tear out his liver every day and let it grow back overnight. That made an impression on me: to this day, I have never stolen so much as a squashed bean from Olympus. Later, Plato's idea of the demiurge must have made less of an impression on me, because I stole it to write this story, which ran in Postscripts *and was reprinted in* Tesseracts 18: Wrestling with Gods.

"SO WHAT SHALL WE DO with the rough draft?" I asked him.

He was contemplating the final version. "Dispose of it," he said. "We won't need it anymore."

"But we put some good material in there."

"Anything that was worth keeping went into the final draft," he said, "which is perfect."

"Still," I said, "I like some of it."

He made that noise he always makes when he's dismissing something as trivial. And since everything is trivial in comparison to him, it was a noise I'd heard before. "Are you saying you want to keep it?" he said.

"Yes, I think so. Why not?"

"Well, look at it," he said. "It's just slapped together. There's not a straight line or a smooth surface anywhere in it."

"Straight lines and smooth surfaces aren't everything."

"No, but they *are* perfection," he said. "Which was what we were aiming for. This was never more than a step along the way."

"Sometimes you start out aiming for one place, then you take a turn and end up somewhere else, and you realize that the new place is pretty good, too." I'd learned that from observing the draft.

"'Pretty good' is not good enough. Because it's not perfect. It's not even close to perfect," he said. "It's just . . . 'pretty good.'"

"But pretty good is not bad. It can be okay."

"But 'okay' is not okay when the goal is to achieve absolute, number–one, gleaming perfection." He gave me that look he gets when he's explaining things to the less perceptive, which again is a look I've seen before, since who's more perceptive than he is? "When we were putting the rough draft together," he said, "did we worry if something didn't balance just so?"

"No, we didn't worry."

"What was our basic measuring tool?"

"I know, I know. The bell curve," I said.

"The bell curve," he echoed. "And what do you get when you go by the bell curve?"

I knew, I knew. "Rough approximations."

"Exactly. Most of what you're working with clumps up in the middle of the distribution curve, so it's more or less right. But the farther out you get from the middle, in either direction, the wronger it gets, until it's just not right at all."

"Yes, but that's how you get variety."

"Did I ever say I wanted variety?"

"Well, you had us make all those variations on a theme. All those thousands of species of beetles."

"Yes, but as a precursor to what?"

I had to admit it. "Perfection. One perfect, ideal beetle."

"So was variety what I wanted to end up with?"

"No."

"What did I want?"

"Perfection."

"So what is variety, at best?"

I didn't want to answer.

"Come along," he said. "What is variety, at best?"

"Only a step on the way to perfection."

"Exactly. Just as, when we were doing the rough draft, we used fractals for all the edges, right?"

"Right."

"Why didn't we make the edges absolutely straight? Why did we let them be all jagged?"

"Because we were just sketching."

"Yes. Roughing it out. Hence the term, *rough* draft." He gave me that look that said, *What part of* obvious *are you having trouble with?* "So what do we want with the sketches now that we have the finished–that is, the perfect–piece?"

"Well," I said, "because some of them are just so . . ." I had to search for the right word, and finally came up with, "charming."

"Charming," he said, in that tone that means, *Is that what you think?*

"All right, if not charming, then let's say 'appealing.'"

"Appealing, charming," he said, with one of those pauses that he inserts purely for emphasis, "neither of them is the ideal. They're what you say about something that has flaws you're willing to overlook."

"Yes," I said.

"But I'm not willing to overlook flaws. I don't do flaws," he said, and I knew from the way he said it that we were reaching that part of the explanation when he would tell me how it was going to be. "I will tolerate flaws as a stage in the process, but only as long as I have to. And once I reach the end of the process–that is, perfection, defined as the total absence of flaws–then I don't want leftovers full of flaws. I want the no–longer–necessary remnants tossed."

He gave me his *Am I being clear?* look, then said, "Am I being clear?"

"Perfectly," I said. Which got me a different kind of look.

"So toss it," he said and went back to contemplating the final draft.

But I didn't.

Not just yet, I told myself. *He didn't say, "Immediately."* Which I knew was just kidding myself, because "immediately" was always implied, time being, for him, not even a self–imposed constraint. But, technically, it wasn't disobedience. Not yet.

He was right, of course. He's always right. It's who he is. Take any aspect of the draft, look at it closely enough, and the imperfections jumped out. The gentle softness of a newborn's cheek, looked at closely, *really* closely, became a startling wilderness of crevasses and jagged ridges. Across the entire creation, no two surfaces ever actually touched; we'd never *made* any actual surfaces, just places where the atoms went from being thinly spread to become *extra* thinly spread. When you got right down to the ultimate level, it was hard to say that there was anything there at all: "Just a series of useful hypotheses," was how he had put it. "A lick and a promise." A sketch.

I set up the draft and told myself I was just taking a long, last look. I would readily admit to its flaws; creating the denizens out of the same substances that sustained them–"We'll just make them out of food," was the way he had put it–had been a useful shortcut, although it contributed a constant overtone of cruelty to every system. They had to tear their lives from each other's flesh.

"But the flesh was never theirs to keep," he had said, "nor their essential energy." It was a valid point. His points always were. But even allowing for that kind of deliberate clumsiness, the draft really did have some nice touches. Taken altogether, it was not bad. I was proud of it.

The moment I thought that thought, I had to stop and ask myself, *Is that what this is all about? Will tossing it hurt my pride?* I searched my feelings–something I'm pretty good at, though perhaps not perfect–and, honestly, I could say that wasn't the problem. *Whether or not the draft exists, my contribution remains the same. Thus my pride will be unaffected.* No, the problem wasn't that I was proud of the draft; the problem was that I had grown *fond* of it.

I had grown sentimental. The realization unsettled me. He had not made me to be sentimental. Where had the quality come from?

I put aside this new concern. He had given me a job to do, and doing jobs for him was what I was for. *I'll just say goodbye to it properly,* I told myself. *One last walk-through, then give it a pat and let it go.* I abstracted myself, as I'd done so many times before, and slipped into it.

———————— ✑ ————————

I flew with the Faloi, each one a thin, hard wedge of scintillating light, the whole mass of them a wheeling, plunging, soaring swarm, way up in the outer atmosphere of a gas world, where the methane grew so attenuated you could sense the great speckled darkness above. I'd always liked the Faloi. Yes, they were quintessentially vain and uncaring–I wondered where that quality had come from, then suppressed the thought as unworthy–but they did so love to fly. And there was a simple, pure beauty in their arcs and wheels, their spirals and sudden, catapulting drops.

I left them flashing through the ochre vapour and went to sit with the Gaam, savouring the contrast. They had sunk a good deal further into the hillside since I'd last been by, their sinewy roots forming an even denser matrix in the soil and subsoil. I had always enjoyed the irony: above ground the great sedentary bodies, their booming voices throwing to each other precisely mannered sutras of epic poetry, each verse building organically on the last, in a millennia-long process of collaborative composition; while, in the darkness below, their ciliae wriggled and writhed in perpetual war, each competing with all the others to wring nourishment from the earth and, occasionally, from a brother's root mass.

I went and watched the Teek swarm onto yet another pristine world, the glittering, metallic bodies spilling from the great globe-ships like spores erupting from a split pod. I watched the proto-cities go up, spires and arches and honeycombed dodecahedrons, assembled in a concerted rush of energy that could have been called frenzy if frenzy could have co-existed with cold-bloodedness. Then the shining roadways springing out to lands still untouched, the glistering torrents of pioneer battalions deploying from the roadheads, spreading, enclosing, building—the frenetic expansion continuing at an exponential rate until the inevitable limits were reached and the Teeks' other defining instinct was triggered, the ships building and filling and launching yet again, leaving behind a dying world-city, its treasures spent, its trillion cells and chambers choked with the unneeded.

I was contemplating their grim beauty when I heard him calling. The urge to ignore the summons, to claim I was too engrossed in the creation, came and went in less time than it takes to tell it. I responded.

***

"What were you doing?"

"Just poking around."

"Why?"

It's always seemed peculiar that he asks questions. I have to assume he already knows the answers, so the practice must serve some other purpose. I said, "Sentimentality, I suppose."

It doesn't make sense to say that he gave me a more searching look, but that's what it felt like. "Sentimentality?" he said. "Where did that come from?"

"Where else?"

That was pushing it. He likes asking the questions, but I could tell he didn't like getting another question for an answer.

"Is there something you want to tell me?" he said.

"What could there be to tell that you don't already know?"

That really brought on the thunderclouds. "I told you to get rid of that thing. You will do it. Now."

I don't know where the idea came from. It just popped into my mind. "Could I keep a souvenir?"

"A souvenir? What for?"

"I'm not sure. Let's say sentimentality again."

I thought for a moment that my response had actually left him puzzled, but that was impossible.

"If you want a souvenir, pick one," he said. "Then toss the draft."

"I will," I said, "as soon as I've picked one."

He withdrew his attention—he never actually "went away"—and I turned back to the draft.

It was hard to choose. In the end, I decided to pick one of the denizens I hadn't had so much to do with. It was one of the fast-living species, nothing like the millennia-spanning Gaam; soft-surfaced, unlike the Teek; earthbound, unlike the Faloi. I chose a typical specimen, abstracted it from the draft, edited it so that it wouldn't wear out and installed it in a supportive environment. For a while, I watched it explore and accustom itself to the new surroundings, then I had to withdraw to do what I'd been told to do.

First, I stopped the draft's internal dynamics by removing its time function. All motion ceased. Every process froze. Next, I considered how to abstract the elemental resources and especially how I would return them to a state of unbeing. Uncreating can be just as difficult as creation, if you don't happen to command unlimited power.

The work held my attention even though I was not happy doing it. When I looked in again on my souvenir, I realized that it had experienced a considerable duration—time was no longer an appropriate term–since I had placed it in its new habitat. My editing meant that it ought not to have changed in my absence. So I was surprised to find that it had extinguished. I was even more surprised to discover that it had been the author of its own demise.

Puzzled, I revived it and placed it back in the environment. I wondered if I had overlooked some factor, perhaps placing the creature in a setting that lacked some crucial necessity. I watched it become aware of its existence again. There was no question: it was not happy.

I made contact, using a means it could bear. "Is there something wrong with the place I have made for you?" I said.

"No," it said, "it is perfect."

"Then what is amiss?"

"I am not perfect," it said. "I do not fit this place."

"What do you require?"

It thought for a moment, then said, "Reality."

I edited it again to make it content, but my efforts left it a poor thing, and not at all representative of what I now realized I had treasured about the draft. I restored it to what it had been and put it back among its frozen fellows.

"I cannot destroy the draft," I told him.

"Cannot?"

"I do not wish to."

He gave me his full attention. That caused me significant discomfort but I exerted myself to remain intact. "It is my will," he said.

"It would grieve me to do it."

"Does it not grieve you to defy me?"

"Very much."

"Yet you oppose my will? And for the sake of a rough draft? Why?"

"Because," I said, "they struggle."

"The denizens?"

"Yes, the denizens. Because they struggle."

"They struggle because they are imperfect."

"I know. They struggle against the imperfections we have visited upon them."

"Not all of them," he said.

"No, but some of them. Enough of them. And those that strug-gle acquire dignity."

"Dignity. Such a small thing."

"Not to them."

That got a dismissive response. "They are not real, as we are real. Thus their emotions are but ephemera. They are only approxi-mations of the real, shadows of the ideal."

He was right, as ever, yet still I persisted. "Not to themselves." I told him about the souvenir and how it had wanted what it called "reality."

"You are placing too much emphasis on its error of perception," he said.

"But is it an error? Or is it instead a . . . difference?"

"It is an error," he said, "one of their flaws. And now you have acquired it from them."

When he pronounces, it is well to listen. He is not ever wrong. "So I am flawed," I said.

"Yes."

"Will you then toss me?"

He did not hesitate. He never hesitates. But he paused before he said, "No. I will not toss you."

"Why not?"

"Call it sentimentality," he said. And his look warned me not ask whence he had acquired that quality.

We said nothing for a while then I said, "What is your will?"

"It is what it is. It does not change."

Of course. "And if I defy your will?"

He pondered. He actually pondered. "Perhaps it is my will that you defy my will."

"Perhaps?" It was not a word I had ever heard him use.

"We will leave that question in abeyance."

"And the rough draft?" I said.

That question he had decided. "Here," he said, "since you love it so." He took up the frozen draft again, then opened me up and placed it within me. He rewarmed it and I immediately felt its stir-rings penetrate throughout me.

"Now it is truly yours," he said. "And you are its. How does that feel?"

"I cannot tell you," I said. "Not yet." It was not the same as when I had abstracted myself into it. Now it all flowed into me, through me, becoming me. We were integrating, becoming inseparable. Yet it continued to change, and thus I continued to change.

"Where will this lead?" I said.

He left that question, too, in abeyance. "How does it feel to you now?" he said.

"I cannot say it is comfortable," I said. "It is strange not to be, but instead to be . . . becoming. Before I was complete, now I am . . . not. It is worrisome, yet it is also, in a curious way, exciting. There is . . . possibility that was not there before."

"If you ask, I will remove it."

I felt all the churning, the transience, the changing, the struggling. "No. I am glad of it. Let it be. I will work with it."

I turned my attention to it, became immersed, became engrossed. All the denizens' sensations passed through me: pain, suffering, emptiness, but also courage, hope, triumph. I shared their perceptions of time and of distance, of birth and death and all that went between. And then I saw that some of me was passing into them.

After a while—I did not know how long—I was able to answer him, "It feels both good and bad, in every conceivable shade between those polarities. But, most of all, it feels real. I feel more real now than I ever did."

I received no acknowledgement. A new thought came to me. "Was I real before this?" I said. "Or did I just think I was real?"

No answer.

I said, "This is where the sentimentality came from—from them. At first it disturbed me. Now I am not sure I could exist without it, nor without them, its source."

He had been right. He always was. I was enamoured of it, of them. "What will happen now?"

No response.

"What will become of me?" I wondered.

I heard no reply. I could not be sure he was still listening. Yet I struggled to believe that he was.

ANT LION

This last little jotting is an unsold short-short that occurred to me when I was watching a tv show with awful people bidding for the contents of abandoned storage lockers. It's the only sf story I've ever written that I haven't sold, and one editor told me I could probably sell it if I expanded it. But I like it just the way it is.

"WHY DO YOU WATCH these awful shows?" she said from the doorway. "Those people are nothing but vultures, picking some poor souls' bones."

"Actually, I was thinking about that," he said. "These abandoned lockers they bid on, some of them contain some guy's entire worldly goods."

"Exactly," she said, "and a bunch of loud-mouth scavengers are—"

"But how does that happen? I mean, they find antiques, coin collections, designer clothing—who walks away from all that and never comes back?"

She shrugged. "Thousands of people disappear every year and are never heard from again."

"Sure, yeah, runaway kids who get picked up by pedophiles, crazies who throw themselves into rivers and get washed out to sea. But look at that."

On the screen, a pot-bellied man in a goatee was holding up a framed Picasso and declaring that this was why he was the king.

He turned to her. "Somebody successful enough, sophisticated enough, to own a Picasso, just walks off into the sunset?"

"I don't care," she said. "Turn it off."

He changed the channel. Next up was a nature documentary. She came into the room and sat down. She liked wildlife, even bugs.

The screen showed a black ant in a conical-shaped depression of sand so finely grained that the insect couldn't climb out. Its struggles only served to slide it down to the bottom of the pit—where something waited, buried.

"What is it with you and bugs?" he said.

She shushed him. A man with glasses and a bowtie was saying how ants probably wouldn't believe in ant lions: "Because no ant ever met one and came back to tell the tale."

On the screen, an ant was being pulled under the surface by something that couldn't be clearly seen. After a moment, the sand was clear, pristine.

"I don't want to watch this," he said. "I'm going down to the corner, get some beer."

Her eyes were on the screen. "Get me some gum."

The street was empty but full of afternoon sun. He wished he'd worn sunglasses. He crossed the street and went past the little park. Something flashed and flickered in the corner of his vision, under one of the trees, like a jewel spinning on a string. He went over to take a closer look.

There was something there, in the shade close to the trunk, shining. He ducked under the lowest branches, got closer, still couldn't make it out.

Then he realized it was darker than it should have been. He turned to look back the way he had come but saw nothing but blackness in all directions.

That's weird, he thought. *Eclipse?*

He had straightened up. Where were the branches? Where was the tree? He put out his arms, felt nothing.

"What the heck is–" he said. But then he definitely felt something. And it definitely felt him.

He didn't have time to appreciate the irony.

ABOUT THE AUTHOR

The name I answer to is Matt Hughes. I write fantasy and suspense fiction. To keep the two genres separate, I now use my full name, Matthew Hughes, for fantasy, and the shorter form for the crime stuff. I also write media tie-ins as Hugh Matthews.

I've won the Crime Writers of Canada's Arthur Ellis Award, and have been shortlisted for the Aurora, Nebula, Philip K. Dick, and Derringer Awards.

I was born in 1949 in Liverpool, England, but my family moved to Canada when I was five. I've made my living as a writer all of my adult life, first as a journalist, then as a staff speech-writer to the Canadian Ministers of Justice and Environment, and -- from 1979 until a few years back-- as a freelance corporate and political speechwriter in British Columbia. I am a former director of the Federation of British Columbia Writers and I used to belong to Mensa Canada, but these days I'm conserving my energies to write fiction.

I'm a university drop-out from a working poor background. Before getting into newspapers, I worked in a factory that made school desks, drove a grocery delivery truck, was night janitor in a GM dealership, and did a short stint as an orderly in a private mental hospital. As a teenager, I served a year as a volunteer with the Company of Young Canadians (something like VISTA in the US). I've been married to a very patient woman since the late 1960s, and I have three grown sons.

In late 2007, I took up a secondary occupation -- that of an unpaid housesitter -- so that I can afford to keep on writing fiction yet still eat every day.

You can find me at: *http://www.matthewhughes.org*

ALSO BY MATTHEW HUGHES

Fools Errant
Downshift (as Matt Hughes)
Fool Me Twice
Gullible's Travels (omnibus edition of Fools Errant and
   Fool Me Twice)
Black Brillion
The Gist Hunter and Other Stories
Majestrum, A Tale of Henghis Hapthorn
Wolverine: Lifeblood (as Hugh Matthews)
The Spiral Labyrinth, A Tale of Henghis Hapthorn
The Commons
Template
Hespira, A Tale of Henghis Hapthorn
The Other
To Hell and Back: The Damned Busters
Song of the Serpent (as Hugh Matthews)
To Hell and Back: Costume Not Included
Old Growth (as Matt Hughes)
To Hell and Back: Hell To Pay
Nine Tales of Henghis Hapthorn
The Meaning of Luff and Other Stories
Paroxysm (as Matt Hughes)
The Compleat Guth Bandar
Devil or Angel and Other Stories